CW00828543

Collected Halloween

Trick 'r Treat

Collected by Kevin J. Kennedy

Collected Halloween Horror Shorts © 2017 Kevin J. Kennedy

Collected by Kevin J. Kennedy

Edited by Brandy Yassa

Cover design by Lisa Vasquez

Each story in this book has been published with the authors' permission. They are all copyrighted by the author. All rights reserved. No part of this publication may be reproduced, distributed, or transmitted in any form or by any means, including photocopying, recording, or other electronic or mechanical methods, without the prior written permission of the publisher, except in the case of brief quotations embodied in critical reviews and certain other non-commercial uses permitted by copyright law.

First Printing, 2017

Table of Contents

Foreword

By

Nev Murray

"It's the most wonderful time, of the year." – Andy Williams

Now…..you may think I have got my seasons mixed up, but I haven't. And yes, I did use that same opening line for my foreword in the Christmas edition. I wasn't expecting to be invited back, so I'm running out of material. The above song is certainly associated with Christmas, but if you read my Christmas foreword, you would remember that I was firmly in the 'hate Christmas' camp! So, I am bringing this song out again to apply to Halloween!! I mean, let's face it, we are all horror fans, so it *is* the most wonderful time of the year. Isn't it?

I am, what we call in this neck of the woods, a late bloomer, in my love of Halloween. The main reason for this is my upbringing. I was brought up in a very religious family in Northern Ireland. We were the protestant side of the fence, the old fire and brimstone Presbyterians. Now – before I go any further – please don't judge me purely on that front. I was the true definition of the black sheep of the family. Although many people consider Halloween to be the Christian version of the more pagan celebration, Samhain, that was not what my family, nor their congregation, believed.

Yes, we would get a scary mask but would only wear it in the house. Yes, we would bob for apples, but that was it. There was no trick-or-treating or anything like that. We just didn't do it. Although, to be fair, in those days in Northern Ireland there was a little bit of a kerfuffle going on with something called "the troubles". That basically meant that if someone came to your door wearing a mask, you had to run for it. Throwing Mars bars at them just wouldn't have worked. Maybe that was the reason why no one did it. In later years, when "the troubles" sort of went away, trick-or-treating became a thing. By this stage I was too old for it, so I really missed out.

Then we had the issue with fireworks as well around that time of year. You weren't allowed them in Northern Ireland unless you had a licence. This was because the aforementioned men in masks used fireworks for other reasons! But, again, I digress. Halloween just wasn't celebrated the way it is now. It has become huge. In the UK, we would use the phrase "it has become Americanised" to describe Halloween these days. We in the UK have really only caught up with the rest of the world in this last twenty years or so with the whole razzamatazz of the event. For example, in the really olden days,

Irish pagans used to carve faces into turnips instead of the old favourite pumpkin jack o' lantern of our modern times.

So, what did Halloween mean to me growing up, as well as in recent years? Scary stories. That's it. Maybe I would watch the odd film or two but they were never my thing. I know loads of you would binge watch as many horror films as you could at Halloween. It just doesn't float my boat. Scary stories is where it's at.

I love the whole idea of ghosties and ghoulies on the prowl on Allhallows Eve, ready to steal away the innocent, and punish the guilty. Old scores settled in the dead of night, by demons and lost souls who have slipped through the divide between our world and the mystical.

Books are magical things when you let your imagination run riot, as you take in the sights and sounds, and even the smells of a story. The Halloween season is one of the greatest times of all to make use of all of those senses, and ingest everything a story can bring you.

One of the greatest Halloween nights I have ever had was a couple of years ago when myself, my wife, and our not so little man went to a place called Auckland Castle. They run an event at Halloween simply called, All Hallows. It is one of the eeriest events I have ever been to in my life. You walk around the castle grounds in small groups, in the pitch dark, led by a guide with a torch. At certain points on the walk, he will turn his torch off and soft lights come up as local school kids, dressed in olden days clothing, sneak out from behind the trees and act out a ghostly story to try and scare you. Others just read a story or a poem to you in the evilest voice they can muster. It is a wonderfully eerie and devilish night that sends chills running up your spine, that remain long after you have left.

And what is the main theme, the one thing that gives you those frights and feelings of unrest and fear? Stories. Nothing more. Nothing less.

You don't need Hollywood's multi-million-pound blockbusters to scare you at Halloween. All you need is a well-written story and an imagination to go with it, and all your fears will come true.

In the pages you are about to read through, there are such stories. These stories all deal with traditional events and themes to do with Halloween. But, as with the earlier Christmas and Easter anthologies, these stories grab those traditions and turn them completely on their heads.

Don't be expecting Halloween parties where dunking for apples is a fun game that everyone enjoys, those apples may just bring evil to the fore. Don't be expecting trick-or-treating with friends where everyone wears beautifully elaborate costumes that get taken off and thrown in the cupboard until next year, those costumes may just be real. Don't be expecting cheap imitation decorations from the dollar store; you can never trust whether something is real or not.

Do be expecting a wide-ranging mixture of stories from some of the brightest young horror writers that are making names for themselves all over the world. There is no razzamatazz in any of these tales. Darkness prevails from the beginning, to the end. You will feel the ice trailing down your spine. You will feel the tickle of the spiders' web on your face. You will be checking over your shoulder to make sure no one is there. You will be thankful when the tales within are over, and you can breathe in peace once more.

Kevin J Kennedy and the plethora of people who help put this series together should be extremely proud of themselves for what they have achieved once again. The stories held within this book put twists and turns into popular tropes, making them fresh, and scary again, without losing the flavour and tradition of the Halloween season.

When you are reading this, I may just be wandering around in the dark at Auckland Castle again, having the bejeesus scared out of me!

This book will do the same to you!

Happy Halloween.

Nev Murray

September 2017.

Black Widow

By

Christina Bergling

"Dress-Like-A-Slut Day! My favorite day of the year, man!" Dane shouted, as he bounded into the common room.

His voice boomed through the still-waking Delta Beta house, rippling along the lingering traces of smoke and the thin acidic odors of stale booze and forgotten vomit on the air.

The soles of his skater shoes gripped the hardwood floor, making a subtle rip with each step. He found Brent sprawled out on the couch in front of the ornate yet battered fireplace mantle. Sunlight poured abrasively through the large, smeared front window almost making the light warble like the hangovers they shared.

"Dude," Brent started, "you know, if our society didn't shame women about their sexuality or their bodies they might not need an excuse to dress like a slut. It could be Dress-Like-A-Slut Day every day."

"Whoa, bro. That Women's Studies class is, like, infecting your brain and shit."

Dane slapped Brent's feet off the matted, stained cushion and dropped down beside him. A cloud of something puffed up beneath him, and the particles danced in the harsh light.

"It's a required credit," Brent replied.

"I know it's required, but you're actually learning this feminazi shit."

"Dude, it's impossible not to. I am, like, the only guy in there. All eyes are on me. And I can't really talk or participate. I tried the first day."

"What happened?"

"It did not go well." Brent pulled himself up to sitting.

"Yeah?"

"Anything I said, some chick would interrupt me and say I was 'mansplaining.'" Brent lifted mocking air quotes. "I don't even know what that means! So they just shut me down every time, and I just said fuck it. Then, after class, this smoking hot girl with dreads leans over to me and tells me, 'now you know what it feels like to be a woman' and walks off."

"How are you still going to this class? Man, sounds like bullshit."

"Consider it counterintelligence. You know how many chicks I've pulled by saying buzzwords like 'male privilege.' And it's required."

"Yeah, yeah, you mentioned that."

"So, what are your big plans for Dress-Like-A-Slut Day? You trolling the annual kegger here, as usual?"

"Nah, man. The place is tapped. Senior year. I have been through all the slutty cops, slutty school girls, slutty nuns, slutty nurses, slutty cats, slutty devils, slutty pirates, slutty Harry Potter characters from the lit majors, slutty costumes I don't get from the science majors, slutty Freudian puns from the psych majors. The only new crop is the freshmen, and they get too damn drunk to be any fun."

The freshmen did get way too drunk, at every party, not just Halloween, but Dane would never make the freshman mistake again. Not after the slutty angel turned up pregnant right before Thanksgiving break. He could not bear another round that ended in juvenile crocodile tears while lobbying to keep the baby. Once he had said he would not be involved at all enough, she had found her way to the clinic.

"So, what are you doing instead?" Brent asked.

"I got a line on a good party."

"A line? What is this line?"

"I got this invitation."

"In your email? On Faccbook?"

"Nah, like a legit paper invitation. Someone slipped it under my door at the bash last weekend."

"Who uses paper invitations?"

"I don't know, but I've been doing these parties all year, every year. I've been banging these same sorority sisters and girls stumbling over from the dorms. If I fuck one more slutty animated princess or slutty storybook character, I may just sleep through the shit. I have a bucket list I am trying to check off here."

"I forgot about that. Last year was...?"

"Slutty cheerleader."

"Ah yes, I vaguely don't remember her."

"Yeah, me either."

"So what is possibly left on your Dress-Like-A-Slut Day bucket list?"

"I don't know, man. I guess I'll have to be surprised. Not a whole lot of the animal kingdom on my roster."

"Little pseudo bestiality. You're lucky I don't have a psychology requirement too. Have a field day on your ass today."

"Get your ass a beer, man. Before you go sprouting a vagina."

"Then I could be your slutty werewolf or whatever."

"You couldn't handle me, bitch."

Brent busted into ripples of sloppy laughter, slapping his knee and hacking on the lung char from the previous night's cigarettes. He shoved Dane harshly with his forearm.

"I have to get some hair of the dog in me to blast that image right off my brain cells." Dane laughed, standing. "Plus, I have to be prime tonight to find my slutty pumpkin or whatever."

"Now you're on to fruits and vegetables? Make up your mind, man."

"What are you going as tonight?"

"I am busting out Professor Poindickster, as usual." Brent tugged on the front of his shirt as if to pop the collar of his blazer with leather patches on the elbows.

"A classic. Works every year."

"You?"

"Doctor Feelgood." Dane let a hand slide down his chest with the name, stretching it slow.

"Nice, man. Well, tomorrow, you'll have to tell me what slutty costume you pulled."

"Over bloodies, no doubt."

"Right now, let's crack the brews and start working on these decorations."

"You want me to help on a party I won't even be attending?"

"Not our fault you're absconding. You got duties, bitch."

The alcohol licked below the surface of Dane's skin as he stood before the cracked mirror in the communal bathroom. The pregame drinks he had with the boys as they adorned the house with cheap and abused Halloween decorations throbbed in his veins, just like he wanted. Comfortably numb, appropriately relaxed, ready. He dug his fingertips into the hair wax and raked and tugged his hair into a pointed fauxhawk. Then he pulled on his lab coat and adjusted the empty glasses frames on his face. Doctor Feelgood, indeed.

As he checked, rechecked, and checked his appearance again, turning and angling himself in the unforgiving light, his phone chirped on the counter. His Uber was outside, waiting to whisk him away to a new and untold crop of scantily clad, costumed women.

The invitation led Dane far off campus. Flocks and droves of students swarmed over the dark lawns and weaved between the old buildings. He could hear the laughter and the thumping of party music through the car window. Dane slipped the flask from inside his lab coat and maintained a pleasant buzz on the bouncy seat.

The driver's GPS squawked commands that had the car twisting and twirling through the night streets. The driver was not a chatty one, like so many Uber drivers. He watched the road silently, leaving Dane to his lack of thoughts, until the small sedan rolled to a stop on a gravel parking lot. A large, warehouse-like building occupied the sky. The structure would have loomed dark and ominous as a horror movie set had the lights, music, and festering guests not enlivened it.

The music throbbed and the lights pulsated in the large room. Some enhanced mix of Monster Mash undulated through the air and the bodies on the dance floor. Spiderwebs laced every joust, wall, and corner, crawling out of the ceiling.

The bar stretched the length of the back wall, dark black and illuminated with vivid orange lights. Fake pumpkins adorned every few feet with carved eyes aglow. The bodies gyrated in circles on the flashing dance floor or clumped together in groups at the peripheral. Dane could make out the twisted shapes of wings, horns, scythes, capes in the strobed silhouettes.

This was no frat house party.

Dane took a deep inhale, the air humid with so much body heat and exhalations, and stepped toward the bar.

"What's your poison, sugar?" A tall vampire with bloodied cleavage up to her chin asked.

"Surprise me," Dane replied to her breasts.

Vampira pretended not to notice and smiled fangs at him just the same. She whirled around, her cape empathic to her turn. After a lifting a couple bottles, she turned back, dropping a clear plastic cup filled with a deep red liquid in front of him.

"Werewolf blood, honey. Ten dollars."

"Ten dollars?" Dane exclaimed.

"Don't worry, doctor," Vampira smirked. "The buzz is worth the price."

Dane reluctantly tossed a handful of bills on the bartop. Drink in hand, he drifted away from the laughing jack o' lanterns on the bar and toward the enticing mass of moving bodies on the dance floor. The tangle of dark shapes was mesmerizing. He pulled a deep sip of werewolf blood into his mouth. His tastebuds seized, and the back of his throat watered. Vampira did not lie; the blood packed all the bite she promised. He could feel the heat bloom instantly along his nerves, blurring and blending with all the other drinks he already had riding his bloodstream.

He found a tall table and leaned his elbow against it. A flock of angels wisped past him. Their hemlines danced above long, taut thighs, flirting at the terminal curve of their torsos. Their necklines plunged deep to expose the slow stretch of breastbones down to their navels. Tall, exaggerated wings towered above and molted feathers with every saucy step on impossibly high heels. Dane felt his eyes, and his penis, snap to attention. Until he remembered the little pregnant freshman had been an angel too. The memory negated his blossoming erection immediately, and his eyes returned to the crowd.

A fetish nurse emerged from the bar patrons. Sweat glistened on the shiny material cleaving to her like skin. Two red crosses covered her nipples beneath a tube of fishnet. Matching stockings climbed her legs into garters with red bows. She had coordinated these distracting bits with a PVC surgical mask and tiny traditional hat. She was the candy striper's damaged, slutty sister.

Dane could already hear the lines about how perfect she would be under the employ of Doctor Feelgood, yet her eyes were so fierce edged deeply in black. Her saunter was too confident and smoldering. An unfamiliar anxiety swelled at the sight of her. She was no insecure sorority sister, no drunken college girl. She stomped past Dane without even a glance in his direction.

Dane plunged into his drink, gulping at the liquid as if he were blood-thirsty. He permitted the buzz to penetrate deeper than his skin, creeping and pooling in his bones, permeating his brain. The larger the alcoholic wave swelled, the less he thought of the freshman nurse or the inadequacy that hinted among these women.

He was here on a mission. Doctor Feelgood would not be going home lonely tonight.

As he lifted his cup to his lips again, something collided with the back of his head. His nose slammed into the rim, and werewolf blood splattered down the front of his crisp, white lab coat.

"What the fuck?" Dane said, whirling around, already balling up a fist at his side.

"Oh my God, I am so sorry!"

Dane saw her eyes first. They practically glowed in the shifting light, a blazing amber under a bristle of long eyelashes. At contact with them, suddenly there was no air in the room. He gaped at her for a long, pregnant second until she reached forward and started brushing at his lab coat, snapping him back to the flesh.

"I am so sorry," she said again. "These things have a mind of their own."

She rolled her gleaming eyes in the direction of the long, angled appendage that had clocked Dane in the head. Still mute, Dane glanced up at the long leg and followed it from where it dangled in the air above her to where it intersected her body with seven matching siblings. At some point, he noticed his mouth gaped wide.

"Maybe a spider wasn't the most appropriate costume for such a packed party," she laughed as she still dabbed at the blood drops on his coat to no avail.

"No," Dane finally stuttered. "You look amazing."

"Oh, thank you." She smiled. Genuinely. Her eyes radiated all the brighter on top of her rising cheeks.

"How did you even make all this?"

Dane looked over the grand, dangling eight legs again. Each leg was hearty, climbing into the air from her back before plunging back down. The black segments were smooth, almost sharp. Dane could not make out what material they were made from in the low light. The legs moved in chorus to the sway of her perfectly shaped torso. She wore a black bodysuit that left absolutely nothing to the imagination. Even in the dim and flashing light, Dane could make out the contours of her muscles against the fabric. The cloth terminated at the edges of her torso, leaving her own legitimate appendages completely exposed. Her dark skin was flawless, perfect in a way Dane did not know was possible. There were too many appealing points on her body for him to take in without awkwardly gawking.

Her costume was as jarringly amazing as it was starkly sexy.

"Well, if I'm being honest, I'm kind of obsessed," she answered. "Spiders are kind of my thing. All the time. Not just around Halloween."

Spiderweb earrings dangled from her earlobes. A sparkling, beaded spider pendant adorned her bare chest. When she turned her head, Dane noticed that her braided hair had been segmented and connected to weave a web down the back of her head.

"Wow," he said, feeling his heart climb back down into his chest. "I see that might just be an understatement. But you look amazing."

"Thank you," she said again, another true smile.

The attraction blared through Dane's brain, loud enough that he could feel it reverberate on his nerves. Bucket list or not, missing spider checkbox or not, this was the girl. He could forget it was Dress-Like-A-Slut Day at all looking into those fierce eyes of hers. He felt more drawn in, more distracted than he ever remembered.

"Let me buy you a new drink," she said. "What is that? Werewolf blood?"

"How did you know?"

She raised a matching cup of the same deep red. Dane laughed.

"You're right, but let me get it," he said.

"No, I knocked your drink all over you."

"You did, but if you try to plow your way to the bar with those things, you're going to be buying the room a round. Let me."

"I guess you have a point."

"Two werewolf bloods?"

The spider nodded.

Dane's heart pounded in his ears as he reached the bar. He felt oddly winded, again gasping at air that seemed to have vanished. What the hell was wrong with him? Women never had this effect on him. Yet there was an undeniable flutter on his nerves. He could not stop thinking that she was the one tonight.

"Thank you, sir," the sexy spider said, reaching her human arm towards the cup.

"Dane," he said over the music.

"Charlotte," she replied, slipping her smooth, warm hand into his.

Charlotte hinged forward onto the table, swaying her hips as they talked. Her spider legs moved behind her, almost drumming like fingers. Dane found the way they crawled in the air as mesmerizing as it was unnerving, thrilling in the way it nibbled at instinctual danger. Dane mirrored her position to bring his face as close to hers as possible. She smiled out of the side of her mouth at him as they drained the werewolf blood.

"So Charlotte," Dane said, "why the spider obsession?"

"It's what I do," she replied. "I got my degree in entomology, but spiders are not insects. I am now getting my Master's in zoology with a focus in arachnology."

"That is impressive." Dane hoped Charlotte would not ask about the bullshit degree he had been half pursuing in his lackluster college career. He leapt to a new question before she had the opportunity. "What will you do with an arachnology degree?"

"Study spiders, of course," she laughed. "Spiders can indicate whether an ecosystem is in balance. They play a huge roll in insect population control. They are necessary."

Dane thought of the endless parade of spiders he had smashed beneath his sneaker sole and flushed down the dingy toilets in Delta Beta house. Something like a pang of guilt pooled in his throat.

"I guess I never thought about that."

"Most people don't. Most people just squash them with a shoe and flush them down the toilet. Then they bitch about all the mosquitoes or flies."

Dane swallowed that remorseful lump in his throat, smiling instead. Charlotte tipped up her glass and let the last of the blood drain into her throat. Dane chased the gesture, feeling the culmination of all their rounds of drinks pile on top of his forehead. His skin itched to touch her, yet his tongue fell impotent in conjuring a line to seduce her. Charlotte set her empty cup heavy between them as she leaned forward.

"Dane," she said, thick and slow.

"Yes?"

"Would you like to come home with me?"

Dane and Charlotte crammed in among her eight spindly legs in the backseat of another Uber. The legs seemed to grope at Dane as the road rolled beneath them. They curled the two of them into a grotesque cocoon as Dane felt Charlotte's warm, smooth hands exploring the fringe of his flesh. The heat of her mouth licked chills down his back as she let her teeth gently graze his neck. His nerves were vibrating with how much he wanted her.

Charlotte giggled seductively as Dane compulsively pawed at her up the stairs to her apartment door. Dane struggled to weave his arms beneath and between those twitching legs to put hands on her human body beneath. The alcohol pulsating and swirling through his system made him sloppy, desperate, hungry.

"I'm going to go slip out of this costume," Charlotte said against Dane's mouth as the door clicked shut behind them.

"Let me help you." His hands again at her.

"Down, boy." Her voice was so thick Dane could feel it caressing his ears. "You have no idea how complicated this costume is. It would not be a sexy thing to see me struggle out of it. You go there."

Charlotte extended a finger as spindly as her costume legs towards an open door in the dark. As she swept all her quivering legs into the bathroom, Dane stumbled into her bedroom.

Charlotte had not exaggerated; she was obsessed with spiders. Her bedroom looked like a seductively lit, painstaking Halloween display. Electric candles with flickering purple flames quivered on top of swirled metal candlesticks styled to resemble elaborate webs. Ornate black webs crawled in embroidered stitches across a pale bedspread. More sparkling beaded spiders, like the one scaling Charlotte's chest, dangled from glittering strands.

Dane took a deep breath, inhaling the same sweet scent that had radiated from Charlotte's skin all night. His consciousness struggled to swim up through the alcohol, all his liquid courage now weighing him down. He could not be down now, not weighted; he needed to be up. He needed to be as hard as possible for his first slutty spider.

Starting at his sticky shoes, Dane stripped himself down and spread himself over the swirled spiderweb pattern on the bed, like a fly trapped and waiting. He battled his sagging eyelids until Charlotte emerged to snap them open.

Her hidden skin carved her shape just as flawless and enticing as the exposed helpings had suggested. Without the distraction of so many bobbing, wayward legs, Dane could fully appreciate how gorgeous she was, perhaps the most dazzling he had ever bedded. Charlotte was no drunken slutty college girl.

She lingered in the doorway for a breath, filling the space and posing against the frame. The glowing orbs in her perfect face eyed him fiercely, a hunger of her own in the way they narrowed. A smile slyly crept over her face before she lowered her head and crawled over to him.

She felt too good. Her skin was too soft, too warm. Her moans too sweet and escalating. He could feel himself climbing as well, building toward that edge. He tried to breathe, tried not to think how painfully intoxicating she was enough to hold out. He struggled so desperately, he scarcely noticed her buck him off from her and flip on to her stomach.

As he slid back inside of her, he saw the design low on her back, as low as it could be. Two red triangles connected at the points, the red somehow bright against her dark skin.

"Holy shit," Dane laughed before he could catch the words between his teeth.

Charlotte tossed the web of braids over her shoulder and brought her piercing eyes to him. He nearly finished when her pupils seized him again.

"What?" she asked, smirking sexily.

"A black widow?"

She smiled authentically again, sliding the tip of her tongue along the ridges of her teeth.

"Oh, you have no idea," she grinned.

Seconds later, Dane could not contain himself any longer.

Drained of his drunken lust, Dane immediately felt the desire to toss on his bloodied lab coat and flee the scene rising. A familiar habit, muscle memory to his orgasm. Yet when he emerged from the bathroom, the curve of Charlotte's body crested from beneath the blanket. The rolling landscape of her flesh remained enticing. What if she wanted to go again? Could he count her as additional notches on the bucket list if they went additional rounds?

Charlotte's amber eyes locked onto his as she extended her hand out in the dark. Her fingers entwined and tangled his, dragging his body around hers like a blanket. Against her smooth form, he drifted off to sleep.

The pain signaled the alcohol's departure from his body, shriveling up his cells as it abandoned him. It hurt everywhere, from the dry heaviness of his brain in his skull to the frayed edges of all his nerves. Yet it pooled in his abdomen, heavy and pointed.

The sun had not yet breached the sky. The bedroom window remained a black view out into the night. Charlotte breathed heavy and slow beside him. Dane recognized his moment and took his clothes and his hangover out the door as she slept.

"A slutty spider?" Brent asked, sipping at the Bloody Mary in the red plastic cup. His eyes were veined as crimson as the liquid he gulped.

"Yes, a slutty spider," Dane confirmed, slurping his down as well.

"How does that even work, dude? How do you make a spider sexy? I am trying to picture it."

"She pulled it off. She had this tight little bodysuit on this tight little body then these huge legs coming out of it. She actually clubbed me in the head with one. That's how I got my in. Then when I flipped her over, black widow tramp stamp."

"Damn, man."

"I think this might have been my best and most successful Dress-Like-A-Slut Day yet."

"Who knew the gold would go to a fucking spider?"

"Literally. A fucking spider."

Brent lifted up his cup, and Dane cheers'd against it. As he brought the plastic rim to his lips, he winced. The pain stabbed at his stomach again, needling him deep below his belly button. The sensation started sharp, then slammed back against his spine. He steadied himself then took a deeper drink.

"You all right, man?" Brent asked.

"Yeah, yeah, totally fine. Just got a bitching hangover. We got down on a lot of some random drink called werewolf blood."

"Better drink up then. Hair of the dog. Or, I guess, werewolf."

The pain made a home in Dane's gut. The hangover washed over him like the tide, with another swelling up in its wake. Even beneath the fuzzy haze of keg beer and tequila body shots at the Dia de las Cervezas party chasing Halloween, Dane felt the persistent ache drilling into him, clawing as if it had legs. He could not even bring the sexy little blonde with sugar skull makeup smearing white kisses down his neck to his room. The pain doubled him over as he tried to stand.

Dane's head swelled as he placed his cup on the nearest surface. He could not tell if the alcohol had reclaimed the balance in his bloodstream or if he was straddling another hangover. As blondie turned and shook her very culturally inappropriate maracas in another's direction, Dane felt an unexpected and foreign pang of emotion crawl under his face. How could she just leave him like that? Could she not see that he was hurting?

When the alien sensation of tears burned at the rim of Dane's eyes, he fled through the grinding bodies and upstairs to his room.

"What the fuck are you doing, man?" he yelled at himself, stomping in ugly circles around the small space.

He pinched violently at his eyes, flinging the offending tears away from him.

"She's just some Zeta bitch. Thousand other just like her."

Anxiety twitched in Dane's legs. His pace swept frantically across the warped floorboards. His mind teemed with absurd thoughts as unfamiliar emotions collided in his chest. He did not feel himself. He felt infected somehow.

The pain punched him again in the stomach, halting his stride and folding him over it. The sensation flared at a point then crawled out in an itching burn along his nerves before weaving itself around his addled brain. He wanted to vomit; he wanted to cry. Sweat prickled over his scalp.

Frantic and sloppy, Dane groped at the hem of his shirt, tugging it up to his neck.

"What in the..." The words dropped out of his mouth.

The epicenter of his pain drew into a wound. The tiny scabbed circle pulsated swollen and angry. It rose up from his skin, and from its summit, red, branched veins drew lines in wayward directions across his stomach. Dane tentatively raised a shaky finger toward the lump, hesitant to probe it. When he finally brought his touch to his perverted skin, it stuck there. He retracted his fingertip, and a shiny strand cleaved to it.

Panicked, Dane swung and slapped his finger against his pants. The pain surged again from the livid pinprick and dragged Dane to the floor in a heap. His nerves crackled, and his muscles seized. Then the night opened up to swallow him.

Dane woke up in a heap as brutal sunlight rained down from the narrow window. Brent's bunk bed lay rumpled yet vacant. He must have found a bedmate at the party, probably the blonde sugar skull who abandoned Dane.

Dane felt the hangover in his bones, but his head pounded in a different rhythm. His eyes burned exhausted. Then the image of his spidery wound flashed over his mind. He snapped from the floor and scrambled to his feet. He ripped his shirt off over his head.

The circular red scab remained, yet the red spindles reaching out from it were gone. He shook his fingers then ran the tips over the wound. The surrounding skin held a sympathetic heat. The flesh was tender. Yet it was merely a scab.

He must have dreamt the sticky strand and creeping veins. Dane laughed in spite of himself and hurried downstairs.

The semester began to close, not that Dane ever paid attention. He only noted the waning in party frequency in the echo of Halloween and in anticipation of the Thanksgiving break on the horizon. He did not feel himself. That Halloween hangover, whatever it was, persisted on the edge of his mind, in that little scab that would not seem to heal.

Mostly, Dane felt nauseous. All the time. And exhausted. It felt like his muscles were packed with lead to match the weight in his eyelids. His stomach frothed and boiled in constant distress. Nothing smelled good or tasted good, except fried chicken and dark chocolate—separate or together.

He found himself wholly uninspired. The thought of alcohol made his throat seize. The idea of parties gave him a headache. He did not even consider chasing another tail. All he wanted was to curl up on the communal couch and dissolve into a movie. None of his brothers seemed exceptionally interested in that idea. They rolled their eyes as they left him for more active pursuits.

"Dane, man, what in the hell is going on with you?" Brent said, finding Dane again dozing on his bed between the classes he was skipping.

"What are you talking about?" Dane whined from the pillow.

"Are you fucking kidding me, dude? You stopped drinking. You stopped hustling bitches. I don't think you've gotten your dick wet since the slutty spider."

At the mention of the spider, Dane felt a burning nausea creep up the back of his throat.

"And that gut, dude," Brent said.

"What?" Dane gasped, shooting up from the mattress.

"That *gut*! Last month, you were rocking a six pack. Now, you're jiggling a straight keg."

Dane's face contorted in offense. His mouth remained ajar as he turned to the side and groped at his waist line. Maybe it was a little softer these days, but a keg?

"How could you say that to me?" Dane's voice wavered.

"What? Who is sprouting the vagina now? This is what I'm talking about, man. You haven't been the same since Halloween. What did that spider do to you?"

Brent waited for Dane to reply. Dane could only stare at him mutely with glistening eyes. Brent scoffed as he tossed up his hands and left the room.

Dane felt the burn through his sinuses climb into his tear ducts. He shook his head, utterly baffled by himself. As the first tear squeezed through his reluctant lids, the pain exploded over him again. His nerves sizzled at the point of the scab on his stomach and curled the rest of his body around it. The pain was hot, burning, moving, writhing. He coughed at it as he collapsed again to the mattress.

Then Dane threw up on the floor. Not the first time he had vomited in this house or on this floor specifically, but it was the first time he got to experience it with the razor edge of sobriety.

The next day, the movement began.

The sensation started at the root of the unhealing scab, branching out like the red veins Dane first hallucinated after too many cerverzas. It pushed and pulsated in the swell of the keg Brent identified on Dane's abdomen.

It started as a pressure to accent the dull pain that returned to hum up to his brain. Like his skin was not big enough, like something wanted to get out. Or in. Then it diversified. The blunt, rounded pressure grew points that wriggled independently. It felt like he was teeming.

Dane reached down to examine the feeling. The movement responded to him, pressed and clawed against his touch. His entire body seized. He stopped breathing.

This time, Dane made it to the toilet before he retched again.

What did that spider do to you?

Charlotte's apartment building looked different in the daylight. From what Dane remembered anyway. He was not even sure how he remembered how to get there. Yet he stood in the same parking lot where he grabbed through her many spider legs on that Halloween night.

He kept hearing Brent in his head. *What did that spider do to you?* Brent was right; he had not been himself since that night, since her. She had done something to him, given him something. Something was wrong with him, and the only thing he knew was that Charlotte was the start.

Charlotte did not answer the door when he knocked. He tried to wait but found himself pounding with his fist, desperately. When his force increased, the door slipped off the latch and squeaked open ominously.

Dane did not think. He shoved against the door and burst into the apartment. Yet he only penetrated the threshold before stopping cold, the door swinging closed softly behind him.

Long, sleek, glittering spiderwebs consumed the apartment. They reached spindles along the floor before climbing the corners and cleaving to the ceiling. They intersected and branched out over the furniture, framing the entire room in their wispy edges.

Dane felt his skin begin to crawl as the shifting in his abdomen became frantic. He cupped his belly, hoping to calm the scurry. He gulped down against the pain and forced his eyes to scan the room, taking cautious and reluctant steps forward.

Charlotte's bedroom was equally shrouded in web but was also layered in darkness. Shadows carved along the lines of the webs and created caverns out of the corners. Yet something glinted in the deepest recess, something amber and fiery.

"Charlotte?" Dane's voice quivered more than he wanted.

The glowing circles moved at the name, floating closer out of the darkness. The curve of Charlotte's face emerged from the shadow, still as sharply beautiful as when the alcohol hazed Dane's vision.

"I knew you would be back, Doctor Feelgood," Charlotte laughed, her white teeth catching the edges of the light. The chuckle on her tone was seductive and unnerving.

"Charlotte, what is going on here?"

"I'm redecorating. Do you like it?"

"No, not really. It's really creepy. Halloween is over."

"Your Halloween was over after you came inside me and vanished into the night. My Halloween is never over."

Oh no, Dane thought quickly. *She's a psycho.*

"Look, Charlotte. I'm really sorry about that. I figured with," Dane stopped himself. He did not know how to phrase it. He rarely had to have this conversation. Except with that freshman angel. "With how fast you went that you wouldn't mind me taking off."

Charlotte laughed again, sharper.

"You thought since I invited a stranger home with me I wouldn't expect a morning goodbye?"

"Something like that. I guess."

Dane felt heat in his cheeks. He looked down. The squirming in his belly became more agitated.

Charlotte moved closer again, her chest and shoulders cresting out of the darkness.

"Why are you here, Dane? You didn't think you could come back for seconds, did you?" Charlotte asked.

"No." Dane struggled to compose his thoughts. He could not form ideas with that clawing sensation on his insides. "You did something to me. You gave me something, Charlotte. Something is very wrong with me."

"Gave you something? You think you caught some STD from me? Something is very wrong with you, but it is not me."

"No, it started after I was with you. I have this scab that won't heal on my stomach. I'm getting fat even though I keep puking. All I do is sleep and cry. I haven't cried since the 7th grade. When my dog died. And I have cried multiple times just today. There is just horrible pain all the time. There feels like there is something inside me. Something clawing to get out."

"Oh poor Dane. You sound pregnant, sweetheart."

"I am not pregnant! I used protection."

"A condom was not going to keep you from getting pregnant."

"No. You know what I mean. I can't get pregnant."

Charlotte's smile carved deviously into her cheeks. Her blazing eyes laughed against Dane's. Her shoulders began to serpentine as she moved out of the shadows. She glided over to him quickly on her eight long legs.

"Charlotte, what the fuck? Why are you wearing that costume?" Dane yelled.

"What costume?"

Dane looked down to notice the legs did not sway and dangle the way they did on Halloween. They skittered across the ground, lifting Charlotte up and whisking her to him.

"What the f..." Dane lost the words. He lost thoughts.

"I'm not a slut dressed as a spider, Dane. I am an actual, literal slutty spider. And you're wrong; you can get pregnant. Those are thousands of my babies, our babies, scratching around inside you."

Dane lost breath. He gaped at Charlotte in all her arachnid glory as the swarm in his gut stirred to a frenzy. He could now feel all their tiny legs, the sensation given shape by identification. They moved together, in concert now, pressing hungrily toward their mother. He gritted his teeth against the pain and tried to deny the treacherous tears that returned to his eyes.

"How? How could you? How could you *impregnate* me?"

"How?" Charlotte mocked with a maniacal laugh. "You had sex with me."

"I didn't agree to this," Dane's voice cracked high and panicked. "This is my body. I don't want this."

"Oh honey." Charlotte took Dane's face in her hands. "Then you shouldn't have had sex with a spider."

Charlotte kept her human hands on his cheeks as her front spider legs reached out and raised him before her. Her touch sedated him. Her smoldering eyes mesmerized him. He scarcely noticed the thick web cord being stuck to his shoulder. When she began turning him over between her legs, winding the web around his body and encasing him in a sticky shaft, he began to feel drowsy.

"You know," Charlotte said as she worked. "Normal spiders don't lay their eggs in a host. That is the stuff of horror movies. They weave an egg sac and hatch them there. But I am something else. I am more evolved. I knew you were the one for this."

Dane murmured softly and incoherently as Charlotte placed him in a web sling, suspending him from the corner. He flirted with consciousness. Charlotte could hear her young teeming beneath his surface, growing stronger and closer. She perched back on her legs and waited.

Suddenly, Dane's eyes snapped open. A scream erupted from his lips, followed by a wave of blood. He sputtered on his own liquid, coughing to keep screaming. Charlotte's eyes lit up and grew wide. Even as Dane's body struggled against the webbing, she could see his abdomen puckering and swelling. His back arched violently as the first small, black spider perforated his skin.

The baby spider traversed Dane's landscape straight to Charlotte, followed by an avalanche of its writhing siblings. Charlotte extended her finger to her firstborn. Her eyes swelled with affection as she lifted it to her face.

"Eat," she whispered. "Eat, my babies."

She replaced her young onto Dane's shoulder amidst the swarm of her other children. The crawling mass poured out from Dane's split stomach, riding bloody waves out of his body. They climbed swiftly up the web strands constraining him. Dane continued to scream as they sunk an army of tiny fangs into his face.

The End

Mister Parker

By

Richard Chizmar

Benjamin Parker – Mr. Parker or Bulldog Parker, behind his back, to his eighth grade English students – lived a simple life.

By choice, he had no wife, no children, and no pets. He lived in a practical two-story house in the suburb of Forest Hill. The house was practical because it was located three miles from the middle school at which he taught – close enough to save on fuel costs, but far enough so that he didn't have to live amidst his pupils -- and because it was a perfect fit for his daily needs and extensive library.

Parker mostly kept to himself, although he attended a weekly book club every Thursday night and a monthly Friday night poker game with five other teachers from nearby schools. He spent most afternoons reading student papers and grading tests; most evenings in the library or in the back yard with his telescope.

Parker had two great loves in his life: books and astronomy. Naturally, his library featured many volumes that focused on his lifelong obsession with the night sky, but it was hardly limited to that subject.

Classic literature. Poetry. History. Biographies. Folklore. True crime. Photography. Cooking. Pop culture. Even modern fiction.

It was all there. Each volume categorized by genre; each author alphabetized; each book protected within carefully applied Mylar sleeves.

When Parker was a younger man, he often spent his weekends driving to various rare or used bookshops, searching for hard-to-find titles to fill out his collection. Of course, he could have done much of this buying via the telephone or mail order catalog, but he enjoyed his treasure hunts, as he referred to them. He never felt lonely on these road trips; quite the contrary. He enjoyed driving the winding back roads and listening to music while the wind whipped through his hair and cooled his cheeks.

But, as the years passed and the internet forced many booksellers out of business, these trips dwindled from weekly to monthly to every other month until finally, Parker barely managed two or three road trips a year.

Now most of his book purchases were completed through numerous online websites and occasional slumming on eBay – which is precisely what Parker was doing when Kelly Rutherford walked into his classroom after the final bell on Friday and interrupted him.

***

"I'm sorry to bother you, Mr. Parker."

Parker started and looked up from his computer screen in surprise; he hadn't heard anyone come in. He closed the laptop and put on his best English teacher smile.

"No bother at all, Miss Rutherford. How can I help you?"

"I was wondering…" The girl started shuffling papers out of a bright pink notebook. "…if you wouldn't mind reading my paper this weekend if you're not too busy." She dropped one of the pages onto the desk, quickly grabbed it and almost knocked over Parker's coffee mug. "I know it's not due until next Friday, but I finished early and I'm a little worried if I'm on the right track or not."

Kelly Rutherford was a straight "A" student, class president, and *always* worried if she was on the right track or not.

Parker stood up and walked around his desk. Took the outstretched pages.

The girl shrugged apologetically. "I understand if you're too busy, I just thought—"

"It's fine, Miss Rutherford. I'd be happy to give it an early read." He opened the briefcase on his desk, placed the paper inside, and clicked it shut again.

The girl beamed in relief and squeezed her hands together in a gesture Parker found both odd and charming. "Thank you *so* much, Mr. Parker. I really appreciate it."

Parker, for reasons he couldn't have explained if he tried, steepled his own hands together and gave a polite, little bow.

The girl looked momentarily confused, then broke out in a giggle. "Well, thanks again, Mr. Parker."

She practically skipped out of the classroom before pausing by the door and looking back over her shoulder. "Oh, yeah, and Happy Halloween." She flipped him a wave and was gone.

The smile faded from Parker's face, his eyes troubled. He picked up the mug from his desk and took a long swallow of lukewarm coffee. "Happy Halloween, indeed."

***

Benjamin Parker lived a simple life. He was a strict and respected teacher. A quiet and courteous, if not overly friendly, neighbor. And a kind and trustworthy friend within his small circle; even if they all tended to tease him about his eccentricities and overly private nature.

Parker was a man of moderate taste, temperament, and behavior. He was, as the self-help gurus liked to say, very comfortable in his own skin. In fact, he often thought to himself: *I have my stars and my books and my peace of mind; that is more than enough for any man.*

Most people would have been shocked to learn that there were indeed two matters Parker despised with enough passion to upset his calm exterior: drunks and Halloween.

His father had been a drunk -- a violent one -- and Parker had suffered at his hands. A broken arm one night after the old man had lost yet another job. Three broken fingers when Parker had made the mistake of sticking up for his mother after she burned a pot roast dinner. Permanent scars on his back and buttocks after Parker had accidentally knocked his father's beer off a tv tray or left his bicycle in the front yard overnight. More black eyes and bruises than he could count or remember. Parker eventually learned to antagonize his father when he had been drinking, to invite his aggressions, in an effort to spare his mother. All this by the time Parker was eleven years old.

The nightmare lasted until his father's death in a hit-and-run accident shortly after Parker's fifteenth birthday. The old man had been drunk, of course, staggering home from a bar in the middle of the night -- *and* the middle of the road. Someone simply came tearing around the bend on old Route 22, drove him down like a stray cat, and kept right on going.

Two days later, they buried him on a rainy Sunday morning. Only three people stood at the gravesite: Parker, his mother, and the preacher. His mother had a black eye. There were no tears that day.

***

Parker took a left on Hanson Road and drove slowly down his street. It was too early for trick-or-treaters, but he was by nature a careful man. The speed limit was 25 miles per hour, so he drove 25 miles per hour.

He focused on the road ahead of him, doing his best to avoid looking at the garish Halloween decorations adorning his neighbors' houses. He was particularly grateful that it was still light out and none of the fat orange pumpkins sitting on front porches were smiling their jagged, glowing grins.

Parker signaled a right hand turn, slowed, and pulled into his driveway. He turned off the ignition and sat behind the wheel for a moment. He didn't feel quite right. At first, he had thought it was the usual trepidation he felt toward the final night of October, but now he was starting to believe he was coming down with something. His heart was beating too hard and his head felt swimmy and unfocused.

He grabbed his briefcase from the seat next to him and got out of the car. As he was walking up the front walk, a voice called out to him from across the street.

"Happy Halloween, Benjamin!"

He turned and saw his neighbor, Carol Perkins, raking leaves into narrow, makeshift burial mounds, each one centered in front of a fake, Styrofoam tombstone.

Parker gave her a half-hearted wave and continued onto his front porch and into the house. His briefcase felt heavier than usual. He needed to rest.

***

If Parker were ever forced to acknowledge and then explain his loathing of Halloween, he probably would have opted for the simplest explanation: it was a frivolous tradition that bordered on the sacrilegious; a greedy retailer-manipulated holiday based on cheesy decorations and cavity-inducing sweets.

But Parker knew that day would never come. Only two people in the world knew about his true feelings toward Halloween. He was the first (and he wasn't talking), and his mother was the second (and she wasn't either; Parker had buried her two decades earlier in a cemetery far away from where his father's corpse lay rotting).

The truth of the matter was Parker hated Halloween because of his father. No surprise there.

Parker's father wasn't big on holidays. Most Christmases he was solidly in the bag by the time presents had been opened and the smell of ham was just beginning to waft out of the kitchen. Thanksgiving was a blurred nightmare of football blaring on the television and loud, drunken complaints about food preparation. The fourth of July was more than likely a fistfight at the neighborhood picnic and an early exit, thus guaranteeing that Parker would once again miss the fireworks display after dark.

But Halloween was the worst of all...because Parker's father actually *liked* it. He would start decorating the house and planning his costume by mid-October -- paying little attention to Parker's own costume or excitement -- and by the time the thirty-first rolled around, their house was a gaudy mess of fake spider webs and ghosts hanging from trees; plastic tombstones scattered across the front yard; and nearly a dozen glowing jack o'lanterns lining the porch and front walk.

As dusk darkened the October sky on Halloween night, Parker's father would appear in full costume -- the most memorable being an incredibly life-like Frankenstein, complete with stitched, green skin and nuts and bolts in his skull -- and inevitably he would be reeking of liquor.

When Parker would come downstairs dressed in his own costume -- a hobo or a clown or a fighter pilot; usually something his mother helped him make -- his father would make merciless fun of him, calling him "fag" or "sissy" or "homo."

Then he would spend the rest of Halloween night sneaking sips of whiskey and jumping out from behind the tall shrubs that bordered the front porch and terrifying unsuspecting trick-or-treaters. Many of the children would scream in terror and run crying back to their parents waiting on the sidewalk -- but very few of those parents would complain; Parker's father was a very large man.

Eventually, as the years passed, fewer and fewer children came trick-or-treating to Parker's house, and he knew his sadistic father was to blame.

Parker learned to hate his father even more for ruining Halloween.

***

Parker double-checked that the front porch light was turned off and retreated to his library. Dropping his briefcase to the hardwood floor, he practically collapsed into his favorite reading chair, immediately feeling at home in its soft leather embrace. He closed his eyes for a moment and tried to settle his breathing.

He was feeling worse. He'd decided to skip dinner -- he wasn't very hungry at all, which was unusual -- and spend his evening reading and listening to music.

Parker pushed on the armrests and the chair readjusted itself into a lounger. He reached over and took his book-in-progress from the end table and rested it on his lap. He closed his eyes again (*just for a second*, he thought), and just as he heard the first distant chatter of trick-or-treaters out on the street, he drifted off to sleep -- and dreamed of his father dressed as Frankenstein chasing him down a dark sidewalk.

***

It was little surprise that a beloved book resting in his lap had helped to lull Parker to sleep. In many ways, books were his security blanket and salvation.

Not surprisingly, he had learned his love of literature from his mother. As far back as his memory stretched, he could remember his mother borrowing stacks of books from the local library and reading to him in his tiny bedroom. Reading wasn't limited to bedtime in their house; it was an any-time-of-the-day activity. It wasn't until Parker was a little older -- and reading himself -- that he understood what his mother was doing, what she was *providing* for them both.

An escape.

An escape from the nightmare world they lived in.

An escape to faraway worlds and experiences that were often magical and mysterious and, most importantly, *happy*.

This certainly explained why his mother read two or three books herself each week. She couldn't defend her son from the almost daily physical blows and psychological torment, but she *could* teach him that other worlds -- better worlds -- existed within his reach.

After she was gone, Parker realized that his mother had blessed him with the most precious gift of his lifetime -- hope.

***

Parker awoke with a start, heart thudding in his chest, face bathed in a sheen of sweat. He jerked to a sitting position, and the book tumbled from his lap onto the floor. He couldn't remember his nightmare, but he knew it had been a bad one.

He looked around the dark room, confused, the flickering orange flames from the gas fireplace the only available light.

Something was wrong -- with him *and* the room.

I could've sworn I switched on the lights in here...and I know I didn't turn on the fireplace...and why was everything so damn blurry and out of focus?

Parker bent over and picked up the book and placed it back on the end table. His hand was shaking. He carefully got to his feet, steadying himself against the chair. He was dizzy and could feel a blue-ribbon headache blooming in the back of his head.

I'm dehydrated, he thought. *Need water.*

He started to shuffle his way out of the library -- but stopped abruptly, legs frozen, eyes wide, when one of the shadows in the corner of the room detached itself from the wall and slithered behind a tall potted plant.

"Who's there?" Parker asked in a trembling voice. "I saw you. You can't hide in here."

There came no response.

Parker held his breath, listening for a sound of any kind.

Nothing.

Summoning courage, he took a slow, silent step forward -- just as someone banged three times on the library window.

Parker let out a little scream and almost knocked over the big, museum quality globe that was the centerpiece of his library. He steadied himself again and focused on the lone window in the room, a dark square floating against an even darker backdrop. *Had someone knocked on the outside of the window -- or the inside?*

The thought made Parker's head spin, and he brushed it aside.

Enough of this, he thought, and deliberately made his way out of the library and into the hallway. The foyer ceiling light was on, and he shielded his eyes from the sudden brightness. He started for the kitchen--

--and the front doorbell rang.

Parker froze and looked at the door. *Stupid kids.*

The doorbell rang again.

"Go away!" he bellowed. "No trick-or-treaters allowed!"

He was answered by a violent pounding on the door -- BOOM! BOOM! BOOM!

Using the wall to support himself, Parker shuffled into the foyer and took out an umbrella from the base of the coat rack. He held it high over his shoulder, poised to strike, and reached for the doorknob.

***

Parker yanked open the front door -- "I told you kids to get out of here!" -- and found the porch empty.

He squinted into the darkness, peering up and down the silent street. It was later than he thought -- *how long had he slept?* -- and the sidewalks were devoid of trick-or-treaters.

A sudden rustling noise came from the bushes that bordered the right side of the porch. Parker lifted the umbrella high above his head. "Who's there? Come out and show yourself!"

When no one answered, Parker leaned back inside the doorway and flipped on the front porch light.

He turned back to the bushes on the side of the porch -- and froze in terror.

His eyes locked on a large, green puddle of rubber -- *a Frankenstein mask* -- lying on the edge of the concrete porch, and right next to it, scrawled in big, dripping red letters, a single hateful word: **FAG**

"Nooo!" Parker wailed.

He stumbled toward the mask, his face twisted in disbelief, and then he sniffed the faint scent of liquor in the night air. The smell struck him like a physical blow and he slammed back against the house, hitting his head against the brick and dropping the umbrella. *Dad?*

Rustling came from the bushes again, and this time, Parker could see the shrubs moving.

"Dad?" he whispered, not recognizing the sound of his own voice. "Is that you?"

The shrubs abruptly stopped moving. A gentle breeze stirred the bare trees. A dog barked. Somewhere down the street, a car started and drove away.

"It can't be you." Parker took a step forward, his voice louder now, already edging into panic. "You're dead. It can't be you."

Another step -- and the smell of liquor touched his nose again. "Nooo! It can't be! I killed you, you son-of-a-bitch!" He surged forward. "I ran you down like the junkyard dog you are!"

He dropped to his knees and picked up the mask in both hands -- and that's when his tired heart finally burst inside his chest.

Parker, a simple man with simple hopes, had just enough time to look at the mask and think *Wait, this isn't Frankenstein; it's Shrek, isn't it?* before everything went black and he collapsed dead to the porch floor, still grasping the rubber mask in both of his hands.

***

November 6, 2016 edition of the Baltimore Sun newspaper:

JUVENILES ARRESTED FOR HALLOWEEN PRANK GONE AWRY

Baltimore County Police Detectives made several arrests yesterday in the tragic, accidental death of Forest Hill resident and longtime Fallston Middle School teacher, Benjamin Parker.

Names are being withheld because the suspects are juveniles, but numerous sources report that three arrests were made yesterday afternoon at Fallston Middle School, including one female and two male students.

Parker, 51, a resident of the 1900 block of Hanson Road, was found dead on his front porch the morning of November 1, 2016 by concerned neighbors.

An investigation was launched after police found a hate message sprayed on Parker's front porch and a mysterious rubber mask still grasped in the deceased's hands.

While the coroner's report listed cardiac arrest as the official cause of death, subsequent toxicology reports indicated the presence of an unusually high dosage of a yet-to-be-named drug, which most likely caused blurred vision, severe confusion, heightened anxiety, and hallucinations.

An unnamed police source revealed that one of the students allegedly spiked Parker's coffee during school hours, then all three students allegedly appeared at Parker's Hanson Road home later that October night to play a Halloween prank on him.

All three suspects are being held in the Baltimore County Eastern Precinct until a bail hearing can be arranged...

The End

Girlfriend

By

Andrew Lennon

Simon awoke feeling refreshed. This was the first Saturday, for as long as he could remember, that he hadn't been ripped from his sleep by the sound of an alarm. He picked up his phone, as was always the first thing he did each morning. The time read 11:48. No wonder he felt refreshed, his alarm had always been set to 8:00. In the middle of the phones screen was a message.

Four missed calls.

He didn't need to check who it was. It was the reason he had turned his phone to silent before going to bed. He placed the phone back on the side, and went to the bathroom to empty his bladder.

After retrieving his phone from the bedroom, he walked to the kitchen wearing nothing but his underwear, filled the dirty, old, white kettle with water and then flicked the switch. While waiting for it to boil, he stood staring out of the window. The day outside captured his mood perfectly. The sun was shining, the sky clear blue. Even the grass looked greener. Unseasonable for this time of year, but that made it feel better.

The sound of a vibration pulled him from his thoughts. He turned to see the light on his phone flashing on and off. The display said, *Susan.* Simon let out a sigh, and then answered the phone.

"Hello, Susan."

"Simon, I was hoping we could talk."

"There's nothing to talk about."

"But there is, I wish we hadn't split up."

"But you split up with me!"

"I know, and I wish I hadn't."

"Well, you should have thought about that beforehand, shouldn't you?"

"I want to give us another try."

"No."

"It's Halloween."

"What does that matter?"

"You know how much I love Halloween, how much I love to scare you." She giggled.

Simon put the phone down by his side and took a deep breath. He then lifted it back to his ear.

"We've already been through this."

"I know, but..."

He hung up.

Still wearing nothing but his underwear, Simon sat in front of the television on a floral patterned couch. He didn't even like that couch. The only reason it was there is because Susan had chosen it. Why he had let her choose *his* furniture was beyond him. At the time, he agreed with her that it made sense since they would probably end up sharing furniture one day, anyway.

How wrong they had been.

Looking at his watch, he noticed it was almost 12:45. He changed the channel to *Sky Sports 1* in anticipation of the Everton v Chelsea game. He couldn't remember the last time he had actually been able to sit at home and watch the football. In fact, he'd only called to renew his *Sky Sports* subscription last night to ensure that he was able to watch this game.

Simon had always been a big Everton fan. Using his season ticket, he would go to every home game. He also forked out the money every other week to go and see the away games. That was years ago. After he had gotten with Susan, the first thing to go had been his season ticket. She had said that it was too expensive, for what it was anyway, and seeing as they would spend weekends together, he wouldn't even have time to go to the games.

At the time, they'd been spending most weekends having sex as much as they could. He loved football, but even Simon was willing to sacrifice it, if it meant he could watch Susan's ass bouncing up and down on his cock. Or grab her red hair in his hands as she went down on him. Simon started to harden at the montage of sexual memories. He moved his hand down and gripped himself.

Not done this on the couch for a while

He smirked. Slowly, he started to stroke himself when the phone started ringing. He looked at the display and immediately lost all interest in pleasuring himself. He tucked himself away and then answered the phone.

"What?"

"Don't be like that," Susan said in almost a whisper. Simon could tell she had been crying.

"Susan, the footy is about to start. What do you want?"

"Oh, so you got *Sky Sports* now, then?"

"Not that it's any of your business, but yes."

"Perhaps I could come over and watch something with you?"

"Don't be bloody stupid, Susan. You don't even like the footy!"

"Well, I would do something else while you watch it." Her tone had changed now. It sounded sultry, provocative.

"Well..." Simon paused and smiled. "I wouldn't fucking want you here." And then he hung up.

The football match had been and gone. Simon had been drinking while he watched it. This was something he used to do all the time. He would start drinking, no matter what time the game started, and then he wouldn't stop until he could drink no more. Nowadays, he was a bit more sensible. He had drunk a couple of cans and that was his limit. Still, he was feeling a bit tipsy. His tolerance for alcohol wasn't what it used to be, his age a deciding factor in the limited consumption throughout the years. He decided to browse through the TV Guide and check out what horror movies were scheduled for later. There's always some good slasher movies on around Halloween. Something to take his mind of that pain in the ass, and the Everton game.

During the game, Simon's phone rang several times. He'd deliberately ignored it, already annoyed with Susan. He didn't want her ruining the football match as well. As it turned out, Everton had lost anyway and given a terrible performance, so it probably would have been more fun arguing with her. The phone lit up again.

Ah, speak of the devil.

"Well, hello again."

"Simon, I want to…"

"I was hoping you would call," Simon said, trying not to sound smug.

"Really?" Susan couldn't hide her excitement.

"Yeah, I was just thinking. I haven't spoken to that bitch, Susan, in a while."

"Simon, why are you talking like that?" He could hear that she was crying again.

"I was hoping you would call just so I could hang up on you again. Bitch."

He hung up the phone. It rang again, almost immediately, but Simon just threw it on the glass coffee table. He couldn't help but notice how filthy that table was. He had never bothered with cleaning around the flat. He supposed that he should start doing a little bit, now that Susan wasn't there to do it for him.

The phone rang again; he ignored it once more.

On the table he noticed a magazine. It must have been Susan's, as he never bought magazines. At the top of the front page was a picture of a large red stamp, the kind that was used years ago to seal envelopes; one of those proper, old-school wax stamps. The bottom of it was dripping, like blood, and in the centre of the stamp was a name, *Dark Chapter Press*. The rest of the front cover was filled with horror pictures; a creepy doll's head with blood dripping from an empty eye socket, a picture of a surgeon holding a bloody knife. Simon opened the magazine and flicked through until he reached the centre page. There was a story filling one of the pages – *Intruder*.

Andy sat on the king-sized bed, alone. He had gone up to his room early to watch a movie. Wearing pyjamas that were covered with pictures of Animal from The Muppets, he sat, his legs crossed next to the remotes on the purple and cream duvet cover.

He picked up his two litre bottle of Pepsi and took a big gulp. After letting out a loud belch, he grabbed the remote and flicked through the channels. Once he'd scrolled through the entire TV guide and realised that, as usual, there was nothing on, he settled on the Horror Channel.

The front door squeaks, while being opened downstairs. It squeaks again, when being closed. The latch is turned, so as to make sure that the door does not slam. The house has thin walls and ceilings. Andy hears every noise that the door makes. Thinking that it is nothing more than his son coming back from a friend's house, he ignores it.

The movie on tonight is The Dead Zone. Being a big Stephen King fan, Andy gets excited for this viewing, but first he has to put up with old Doctor Who episodes. Having never been a Doctor Who fan, he only half-watches it, looking up every now and then while playing on his iPad. The episode tonight has weird clowns that keep attacking the doctor. There is something sinister about clowns that just rubs Andy the wrong way.

Downstairs there is more noise. Each door was being opened, and then closed again. As if someone is entering each room, looking for someone.

"Craig!" Andy shouted. "I'm upstairs, everyone else is out."

No answer comes. Perhaps Craig didn't hear him, although that's very unlikely because of the thin walls.

After a few minutes, he hears footsteps coming up the stairs. His bedroom door opens and a large man enters wearing a balaclava. In his hand is a large machete.

"What the fuck?" Andy screams.

He falls sideways off the bed.

The intruder tries to make his way around the bed, but there is a wardrobe up against the wall at the end of the bed. There is a gap to get around, but it's very small and the intruder is too large to fit. Before he can process the thought and go over the bed instead, Andy jumps up and grabs the baseball bat that he has propped on top of the head board.

"You fucker," Andy shouted. "You're not gonna cut me!"

He jumped at the intruder and swung the bat, connecting with the side of the head. He can't see the extent of the damage from the blow because of the balaclava, but the intruder collapsed to the floor, dropping the machete. Andy knew he'd done enough to give himself the upper hand.

Andy quickly reached down and grabbed the machete before the intruder regained consciousness.

"Break into my house will you? You fucker!"

Andy raised the machete into the air. He pushed his foot on the shoulder of the unconscious body, so that it rolled over and lay on its back. Then Andy drove the machete down into the chest. He could see the eyes open wide with shock, the mouth opened as if to let out a scream, but all that followed was a gurgling sound.

In a rage-fueled frenzy, Andy repeatedly stabbed the machete into the intruder's mid-section, over and over again. He could smell shit from where he had pierced the bowel. Still, he stabbed again. After what seemed like hours, but was, in fact, only a few minutes, he stopped. Panting for breath, Andy walked around the body and leaned down to look at the head. He stared straight into the dead man's eyes.

"Right you, fucker. Let's see who you are."

He pulled the balaclava from the head. Andy's jaw dropped … he was staring face to face with his brother.

He stepped slowly and zombie-like, in a daze, down the stairs. When he reached the bottom, he turned to enter the living room. As he opened the door, the lights were turned on and a crowd of people jumped up from all around the room.

"SURPRISE!" They all yelled.

"Ha, look at your face!" Craig said. "I knew that Mike would scare the shit out of you with that burglar trick. I can't wait to see it."

"What?" Andy asked, still in shock.

"I hid the camera in your room so we could see the prank. I'll bet it was golden." Craig laughed. "Mike bring the camera down!"

"He's not there." Andy said, almost in a trance-like state.

"Where is he?"

"Well, that was fucked-up. Still 'tis that time of year, I guess." Simon threw the magazine back on the table. A cold shiver ran down his spine, forcing him to turn and look behind him.

"Stupid, fucking story."

He walked to the kitchen to get himself a drink, stopping to check behind him, feeling that he was being watched. He looked down at his phone and started browsing through his news feed on *Facebook*. The whole feed seemed to be filling with pictures of pumpkins or *Michael Myers;* people can't even come up with something original anymore. In his peripheral vision, he thought that he saw something move. He turned to look, but nothing was there. The only thing there was a cupboard. It wouldn't be possible for anything to move.

His phone rang, making him jump, and then drop the handset. Luckily, he managed to crouch down and catch it before it landed on the hard, tiled floor. He quickly swiped to answer and put the phone to his ear.

"Fuckin' hell, Susan. You scared the –"

"– Simon, it's Maria."

Simon pulled the phone away from his ear and looked at the display. The display confirmed that it was Maria. He wasn't sure why he'd questioned it, even for a second. It was only a matter of time until she called. Maria was Susan's sister. Now that Susan had gotten nowhere with her calls, she had asked Maria to call for her, instead. This just made Simon even angrier. So now they were going to try and gang up on him? He put the phone back to his ear.

"Have you called to wish me a fucking, happy Halloween as well?"

"Simon, I..." She was crying.

"Oh, don't you start as well! Listen, Maria, I'm not being funny but..."

"She's *dead*, Simon!"

Simon felt the blood drain from his face. He felt numb. "What did you say?"

"Susan is dead, Simon. She was upset and wanted to make up with you. You wouldn't answer her calls. So she decided to drive over and talk to you, face to face. I...I don't know exactly what happened. I haven't even been given any proper news yet. I've just had some woman who said she was a police officer call me from Susan's phone. Apparently, there's been an accident involving her car and a lorry. They're going to call me back later to..."

By this point, Simon had stopped listening. He placed the phone on the side next to the kettle and walked slowly, in a daze, to his bedroom. He dropped down on the bed and shoved his face in the pillow.

He cried.

Simon awoke disorientated. He hadn't meant to fall asleep. He slid out of bed and shuffled through his flat towards the kitchen, seeking coffee.

Flicking the switch on the kettle, he noticed his phone lying on the side next to it. He remembered the phone call. *Had that really happened or was it just a dream?* He knew that he had been slightly drunk after watching the football, plus that story creeped him out. Between that and all this crap with Susan lately, it could have been playing on his mind. That's how nightmares come about, isn't it?

"Please, God, let it be a dream."

He picked up the phone and swiped to unlock the screen. The display said, *Eight missed calls.*

"Ha ha, yes!" Simon's shout echoed from the kitchen walls.

It was a dream. Recently, the sight of those missed calls and messages had driven him to the point of insanity, but now he couldn't be more relieved.

In the back of his mind, there was still a lingering shadow of doubt. He felt like he had to double check. He didn't want to be with Susan anymore, but he couldn't bear the thought that something had happened to her. He wanted to be sure, but he didn't want to call Susan, either. That would give her false hope. Instead, he scrolled through his contacts to Maria and called her.

As the phone started to ring, he began to think that this was a bad idea. *What exactly would he say?* He hadn't thought this through. Before he had chance to think any further the call was answered.

"Hello."

"Hello, Maria. I was just calling to see if everything was OK?"

"What?" Now he could hear that she was crying. "I'm sorry, Simon. I still haven't heard anything else if that's what you mean."

Simon felt like his stomach was twisting inside out. His knees began to shake along with his arms. It wasn't a dream.

"Maria, I'm sorry." He cried. "I'm so sorry."

"It's not your fault, Simon. I tried to tell her to just leave it. But she loved you so much. She just wouldn't let it go."

Simon's cry had now turned into a full sob. His words were completely unintelligible. He finally managed to force out. "If you need me to do anything…"

"I'll let you know. Listen, Simon. I have to go. Good bye."

The phone went dead. Simon stood staring at the blank screen. He felt completely helpless. He had no idea what to do. Perhaps, if he had just given her a little bit more of a chance then she would still be alive. The phone in his hand vibrated and then started to ring again. He looked at the display.

Susan.

Trembling, Simon put the phone to his ear.

"H, h, hello?"

"Happy Halloween, lover." It was Susan's voice, but it sounded strange. Like it was under water.

"Susan!" Simon shouted.

"Simon, I want us to be together again." It was so faint.

"Susan, I can hardly hear you. Are you OK? Maria said you…you were."

"Don't worry, Simon. I'm on my way now."

"How are you calling?" Simon was sobbing again, now. "You are…Maria said you are dead"

"I'll be there soon." This time her voice was very clear, and then the phone disconnected.

It didn't take long before Simon's grief and despair turned to anger. He paced back and forth through the living room, walking around the couch and the glass coffee table.

"Fucking bitches. What a horrible fucking joke."

He picked up his phone and called Susan. It went straight to voicemail.

"Fucking typical."

He dialled Maria. This time it rang.

"Hello," she answered.

"Do you think that was fucking funny?"

"What?"

"You know what!"

"Simon, I..."

"Susan just fucking called me! Being all spooky and everything. Ohhh, Simon, I'm coming over. Ohhh, Simon, it's Halloween. You know how *sick it is* to pretend someone is dead? You are both vile. Tell her that she best not come near this place or I'll kill her myself!"

He hung up the phone before Maria had chance to say anything else. Still shaking with rage, Simon threw his phone at the glass table. He was hoping that the table would smash, feeling that breaking something would relieve him of this anger. What happened was far less satisfactory. His phone just slid along the table, knocking the magazine off, before eventually sliding under the couch.

"Oh, for fuck's sake."

He pulled the table out of the way. It made a horrible screeching noise as he dragged it along the laminate flooring. He lay down on the floor and looked under the couch to see where the phone had slid. It was so dark that he couldn't see anything. He reached his hand under to feel around for it.

From under the couch came a hand. It grabbed Simon's arm. Simon looked at the tight grip of the fingers wrapped around his forearm. He jumped up from the floor, screaming and shaking his arm. Nothing was there.

Simon looked down at the couch. Still shaking with fear, rational thoughts began to enter his head again. The gap under the couch must be three inches at best. There is no way that anyone, or anything, other than his phone, could fit under there. The doorbell rang, making him jump again.

"Jesus Christ, I'm going to have a heart attack today."

He stormed to the door, shaking, trembling. He looked through the peephole. Magnified by the circular glass was Susan's smiling face. Simon could feel the blood rush to his head again. He was glad that she'd finally turned up. He needed a good argument to get rid of all this anger and stress. He dragged the door open.

"Right, you..." He stopped.

No one was there. For a split second, he felt terrified, but then the anger came rushing back, again. So now they were being so childish as to play knock and run. Simon slammed the door shut so hard that it echoed through the living room. He wanted to grab his phone and call them to give them a piece of his mind for being so childish. But, even though he didn't want to admit it, the thought of reaching under that couch still creeped him out.

He decided to have a shower. The soothing heat of the water against his body usually calmed him down when he was in moods like this. He turned the shower on and began to strip while the water warmed up.

With the bathroom steaming up, Simon reached in to feel the water. It was nice and hot. He pulled the shower curtain back and stepped in. He lowered his head under the spray and closed his eyes, letting it run along the top of his head and down his face. Suddenly, he jumped back in a fright. The water was freezing.

He opened his eyes and saw Susan staring back at him. She stood naked with the water streaming across her body. It wasn't the perfect, beautiful body that Simon had looked upon so many times. It was covered with deep lacerations. Her lower left arm hung loosely by what looked to be a piece of skin. Simon could quite clearly see the bone.

"I want us to be together, Simon." Her voice came out like a whisper, but it was loud as well. It seemed to echo throughout the bathroom.

Simon fell out of the bath, dragging the shower curtain with him. Lying naked on the bathroom floor, he looked up to see that the room was empty.

"I swear to God, I'm going fucking crazy. It's her, she's not even here anymore, but she's finally pushed me over the edge." He laughed. "Look at this. I'm even talking to myself now."

He didn't even bother to get dry. He threw the clothes he had been previously wearing back on and marched straight to the fridge. His face was a picture of determination. He looked like a man going to war.

"Right, that's it. I'm going to sit here and get drunk. And then I'm going to laugh non-stop until I go to bed."

He grabbed his box sets of *Halloween* and *Friday the 13th*, but quickly changed his mind and opted for *Only Fools and Horses* and *The Young Ones*. He put the first disc in.

After several hours of drinking and very forced laughter, Simon threw his last can on the floor. He had already dropped several while drunk and trying to place them on the coffee table, completely forgetting that he had moved it earlier.

He staggered to the bedroom. Barging the door open, he built up to a sort of hunch- backed run. Then, he flopped onto the bed. He lay there, still fully dressed, on top of the covers.

"Fucking bitches," he mumbled.

He didn't close his eyes. He just stared at the patterned wallpaper, watched it spinning round. Another side effect of his night's drinking. Plus, he didn't even like that wallpaper. That was another thing that Susan had chosen.

As he was starting to drift off, Simon could feel the cover being pulled from beneath him. Slowly, it was being pulled back over and then starting to cover him.

"Don't worry, darling. I'm just tucking you in." A whisper in his ear.

"Thank you. I love you," he whispered back.

"I love you, too."

Simon's eyes opened wide when he felt a kiss on his cheek. He bolted upright, throwing the covers off, and looked around the room. It was empty.

"No. This is enough. I need to find out if I'm going crazy or if she's dead."

He stumbled out of bed and zig-zagged into the living room to grab his car keys. "I'm going to Maria's," he shouted. "Fucking ghost."

He struggled to get the key in the ignition at first. He was still seeing double and everything was moving round. Finally, he got it in. He revved the engine and then shot down the road. He didn't even notice that he had knocked a wing mirror off one of the parked cars.

Pulling onto the carriageway, Simon opened the window, hoping that the cool air would sober him up a bit. The air coming through the window was still quite warm for this time of night. "That's not going to do it," he muttered. He accelerated from forty miles per hour up to sixty. "Ah, that's better."

The lights behind him caught his attention in the rear view mirror. He glanced up to check that the police weren't behind him. Sitting in the back seat was Susan, smiling at him. Simon turned round, panicking at the sight of her. As he turned, he dragged the steering wheel, pulling the car across to the opposite side of the road.

He didn't even see the lorry before it crushed him into nothingness. The last thing he saw was the smile on his dead girlfriend's face. The last thing he heard was her whisper.

"Happy Halloween."

The End

The Coffin Man

By

Mark Lukens

"You're saying that there's no trick-or-treating allowed here tonight?" Dennis asked. He stood in the middle of the murky second-floor bedroom.

Kara walked over to a set of windows and pulled the curtains back. Dust motes danced in the golden afternoon light all around her.

"It's against the law?" Dennis asked.

"I didn't say that," Kara answered without turning around to look at him. She stared out the windows that looked down onto the street. "It's hard to explain. It's just something they don't do here."

Kara had said the word "they" like she wasn't one of "them" even though she'd lived in this village as a child. Dennis had agreed to come up here to this tiny town tucked away in a forgotten corner of Maine after Kara told him that her grandmother had passed away. She'd said her grandmother was wealthy and had left her some stuff in a will, but so far Dennis wasn't very impressed. He guessed the woman had been wealthy in the context of this little town.

Dennis had noticed as soon as they'd entered the town earlier in the day that there were no Halloween decorations anywhere, even though it was Halloween. Well, there were decorations, but strange ones: pumpkins with no faces carved into them, stalks of dried corn and bales of hay stacked up near the pumpkins, little straw men and stick figures crafted from twigs and twine hanging on front doors and windows. They had driven into town on a remote county road that intersected with the other main road at a town square. In the center of the square was a large field, and in the middle of that field a fifteen-foot-tall stick figure had been constructed with more stalks of dried corn and bales of hay bunched up at the figure's feet. There was a school/church at the far end of the town square, and a few businesses lined both sides of the square including a city hall, a post office, and a volunteer fire department. The homes around the square and the ones on the side streets looked old, maybe at least a hundred years old, but everything looked meticulously taken care of. On the outskirts of the village were some farms—some large, some small—and then there was nothing but woods as far as the eye could see.

The village was quaint, even beautiful in its own timeless way. The few people he'd met earlier in the day seemed friendly, but there was something conspiratorial about them. He felt watched, like he was an outsider to be wary of. He didn't know how to describe it, but they all seemed nervous and tense, like they were scared of something.

Kara's grandmother's home was only two blocks away from the center of town, on the corner of the main road and a side street. It was a three story Victorian-style home.

"What about the kids?" Dennis asked as he watched Kara at the windows of her grandmother's bedroom. "Halloween should be for kids."

"We just don't do it here," she practically snapped at him.

Dennis didn't say anything for a moment. Kara was tense; she was obviously upset about her grandmother and he thought he should leave her alone. She had missed her grandmother's funeral a week ago and now she was here to take care of a few legal matters and pick through some things at her grandmother's house.

He thought about walking over to her and touching her, holding her, comforting her in some way, but he didn't.

She turned around and looked at him. "I'm sorry. I'm just . . ."

"Hey," he said and now he was across the room in a flash. "It's okay. I understand."

Kara had already lost her mother a few years ago, but she'd never gone into too much detail about her death. Her dad had run off when Kara had been a baby and she'd never heard from him again. She didn't have any brothers and sisters; her grandmother was all she had left in the world.

And Dennis knew how she felt. He wasn't close to his family—most of them gone now, too. It was one of the things that had drawn them to each other.

He wanted to change the subject, start over somehow. Instead, he hugged her, a gentle squeeze. "I'm going to grab a beer," he said, thinking he should give her some time alone up here. He had a cooler full of beer downstairs. Kara had told him to bring his own beer because they didn't sell alcohol in town.

She nodded and turned back to the windows, staring down at the street.

Dennis left her alone.

*

They ate a dinner of sandwiches they'd brought with them in the cooler, and Dennis was finishing up his fourth beer. The sun was setting, the shadows of the spooky old house growing long, taking over. Kara had turned on the kitchen light and lit some candles in the living room, but they struggled to push back the oncoming darkness.

Kara got up and walked to a coat closet in the living room across from the front door. She pulled out one of those stick figure things that Dennis had seen hanging on other people's doors and windows all over town.

"It looks like something from *The Blair Witch Project*," Dennis joked as he watched her.

"Grandma would've wanted it on her front door tonight."

"What are those stick figures supposed to mean?" he asked.

She shrugged as she opened the front door and hung the figure on a hook over the pane of glass. She closed the door and locked it. "It's just a tradition. Something we've always done on Halloween night to keep the . . ." She stopped like she'd said too much. She had that nervous look in her eyes like everyone else he'd seen in town.

"What?" he asked.

"Nothing."

"Tell me."

"You wouldn't believe me."

They went back to the table in the kitchen, back to the light. Dennis opened another bottle of beer. "Tell me," he pressed.

Kara sat down at the table. "It's kind of scary."

"I could go for a scary story on Halloween night." There was nothing else to do here. No TV or internet, no cell phone service. And in the despondent mood Kara was in, he wasn't even going to suggest sex.

She was quiet for a moment, like she was trying to find the right way to explain things. "We don't celebrate Halloween tonight, but there's this . . . this tradition we have."

"The stick figures," Dennis said.

She nodded. "They're supposed to ward off the Coffin Man."

Dennis almost laughed. He *wanted* to laugh, but a twinge of fear knifed through him from the expression on Kara's face—she was really scared.

"The Coffin Man always comes on Halloween night," Kara said, her voice lower, eyes cast down. "We'll be okay as long as we stay inside."

Dennis was quiet for a moment as he watched Kara. "Come on, you don't really believe that kind of stuff, do you?"

She stared at him, dead serious now. "Whatever you do, don't peek out the windows tonight. If you hear noises outside, don't look. The Coffin Man will ride through town on his flat cart that's pulled by two black horses. He's dressed all in black with a black hood over his head, like an executioner. He has four lanterns on his cart, at all four corners. And on the back there's a coffin. If he sees you . . ." She let her words trail off.

Dennis wanted to ask how she knew what the Coffin Man looked like if no one was allowed to peek out the windows at him, but he didn't want to push his luck. She seemed different now, not the same Kara he'd fallen for over the last eight months. He wondered if she was really this disturbed from her grandmother's passing. She was alone now, but he promised that he would be there for her. They were both alone now, but they would always have each other.

He got up and gave her another gentle hug, and then a kiss on the top of her head. "Don't worry, I'll protect you from the Coffin Man."

But Kara wasn't laughing.

*

Dennis woke up in the dark. He and Kara had gone to bed around nine thirty, sleeping in a guest room upstairs that he suspected used to be her bedroom when she was a child even though she hadn't said as much. Moonlight managed to stream in around the curtains drawn over the window, and he saw that he was alone in the bed.

He was thirsty, a little dehydrated from the eight beers he'd downed earlier in the evening. He'd fallen into a fitful sleep next to Kara but now she was gone.

"Kara?"

No answer. Maybe she'd gone downstairs, or she'd gone across the hall to her grandmother's room.

He sat up and then got to his feet. Something had woken him up, some kind of noise. He checked his cell phone on the table next to the bed. It was ten thirty—he'd only been asleep for an hour. He still didn't have cell phone service here, but he used the illumination from his phone like a flashlight to guide his way to the bedroom door.

He stepped out into the hall. The door to Kara's grandmother's room was halfway open and Dennis heard a noise coming from inside. Maybe it was the same noise that had woken him up.

"Kara?"

Still no answer.

He crept across the hall, the floorboards creaking beneath his footsteps, ancient wood popping. He pushed the door all the way open and his phone shut off, plunging him back into darkness.

"Shit," he whispered and pressed the button to light up his phone again. He shined the meager light in front of him and entered the bedroom. Moonlight filtered in through the flimsy curtains over the row of windows that looked down onto the street. Kara wasn't in the room.

Noises were coming from outside, a steady noise, and it took him a moment to recognize the sound . . . the clopping of horses' hooves.

Dennis was drawn towards the windows, almost like he was in a trance. Before he even realized what he was doing, he had one of the curtains pushed aside. He stared down at the street and saw the Coffin Man. The lanterns on the cart illuminated the man dressed all in black. He sat on a buckboard with the reins guiding his horses in his gloved hands. He wore some kind of black mask over his face underneath a tall hat. And on the back of the cart was a simple wood coffin.

The Coffin Man pulled gently on the reins, halting his horses. He stared up at the window, right at Dennis.

Dennis let the curtain fall back in place over the window and backed away quickly.

"You let him see you," Kara said from across the room.

Dennis jumped, turning around to look at Kara in the doorway. "You scared the hell out of me," he breathed out as he lit up his phone again and walked towards her. And then he stopped; he saw the horror on her face. She was trembling, shaking her head no. She had a look in her eyes like all hope was lost now.

"Kara . . ."

"You weren't supposed to look out the window." Her eyes were wide and moist like she was about to cry. "I told you not to look out the window."

"That guy out there . . . this has to be some kind of prank or something."

A pounding sounded from downstairs—someone was banging on the front door.

Kara stifled a scream. "He's at the door now. He's going to keep coming for you. He won't stop. He'll never stop."

"This is crazy," Dennis told her. "We need to call the police." He dialed 911 on his cell phone but the call wouldn't go through—he still didn't have any service to his phone. "Does your grandmother have a phone?" he asked even though he didn't remember seeing one.

She shook her head no.

The pounding downstairs was louder, it sounded like the man was going to break the door down.

"Come on," Dennis said. He used his cell phone to light his way back to the guest bedroom. He found his jeans crumpled up on the seat of an antique chair and he pulled them on, and then he slipped his feet into his sneakers. He made sure he had his car keys in his pants pocket. Kara was still fully dressed.

They hurried downstairs. The pounding on the door was even louder down here. The large pane of glass in the front door rattled every time the Coffin Man beat on the wood with his fist.

"Go away!" Dennis yelled at the man beyond the door. The Coffin Man looked tall; he looked bigger now that Dennis saw him up close—just a black and bulky shape outside the door. "We've called the police!" he lied.

The relentless pounding continued in a maddening rhythm.

"Leave us alone!" Dennis yelled at the door, backing up deeper into the living room.

The Coffin Man smashed his gloved hand through the glass in the front door, knocking the twig man Kara had hung on the door out of the way. He reached inside, groping for the doorknob.

"What the hell?" For a moment Dennis was too shocked to move, staring in disbelief as the Coffin Man twisted the lock on the doorknob, opening the door. This was no prank.

"Come on!" Dennis grabbed Kara's wrist and pulled her into the kitchen.

"There's nowhere we can run to," Kara said, pulling back on Dennis. "You shouldn't have looked out the window. I told you not to look!"

"Stop it, Kara!" he snapped. He pulled her towards the back door in the kitchen that led outside. They just needed to get around the house to the driveway, to his car. Once they were in his car they could get away.

They got to the door and Dennis heard the Coffin Man stomping through the house, getting closer. He pulled Kara outside, down the steps towards the side of the house. It still seemed like she was resisting, pulling on him as hard as he was pulling on her.

When they were twenty feet away from the door, Kara yanked her hand out of Dennis' hand.

"What are you doing?" he hissed at her, and then he saw the Coffin Man in the doorway to the kitchen. The Coffin Man just stood there, watching them.

"He's right behind you!" Dennis told Kara. "We gotta go!"

Kara stood in the darkness, the moonlight shining down on her and Dennis saw the realization dawning on her. "He only wants you," she said.

Dennis heard a noise right behind him, the snapping of a twig from a footstep. He turned around and saw the Coffin Man right in front of him, a sickle gripped in the man's gloved hand. The last thing Dennis wondered was how the Coffin Man had gotten behind him so quickly, and then the butt of the sickle's handle struck him in the side of his head and the world went black.

*

It was close to midnight when the Coffin Man drove his buggy up towards the gigantic stick figure in the middle of the town square, the stick figure already ablaze, burning brightly in the night. The townspeople had gathered, all of the men dressed in black with hoods and hats—they were all the Coffin Man.

Kara, now dressed in white along with all of the other women in town, watched as the coffin men unloaded the coffin from the buggy and laid it down on a bed of straw in front of the gigantic burning stick figure. She knew that the coffin had already been drenched in a resin that would allow it to burn easily. She could hear Dennis thrashing around inside the sturdy pine box, bashing himself against the walls, beating at the top of it . . . screaming.

But there was no escape for him.

Kara's grandmother approached her. She touched Kara gently and then they watched together as some of the coffin men grabbed at the ropes attached to the gigantic stick figure and pulled it down on top of the coffin as the midnight bell rang out from the church steeple. The coffin caught fire immediately.

This sacrifice would help the town through the winter, appease the ancient gods in the spring and make the ground fertile, allow for a bountiful harvest in the fall.

"Is this the last one for me?" Kara asked her grandmother.

"No, my child. Bring us another sacrifice next Halloween."

The End

The Devil's Fruit

By

Suzanne Fox

"You've got to be fucking kidding." Josh took a swig from the bottle in his hand and stared at his friend. "I'm thirty-one years old, not eight. When you said come over for a Halloween party I thought you meant a proper party. Booze, women, a spliff or two, but… this?" He jerked his bottle in the direction of the large tub of water. Lager splashed from its lip, splattering the kitchen floor with foam. "I mean… apple bobbing?"

Sam walked around to the opposite side of the tub, plucked out one of the apples and held it toward his friend. "This may look like an ordinary apple, Josh, but tonight is Halloween and this piece of fruit is the key to getting the knickers off whatever woman, or women, you fancy tonight."

"I'm supposed to believe that a piece of fucking fruit is going to get me laid?" Josh shook his head, convinced that his friend had lost the plot, and that his love of weed had finally destroyed too many grey cells.

"Hear me out." Sam's eyes burned with excitement. "We turn a stupid kid's game of apple bobbing into a drinking game."

"And, getting drunk is going to get me laid how?"

"Not you, twat. Let me explain. You pick someone to play against and take turns to try and get an apple using only your mouth. If you get a green apple, your opponent has to down a shot. But…" He paused to give Josh time to absorb his words and realise the genius of his plan. "If you get the only red one, they have to drink two. Have you still got your eye on Stacey?"

Josh's lips twitched at the thought of the long-legged, brunette from the checkout at Tesco. He imagined those legs wrapped around his waist, pulling him in deeper, squeezing tighter until …

He stumbled sideways and yelped as Sam's punch connected with his upper arm.

"Have you listened to a single word I've said?" Sam shook his head. "You were practically drooling. If you want to fuck her so badly, challenge her to a game of apple bobbing. You can't lose."

"She might be better than me." Josh rubbed his arm. Sam hadn't held back with his punch.

"It makes no difference. Take a good look at the women here. Every one of them will have spent hours perfecting their hair and makeup, each trying to be the prettiest to get us jerks to notice them. Do you really think a single one of them will dip their face in tub of cold water and risk messing up their hard work?" He laughed. "So long as *you* don't care about getting wet, you can't lose. As soon as they've had a few shots, they won't be able to drop their knickers quick enough. They're all after a good fucking, but won't admit to it."

A vision of a drunken Stacey haunted Josh's mind. He knew that most girls were easy with a few drinks inside them - their true natures shining through a boozy haze. He wished that they'd just admit they were every bit as horny as he was but, if they wanted to keep up the façade, he was happy to push a few drinks on them first. He ran a hand over his prematurely thinning scalp. "Do I look like I'd worry about getting this wet?"

Sam laughed. "You don't have enough to worry about, mate."

"Cheers. One thing's bothering me though."

"Yeah? And what's that?" A frown creased Sam's forehead.

"What dark magic managed to get Sam, 'Mr. Takeaway,' Harris to finally venture down the fruit and vegetable aisles?"

"What kind of sick freak do you think I am?" Sam flipped the top off another bottle of lager and gulped down a mouthful. "Didn't have to. Found a big bag of apples on the doorstep this morning. I reckon the old guy down the road left them there. You know, the one with the long, grey beard?"

"The one who grows all of his own fruit and veggies? Gandalf's granddad?"

Sam nodded.

"Are you sure? Any freak could have left those apples there."

"It *was* him. I saw him shuffling back to his house when I opened the door. I shouted 'thanks,' to him and he waved back."

"And he only gave you one red apple?" Josh frowned.

"But it's a beauty..." Sam selected the scarlet apple from the tub. "...if fruit's your fetish." He dropped it back into the tub with a splash and walked toward the door. "I'll round up some players."

* * *

Josh's knuckles paled as he gripped the sides of the tub. He winked at Stacey who stood opposite him. "Better fill your glass, sweetheart, because I'm not coming back up without an apple in my mouth."

She stuck out her tongue and rolled her eyes. "Do your best but, I'm pretty good with my mouth."

Sam snorted, spraying beer on his shirt as he choked back his laughter. "Yeah, Josh's counting on it, Stace."

Before Stacey could protest, Josh drew in a breath, plunged forward, mouth wide open, and targeted the nearest apple. The smooth-skinned fruit bobbed and bounced away from him. It had been years since he had played this game and he had forgotten how difficult it was to retrieve an apple. Each time he made contact with a fruit, it evaded his bite like a fish teasing an angler. He chased it around the tub as other apples ricocheted around him. Josh was oblivious to the wave he created that flipped over the edges and splattered his spectators, and was only dimly aware of the muffled yells and laughter that sank through the water to his ears.

Breath fading, he made one last attempt to catch an apple. It scooted away and he lunged forward, trapping it against the side of the container. He held it in place with his lips and sank his teeth into its crispness.

"A green one!" Sam shouted as Josh emerged from the water, shaking his head and soaking everyone within a three-foot radius. "And well within the sixty-second time limit. Down in one, Stacey." He pushed a glass towards the girl and cheered as she tipped back its contents without flinching. "Your turn."

Stacey moved closer to the tub. Pushing her hair behind her ears she leaned over and opened her mouth.

"That's a pretty mouth, Stace." Josh sleeked back his wet hair and watched as she edged closer to the apples. Sam had been right, he realised, as Stacey hovered above her target. She dipped her head towards the fruit but, each time her lips brushed one and it briefly sank, she recoiled as though the tub was filled with acid. She had no intention of ruining her impeccable makeup or ironed hair.

"The clock's ticking," warned Sam. "Fifteen seconds left."

Stacey wrinkled her nose and nudged another apple as she attempted to fix it between her teeth.

"Five, four, three, two, one. Beep. Time's up. Round one to Josh. Are you ready to go again?" said Sam.

Josh's grin widened. He knew Stacey didn't stand a chance. He was going to capture an apple every time and, as long as she was too vain to risk spoiling her image, she would lose.

"I'm ready." He took another deep breath, plunged into the water and chased his prey until he held it in his teeth. He surfaced with another green apple and dripping hair. His opponent picked up her second shot and swallowed it.

The two adversaries faced off again and again, and each time Stacey failed to retrieve a single fruit whilst Josh claimed more prizes. As Stacey's eyes took on a glassy stare Josh realised that if he won a couple of more rounds she was going to be easy meat for him to devour. He braced himself for his next attempt. This time the red apple was his target. If he could pull that one out and force Stacey to drink two shots he would back down, throw in a little fake concern for her wellbeing, and take her somewhere private to recover.

Eyes wide open, he thrust his head below the surface. Blurred green shapes flitted out of reach as he twisted and turned seeking out the solitary red fruit. It seemed to take on an energy of its own. As soon as Josh located it, his elusive prey dodged his assault.

The pressure in his chest began to build as the air in his lungs diminished. He realised he had to make a choice. He could concede defeat or he could pursue an easier target. *At least a green apple will get me another step closer to fucking her,* Josh thought as he turned toward an approaching emerald blur.

He opened his mouth in readiness to bite when the red apple pushed the green one aside. He closed his eyes and clamped his teeth against the firm flesh. *Yes!*

His nose smashed against the base of the tub as a great weight pressed down on the back of his head.

Josh tried to pull back but, he couldn't move. Terror pushed its icy fingers into his heart. His lungs burned, screaming for fresh air to replace the depleted gas inside him.

He flattened his hands against the table top and pushed, muscles straining to release himself from his watery snare, but it was a futile attempt. Whoever was holding him down was strong and unrelenting but, in his confusion and fear, he could almost believe that something was pulling him under.

Brilliant red scored his vision and a tide of anger rose through him at the stupidity of the prank. Josh couldn't hold his breath for much longer. His chest heaved as it fought to suck in life-giving oxygen and he clamped his teeth together trying to resist the urge to draw in a liquid breath.

Crunch.

A foul slime filled Josh's mouth. Its putrid heat oozed down his throat and his gullet spasmed as it tried to expel the loathsome liquor.

Panic pushed anger out of its way. Josh knew he couldn't hold his breath a moment longer. The silly game had turned into a fight for life. In desperation, he began to suck in a watery breath through his nose and ...

He crashed backwards into the kitchen wall still holding the red apple between his teeth. Water washed over the sides of the tub, cascading to the floor and drenching everyone nearby.

Josh doubled over and spat out the fruit before spewing a frothy combination of lager and apple pieces over his shoes. His air-starved chest heaved as he took in a deep breath before coughing it back in the direction of a shocked audience. The tang of putrid decay coated his tongue, and his stomach rolled and retched. More vomit splattered the floor. As he regained his breath his anger flared.

"Which fucking bastard held me down?" Josh's voice rasped as though invisible hands gripped his throat. He turned his glare toward Sam. "You, fucking twat."

"Hey, man. Calm down. What the hell are you playing at?" Sam raised his hands as he stepped toward his friend.

Josh shoved him aside. His face blazed red as he spat more of the foul taste from his mouth. "What am I playing at? You could have killed me, you bastard!" He smeared snot across his face with the back of his hand. "Was it a big joke? Hold me under the water until I can't hold my breath a second longer. Have you any fucking idea how that feels?"

"What?" Sam shook his head. "You were under the water so long I was scared you had passed out. I was trying to pull you out. Jesus, I don't know how you managed to stay under. I couldn't move you."

"Don't fuck with me." Josh spun around toward a white-faced Stacey. "I suppose you were in it with him?"

Stacey recoiled from his onslaught and fled the kitchen.

"Not so funny now, bitch!" he yelled after her.

"For God's sake, calm down, man. She didn't do anything. No one did. I thought you were showing off to Stace. Showing how long you could stay under for. Maybe you blacked out?" Sam placed a hand on his friend's shoulder only to have it shrugged away. "You can be a complete arse sometimes, Josh. Go dry off and sit down for a while."

The door bounced off the wall as Josh stormed through it, and a picture slipped askew. Pushing aside anyone who got in his way, he staggered upstairs and threw open the bathroom door.

"Hey. I'm not done." The guy peeing in the toilet returned his attention to what he was doing.

"Get out," slurred Josh. His stomach rolled, and fat beads of sweat mingled with the water that dripped from his face.

"Jesus, man. You look sick." The man tucked his cock away and zipped his jeans.

Josh lurched forward as the contents of his stomach rose in a burning fury and splattered his bathroom companion's jeans and trainers with luminous bile.

"Aw, fuck. You dirty bastard." The man looked down at his soiled clothing and blanched. Retching, he grabbed a damp towel, pressed it to his mouth and fled the bathroom.

A wriggling on the floor drew Josh's gaze. He froze.

Blood-red grubs writhed in a sickly sea, trying to gain traction on the tiled floor. As he watched, transfixed by the grotesque image of what had erupted from his stomach, one of the grubs began to stretch. Each end pulled and squirmed, stretching its soft body in a solo tug-o-war. Its middle thinned and lengthened until...

Pop.

One grub became two.

Revulsion shrouded Josh, rendering him briefly catatonic. Then, he brought his foot down hard on the obscenities that were multiplying in the puddle of vomit. The red grubs smeared beneath his boot leaving crimson streaks in their wake.

Josh doubled over as a blade of pain cut through his gut and he gripped the edge of the bathtub, clawing his fingers at the unforgiving enamel. His teeth ground together as he battled to stop himself from releasing the agony in a scream.

Blackness swallowed him.

* * *

Josh opened his eyes and gazed up at the bathroom ceiling. His pain had evaporated like morning dew in an August heat wave. He rolled over, pushed himself to his knees, and looked around. The bloody grubs had vanished along with his nausea. A residual ache thrummed through his abdomen but now, this was merely a discomfort.

As he continued to climb to his feet, a pressure grew around Josh's groin. He let his fingertips slide across his crotch and discovered a stone-like erection pressing against the zipper. This was no manifestation of lust. This was a symbol of his wrath. A seed of rage was growing inside him, carried on a surge of white-hot blood that coursed through his body, igniting every nerve with its fury.

He gripped the wash-basin and glared at his reflection in the mirror. Malignant eyes burned back at him. He bared his teeth and snarled.

The queue for the bathroom scattered as he stormed from the small room and cries of, "Fuck you," echoed behind him. Josh didn't care who he pushed from his path as he forged his way to the scene of the crime - the kitchen.

He walked in to see Stacey and a couple of her friends drinking and chatting. They lifted their heads simultaneously as he stalked toward them, and the sight of their expressions of surprise turning to fear, fuelled the hardness of his cock.

"Josh." Stacey's voice trembled. "Are... are you okay? You don't look yourself."

"I'm feeling more like my true self every minute."

He leaned forward, his nose inches from hers. He smelled her fear with the discernment of a sommelier sampling a fine wine and he drew in a long, slow breath. The cheap, chemical fragrance she wore failing to smother her anxious, sharp tang.

Stacey recoiled but her retreat was blocked by the wall.

Josh licked his lips.

"You seem a little afraid," he whispered.

"No. I'm not." Stacey slipped sideways along the wall and looked toward her friends for assistance, but alcohol had clouded their eyes and judgment. They were blind to her distress.

"You're lying. I can smell it."

She flinched as he grasped her chin and stared into her teary eyes.

"You're scared, bitch. You're scared that no man is ever going to want you. That's why you spend hours layering on thick make-up, trying to hide this." He scraped a fingernail along her cheek lifting a layer of brown foundation and powder. "Did the nasty doggy bite you, little girl?"

Colour drained from the terrified woman's face despite her thick layer of makeup. "How... how did you know?"

Josh grinned, a malign rictus that stretched wide and hungry. He had no idea how he knew about the dog attack when Stacey had been a child. She had kept the scarring hidden from everyone. But the knowledge was there, deep inside him, and waiting to spill from his lips. It cut through the layers of armour she had spent years constructing. Fat tears splashed her face tracing black streams of mascara across the white scars.

Pain squeezed his right arm and Josh stumbled backward, spinning around to see a hard-faced Sam.

"Leave her alone, Josh. What the fuck is wrong with you tonight?" Sam stared, unblinking, at his friend. "I think it's time you went home."

"And I think the party's just starting to get interesting," sneered Josh.

"Not for you, mate. You're acting like a dick. Go home. Go to bed."

"And what if I don't want to?"

Two heavy-set men stepped closer. Josh vaguely recognised them. They were far bigger than him, but tonight he felt different. Invincible. Capable of taking on any adversary and crushing them to a fine dust.

His fingers curled into a fist and he drew back his arm.

He wasn't invincible.

The two musclemen grabbed him by the upper arms and dragged him to the door. Sam followed. "Go home, Josh. Have some coffee and go to bed. You're going to feel like shit in the morning. Don't make it any worse by doing something you'll regret, too."

At the door the goons pushed him away and he stumbled into the darkness. The door slammed and he was alone, apart from the faces that stared at him from the window. Josh flashed two fingers at his audience, swaggered down the driveway and followed the road.

The sharp air snapped everything into focus. The black silhouettes of branches swaying against the glow of the dead moon. The scent of foxes as they raided unguarded waste bins. Even the slither of worms as they oozed their soft bodies through the dirt. Josh heard, felt, and smelled it all, including the dusty breath of the grey-bearded man who watched from the deep shadows of an apple tree. A man so old he had defied death, generation after generation, waiting for this cursed night.

The two men were now entwined in the dark underworld that flourished on all Hallow's Eve. Josh felt the blood of night creatures running through his veins, and the breath of long-lost dragons' in his lungs. Songs in an ancient tongue filled his mind. His night, his time, was just beginning.

Slipping down the driveway of a neighbouring house, Josh made his way to the rear garden keeping under the cover of gnarled fruit trees. Hedges divided one garden from the next. He forced his way through the privet rows until he reached his destination. Music, laughter and flashing lights spilled from Sam's house.

Josh paused by a window and looked through his own terrible reflection at the people inside. Sam sat on an armchair with Stacey draped across his lap, their tongues probing each other's mouths and his hand disappearing beneath her skirt.

A feral growl rumbled in his throat and, deep inside, a gnawing began, like tiny, needle-sharp teeth devouring his self-control. The sensation radiated outward from his abdomen chewing a path through his chest, groin and limbs. Josh raised a hand and flexed his fingers. Tiny maggot-like creatures swarmed beneath his skin both feeding from him and filling him with a preternatural wrath.

As he approached the door it opened and a drunken girl staggered out. She raised her head, her blurred eyesight sharpening the moment she saw Josh.

She screamed and ran, like a terrified Cinderella, leaving only a stiletto-heeled shoe embedded in the lawn.

Josh walked toward the door and, with each step, he felt a darkness rising from the depths of the earth, through his feet, and into his body.

His soul.

The door flew open at the lightest touch of his hand and he re-joined the party.

A burst of static discharged through the speakers, shattering glasses before finally falling silent. Sam leapt from his seat spilling Stacey to the floor, her skirt hitched exposing her long legs.

"What the fuck are you doing here?" Sam spluttered. His eyes widened and he paled as he stared at the form that resembled his friend. He stumbled backwards toward the other doorway bumping into a girl coming through it.

"Hey, mind where you're go…" Fear paralysed her body, but not her mouth. Her lips parted and her screams filled the room.

The two musclemen who had ejected Josh from the party ran into the room. Josh raised a hand and they collapsed to the floor, thick clots of blood oozing from their ears and noses as they writhed and squirmed in agony.

Furniture trembled.

Smash!

A mirror tumbled from the wall, shattering into a million diamond shards, and a low rumble started to rise.

Josh howled and doubled over, raising his hands to his head. Bony prominences pushed their way through his skin, spilling grub-flecked, dark blood down his face. The bone spicules grew and contorted until long twisted horns emerged from his skull. Rising, he threw back his head and roared.

The air crackled and everyone within the room felt the hairs on their neck stand up and their bowels relax.

The thing that used to be Josh surveyed the room, pausing when he saw Stacey. He stepped closer to the sobbing girl and stretched out his hand.

"Here. Now!" The voice was unrecognisable as being Josh's. Its vibrations shook the room and ruptured blood vessels in anyone who heard it.

Stacey drew her legs into a foetal curl, and wept blood-stained tears.

"Puh… please, leave me alone," she begged.

"I'm taking what's mine." The Josh-demon's voice boomed. "And no one can stop me."

Whimpers and cries filled the room as people attempted to crawl from the devil in their midst. But one man battled against the tide of terrified partygoers. Sam. He dragged his pain-ridden body toward where Stacey lay sobbing.

Josh noticed.

The demon raised its hands and silence descended for a brief moment before the screaming resumed.

Pain burned their ears as crackles split the air and a neon snake of blood-red sparks erupted from Josh's fingers, circling the room before finding its prey in the form of a cowering Sam.

Flames engulfed Sam and, as his body blistered and blackened, his screams rose above all the rest.

While the human fireball thrashed and twisted in its torment, igniting curtains and furnishings, a dark void began to grow and open in the far wall, emitting a sulphurous stench into the room.

The demon grabbed the girl by an ankle and dragged her toward the hole.

Stacey's fingernails clawed at the carpet as she tried in vain to halt her journey into the darkness. The nylon threads snagged and tore at her nails, leaving bloodied trails in her wake.

As she crossed the threshold into a different hell, the void closed.

* * *

"Get that hose over there. Now!"

The young fire fighter obeyed the order, getting as close to the shattered window as possible and playing the water into the room beyond. He had never seen a fire like this before. Every time they edged their way closer, the flames seemed to know and grew bigger, forcing them to retreat once more.

His commanding officer moved to his side. "The neighbours say it was one hell of a rowdy Halloween party. They also say no one's come out of there since the fire started." He turned toward a wrinkled, grey-whiskered man who stared and smiled at the inferno from his garden. "Get back, sir. It's not safe!"

The rookie nodded as he fought to keep the hose on target.

"It's too fierce to send any of the team inside," he continued. "No one's getting out of this one alive."

"No, sir," said the rookie.

The senior officer shook his head and mumbled to himself, "If I was a believer, I'd swear we were trying to put out the fires of Hell itself."

The End

The Halloween Playground

By

Christopher Motz

Marty stopped at the red light and scanned the empty street in front of his station wagon. His window was down and the car's vents were blowing frigid air into the interior; it was October, after all, not a sunny, July afternoon. Halloween was less than a week away, and the air was chilled with the last dying vestiges of autumn. All the trees in town had already shed their leaves, and every morning, Marty's overgrown lawn was coated in a thin layer of frost.

He shivered beneath his heavy, wool coat as a couple hurried along the crosswalk, watching him through the foggy windshield. *Nothing to see here*, he thought. *Just keep moving.* They hurried onto the sidewalk and disappeared behind a row of houses. He was like them once; a happy, young guy with a pretty girl on his arm, and a lifetime of memories yet to be discovered. That was a long time ago. The only memories he had now were of fights at the dinner table, vacations dripping with the stink of lingering arguments, and holidays spent in a bottle of brandy, getting pleasantly drunk while his wife reminded him of his inadequacy as a husband and a human being.

"I bet you regret that now," he said, checking his rear-view mirror.

His wife, Jenn, sat in the back seat, wrapped in clear plastic, staring at him accusingly, with eyes that had become milky in death. Just this once, Marty had gotten the last word, and it filled him with unbridled joy and a sense of relief so profound, he couldn't help but laugh. Waiting at home was an unopened bottle of Gray Goose he'd use to wash down the leftover shepherd's pie Jenn had made two days earlier.

Their last supper.

Marty pressed on the gas when the light turned green, and guided the station wagon over streets still rutted with the season's first snowfall. Small, suburban homes surrounded him, decked out with every possible variety of tacky Halloween decoration imaginable: cardboard skeletons, crudely carved jack-o'-lanterns, strings of orange twinkly lights, department store mannequins dressed as ghouls and goblins. He scoffed and turned onto his street, parking the wagon in the driveway and rolling up the window. He couldn't wait to get warm, but first, he had business to attend to; his vodka and shepherd's pie would have to wait.

"Marty!" a voice shouted from across the street. "How the hell are you? I haven't seen you around much lately."

Justin. One of Marty's less pleasant and far nosier neighbors. "Oh, I'm doing well," he replied. "Been working a lot."

The man walked into the street and slowly came toward him. Marty walked forward to meet him; he certainly didn't need Justin poking his nose around and seeing his motionless passenger in the rear seat.

"You and the wife handing out candy to all the little ghouls and monsters this year?" Justin asked.

"Uh, yeah, we're just a bit behind, you know?"

"Behind? Looks you haven't even begun."

Smug son of a bitch, Marty thought.

Justin eyed Marty's overgrown lawn and frowned.

"Listen, I have to get inside. Jenn has held dinner long enough."

"Oh, sure," Justin said. "I just wanted to say hello." Marty watched as Justin slowly turned and knew right away this was going to be one more headache he didn't need. The man spied the plastic covered corpse in the back seat and stopped dead in his tracks. "Is that a decoration?" he asked. "It looks so real."

"You'll just have to wait and see," Marty said. "Really, I have to go now..."

"Is that *blood*?" Justin interrupted. "It looks so real, Marty. It looks just like your..."

Justin's eyes opened wide, as fresh blood dribbled from Jenn's nose and coated the inside of the plastic bag. He bent closer, horrified, leaning on the car for support. *That's no Halloween decoration, that's...*

"...your wife," Justin said. "Oh my god, that's Jenn! Marty..."

Marty didn't give him a chance to cry out, or even turn around. He slammed Justin against the station wagon, hearing his neighbor's breath escape in an explosive burst. He pulled his keys from his pocket and swung his arm in a sideways arc, hearing the loud crack as the ignition key parted the flesh at Justin's temple and punched through his skull. The large man jumped, his body trembling from the sudden strike; he fell to the driveway with Marty's keyring jutting from the side of his head.

"You nosy bastard," Marty hissed. "You just couldn't take a hint, could you? Now look what you made me do." He grabbed hold of the keyring and pulled it from Justin's head with a wet crackle; blood slowly leaked from the wound and pooled on the concrete as he looked around the neighborhood to make sure he hadn't been seen.

More work for me, Marty thought. *Just what I need.*

He dragged his dead neighbor up the driveway and around the side of the house, propping him against a garbage can while he undid the lock on the cellar bulkhead. Grabbing him by the arm, Marty tumbled him down the stairs where his body came to rest on the basement floor.

Marty locked the bulkhead door and returned to the front of the house; panting, he wiped a thin line of sweat from his face and set about removing Jenn from the back seat of the station wagon. He carried her to the front door, hung over his shoulder like a sack of potatoes. He wasn't about to put her in the cellar with the spiders and rats; she was his wife, after all. She was too good for that.

Once inside, Marty flicked on the dining room light and deposited Jenn's lifeless body in a straight-backed chair at the dinner table. He rummaged through the refrigerator, grabbed the leftover shepherd's pie and bottle of vodka, and removed his jacket. He unscrewed the cap and drank right from the bottle; he was too tired to grab a glass from the kitchen cupboard. When the microwave beeped shrilly, he grabbed his plate and sat at the table across from Jenn, watching her, warily.

He couldn't remember a time she'd been so quiet. He ate his dinner in peace, feeling the vodka go to his head and slowly blur his vision. It had been a long day; all he wanted was a hot shower and the soft embrace of his wool blanket. It would be the first time in many years he didn't have to share the bed with anyone, didn't have to fight for space or retrieve the covers from his loudly snoring wife.

He put his plate in the sink and returned the bottle of vodka to the refrigerator, sighing contentedly with a full belly and a fuzzy mind. He glanced at Jenn a final time before turning off the lights and heading upstairs. He could always remove the plastic in the morning; his wife certainly wasn't going anywhere.

It felt more like Christmas than Halloween.

Tomorrow he'd unwrap his present early.

***

The first thing Marty noticed, when he entered the kitchen the following morning, was the pervading smell of sour urine.

Jenn's body sat where he'd left it, marinating in her own fluids, staring out the kitchen window with blue eyes that had faded in death. Before anything else, he'd need to clean the puddle of piss from the linoleum. He passed his wife's corpse with a grimace and grabbed a towel from the small linen closet in the hall. If he'd known ahead of time this was going to become such a hassle, he would've dumped her in the cellar with the *others*.

The others.

He'd almost forgotten how much work there was to do before Halloween. It was barely after seven in the morning and Marty was ready to reach for the bottle of Grey Goose.

Jenn had always hated Marty's drinking; not that he was an alcoholic, but he did often find himself stuck in a rut. Behind on the bills, drink. Passed over for a promotion at work, drink. Jenn reminding him of how awful he was at almost everything, drink a *lot*. Now, Jenn wasn't here to nag and moan about how much booze he had after work, or if he really needed that extra beer while he grilled their dinner.

She would never nag him again.

Neither would nosy Justin from across the street.

Neither would Rebecca Braun from work.

Neither would that son of a bitch, Al Grosskopf, who always let his Pekingese shit all over Marty's lawn.

Marty was taking care of business like Bachman Turner Overdrive; his bullshit meter was in the red; the proverbial cup had runneth over.

By the time he had cleaned up the mess his late wife had left for him, and removed the plastic from her stiffening body, he realized it was nearly nine o'clock. He wasn't going to make it to work on time, which suited him just fine; he hated the place, had for years, ever since Jim Stark had been promoted to Manager, a position that *should* have been offered to Marty.

"Ass-kissing bastard," Marty grumbled. "Who does he think he is? Jesus Christ, Himself?"

He looked at Jenn, half-expecting a response. He shrugged, grabbed the bloody plastic and crammed it in the garbage can. He scanned the neighborhood and saw no one; they had all gone about their day like the corporate sheep they were, bleating their way to the water cooler so they could discuss what happened on *Dancing With The Stars*.

God, he hated them. All of them. He couldn't wait to see the looks on their faces when...

His thoughts were interrupted as a woman crept up his front walkway. He barely recognized her; she'd lost weight and hadn't applied her usually ridiculous amount of makeup to cover the pocks on her face. Amy Balin, Justin's long-suffering wife. She had a fuzzy housecoat draped over her shoulders and a baseball cap pulled down over a mop of unwashed hair. She stopped a few feet away, cradling a rolled newspaper and dancing from foot to foot.

"Morning, Marty," she said shyly.

"Amy," he replied, with a nod.

"I don't mean to bother you, but have you seen Justin around? He went out last night and hasn't come home."

Marty played along, stroking his chin as if in deep thought. "No, sorry, I haven't. Last night you said?"

"I was already in bed, but I heard him leave. I assumed he was taking out the trash or something, but when I woke up he still wasn't here."

"I'm sure there's an explanation," Marty offered. "He'll probably turn up any time, now."

He really wanted to wipe that stupid, 'lost puppy' look from her face.

Listen Amy, he thought, *your dumbfuck husband is in my cellar, bleeding all over the concrete. Don't be sad, he has company.*

"I should call the police," she said, turning to leave.

"The police won't do anything, Amy," Marty said. "He hasn't even been missing twenty-four hours."

"It's not like him to just disappear," she said. "It can't hurt to give them a call."

Having the police involved was the absolute *last* thing Marty wanted; he had to think fast.

"It's Halloween in a few days," Marty said. "The cops probably have their hands full right now with childish pranks. Why don't you wait a little longer and see if he turns up before you go bothering them?"

"If something has happened to Justin, I want them to know."

There was only one way this could end.

"Why don't you come in and use my phone? I have coffee on."

Amy thought about it for a second before nodding and turning back to Marty's house. "Thank you, Marty, really. I know I'm being silly, but I worry."

"It's understandable. If Jenn took off without telling me, I'd be a ball of nerves." It took everything he had to not laugh aloud.

Once inside, Marty quietly closed the front door and locked it behind him as Amy crossed the living room and paused. "Where's your phone Marty?"

"In the kitchen, but you probably don't want to go in there."

"What? Marty?"

"I have Halloween decorations everywhere," he giggled.

"You're acting weird, Marty, what's going on? Is Justin here? Are you two pulling a prank on me or something?"

"No pranks, Amy. This is all very real. I have something *very* special in store for Halloween this year, and you and Justin are going to be part of it."

"You're not making any sense," she said, exasperated. "Is Justin here, or not?"

In a flash, Marty crossed the room and grabbed the cloth belt from around her waist. He wrapped it around her neck several times and pulled until his tendons creaked. Amy dropped her newspaper and clutched at her throat as Marty pulled her into the kitchen. When she saw Jenn's pale, blue corpse sitting at the dinner table, she squawked and doubled her efforts to escape Marty's grasp.

"Don't fight, goddammit," Marty hissed. "Just let it happen. This year is going to be special, Amy. The entire neighborhood will remember Halloween for years to come."

She struggled weakly as her feet slipped on the smooth, linoleum surface. She sat between Marty's feet, tearing at the flesh around her neck as her vision dimmed. Marty looped the excess belt around her neck and pulled as hard as he could; Amy's whistling breath was silenced, once and for all.

"We all have to make our mark in this world," he said, breathing heavily from exertion. "I'm going to make mine."

Marty had no idea how long he stood there; his hands hurt from the strain and his back ached. He exhaled loudly and let go of the belt, as Amy toppled over and banged her face on the leg of the kitchen table. He watched her carefully for several minutes, waiting for the telltale rise and fall of her stomach, but it never came.

He laughed loudly, startling himself in the silence of the small room.

The body count had risen by one.

It would soon be time for a little yard work.

First, he needed a costume.

***

The drive to the store was a pleasant one.

For years, whenever Marty went anywhere, Jenn tagged along, like she had some fear of missing out on something. She'd roll down the window and stick her head out into the wind just like Scout, the Beagle his father had when Marty was a child. The first few times he saw her do this, it was odd and cute at the same time. After the first hundred times, Marty wanted to push her through the window and let her tumble out onto the highway.

Today, his view was unobstructed. It felt refreshing to have the ability to enjoy a few moments of peace without Jenn whining about politics, or the antics of her moronic coworkers at the tax office. He clicked on the radio and hummed along to an old country-western song, driving slower than normal, just taking in the peace and quiet.

It was just yesterday when Marty strangled his wife with his bare hands.

It started as a trip to Wal-Mart; it should have taken twenty minutes, but ballooned into two hours, as Jenn poked through the free samples at the make-up counter. When in her thirties, Jenn would scoff at women who wore too much make-up, turning her nose up in the obnoxious holier-than-thou attitude she had. Once she hit forty, she wouldn't leave the house without staring at herself in the mirror for an hour at a time. She had become one of the women she once hated.

What started as a simple discussion about what candy to purchase for the trick-or-treaters became an all-out war about gender equality. Jenn often climbed on top of her soapbox, but yesterday she was in rare form.

Marty couldn't take one more minute of her vitriolic blathering; he pulled over to the side of the freeway, put on his four-way flashers, and slammed her head on the dashboard in mid-sentence. He repeated this several times until she lost consciousness, and once he was sure she was unable to put up a fight, he pinched her nose closed between his fingers and held her mouth closed with his other hand. After a few minutes, the deed had been done. She wouldn't get up on her high horse, ever again.

Now he wouldn't have to be so secretive about the bodies he had locked in the basement. He killed two birds with one stone.

Marty squeezed the station wagon into a parking slot near the front of the store and walked to the entrance as flurries drifted down from a slate-gray sky. Wal-Mart never had a great selection of Halloween costumes, but it was one place he could blend in, one where no one knew him.

He was in and out within minutes, settling on a cheap, plastic skull mask and matching skeleton pull-over. It wasn't a matter of wearing the best costume; it was all part of a much bigger plan.

On his way home, Marty slowed the wagon as he passed the gravel turnout along the side of the highway. He looked at the patch of ground reverently; it marked the passing of his old life and the beginning of another.

It was his life, and he was taking it back, kicking and screaming, if necessary.

***

Later that night, Marty stood on the basement floor wearing a pair of hip-waders, his 'Kiss The Cook' apron, and a welder's mask. The upcoming job of dismembering his kills was going to be a messy one, but one he thought he'd enjoy under the circumstances. Not Jenn. She was going to remain intact; cutting her into pieces would be bad etiquette.

He pulled a hatchet and a small machete from the pegs on the wall. First to go were arms and legs; he tossed them in a pile nonchalantly, as if he was doing nothing more than separating chicken bones from a meal. The smell was awful; his neighbor's corpse had begun to putrefy and leak a multi-colored, viscous fluid onto the cellar floor. Marty dragged his shoe across the concrete to remove the foul slime after accidentally stepping in the coagulated mess.

Thank God this is almost over, he thought.

Jenn had often nagged him about his lack of inspiration and ambition.

"If this isn't ambitious, then I don't know what the fuck is," he said to the empty room. He wiped blood from the front of his apron and raised the welder's mask with one gore-covered hand. This was the easy part.

Marty took a quick, steaming shower to wash off the sweat of his labors and went to sleep completely exhausted.

Twenty-four hours later, with shovel in hand, Marty tramped through his overgrown yard and started digging. He made sure to judge each separate hole accurately; now was not the time to screw up the fine details.

As Marty stopped digging, he noticed a car creeping down the street, causing him to exhale a nervous plume of white vapor.

Not now, he thought. *Keep moving, pal.*

The car disappeared around the corner and Marty went back to the task at hand. His heavy coat had become stifling as sweat leaked from his pores and soaked through his shirt. Clear snot dribbled from his nose and dripped from his upper lip. It was nearly one in the morning when Marty finished digging; his arms and legs shook from exertion, yet there was still so much to do, and very little time to do it.

***

Halloween day dawned chilly and overcast.

Marty's neighborhood had always come to life on Halloween; not just the usual trick-or-treating at sundown, but an all-day event, where parents paraded their children around the streets in their cheap, plastic costumes, showing them off to each other like they were fighting for some grand prize. This year was no different.

Marty sat perched in the bare elm tree in his front yard, trying not to gag from the overwhelming smell of gasoline. Several families had passed his lawn, but no one had, thus far, paid much attention. If he was going to make this a holiday to remember, Marty needed an audience.

"Come one, come all to the Halloween Playground," he shouted.

A couple stopped with their young son and gawked up into the tree where Marty stood, clinging to a branch and wearing his pullover skeleton costume. Others along the street began to pay attention, afraid they were missing out. Before long, Marty's sidewalk was lined with curious onlookers dressed in a variety of silly, cheap, thrift-store costumes; boys and girls were slathered with grease-paint and fake blood, holding plastic machetes and empty plastic bags just waiting to be filled with teeth-rotting candy.

"Step right up, friends and neighbors, and see the wonders of the Halloween Playground, a lesson in life and death."

"What are you selling, Marty?" a man asked. He was greeted with scattered laughter.

Marty didn't answer, smiling beneath his mask as one of the neighborhood children slowly made his way across the lawn.

Only a matter of time.

Marty's hedges were draped with red, tattered lengths of frost-covered intestines.

His wife's corpse hung stiffly from a large wooden post hammered into the ground; a scarecrow of flesh and bone. Straw was tucked into her clothing and crammed into her mouth; large black buttons were crudely sewn into her eyelids.

The grass was coated in a layer of coagulated blood like the floor of an abattoir.

"Come out of there, Dale," a woman shouted. "You're getting that crap all over your new shoes."

"Oh, relax," Marty said. "Sometimes you have to get a little dirty to appreciate the beauty of being alive."

The woman frowned and went after her son, glancing around at the *decorations* spotting the overgrown yard. The ground was dotted with freshly turned earth, large lumps meant to signify fresh graves. At the end of each mound was a buried head, each wearing a different mask to cover the slowly withering flesh beneath. Laid out on either side of each fresh grave were dismembered arms and legs; a random placing of limbs that didn't match the bodies beneath.

One head wore a clown mask with frilly, orange hair; a man's arms were mixed with a woman's smooth legs, red stilettos still attached to a pair of gray feet. Another head wore a matted, tangled werewolf mask; on each side were three arms a piece, laid out like some mutant spider scuttling across a sea of shiny blood.

Eight heads were buried beneath a thin layer of dirt, each wearing a different mask and surrounded by stiff appendages that had turned blue or gray in death. Lumps of crimson jelly and brownish-red muck clung to the woman's shoes and cuffs of her pants as she tiptoed across the lawn to retrieve her curious child. She put a hand over her nose and mouth, and wrinkled her brow at the awful stink of decay.

"My God, Marty, what have you done? This shit is never going to wash out!"

"What is that? Pig's blood?" asked a man from the sidewalk.

"That all depends on what you define as a pig," Marty chuckled.

"Come on out of there," a woman called. "It's absolutely disgusting."

"For years, you've all scared yourself with slasher films and cut-rate haunted houses, but have *any* of you ever felt the exhilaration of actual fear? I'm doing you all a favor, one you'll never forget."

"You've gone off your rocker, Marty!" a man shouted. "Someone's going to call the cops this time."

"Oh, I'm sure of that," Marty replied.

The woman finally reached her son and grabbed him harshly around the arm, as he squealed and cried in protest. Her legs were spattered with thick red dots from her shoes up to her knees, and she tried hard not to vomit from the awful stink. She paused and glanced up at Marty's scarecrow; a look of pure horror twisted her features as she started screaming.

"Oh my God," she wailed. "It's Jenn! It's his fucking wife!"

She stepped back and tripped on a meaty arm that had grown rigid from rigor mortis, then fell into the grass and became instantly coated in thick, red slime. She began writhing on her back, rolling around in the sticky concoction and spitting the congealed sludge from her mouth. No one came to her rescue; they stepped back silently, hands over their faces, watching the display unfold as Marty laughed from his nest, ten feet above. Now, it was all about the screaming and crying, and years of therapy.

"Now you see what I mean!" Marty shouted. "Real fear! If you could see the look on your faces right now. Do you feel your hearts hammering in your chests? The cold sweat running down your spines? I did that! All me!"

The woman crawled across Marty's lawn, dragging herself through the grass by her fingers as her son jumped up and down on the sidewalk, calling for her in between choking sobs. Marty heard the distant approach of sirens and knew his time was short.

"I'm so glad you all came to witness my special project, but what show would be complete without a grand finale?" Marty reached down and grabbed a green, plastic lighter he'd placed in the crotch of several joining branches. Small groups of people had already dispersed in several directions, running up and down the street. If he was going to make an impression, it had to be now.

"I hope I've given you all a Halloween to remember, something to write home about! Tell your friends; my little display will likely be here for a while!"

The sirens were closer, drowning out the frantic cries of Marty's neighbors as they scrambled for safety.

Marty looped a thick noose around his neck and pulled it tight, grimacing as it dug into the flesh under his jaw. Before he'd taken his position in the old elm tree, he'd not only secured a thick rope to one of the sturdiest branches, but had also doused his costume in gasoline. The only way to make a real impression was to go out in a blaze of glory.

"Farewell, everyone!" Marty shouted. "And Happy Halloween!"

He looked down one final time, watching the woman dragging herself across the sidewalk, leaving a red path in her wake.

He smiled and struck the lighter.

As Marty swung down from the tree in a wide arc, his clothing and flesh blazed in a bright orange ball of flame.

He'd tied the noose incorrectly, and instead of breaking his neck instantly, it only cut off his airway, forcing him to dangle there helplessly, slowly suffocating as his body cooked.

In the end, he couldn't even scream.

After a few minutes, his body stilled, and the flame burned through the rope, tumbling his blackened body to the bloody lawn with a crunch. His neighbors watched in shock and horror, as they hid behind parked cars and hedges; others ran up and down the street, as if they were the ones on fire. Marty had gotten his wish -- to show them real fear and give them a Halloween to remember.

The son of bitch surely paid for it.

***

"On tonight's News at Five, a Halloween massacre for the history books, and right here in our area. Find out the details in this shocking story, right from a Hollywood horror film."

The pretty news anchor looked into the camera with a smile. She, too, had a child to get ready for trick-or-treating that night, and she certainly wasn't going to let this get in the way of little Ashley's fun. Besides, this kind of thing could *never* happen in her neighborhood.

"Why was Halloween cancelled in one small town, and could your town be next? We'll be back right after the break."

The End

Jenny Greenteeth

By

James Matthew Byers

The rustle of the eager bag

Bespoke of autumn days.

The window veiled a spooky hag,

Entrenched in deep malaise.

Exposure to the sun had fried

Her muddy, wrinkled skin,

And though she often had it dyed,

It never matched her chin.

The hair about the knobby bump

Propelled an inch or so.

A mirror always made her slump-

She hid, but felt it grow.

Congealing reptiles chopped and stirred

Distracted her a bit.

And though she burned and bobbed and blurred,

The nagging would not quit.

A thousand years or more, it seemed

Invoking Halloween

Supposedly was all she dreamed-

A doting, witchy queen-

And still tonight, the energy

Evaded her in full.

Prospective mythic synergy

Encroached amid the pull

The night would bring as all around

In laughter, children strode.

A leery peering gesture found

Enough to coax and goad.

The swelling hunger in her throat

Reminded her the way

Millennia had passed afloat;

Succumbing to the sway.

So many names had come and gone;

The changing times and all-

But Jenny Greenteeth stuck like bone,

Reclusive until fall.

As waters wilted into mud

And swamps and rivers drained,

A fever swarmed her frozen blood;

The yearning that remained

Propelled her into days of old;

A people lost to lore.

Intense emotion found a hold;

A knock came at her door.

Succinct and pure, the chattel rose.

Aroma, rather sweet,

Escaped and entered in her nose.

A subtle, "Trick or treat?"

Erupted like a sonic boom

As Jenny planned a ploy.

Beside her stood her trusty broom;

Without, a girl and boy

Awaited her to open wide

The gateway to their death.

A bucket and a bag denied;

A gifted final breath

Compiled the rush in Jenny's heart.

A snap, and with a grin

The witch of old engaged her part,

Inviting them both in.

"So pretty, yummy, scary, dear!

The both of you look lush!

Why don't you gather over here;

No need for you to rush!

Old Jenny has a treat in store-

The candy you will taste

I bet will leave you wanting more;

A joy you will not waste!"

A fairy and a goblin strode

Into the house in glee.

The witch began to tease and goad

As what she came to see

Inspired the thirst and hunger, deep

And throbbing in her chest.

"So children, here within my keep,

I saved for you my best ... "

The boy stood up in eager bliss,

And yet the girl stood back

"My sweet, my dear, my little miss-

Come- open up your sack!"

Reluctantly, the second child

Unloosed her tension's grip.

A hidden gleam the witch beguiled

Imploded, lip to lip.

Expecting her to follow suit,

The witch began to change.

Around them, dark of grime and soot

Convulsed upon the range.

The living room became a moat;

A swamp within the wood.

Upon the air, a whispered gloat

Expressed, "I've got you, good!"

Uncertainty began to bleed

In words of spells she cast,

And as the children fed the need,

She wandered in the past.

So many faces she had worn,

A title, like a wreath,

About her manner would adorn-

But how she loved "Greenteeth."

Descending from the grindylow

And Grendel's mother's girth,

Originally, she was Gno,

The name she bore at birth.

Releasing nature from the net,

The spell removed the call.

Another year of no regret-

As back behind the wall

Inside the cottage, queer and quaint,

Another missing sign

Upon the morrow marred the paint,

The craft of her design.

And now the hunger swelled amuck,

As two were not enough

To quell the burning blaze that struck.

She rallied in the rough.

Demonic rages, grazing heat,

And evil never seen

Invoked the witch to trick-or-treat

Upon this Halloween ...

Don't Fear the Reaper

By

Steven Stacy

OCTOBER 31st

HALLOWEEN

"Tommy! Tommy... Stop crying," Amber pleaded through her own tears. "I promise you, this is going to work." Amber wiped her eyes and told herself to toughen up. Behind her, the sun was beginning to set on the cold- hearted day. Autumn leaves fell from a large, twisted oak, floating down around her.

"How do you know?" Tommy asked. He was twenty-one, but because of everything that had happened he seemed much younger than his years. In many ways Amber felt like his mother rather than his younger sister.

"You'll just have to trust me," she said, hiding her tears. "You stay strong and so will I."

"You abandoned me!" he angrily accused. Amber had nothing to say to the accusation, because in many ways she felt guilty. "They're coming!" Tommy screamed, and then she could hear him wrestling with someone. She placed a hand over her mouth. Then a stranger came on the line.

"Hello, Miss Strode? This is Donna Trenton, the head nurse at 'Tad's Psychiatric Hospital.'"

"Is he okay?" Amber managed to get out, choking on her words. "You better be treating him well."

"Tommy's fine, honestly Miss Strode. I know it's a rough time of year for the both of you, but I'm afraid your brother's phone time is up," the nurse stated, not sounding like she knew what a rough year was like, and certainly not seeming to care. "I'm afraid I'm going to have to go, unless there's something else I can help you with?"

"No. I don't think there's anything you can help me with. Thank-you," Amber said, coldly. She hung up and closed her eyes. Amber could hear Tommy in her mind, crying. She'd hung up on her sobbing brother, feeling guilty and like a complete bitch. It was just fifteen minutes since she'd finished school, and she was waiting for her best-friends, Emma and Faye. She wasn't in the mood to see anyone. She searched through her coat for some strawberry bubble gum, her favourite.

It was a cold winter's day and the brisk wind was howling. She was sat on the park bench where they always met, because they all walked the same way home. She took out her compact and tried her best to hide the tracks of her tears, wishing she'd bought waterproof eyeliner. Amber had once been a wild child – the girl who liked to party too much. She had always been at the beach, a surfer girl; petite and pretty. She still liked to surf, but she'd grown mistrusting of many people.

School had been full of Halloween good cheer all day. The other teens had been dressed up in one kind of costume or another. Not her. It wasn't a good date for Amber; she'd lost her older sister on Halloween, and her eleven-year-old brother was the only witness and suspect. He'd been dressed as a clown with the murder weapon-- a large kitchen knife-- glued into his hand by someone he said he'd never seen. That was his defence. He refused to speak about that night now. Halloween scared the life out of him, and Amber couldn't really say she blamed him. It scared her as well, and she wasn't even there that night, ten years ago; she'd been at a slumber party with girlfriends. They'd questioned her about the whole thing, even the fact that she'd seen the movie 'Halloween' had been seen as interesting. As if half the Western world hadn't seen it! Since the murder, she'd buried her head in books.

"Hey," Emma said. Amber jumped out of her reverie and up from the bench and spun around, dropping her books in the process. "It's only me, for God's sake." Emma smiled, her voice reassuring. She was a naturally charismatic girl who always had a cause to fight for. Her favourite was her feminist agenda and getting ahead. She worked two jobs just in case she didn't get a scholarship, although she was fairly assured of one.

"I'm so sorry, you know -- *Halloween*," Amber said. "It's a bitch."

"I didn't mean to scare you. Why don't you take a Xanax or a Valium or something?" Emma asked, as she was helping Amber to pick her books up from the grass.

"The doctor would only give me ten. I've been...imagining things again. It's stress, but God forbid I'd get a pill to help me deal with it. Damn doctor! I've already taken two, and I want some for tonight or there's no way I'll sleep. Besides, I'm babysitting tonight – I need to be alert. The Bethanys rang me earlier. They won tickets to go see that new play 'Angels In America' ...something like that anyway."

"They must be *giving* those tickets away; I'm babysitting for Wade Morgan, he's in the house just across from the Bethany's, right?"

"Yeah, I've babysat for them plenty of times. Are we waiting for Faye?" Emma looked up from her phone, her glossy red hair shining in the waning daylight. She shrugged. Amber pulled her coat close, her teeth chattering slightly.

"I'll text her and tell her we're gonna start walking. She's always late. Anyway, maybe I'll borrow one of those Valium and stick one in little Wade's drink," Emma giggled. "He's gonna need it after I scare him to death with a night full of horror movies."

"I thought I was gonna get a lecture to be honest," Amber laughed, stopping to pull her transparent pop-socks up. "Oh my God!" Amber said, just remembering. "Did you know that the boogeyman dates back hundreds of years? We were reading about it today in creative English, ya know, because it's Halloween."

"Well, no wonder I was so scared to go to bed as a kid. I must've seen him. Either that or these people *also* have older brothers who liked to scare them to death in the middle of the night," Emma laughed. "Being the only girl is not much fun, I can tell you that much." Emma's phone went off, the Halloween theme shrieking out in its low and high notes. "Faye says she's '*right behind us*'." Both girls turned to see Faye hurrying to catch up to them, struggling in heels across the muddy field; her long, fair, hair moving left to right as she strode their way. "Besides, why were you expecting a lecture?"

"Hey, wait up!" Faye yelled and both girls stopped. "Why didn't you wait? The paper was flooded after Amber's title piece came in late yesterday."

"Well, we can't wait for *you* all day," Emma said. "Anyway, what piece is this?" Emma asked, looking at both girls in turn. The girls had all met at a party. Emma and Amber had out-grown, or been out-scared, of partying. Faye was still strongly taking part. She was completely care-free, unless it came to her writing. She was head editor of the High School paper. Then, the tall blonde was obsessed with getting it right. The three girls left the school and moved on to Main St., which was usually lined with pink and white blossom trees. The blossoms were either on the ground or floating down in the strong breeze. Amber pulled her long, pale pink, coat together and tied the belt. Faye fiddled with her hair and then pulled a paper out of her backpack and handed it to Emma.

"I swear, I couldn't *believe* it when Amber came into the office the other day, telling me she was the other *Strode* sister..." Faye said, then sighed. "Of course, she told me you already knew, Em." Emma suddenly cottoned on and gave Amber an alarmed, judgemental, look. Then she unfolded the school paper, and there was a picture of Amber and a headline – "My Michael Myers Stalker."

"You told the whole school!" Emma said in a horrified whisper. The three girls stopped. Amber looked away, guiltily. She chewed her gum, blew a bubble and let it pop. "Why didn't you tell me you were going to do that?"

"I *had* to do something, you don't understand the way Tommy is. I have to get him out of there...."

"And the only way you'll do that is if the copycat shows up and kills someone off. That's what you want is it?" Emma asked, furiously. Faye looked confused.

"Of course not! I just want my brother and my family back," Amber shouted, and then started walking ahead. "I am not just going to stand by and watch my brother suffer any longer." Emma followed, then Faye. The sound of heels and trainers mixed with the smell of perfume and hairspray.

"Well, I thought it was very brave of Amber to come forward. You have to see it from her point of view, Em. She's lived with this secret and she --"

"I've seen things from *her* point of view right from the start. It'll be *our* butts on the line if that Michael Myers fanatic comes back. Mine and yours, Faye." Faye pouted, looking dubiously at Amber, whose was chewing more quickly.

"You think I'd do that to you, huh?" Amber said, pointing an accusing finger at her oldest friend. "Well then, you obviously don't know me at all. The police have *finally* let me do this, I've already arranged for the both of you to be put in safe houses for the entire night!"

"What!?" Both Emma and Faye exclaimed together. "You can't do that, I'm busy tonight," Faye said, sweetly. Emma simply flushed red with guilt.

"Y-you what?" Emma stuttered. "Look, Amber, I'm sorry. It was just such a shock."

"It's okay, it's fine! I understand," Amber said, storming ahead.

"I just wish you'd told me."

"It was a last minute decision," Amber explained, turning to Emma. Who immediately grasped her around the shoulders and pulled her into a hug; as Faye cooed in the background about how cute they were.

"Look, I'm sorry – and I don't want to go into a safe house; how will we smoke the fucker out like that? Everything needs to look normal, I gather," Emma said, a strained smile on her lips.

"Well...yes, but I don't want you putting yourselves in danger."

"No safe houses," Emma said defiantly.

"Well, I think it's cool," Faye laughed. "I mean who knew Amber was the Strode sister? A Michael Myers copycat killer, obsessed with your family – it's so creepy, I love it! My readers love it. It went crazy online. It's just too bad your surname's Strode." Emma and Amber walked along not saying anything, but both looking worried. "Anyway, what are you two doing tonight?" Faye asked, changing the subject and attempting to lift the mood.

"Babysitting," Emma and Amber said in unison, then laughed at the irony.

"Well, Richie Taylor asked me out tonight, so we're going to the yearly horror movie marathon," Faye said.

"I didn't know you were dating Richie..." Amber said, her voice serious again. Her nail-bitten hand pushed a strand of blonde hair out of her face - the two girls exchanged embarrassed looks; which Emma noticed. Amber blew a pink bubble.

"I thought you were dating Phil," Faye said, defensively.

As the three girls talked and walked, a 1978 Ford Ltd Wagon started up the street behind them.

"That's...complicated. I just thought it was a rule that we didn't date each other's ex's," Amber explained. Emma rolled her eyes, she couldn't stand drama, especially girl drama. She'd rather fight it out on the hockey field. The Ford started to crawl closer to the girls, though none of them noticed.

"You only went out twice, you said he was a creep and that he tried it on with you," Faye said, mildly annoyed.

"He *is* a creep, Faye; I don't think you should go out with him. He got *really rough* with me when I said no to him. I had to knee him in the balls, get out of the car and walk home..." Amber sighed. "There's enough pressure tonight without Ritchie being involved." Faye opened her mouth to say something, decided against it, and shut it again. She liked Amber, and didn't want to spoil their friendship; especially now that she was verging on movie of the week, star status.

"How you two can wear mini-skirts in this weather, I don't know – it's freezing! And let's face it, you're only wearing them so that men will look at you," Emma teased, changing the subject again.

"Damn straight!" Faye said with a laugh.

"Actually, I like wearing them. They look good, and I wear them for *myself*. Not everything is sexual politics, Emma. It's fashion; if you ever shaved your legs, you might be able to try it." Amber gave Emma a guilty smile and Faye laughed loudly.

"Owned!" Faye giggled.

"Are you the Bible? Because men keep using you to support their own selfish agendas," Emma said.

"*What?*" Amber mocked. "You take that stuff *way* too seriously."

"Definitely," Faye agreed.

"Faye, you are such a parrot," Emma said, frustrated. "Would you stop copying everything Amber says!"

The Ford was crawling down the street beside them now. Amber looked over curiously and felt a mild swell of fear. The sunlight was so bright, she could only make out the shape of the driver, nothing more. She blew a pink bubble and popped it.

"Hey!" Faye shouted toward the Ford, she had obviously noticed it, too. "Take a picture, it lasts longer, you pervert!" Then Faye opened her jacket and flashed a low- cut sweater. A flash went off from just inside the car, where the side window was down a little. The car then sped off. "Well, I didn't actually *mean* it," she laughed nervously. "What a creepy bastard..."

"And why was he driving that old car?" Emma wondered, thinking aloud. She exchanged a worried look with Amber.

"Who cares what car he's driving?" Amber, clearly annoyed. "Now some weirdo has a picture of the three of us." The three girls stood in a row, watching the car drive away. "Faye, seriously, you'd better be careful. One day you'll say the wrong thing to the wrong person."

"I'd have kicked his perverted arse anyway," Emma said. They walked for a few moments in silence.

"Well, to lighten the mood, what are you two going dressed up as tonight?" Faye asked.

"We can hardly show up to look after kids in full costume, honey," Emma laughed. "And *normally*, I wouldn't dress like a tart just to please my man, but... I did promise him this year. So, I'm going fifties pin-up. 'We can do it!'" Emma said demonstrating by curling her bicep.

"Actually, I was thinking of going as a cat. I've got cat ears, and this tail thing which wraps around my waist…" Amber said, chewing. She wasn't really interested in celebrating the holiday.

"Way to go Amber! I'm still choosing between 'duh, I'm a mouse' and 'Suicide Squad' – Harley Quinn. We're going to Jason's Halloween party; I'll pop 'round to the house later, after the kids are in bed."

"Yeah, and don't wake them up by ringing the doorbell, I'll leave the door unlocked…," Emma began, then thought for a second. "Actually, just call me *and* knock at the door, due to current events changing everything."

"Yes, leave the door open, Emma, for any psycho to walk in off the Street. Why don't you take a long shower while you're at it, too, huh?" Amber teased and then laughed.

"Actually, I just might do that – but boo-hoo, I forgot to steal the cash first. Well darn," Emma said, doing her best Betty Boop impression.

"This is my stop. I'll text you two later about tonight's shenanigans," Faye said with a wink, and then walked up her path. Emma looked towards Amber, who was watching Faye leave, and could see she was worrying.

"Faye's a big girl, you know; she can take care of herself." A few minutes later Emma had to walk across the street to her own house. "See ya later, and don't fear the reaper…"

Amber walked the rest of the way on her own, singing "My momma don't like you, and she likes every-one," as she went. Up ahead of her was a hedge and as she looked towards it, she saw a man standing next to it in full Michael Myers, 'Halloween', get up. Her mind soared; she'd been imagining him a lot lately. *Was he real?* "What the hell?" she mumbled to herself as she stopped walking. *He was just stood there; watching her through that creepy white mask with the scruffy dark hair.* She blew a pink bubble gently. Suddenly, a hand clamped down on her shoulder. The bubble-gum popped. She screamed and spun around. It was an older man, stodgy and well built; with a shaved head, in a nice suit. Her trembling hand stayed by her mouth. "Get your hand off me!"

"I'm sorry, I didn't mean to scare you…." Amber said nothing. "Is your name Amber Strode-Rodgers?" the man asked in a gruff voice.

"Who's asking?" Amber asked, shaking off his hand and looking behind her. The Myers figure was gone. A look of bewilderment fell across her face for a moment, before she turned back to the man.

"I'm Detective Bill Weaver, and I'd like to speak with you." Weaver smiled at the petite teen, as he flashed his badge.

"What about?" Amber enquired, studying his badge. They'd placed her undercover years ago. In protective custody, with her aunt and uncle- in- law. She had moved schools and was told not to share information with anyone. Of course, that was until yesterday, and the school paper. Though she was sure someone could've traced her online, if they'd had the inclination. She had told Emma, one drunken night, months back. "Hey, that badge says you're retired... what's this about?" She asked again, and Weaver realised she was a quick study.

An hour later, Weaver had explained the whole story. He'd seen her story had broken yesterday and had been unofficially working her family's case since the beginning. "I'm just in the neighbourhood, working with the local Police Chief; if anyone sees anything strange – they get in touch. I have a hunch the killer will strike again; after all it's been a decade since your sister's death."

"Fifteen years in the movie, though," Amber said.

"Yes, but he goes after Jamie-Lee at the age of seventeen. *Your age now*. And, you might've just scratched his itch with your article." Amber raised an inquisitive brow.

A few minutes later Amber had invited the ex-detective into her aunt and uncle's home. "There are hundreds of Michael Myers costumes around ex-Detective, I'd be calling you every five minutes. After the murder, Myers had a surge in popularity. People seem to like the spooky story, and they've taken it to heart. Like in *'The Town That Dreaded Sundown.'* People are sick." Amber felt goosebumps rising on her arms and lower back. She swigged some iced tea. Her 'parents' were still at work – thank God; they'd kill her for letting the story loose. If they didn't know already, it was good. They'd just try to stop her.

"Would you just take my card and call me if anything strange happens?"

"*Strange*, on Halloween night... c'mon, the irony! Besides, I'm already working with the local police. I'll take it, sure." Amber took one of the dog-eared cards, and started programming the details into her smart-phone.

"We all know how well 'the local police' do in these stories, Amber," Weaver said dryly. Amber sighed, and then looked towards the door. "I'm sure you'll be anxious to know I'm babysitting tonight," she said and popped her bubble-gum. Weaver's back was straight up.

"Who asked you to babysit?" Weaver enquired, immediately on edge.

"The parents, they called me ..." she said, a smile on her wine coloured lips; she'd become very good at hiding her feelings. "I've baby-sat for them before."

"You actually spoke to them?"

"Yes," Amber said, slightly concerned at the worry in this guy's face. "Otherwise, I wouldn't be doing it, would I?" He walked towards the door, and Amber noticed that his suit was crumpled, like he'd been sleeping in his car. "The police seem to think that if I --"

"By the way, you'll be looking for the *original* mask and costume, not the Rob Zombie version," Weaver interrupted, opening the door.

"So, no grubby goth masks, *check*," she said, holding the door open for him. "Try not to worry so much, ex- detective... you'll live longer." He turned back to her and gave her a weak smile.

"I find the opposite to be true, actually. Ring me if you see anything – *you'll* live longer! These guys don't usually change their M.O," he frowned.

"It could've been a one off you know..."

"Hopefully. It was nice to finally meet you, Amber," Weaver said.

Amber dressed in a hurry; this ex-detective had slowed her down. She felt anxious being in the house alone, she should've known better. After speaking to Weaver, she realised that he was right about the possibility of her being in danger. Besides, she had two undercover police following her, and watching her, tonight. Poor Tommy, she felt so guilty that she couldn't be there for him full time; but she was taking the advice of the doctors and the police. Plus, she visited him as much as she could. Amber heard the wind was picking up outside, so she pulled on a short-sleeved sweater. Unexpectedly, her phone started buzzing on her vanity table; she walked over to pick it up. "Hello?"

"Hey Amber, it's me, Emma."

"I know. Your Facebook picture comes up when you call, remember? Not to mention your name," Amber said sarcastically, walking around her bedroom and looking for her black boots. She walked past the posters of punk bands and Emo boys.

"Ha-ha! Very funny, wise guy! Anyway, I was wondering if you wanted a ride, but you're starting to make me regret my kind gesture..." Emma teased.

"Wait up! I'm sorry, you know I love you really... and a ride would be brilliant. A car's going to be following us. Two undercover police, just ignore it, though. Act completely normal."

"What's acting 'completely normal' like? And okay, *what police*?" Emma said, pretending they didn't exist. "You know in the movie; he goes for the best friends..." Emma pointed out. There was an awkward silence on the phone.

"Look, I know – and you can go undercover right now. I have to get Tommy out of there, but this is your decision," Amber said raking a nervous hand through her long hair.

"I don't really feel like I have one because things won't look normal if I go undercover; either way I'm gonna get blamed."

"I will *not* blame you for pulling out of this, do you hear me? Are you in or out?"

"...In!" Emma said finally, and then pretended as if nothing was wrong. "Yes, well you're lucky I've got such a forgiving heart...What time have you got to be there?" Amber was still concerned about the Myers figure she'd seen earlier. It wasn't the first time she'd seen things that weren't *really* there; especially around Halloween.

"I'm scared," Amber confessed. She took her bubble-gum out and threw it in the trash. "Earlier on, I thought I saw a guy dressed as Myers on my street. I wasn't sure if I hallucinated or not. Did you speak to that ex-cop, Weaver?"

"Yeah, my dad passed along the message. Watch out for Michael Myers… like we needed a warning. I heard the guys in school were planning tricks, though. So watch out! It might've been some guy from class. You don't wanna stick a knitting needle in some poor boy's neck. *I know*! It probably *was* Bruce Marker; he has a huge crush on you."

Amber closed her blinds, sat on her bed, and started pulling her heavy boots on. "Yeah, well Bruce Marker *needs* a mask, he's such an ugly sleaze. I hope he doesn't donate his face to science," Amber laughed. Emma started giggling across the line.

"Bitch-ey! Oh my God, Amber, remind me not to piss you off," Emma laughed. "Anyway, I'll pick you up in half an hour, on the corner – don't be late!" Amber hung up. She heard her Aunt & uncle come in downstairs.

"Amber!" her aunt called.

"Coming!" she called, and placed the phone down on her bed.

<u>2</u>

Emma picked her up on the corner, as arranged. They were now on their way to babysit, and the sun was going down in the cloudy, crimson-red sky. Amber stared at Emma in awe. "I feel so under-dressed. You look amazing, I love fifties pin-up!"

"So does Andrew, so I went all out. It took me forever to curl my fringe under. And this lipstick." Emma rolled her eyes. She was wearing a short pink dress and heels with frilly white socks, and a pink bow in her hair. "Are the cops following?" Emma whispered. Amber looked over her shoulder, then nodded.

"Just pretend they're not there, okay?" Amber whispered back.

"Right," Emma smiled. "So, I spoke to Faye and she's upset about the Ritchie situation."

"I'm just worried, that's all. I swear Ritchie would've raped me if I hadn't made my daring escape," Amber said.

"I never thought Ritchie was your type anyway. How about if I set you up with one of Drew's friends. You know he's a nice guy and I'm sure he could recommend someone suitable."

"All of Drew's friends are in college," Amber reminded, as if Emma had forgotten.

"And that's why they're more mature."

"I don't know," Amber said, sticking her cat-eared headband through her hair. "What do you think?"

"You're hardly Catwoman. Wear some of my make-up; there's eye-liner and lipstick in my bag." They turned the corner onto Chariot Road as Amber raided Emma's make-up bag. An alarm could be heard going off on the corner of the shopping district. "What a racket!" Emma turned on the radio and 'Don't Fear the Reaper' by Blue Oyster Cult blasted out. "They play this Goddamned song every Halloween. Does anyone *not* fear the reaper for goodness sake?"

"I know I do. There, what do you think?"

Emma turned to see a completely transformed Amber. "You look fabulous. I love it. Dab that red lipstick though, it smudges."

"In one way, I hope the killer does strike, but I can't imagine actually stabbing someone..."

Neither girl noticed the Ford station wagon turn onto the road behind them and start following behind the Ford police vehicle. "You're starting to sound like a Wes Craven movie, and I don't mean in some self-referential, cool, nineties way. Who says you'll have to stab anyone? He makes a move -- the cops catch him."

"Yeah...hopefully. I think I'd be in a Stephen King book, myself. Really dark, fucked-up shit."

"I think you'd be in some random short story, if you were *that* lucky," Emma giggled again. "I suggest you get indoors with Ariel, and then go 'round the house making sure that every single door and window is locked, so the boogey-man won't get you."

"What about you?"

"I can take care of myself. I have mace in my bag and my dad bought me a gun for my birthday," Emma giggled again; a nervous habit. "Daddy got it for me after my first date. He's such a worrier."

Weaver had tracked down the local police lieutenant and Lt. Saxon had agreed to follow Amber and her friends for the night. Weaver now sat in the lieutenant's car as they followed the girls. The car smelt of new leather, under Saxon's heavy cologne.

"I remember that murder, never did think the boy did it. Such an innocent face, and that knife glued to his hand--weird. Of course, he was easy to blame in a murder which needed solving. And she was such a pretty girl," Lt. Saxon said as he drove.

"It's strange how people always say things like that, as if her good looks make the murder more of a crime," Weaver muttered, looking out at the passing children in their trick- or- treat outfits. He remembered when one had to dress scarily, like Dracula or Frankenstein. Now the children were dressed as Angels and super-heroes.

"You know what I mean," Saxon said. "Christina Strode, I remember her. She was always so polite too. What a waste!"

"The killer will go after her friends first, so I suggest we park just back from both houses." Weaver lit a cigarette, preparing for a long night.

"How do you know the killer will strike again tonight?"

"Gut instinct," Weaver said. Saxon grabbed his radio up from his belt and radioed in their location as the girl's car came to a halt ahead. "He's here. Whoever killed that little boy's sister is back to finish their homage," Weaver continued with conviction, as the car came to a stop. "Has the house sold yet? The Strode house?"

"No, everyone seems to think it's haunted."

"Well, tonight it very well might be." Minutes later, they watched from a distance as Amber and Emma got out of the car. Weaver kept his eyes on Emma. He felt Amber was safe for the moment.

Amber waved the Bethanys off to their 'don't wait up for us' night out. She shut the door, and locked it, and then threw another stick of bubble-gum in her mouth. Ariel wrapped her arms around Amber's thighs. She was a very loving child, though spoilt. She was wearing a ballerina costume.

"You look very pretty," Amber said, hugging the child back.

"I like your cat ears! I love cats. They're so cute." After about thirty seconds Amber had enough.

"Can I have my legs back please, honey?" Ariel released her, and her skinny black jeans. Ariel did a shy attempt at a pirouette, stumbled, and corrected herself.

"I can do it better than that, *look*, I'll show you again," Ariel placed a mouthful of fair hair in her mouth and attempted it again.

"*That* was brilliant," Amber said and clapped, then knelt to look her in the face. She pulled Ariel's hair out of her mouth and gently placed it behind the girl's shoulder.

"What are we doing for Halloween?"

"Well, *first* we're going to make popcorn, *then* we'll watch a *scary movie*," Amber stretched the words 'scary movie' out. "*Then*, we're going to make a jack-o-lantern to scare away ghosts and goblins, and *then* we're going to watch movies until bedtime," Amber said in her best Nickelodeon presenter voice.

"My mum said I can stay up until midnight because it's Halloween," Ariel said, pulling a smaller strand of silken hair back into her mouth.

"Your mother told me your bedtime is at nine, you little fibber. Why don't you finish watching 'Nightmare Before Christmas' while I make the popcorn?"

"Okay," Ariel said enthusiastically. Then she pranced off into the candle-lit living room. With all of the candles and all the different scents, Amber thought Mrs. Bethany must have a share in Yankee Candles. The landline started ringing as Amber ripped the instructions off the Jiffy Pop.

"Hello, Bethany residence..." Amber answered, turning on the oven jet.

"Hey, it's me," Emma said. "I love hearing you sound so responsible."

"I suppose it is a change. What are you up to?"

"The Morgans just left and Wade is in the living room playing Resident Evil 7. I don't know how he does it; those games scare the shit out of me."

"Emma, those games are for eighteen and over. He shouldn't even be playing them."

"Well, I never bought the damn things. I asked him if he wanted to watch a movie, but he's completely wrapped up in it. Anyway, Drew is coming over later, after I put Wade to sleep. So, you gonna come over when Ariel's in bed?"

"What if she wakes up and I'm not here? I can't just abandon her."

"Responsible!" Emma giggled. "A few years ago, you'd have thrown caution to the wind. Ariel could've cried all night." The Jiffy Pop started to pop – casting the foil outward.

"Well a lot's happened... can't you just bring Wade over here and we can put them to bed at the same time? The Morgans are way more relaxed than the Bethanys. In fact, they've probably got those babysitter cameras recording me as we speak." Amber moved the popcorn around the hob as it started to heat up. She popped her gum loudly. "Did you get Jiffy Pop?"

"No, the shop was out. I've gotta make it the old-fashioned way; which means I'll probably burn it. Cooking is not my forté. I'll see if I can talk Wade into spending the night with Ariel," Emma said. She twirled the old- fashioned, coiled telephone wire around her fingers. "I'll talk to Faye and phone you later."

"See ya!" Amber smiled and hung up. As she did, the phone rang again, making her jump - along with the' popcorn. "Amber, calm down," she whispered to herself. "Hello, Bethany residence..." No answer. "Hello?" Amber repeated, her voice higher. Straining to listen over the movie and popcorn, she thought she could hear heavy breathing. She hung up quickly. Goosebumps rose on her bare arms, so she hugged herself. Then she loosened the collar on her short-sleeve, turtle neck. She was creeped-out. She left the Jiffy Pop on the hob and went to plug her phone into charge.

Lieutenant Saxon and Weaver sat in darkness watching the houses. Both were detached and expensive. "Looks a lot creepier in the dark, huh?" Saxon said, eyeing them both warily.

"That it does," Weaver agreed, lighting another cigarette. The arthritis in his knees was playing him up because of the cold weather. Weaver patted the gun in his leather jacket; he wasn't meant to be carrying one, but it made him feel a lot safer. And at his age, he wasn't much good racing after suspects. "I'm going to take a look around, you stay here." Saxon locked the car, from inside, with a beep. He leaned out of the window. "To be honest Det. Weaver, I didn't buy this whole 'Halloween' copy-cat story. I mean, I'm still sceptical. Who would break into a house to recapture a scene from a horror movie?"

"A fanatic. Someone out there *is* obsessed with that movie and I suppose I've been cast as Donald Pleasance. Not very flattering considering the age difference," Weaver laughed. "But hopefully I can fit the bill."

"I think you have a strong resemblance to David Cubitt myself."

Weaver sighed. "I've heard that before, actually. Right, if he's following the plot completely, he'll try to kill Emma Richards first. I'm going to take a look around the house, you okay here on your own?" Saxon nodded. Weaver threw his finished cigarette to the leaf covered street floor.

Amber was deep in thought, carving a jack-o'-lantern, with a kitchen knife, when suddenly Ariel piped up with an instruction. "Make it look pretty," Ariel instructed.

"Ariel, it's meant to be scary, so that ghosts and monsters stay away," Amber laughed.

"Does it keep the boogeyman away, too?" Ariel asked, placing a strand of her hair in her mouth. Amber turned to look at her, slush and seeds falling from the blade back into the pumpkin. The room smelt of fresh popcorn.

"Who told you about that?"

"There's this girl named Alice in the year above me, and her and her friends are always sneaking off to play with their friend Mary-Jane, who I've never *even* seen." Amber snickered, and turned back to fetch the carving materials out of the cupboard. "And anyway, *she* told me." Ariel looked up with haunted eyes. "She said he comes out on Halloween night to get little kids."

"You know; older kids just like to scare younger kids. This Alice sounds like a right little -- a little liar," Amber corrected herself quickly. She popped her bubble-gum.

"She also said that the boogeyman killed a girl in this neighbourhood and a little boy saw him and now he's crazy." Ariel, arms behind her back, was awkwardly playing with her hands, while sucking on a silver strand of hair still in her mouth. Amber sighed before starting to chew faster.

"I don't know where kids hear these things. So much for responsible parents…" she said, more to herself than Ariel. "I told you, Ariel, this girl is just trying to scare you. She really is, honey. Let's not talk about things like that, let's do the jack-o'-lantern before it gets too late." Ariel watched her with curious eyes, her brows drawn together, finally she spoke.

"Okay then…"

Emma stood in the kitchen, cooking popcorn. Her phone vibrated on the work-top and she snatched it up, and saw it was her boyfriend, Drew, calling. "Hey!" Emma said.

"Hello sexy, is Wade asleep yet? I've got a costume that I think is going to turn you on."

"No, he's not, he'll probably never sleep again. I've got the poor little git watching 'Halloween Horror Night' on the movie channel. He's made it through *Psycho*, *Black Christmas*, and he's just started *Halloween*," Emma said, then giggled. The popcorn popped and the Halloween theme played loudly from the living room. "What're you dressed as anyway?"

"It's a surprise. What're you dressed as?" Andrew asked. Suddenly, a loud crash came from outside, stopping Emma's smile and making her walk towards the patio doors. She looked outside, but couldn't see anything but her reflection. "Well?"

"It's a surprise…" Emma said, her tone serious. She took the popcorn off the jet.

"Can you pick me up?"

"What? Why?"

"Some arsehole slashed my two front tyres this morning," Andrew said, moaning like a little boy.

"I'd have to leave Wade with Amber, which I don't think she'd be too pleased about. Besides, have you seen 'Halloween' - the original? The girl gets strangled in her car, going to pick her boyfriend up."

"Last time I checked, this wasn't a movie, Em, and it'll only take fifteen minutes."

"Everything with you takes only fifteen minutes," Emma mocked. Something caught the corner of her eye and she turned back to the patio doors, and stopped giggling. She thought a shadow beside a bush looked very human.

Weaver walked around the side of the Morgan's home. He stopped to rub his knees and then walked across the ice-tipped grass. The numerous amounts of trees and evergreen shrubbery made staying hidden easy. He heard footsteps and stopped where he was; while drawing his gun, he crept around towards the patio and could see Emma on the telephone. He stopped to take in how attractive she was and caught himself thinking, *if only I were a few years younger. More like a couple decades*, he chuckled to himself. He moved to get a cigarette out of his coat pocket. Abruptly, he saw something move beside him. He began to turn, but something—like rope-- was wrapped around his throat, choking him. He bucked and tried to free himself from his captor's grasp. He could hear heavy, excited, breathing. His hand flew out, his gun hitting a hanging basket and falling to the ground. The killer was here and he was going to die. *It can't end like this*, he thought.

A loud smash came from outside and Emma gave a startled scream, jumping in the air at the same time. Her fifties- curls bounced around her shoulders. "What's wrong?" Emma walked up to the patio doors. She looked outside to see that a potted plant had fallen and smashed on the patio.

Weaver's hand flew out in a desperate bid to get Emma's attention as the figure drained the life out of him. As his body went limp, the shape released him. Weaver fell to the cold ground...dead.

"It was one of the potted plants; it fell and smashed outside... probably rust." Emma said, shielding her eyes from her reflection and looking into the night. Nothing. Drew laughed loudly down the phone at her.

"You sounded bloody terrified," he teased, his voice filled with ridicule.

"Oh, I can imagine you. You were damn near screaming like a girl when I showed you *'Candyman,'*" she giggled again, her smile and confidence returning along with the memory.

"Ha-ha! Can you pick me up or not? Otherwise, I won't be able to see you tonight."

"Okay, but I'll have to be quick; Faye and Ritchie are coming over. Wade sleeps like a baby, so I said I'd have the get-together over here." Emma turned around slowly to see Wade standing behind her, a grin on his face. "...*Anyway*, Wade's *here*, so I'll call you back." Emma hung up and folded her arms. "Your popcorn is ready, you little sneak..."

"I wanna stay for the party," Wade said, still grinning.

"Wade, I thought we had an agreement, I buy your comic books and you keep your mouth shut about Drew. Besides, I'm not having a party. I'm just going to kiss Drew all night." Emma wiggled her tongue at wade, playfully.

"Eww, gross! O-kay! Am I really going over to play with Ariel?" Wade sounded excited. Emma had already come to the conclusion that Wade was going to be a little heartbreaker when he was older. He certainly had an eye for the women; even in his Amazing Spider-Man outfit. The cowl was off, showing his wild curly hair and bright dark eyes. Emma nodded and smiled.

She held Wade's hand as they ran across the street towards the large, white house that belonged to the Bethanys. "I'm cold!" Wade shouted over the howling wind. Emma pulled him close as the shape watched from the darkness. His grip tightened on the handle of his large kitchen knife.

Amber pulled open the door. "Well, I should've known I'd end up being the one spending her evening alone with the children." Wade ran past her and greeted Ariel with a hug and then a discussion on their outfits. Emma hurried inside from the weather.

"I know, I know!" Emma said, holding her hands up. "I'm sorry. Look, if you agree to watch Wade for the night, I'll not only give you my babysitting money, I'll set you up on a double date. Me and Drew, you and Justin." Amber shut the door and smirked.

"Are we talking about "*Justin' for Justin'* Justin?"

"The one and the only. Not only is he a medical student, he's a complete gym bunny."

"Probably injecting his tight arse with steroids he gets from med school," Amber laughed. The two children sat on the sofa chatting as the girls walked through to the kitchen.

"Please? Someone slashed Drew's tyres so he can't drive over. I've gotta go and pick him up."

"Wait... this is just like in '*Halloween*,' where Jamie-Lee gets left with the kids," Amber pointed out, her face tense with worry. She couldn't get rid of these irrational, paranoid ideas about masked killers coming after her. She'd never liked scary movies much, but since her family tragedy she gobbled them up; identifying with the usual female lead, who most of the time defeated the bad guy. She was so on edge tonight. Especially after that visit from Weaver. She rested on the kitchen island and continued carving the pumpkin, chewing slowly. "I don't like it, Emma." Amber picked up her prescription bottle and took two Valium out. Then, she chased them down her throat with some cool water, along with her gum.

Emma walked around to Amber and put her hand on her back, rubbing it, reassuringly. "I know you've been through a lot, but you're a strong girl. A *smart* girl. You're gonna get through this, and hopefully catch this guy. If you want me to blow off Drew, I'll stay with you tonight." The two girls hugged. "I've been watching out and I haven't seen anything strange yet, so try and relax. Shall I stay?"

"No, don't do that. He's probably waiting for you. Thanks, though, Em; I don't know what I'd do without you, to be honest."

"You don't have to thank me, that's what besties are for. Besides, I would kick that Michael Myers wannabe's arse. Mostly, for what he's put you through."

"You know what I noticed about all these horror movies?" Amber asked, looking up from her pumpkin. Emma shrugged. "The female characters usually get these long- drawn-out deaths, and the men just get stabbed or something."

"Well, then you obviously haven't seen '*Final Destination*' or '*Jeepers Creepers*' – believe me, the boys get it *just* as bad," Emma said, strolling towards the door. "I'll be right back..." she grinned, with a knowing wink.

Lieutenant Saxon turned the heater down and looked outside. It had been fifteen minutes and Weaver wasn't back. He grabbed the radio to call it in when there was a knock at his window.

He turned just in time to see a hand punch the glass--twice. Saxon went to grab his stun-gun as the glass shattered around him. His scream turned into a gurgle as a kitchen knife came through the window and stabbed the front of his neck and, plunging through him, punctured the head rest. As the killer pulled it out, it tore flesh with it. Blood fountained out over the inside of the windscreen, painting it black in the darkness.

Emma sashayed around from the front of the house to the driveway, watching her dress bounce as she went. She couldn't wait to see Drew's face. *It was actually sort of fun being girly*, she admitted to herself. She searched inside her handbag and pulled out her phone. Hit the picture of Drew, smiling with a slice of pizza, and called him. As the phone rang, she turned to look back the way she'd just come. It was very dark, except for the houselights and Halloween decorations. Her eyes searched the surrounding houses and went back to her phone.

She headed to her car, searching for her car keys. "What the hell...?" Her car keys weren't in her bag. She tried the door to her VW Bug and found it was locked. She tutted and ran back the way she'd come--up the porch, past the Jack-o'-lantern and through the front door. She'd left it unlocked. She kicked some dry leaves off the mat and walked inside. Suddenly, the door pulled shut behind her. She spun around, and to her amazement, she heard the sound of the door being bolted from the other side. Her adrenaline started pumping and she felt slightly weak at the knees. "Hello? Drew, I'll kill you if this is a prank!" she shouted hesitantly, then she tried opening the door – it wouldn't budge. "Shit!" She quickly peered through the peephole to see a large figure moving just out of eyesight. "Fuck!" Emma muttered to herself, beginning to panic. *He's here*, she thought with mounting fear. She turned and went for her phone. She tried Amber's number but it went straight to voicemail. *The bastard must be using a scrambler*, she thought. The house lights went off suddenly, leaving her in darkness. A surge of panic started her heart racing. She moved slowly towards the Jack-o'-lantern that was grinning at her with its ghastly smile and flickering orange candle-light that lit the room. She picked up the landline to hear the dreaded - *nothing*, indicating that the line was dead. Quickly, Emma grabbed the gun from her bag, dropped everything else but the mobile-phone and moved slowly through the house with her phone light on torch. There were two options, shoot the bastard or hide. At the moment, her wavering courage was telling her to hide, but if she could just catch whoever it was... Then she'd be able to reunite her best friend with her brother and clear his name at the same time. Emma entered the kitchen, back to the wall, listening to her own desperate breathing. Her eyes were slowly adjusting to the dark. Outside, someone had placed a jack-o'-lantern in front of the patio doors. Someone obviously didn't want her to head that way. She looked around, and ran for the patio doors. They were locked. She grabbed the keys from her belt, looked back up, inserted the key and saw a figure appear from nowhere, outside. Emma gasped and stumbled backwards in terror. The figure was over six feet tall, broad, and wearing a Myers mask, boiler suit, and black boots. The figure punched through the glass, his large, bloodied, hand going for the keys.

"Stop right there, you freak!" Emma said, aiming the gun at him. "You're not Michael Myers and you're not the boogey-man. So one of these is going to put you down permanently!" He turned his head slowly, tilting it, as if he was examining a new species. He ignored her and carried on turning the key. "I said stop! Stop or I'll shoot you, you crazy bastard!" Emma prepared herself as she'd been taught by her father and shot the figure in the shoulder. He flew backwards, away from the door, glass exploding over the kitchen floor – but he stayed standing. She shot again; this time hitting him point blank in the chest. He stumbled backwards as the gunshot echoed throughout the kitchen. Again, he came back for the door. Emma gasped, turned on heel, and ran for the front door. She flew through the darkness, fear taking nearly full grip of her.

Aiming at the lock, she shot the front-door handle twice. The handle fell slightly. She threw her body against it, but the bolt still held. "Shit...Help me! Somebody help me!" Emma screamed, her sense of strength was quickly evaporating. Behind her, she felt a presence. She turned and saw the figure standing just a few feet behind her; huge and menacing. Emma ran up the stairs, her heart pounding. She was nearly at the top in seconds. Suddenly, a hand flew through the bannisters and grabbed her right ankle. She fell forward, bashing her knees, bruising her chest, and dropping the gun. It skidded forward on the highly lacquered floorboards of the landing. "Oh God, oh God, oh God..." She kicked manically, but his grip was relentless. She looked behind her to see his right arm raise a huge kitchen knife. She moaned in terror and frustration as she reached for the gun, her fingers touched the edge of the barrel. Emma's scream echoed through the house as the knife ripped through her calf. Her eyes watered with pain. "Ugh!" At once, her ankle was free. She started to crawl up the remaining stairs, frantically, as behind her she heard the heavy thud of footsteps. Grabbing the gun, Emma turned onto her back and continued using her elbows and one foot to push herself backwards. She looked down at her ankle to see blood pouring out of the huge gash of ripped flesh. He emerged at the top of the stairs and she couldn't help but gasp with fear at his presence. She aimed the gun at his chest with trembling hands and then thought better of it, aiming for his left leg instead. She shot and hit it. Blood exploded from his calf, and he went down on one knee. As relief flooded her, she continued to crawl backwards. *He was human*. She aimed for his head next, pretty sure she could nail the shot despite everything. She pulled the trigger again. To her horror, she was empty. She whimpered and turned onto her front, gasping, as she crawled forward; her leg throbbing as she lost blood. Swiftly, she felt two hands slide around her neck. Her hands flew to his, as she tried to relinquish his grasp. Then, she was gasping for breath. Her eyes bugged. She ripped at his hands with her nails. The figure pulled out the kitchen knife, and to her dismay, she saw a flash of sharp metal. Then her throat was open.

Ritchie pulled his van up outside the Morgans' house. Faye was drinking her third beer, feeling carefree, and clowning around. Ritchie killed the engine and leaned in to kiss her. She pushed him away after a few minutes. "I need to call Emma to make sure we're okay to go in."

"Why doesn't she just tell the little brat to get to bed?"

"Obviously, *you've* never been in charge of a child," Faye laughed, throwing her head back. "Anyway, shut the hell up," Faye said. "You don't speak to children like that. Did your dad ever speak to you like that?" Her phone was to her ear, waiting for Emma to answer.

"My father abandoned me when I was five...I told you not to speak to me like that," Ritchie said, hitting her arm with the back of his hand. Faye pushed it away in annoyance.

"No wonder you have no manners. Hey, Em, this is Faye – where the hell are you?" Faye rolled her eyes and looked at the pitch-black house. The only light was coming from a jack-o'-lantern posed on the porch. "It's bloody freezing, can't you turn the heater back on?" She turned to Ritchie when he didn't answer. "Well?"

"Don't give me attitude and then expect a damn favour," Ritchie grumbled, turning his head away. Faye smiled, and gently took his hand. She lifted it to her mouth.

"Don't be like that, baby," she said, sucking on his finger. "You know you wanna be nice to me, really," Faye said seductively.

"You are bat-shit crazy, do you know that?"

"I'm gonna go inside and find Emma," Faye said, slurring. She glugged from her beer and placed it on the dashboard. Ritchie's eyes filled with irritation.

"What're you doing? It's leather, ya crazy bitch," he yelled, and hit her arm again. This time she furiously slapped his face.

"You Neanderthal!" she screamed at him. He slapped her softly across the face and placed his finger in the dent of her cheek. He pushed forward.

"Call me that again and I'll slap that pretty little face of yours, and then you'll really feel it," Ritchie said and grinned. "Besides, I think you like the rough stuff. I think that's what you like about me."

"I don't like fuck-all about you," she said, climbing down from the van in her Alice in Wonderland costume. "Stupid shit," she went on screaming, slamming the door. Ritchie rolled the window down and shouted after her.

"Don't call me that! And Emma said don't ring the bell. You're an inconsiderate bitch, you know that?!"

"I'm not inconsiderate," Faye explained, walking up the porch. "I just don't give a shit!" She went to ring the bell, but noticed the front door was ajar. She pushed it gently, and it creaked open to reveal the hallway, dark but for a few candles. She walked inside. "It's totally dark," she said to herself. "Emma?" She walked further inside and turned her phone back on. She dialled Emma's number, and this time it went straight to voicemail. She noticed down the other end of the hall, the back door was open, and so headed down to shut it. As she went, she looked down at her phone to text Emma. The shape appeared in the doorway watching her walk towards him while looking at her phone. He moved to the side, beside the shrubs, and inspected her. Faye pulled the door closed and locked it. Then she turned her back to the door and, still looking at her phone, dialled Amber. The call went through easily this time. He liked to play with his prey.

Amber, was sat watching, 'The Thing' as the kids got ready for bed. She slid the phone out of the side pocket in her purse. "Hey, Faye, what's up?"

"Nothing. I'm across the road – no sign of Emma or Wade. Should I be worried?" she asked. She was making her way back towards the front door. The figure was still watching her from behind. His breath was heavy in the mask. His hand still held the large kitchen knife, though it was now dark with blood. He clenched and un-clenched his fist in anticipation.

"Emma went to pick up Drew, and I've got Wade for the night," Amber said.

"For the whole night?" Faye asked. She straightened her blue and white 'Alice' dress, pulling the fabric out, and smoothing it down. "Are you coming over when they're asleep? We can have a drink and a catch up. Girls have been tweeting about seeing Mr. Myers all night long," Faye giggled.

"People will see him everywhere tonight, I guess. I'd rather that, though, then them not see him until it's too late. Will you let me know when Emma gets back, though? Then I might come over."

"Sure, you've spoken to her though, right?" Faye asked, taking her compact out and checking her make-up. She grabbed the brush from her small hand-bag, and brushed the pale blonde wig with the Alice band. She tidied her fringe and closed the compact.

"She promised she'd let me know when she got back."

"Yeah, but she might have gone off someplace with Drew."

"I guess...but she rarely breaks a promise. How's Ritchie been tonight?"

"A dick. But I can handle him." Suddenly, two arms wrapped around Faye's waist and lifted her from the ground, spinning her around. Faye screamed, digging her nails into the bare skin of the strong arms around her. The arms relinquished their grip, and Faye fell to her feet, spinning around and raising her phone as a weapon. Ritchie burst into laughter, backing into the darkness and falling onto the sofa. "You bastard!" Faye yelled. "You scared the life out of me..."

"Faye! Faye, are you okay?" Amber yelled over the phone after hearing her scream. Faye came back on the line.

"Sorry Amber, this idiot just scared the life out of me..."

"Did he hurt you?"

"No, just my pride," Faye said, turning a lamp on. "Okay, well I'll call you when Emma gets back then," Faye said, smiling. "Try and have some fun," she advised on deaf ears. She hung up and slammed the front door. "We have the house to ourselves, and Amber has got Wade for the night!" Faye smiled, excitedly, turning to Ritchie.

"Awesome," he grinned. She turned on the CD system with the remote control she'd spotted. Michael Jackson's *'Thriller'* started.

"Let's get this party started..." Faye said, opening Ritchie's legs and crawling on top of him. He gave her a dry hump as they started to kiss.

Ariel and Wade were upstairs, their feet thumping along the floor as they ran around playing hide- and-seek. It was Wade's turn to count to ten as Ariel hid. She ran into her parents' bedroom and hid behind the curtains, her feet squeaking on the floorboards. The moon was full and she could see fairly well, so she turned to look at the street, outside. It was deserted now, a huge difference from what it had been a few hours ago when she had gone trick-or-treating with a group of friends. "Coming to get you – ready or not!" Wade shouted. Ariel stood stock-still. She was about to turn around, when something across the street caught her eye. A man, very tall with a bright, emotionless white face was carrying a girl. The girl he was carrying looked like she was covered in blood. *Why would he be dressed up so late*? The man carrying the girl suddenly stopped and looked right up at her. Ariel who had been backing away, now screamed with all her might as pure terror filled her. Wade, who was in the hallway, started screaming, too.

Amber raced up the stairs. "What on Earth is going on?" Ariel sat on the floor, at the end of the bed, hugging her knees. Wade stood by the bed, a look of utter shock on his face. "Wade? What's wrong with Ariel?" she asked, slowly entering the dark room. She turned on the light and Ariel buried her head in her hands.

"She just started screaming, I don't know why." Amber ran to Ariel. She had never seen such fear, and in seeing it, the fear blossomed in her, too; ugly and fierce.

"Ariel," Amber said soothingly pulling the girl up. "Ariel, what's wrong?" Ariel wrapped her arms tightly around her babysitter's waist and Amber tried to hold her trembling body still. It was then she noticed the girl had peed herself. Amber's heart rate increased. "Wade, honey, get the iPad and put on your favourite Disney movie. Can you do that for me?" Wade nodded and wiped the tears from his face with angry fists. "Ariel, come with me. I'm taking her to the bathroom, Wade. You climb on the bed and watch your movie, okay?" She couldn't disguise the uneasiness in her voice.

"Uh-huh," Wade replied, nodding. His eyes watched Amber and Ariel with great interest.

"Wade, I want you to put the movie on and watch it. Okay? Lay down and watch it," Amber insisted with a snap of her fingers. Wade did as he was told. Amber took the weeping Ariel across the landing to the bathroom. "Right, honey, I'm going to get you cleaned up." Ariel didn't want to relinquish her grip, but Amber forced her to. Then, Amber cleaned the crying child with baby wipes and changed her into a clean nightgown.

"Did Wade see?" Ariel asked, pulling at her teary eyes.

"No honey, he was watching the iPad, he didn't see anything. But I need you to tell me what *you* saw…"

"A man outside…. he had a white face and he was carrying a girl, but she, she…" Ariel stuttered. "She was all bloody and dead." Ariel burst into tears and Amber pulled the girl, who looked a ghastly shade of pale, closer.

"Ariel, listen…," Amber insisted. Ariel turned her watery eyes up to meet her watchers. "I know for a fact, that tonight lots of the boys in my school were going to play tricks on people; and I think what you saw was a trick. A very *cruel* trick, but it wasn't real. Do you understand?"

"But it was just across the street! It was the boogeyman!" Ariel cried, pointing her finger at the wall, indicating across the street.

"Ariel, repeat after me. *It was just a trick.*"

"It was just a trick," she repeated, her words sounding defiant and unbelieving. Ariel placed her hair in her mouth, once again.

"Now, I want you to go and watch the movie with Wade on the bed, okay?" Ariel nodded. As Ariel plodded over to the bedroom, Amber went for her mobile phone. She hurried down the stairs. She needed convincing now.

Ritchie and Faye had just finished making love in the master bedroom. Ritchie was smoking as Faye fixed her hair. "Do you have to smoke? It fucking stinks, and besides the Morgans will smell it."

"Screw the Morgans," he sneered.

"We could get Emma in trouble... you're such an ignoramus," Faye said, and added a tut, as she pulled her bra on.

"I suppose you're brain of the century?" Ritchie retorted sarcastically. He took in a drag and held in the smoke before letting it out in little, round, donut shapes, that drifted up towards the ceiling and dissipated.

"Actually, I have a very high IQ - 135. I bet you're an idiot," she teased, her hand on his chest. "How about we go and watch some scary movies?"

"I don't like horror movies," Ritchie said nonchalantly. Faye looked at him in utter dismay.

"Well, that's a stupid thing to say. You can't just wipe out an *entire genre*. That's like me saying I don't like rom-com's; I might not like *most* of them, but there's always an exception to the rule, like '*The Wedding Singer*' or '*Mean Girls*,' Faye stated. "You must like *some* horror movies. Come on, what movie scared you the most?"

"I dunno."

"Come on, it's Halloween," Faye pouted. Ritchie rolled his eyes and took a long drag from his cigarette.

"Fine, 'The Silence of the lambs.' Hannibal the cannibal freaks me out," he admitted. Faye sat up with a grin on her lips.

"I knew there'd be something..." she whispered. "Oh my God, I just had a great idea – let's give Amber a prank Ghostface phone call. I have the APP on my phone. It's amazing – you literally sound like the guy in the '*Scream*' movies." Ritchie was already grinning. He'd wanted to get his own back on Amber since she'd kneed him in the balls and left him frustrated by the side of the road.

"Let's do it!" Ritchie smiled for the first time all evening. "You'll have to give me some horror questions to ask though, you watch that shit over and over." Faye was already pulling her Alice costume back on.

"We'll have to use 140, otherwise my face will come up."

"Fine," Ritchie said, pulling on his white shirt and boxers and following the giggling Faye downstairs. Ritchie looked through the blinds at Amber, in the house across the street. He had a dark grin on his face as the phone rang. Faye watched, her hand over her mouth to stifle her giggles.

Amber sighed, stopped heading for the door, and went back to grab the phone before it woke the children. "Hello, Bethany residence?" she said.

"Who is this?" Ritchie asked, his voice hidden behind the Ghostface APP.

"This is the babysitter; can I take a message?"

"Perhaps… what're you doing Miss babysitter?" Amber recognized the voice scrambler and fear sparked inside her, even though, even though she thought it could be a prank.

"Who is this?" She asked, frustrated.

"Who would you like it to be?"

"Let's see, how about Charlie Cox?" Amber played along, smiling. She walked over to the patio and flicked on the light. Outside, mist trailed over the finely-cut grass, and drifted in-between the trees. "I doubt that's who's calling though, so see ya!" she said and hung up. She sat back down on the sofa and pulled her legs in, underneath her. The phone rang again and Amber grabbed the portable, sighing.

"Hi Miss babysitter, you forgot to take my message for the Bethanys."

"I'd be happy to take a message, if you'd leave me your name?" Amber insisted, her patience at breaking point. She turned the lamp off, stood up, and headed towards the front window.

"Charlie Cox."

"Cute. What's the message Charlie?" Amber said, still playing.

"What's on TV?"

"Ugh… that's a *question*. Look, do you have a message to leave or not?" Amber peeked through the blinds and across the street to the Morgan's house. She squinted; a figure was watching her from the house.

"You're the message you frigid bitch!" the voice screamed into the phone. Amber turned her head away to stop the shrieking voice from hurting her ear.

"Nice try arsehole! From the sound of things, this is Ritchie Taylor. I know Faye has the Ghostface APP on her phone, Ritch. And, by the way, I didn't want to sleep with you because you're a druggie, with a dick smaller than his IQ!" She slammed the phone down, stressed out and upset. She wondered if the police were monitoring her calls, because she did *not* want them to hear that.

"She's such a bitch," Ritchie said angrily. "Plus, she chews like a camel!" He threw Faye's phone back at her, and she grabbed it. Amber may be a sudden bookworm with family issues, but she was good with her comebacks. Ritchie looked angry. Even Faye felt slightly afraid of him. She hugged her knees into herself.

"Well... that didn't go as planned. I wonder where Emma is?"

"I'm getting a beer; do you want one?"

"Yeah, sure. I'm going to go grab my stuff from the bedroom," Faye said, as Ritchie headed out of the room. She wanted to get out of here ASAP. Emma and Drew had gone AWOL, and she didn't think Amber would be too happy to see her now.

Ritchie walked down the hall as he heard Faye thundering up the stairs. *That bitch, Amber, had humiliated him in front of Faye.* He was so angry; he could feel heat creeping across his chest. He opened the fridge and grabbed a beer. Standing in the light of the fridge, he glugged as much as he could back. It was frothy and cold. Behind him, he heard a door crash open. He slammed the fridge door, and went into the hall to look. The back door was open; it slammed back - again and again -- against the frame. He walked towards it. Finishing his beer, he threw it in amongst the garden evergreens. He grabbed the door and pulled it shut. "Emma, is that you playing games? Because I'm not in the fucking mood!" he snarled, locking the door. He turned and saw the hallway cupboard. A smile spread across his lips in the darkness. "Predictable!" he said pulling open the cupboard door. It was dark inside. The stereo all of a sudden started back up in the living room. Some creepy, old song.

"Children have you ever seen the boogeyman before...?"

"What the...?" Suddenly, in the corner of his eye he saw a pale white face emerging from inside the cupboard. His eyes bugged. Michael Myers lunged out, grabbing the shocked Ritchie around the neck, lifting him off the floor with incredible strength. Ritchie dropped the beer, his hands desperately tried to peel Myers' fingers from around his throat as he gasped to breathe in air. "Please..." He saw the knife as it glinted in the moonlight. His feet stretched, trying to find the ground. Suddenly, the knife plunged deep into his heart, pinning him to the wall. The beer exploded, alcohol fizzing and bubbling all over the laminate boards. Myers turned his head slowly to the left, and then slowly to the right, examining his kill. The muscles in Ritchie's feet finally dropped.

Faye grabbed her handbag and started stuffing anything that belonged to her inside. She heard the music start with a beat downstairs. It was some creepy, old tune. "Ritchie, what the hell is that shit?" she attempted to shout over the music, even though she knew her calls would be useless at the level it was playing. Grabbing up her leather jacket, she slid into it and sat on the edge of the bed. She fished her mobile phone out of her bag and dialled Emma. It went almost immediately to voicemail. *Where the hell was she?* A worried thought process slid into her head-- that Emma was dead, that Ritchie was dead, and that she was next. Fear tiptoed up her spine. She scrolled through her numbers looking for Drew's, when her phone rang. It was Amber. "Hello?" Faye said anxiously. "Have you heard from Emma?" both girls asked simultaneously.

"Faye, you can tell me this honestly. I just wanna know. Did you and Ritchie just play a prank on the kids?"

"...No, why?" Faye asked tentatively, looking back at the empty doorway.

"Look, something just scared the shit out of Ariel. She said she saw some Myers-style guy carrying a dead girl."

"What!? No, that was NOT us, I swear to you."

"But the phone call was?"

Faye took a deep breath and sighed. "Well, it was Ritchie...but yes!" Faye admitted. "Amber, I'm scared — do you seriously think that guy is back after all these years?" Faye was anxiously running her hands through her hair.

"I don't know. Listen. I'm just worried. I can't get hold of Emma, and she promised she would call me."

"Sorry about the phone call. I'm coming over right now, okay?" Faye asked apprehensively.

"Hold on, I've got another call. It's the hospital, I'll call them back, though. Yeah, let's stick together," Amber agreed. "Get over here and I'll call that detective." Faye hung up and then, as she turned to leave the bedroom, she cried with fright at the figure stood in the doorway. A tall figure dressed in a white bed sheet – two holes cut out for eyes. It stood there unmoving. Faye's hand went to her mouth to stall a scream as her eyes glazed over.

"...Ritchie? Ritchie, if this is a practical joke, very well done! You've scared the shit out of me, now stop!" The figure was unwavering. Faye looked around in the lamplight for a weapon. The best she could see was a nail file next to the jack-o'-lantern. She snatched it up and stuffed her phone in her jacket pocket. Downstairs, the spooky, old song started on repeat. "Uhmm... I'm going over to Amber's, I just called her and apologised..." Faye mumbled. Suddenly, the land line rang. She looked at the figure watching her and then turned slightly to answer the phone.

"Hello?" she whispered.

"Faye! It's about time! Where's Emma? I haven't seen her all night!" Drew said. Faye turned to face the person, knowingly. Suddenly, the figure hidden in the sheet lunged towards her, arms up. She screamed as she glimpsed a kitchen knife and dropped the phone. She rolled over the bed, landing on the other side and picked up a vase which she threw at her stalker's head. He stumbled in the sheet, as she ran for the door. She sprinted down the stairs, and turned to see the ghost had failed to follow her. She looked around as the music boomed on repeat.

"Ritchie!?" Faye screamed. She ran for the front door to find it bolted. "God damn it!" She cried, banging the palms of her hands against the wood. She reached the iPod speakers and turned the music off. "Ritchie...?" her voice was barely a whisper, shrunken in terror. The hallway ahead of her was dark. A floorboard creaked and Faye searched the dark house with wide eyes. "Ritchie!?" Faye screamed in panic, as she hurried towards the back door and freedom. She looked behind her at the sound of the stairs creaking. Suddenly, Ritchie's body filled the doorway; from above, his arms hanging down limply, covered in blood. His mouth and eyes were wide open. Faye screamed and backed up further into the darkness. That was when she saw the man in the Myers costume stood at the other end of the house. She grabbed the pink rape alarm attached to her costume and pulled the wire. It started a blaring whirling sound. She screamed again, louder, and ran for the back door. She flew through it at a racer's speed. Myers walked slowly after her. He smashed the rape alarm under foot. She ran around the side of the house, kicking off her heels as she went. "Help me! Someone!" she screamed. In the garden, she saw Emma hanging from the washing line by her neck; she'd been torn completely open with a knife. Faye screamed again, her hands coming up to her face –which was widening in horror. She ran, pushing past the body. She made it to the street and looked across to the Bethany's. "Amber!" Faye screamed as she ran. She grabbed her phone from inside her pocket and dialled Amber. She'd made it to the front gate when Amber answered her phone.

"Amber. Someone's trying to kill me! Please, let me in - I'm by the front door," Faye cried, desperately running down the path. Ritchie had forgotten to turn off the APP. Her voice was scrambled.

"Yeah, sure– don't tell me this is Ghost-face, right?" Amber said, standing and walking towards the door. On the TV played the end of 'The Thing.' The monster twirled and distorted on the screen, changing from the many faces of MaCready's friends.

"Amber, I beg you!" Faye screamed. There was something in the voice though, through the APP. Reality. *Faye wasn't that good an actress was she? Especially just for a Halloween prank.*

"If you think I'm falling for it twice," Amber said, walking towards the front door slowly. She hesitated in fear.

Faye looked down at the phone and managed to press the button which turned the voice changer off. Then, she turned to see the Myers copycat by the gate. "On my mother's life! Please let me in! He's gonna kill me…" Faye cried. She was now banging on the door with such force, Amber ran to it. *Fuck it, I'd rather be a good friend and fall for a prank*, she thought. She pulled the door open in time to see Myers slash Faye's throat; blood cascaded all over Amber's horrified face, and sweater. To her, it seemed to happen in slow motion; the plastic white face and dead eyes of the Michael Myers mask. Faye's face, as it distorted from fear to pain, as blood burst forth like a waterfall from her throat – because the knife cut deep.

The Myers copycat threw Faye's dead body aside as Amber slammed and locked the door in desperation. Amber felt revulsion at being covered in her friend's blood, but somewhere, relief washed over her that her brother hadn't made it all up; all these years he'd been telling the truth. *Where was Emma, though? Was she also dead?* She backed away from the door, then turned and grabbed the phone. The line was dead. *Shit, where were the police?* She ran towards the sofa to grab her mobile when the lights went out. She looked up at the dead lights, whimpering, and threw the phone down. By the light of the candles, she ran up the stairs. She pulled her blood-soaked sweater off and ran for the bedroom where the children were, as she heard glass breaking downstairs. Both children were sitting on the bed, hugging each other. When they saw her, they ran to her. She slid open the walk-in wardrobe as Ariel began to cry. "Get inside and lock the door. Ariel, I need you to be a really strong girl and be quiet. Wade, make sure you're both super quiet, okay, honey?" She whispered. She took both children into the walk-in cupboard, and handed Wade a lit candle. "Stay inside until I tell you to come out."

"What're you gonna do?" Wade asked.

"Kill him," Amber replied.

Amber closed the doors, and Wade pushed the two bolts on the inside into their slots. Amber's mind was in a whirl; then downstairs she heard the theme to *'Psycho'* playing - she had a plan. Surely, no horror fanatic could resist, she thought. She ran to the main bathroom and turned the shower on. She locked the door. Then she started searching through the Bethanys' personal belongings by the light of more candles that Mrs. Bethany had placed around. She found what she wanted, and then started pulling her jeans off; they were stuck to her with blood. She threw them in a heap, and, facing the door, gently stepped into the warm shower. She pulled the iridescent white shower curtain across. Amber waited with baited breath, as the water washed away Faye's blood from her body, and soaked her black lace underwear. "Come on, come on, you bastard," Amber whispered behind the sound of water pummelling her flesh. The door handle started to rattle and Amber backed up, her long hair plastered to her back. There was a punching sound, then splitting wood. Amber hardly dared to breathe. Then, she saw a figure enter the bathroom on the other side of the curtain; the large body blocking out the light for just a few seconds. This was for her family; for her brother. A figure approached. Suddenly, the shower curtain was torn back by a bloodied man's hand. Amber screamed. The knife rose. Amber aimed and slashed with all her might. The Myers copycat dropped his knife and it clattered into the shower by Amber's feet. He ripped the curtain from the pole and fell to the floor, grasping for his throat. Amber held the shaving razor steady, by the handle, as she watched the blood pump from the killer's slashed throat. Red blood filled the shower curtain he was laying in, his hands were clutching his neck, attempting to keep the blood from leaving his body.

Amber picked the kitchen knife up, from inside the shower, and stepped towards him, trembling; though it wasn't from the cold. Her one hand held the knife to his chest as her other hand hesitated by his mask. "Now, let's see who you are." She took a deep breath and grabbed hold of the Michael Myers mask. She pulled it off the stalker's face as his body started to still. She dropped the knife and gasped as both hands flew to her mouth.

"Tommy!?" She staggered backwards as her brother stared up at her, gurgling blood. "Tommy!?" She knelt down beside him as the life pumped out of him. "No, no, no…" Amber cried, grabbing a towel and putting pressure on his neck. "It can't be true, … *why*? Why would you do this to me?" He looked at her with eyes dark and deadly, but they soon rolled back in his head and he lay still. He looked so angelic, so handsome, Amber thought. *Looks certainly do deceive.* Amber put the back of her wrist to her crying mouth. "Murderer…. Murderer!" she screamed and punched his chest. She felt the Kevlar under his boiler suit, as she cried. She left him wrapped in the shower curtain and pulled herself to her feet. Slowly, she stumbled to the landing. She was dripping with watery blood, as she heard the Bethanys come into the house downstairs. "Stay strong," Amber told herself.

The End

A Story of Amber

By

Mark Cassell

When Chuck found Grandpa's important papers, I'd told him not to read them. And when he used them to make a Halloween mask, he'd said he'd hang me up with the scarecrow if I ever told Ma. I knew he shouldn't have even been in Grandpa's room, let alone searching through his stuff. As the younger brother, I never told anyone.

I didn't ever want to get him into trouble. Pa was strict, but Ma was even more so.

Chuck's papier-mâché effort was much better than mine: after several failed attempts, I ended up settling for a not-so-scary plastic wolf mask, bought from Walmart in the next town. Whereas Chuck had made a head-mask rather than just a face-mask. It was amazing. Everyone said so, and maybe even Grandpa smiled. It covered his whole head and looked like a real pumpkin. But I couldn't help thinking how Chuck had slathered the glue over Grandpa's handwriting.

It was fast approaching Halloween, and one afternoon my older brother sat in the pumpkin patch wearing his head-mask. I first thought he was looking for ideas on how to paint it. You know, to get the correct shade of colour and texture, but it looked finished already.

I had no idea what he was doing.

Even though Halloween was still days away, he often wore it.

Finally, the night before Halloween, I followed him out to the pumpkin patch and heard voices. He spoke with someone whose deep voice sounded a lot like Grandpa's. Thing was, Grandpa hadn't left his part of the farmhouse since Grandma died the year before. While we were out in the fields, beneath that chill moon, I knew Grandpa remained sitting beside the open fire, smoking his pipe.

I squinted into the evening, surrounded by that subtle smell of pumpkin, wondering why my brother spoke to himself. I hoped he was okay. As the sky darkened and the clouds removed the moonlight, I saw something... a shimmering light through the fog and above tall grass. It was like the shadows swayed with the grassy tufts.

It wasn't a something – it was some*one*.

Grandma.

The cold night air snatched my breath.

Although it was much darker than moments before, I saw that flowery dress of hers, the one she often wore. The one she'd been wearing when she died. Right then, however, she didn't look dead. Her apparition hovered above the ground.

I wanted to run to her. But the mud sucked at my feet, holding me still. My legs would not listen to me; all I wanted was to hug her.

She leaned towards Chuck and grasped his pumpkin head. No more than a second or two later, my brother collapsed and Grandma vanished. Faint traces of fog and light drifted away into the surrounding shadows, while the papier-mâché pumpkin rolled away. The moon returned, bathing the scene in silver.

A strange silence washed over me.

Eventually, I yanked my sneakers free from the mud that hadn't really stopped me from moving. I ran over to the pumpkin head, ignoring Chuck, who had his hands over his eyes and whose groans made faint breath clouds. I snatched up the mask, not even caring to check he was okay, and pulled the pumpkin head over my own smaller head. It didn't really fit snugly, so I had to hold it steady.

The stink of Grandpa's tobacco filled my head, fresh and potent.

I gagged and quickly yanked it off.

Chuck was getting to his feet. He rubbed his forehead.

"Dillon?" His voice was small. "We have to go back home."

I threw the pumpkin head on the ground, glaring at it. The tobacco smell still filled my nostrils.

"Come on!" Chuck grabbed my hand in clammy fingers.

We walked side by side across the field. The cold air bit through my sweater, and I felt as though the pumpkin head watched us. As far as I know, Chuck never retrieved it from among the rows of real pumpkins and I often wonder if Pa ever found it when he came to harvest.

Something glinted in Chuck's hand. It looked like gold or a very shiny rock.

"What's that?" I demanded, reaching for his arm.

He flinched and pulled away. We came to a stop. Whatever it was, was now hidden in his fist.

"Show me!" I went to grab it again, but he twisted away further. "Chuck, show me!"

His eyes were tiny, reflecting the cold moonlight.

"Get…" He shoved me backwards. "…OFF!"

I stumbled and fell on my butt. Mud splashed around me and water soaked into my pants.

Older brothers are supposed to be mean at times, and Chuck had his moments. I knew I could be the annoying younger sibling, so I guess we both had our moments. Sometimes, when things got heated, then Ma or Pa would yell at us. I remember once, he wedged me under the bed with cushions and blankets. Pa came bounding up the stairs after hearing my screams. Oh, how he'd yelled at Chuck.

Right now, Chuck looked down at me, but the look on his face wasn't anything I'd ever seen before. His stare cut straight through me. He brought his hand up to his face, and I watched his fingers slowly curl open. Moonlight glinted from the orange gemstone he held. It looked just like one of Grandpa's – one of his favourites, no less – and I guessed he must've stolen it off the shelf as he had the papers. Those colourful gemstones had always mesmerised me, the way they caught the light of Grandpa's room. He'd collected dozens throughout his lifetime, and often told incredible stories of his travels.

I pushed myself up and onto my feet, then charged at my brother, slamming into his stomach. He staggered back, and sprawled in the mud. I pinned him down with my knees and hands, but he didn't fight back. He only looked through me, as he had moments before.

Also, he no longer held the stone.

From nearby in the shadows, tall grass rustled. Something squelched in the clumps of churned earth. I jerked upright, squinting. Dots of glinting amber shone like a dozen eyes from the mud. Even as I looked, more emerged. It was as though they slithered from the ground like stone worms.

Still pinned beneath me, Chuck groaned. I didn't look at him. Instead, I looked further away, over to where we'd walked from. I could just about see the silhouette of the pumpkin head and I remembered Grandpa once told us a story that involved an amber mask. Though I could not recall what he'd said about it.

Chuck feebly pushed me aside and held his hand up to his face. The skin was black and blistered. I slipped away from him and sat back in the mud. He glared at his hand.

The sky darkened further, silence pressing in like a smothering blanket, and—

Hundreds of voices shouted, blasting in my ears.

The pair of us clamped hands over our ears. Chuck groaned again, spit bubbling between clenched teeth. It was in our heads rather than out there in the field. So many voices, crying and whimpering and screaming. Shrill, deafening.

As one, they shut off. Silence descended like the night sky fell, and I slumped.

Chuck leapt sideways and scrambled in the dirt, raking the mud.

"No!" he shouted.

The amber gemstones had vanished.

"Where did they go?" Chuck demanded from a wet face.

"Why are you crying?" I felt tears prick my own eyes.

He stood, mud falling from his fingers. He clutched his burned hand to his chest and stepped in the direction of home, back to the farmhouse, back to Ma and Pa. Back to Grandpa. He didn't look at me.

"Chuck!" I pushed myself up, wiping sticky hands down my pants, and followed him.

We said nothing to each other, mud squelching with every footfall as we trudged across the field. I stepped where he stepped and only once did I glance in the direction of the pumpkin head, but couldn't see it. Walking... and soon the farmhouse came in to sight. The closer we got, I thought I heard those cries again, only this time it was outside. In the last field, just in front of us.

No, it was from the house.

Home.

The sound of Ma's misery swept towards us.

Chuck still walked, but I barged past him, knocking his elbow, and sprinted for the big tree that led to the pathway.

Pa sat immobile in the rocking chair on the front porch beside an open window. The curtains swayed on the breeze as though in time with Ma's whimpers. The lack of a creak from the chair's aged wooden joints reinforced what I knew was about to be said.

"Grandpa's died," Pa murmured.

After that, Chuck was never the same.

I don't think I was ever the same after that, and of course no one ever believed us. Eight years later, Chuck ran away from home.

* * *

The cell bars rattled and Chuck woke up. He pushed fists into the cold floor and stood. His neck clicked as he squinted into the moonlight that shone through the barred window. Metal clunked again and the ground shook. Probably a passing truck. He adjusted his woolly hat as he struggled to remember at which point during the night he'd ended up on the floor – something he was used to. His mouth tasted like shit. Again, something he was used to. When you run away from home, you don't think of packing a toothbrush.

And when you begin stealing wallets from strangers just to eat, you never think you'd get caught. There was something ridiculous about wandering the state for a few years, pickpocketing to survive, only to return to your hometown and finally get caught.

Again, the ground shook.

Voices, yelling… from outside. All around him the vibrations intensified. What the hell? This wasn't a truck. He staggered, his sneakers scuffing the gritty floor. He slapped a hand against the wall and, as though for the first time, noticed how much dirt had collected beneath his fingernails.

Dust drifted from the ceiling near the barred window, where white moonlight poured through. Between the frame and the masonry, a crack appeared. Like lightning, it shot diagonally downwards to spear the floor. A series of crashes and screams rushed at him from beyond the police station. The lights flickered inside his cell, and out in the hallway. The wall cracked again and something overhead creaked.

Chuck's heart pulsed in his head, nearly as loud as the quake. Should this continue, it was going to end one of two ways: freedom or death.

He charged for the door, gripping the bars, his knuckles whitening.

"Hey!" He felt the door give a little. "Get me out of here!"

Behind him, amid the rumbles, something groaned, crunched, and snapped.

Still with fingers curled around the bars, he turned to see the floor heave. Concrete bulged in a mess of sand and rubble.

Something emerged. A mottled brown rock, rising from beneath the cell floor.

Reflecting the flickering lights, shiny like it was made of orange glass, streaked with dirt, it rose from beneath. Slightly curved, its tip lanced the ceiling. Masonry crumbled overhead, and cables snaked down like multi-coloured vines. Chunks of brick and mortar collapsed in a cloud of bitter dust.

He had to get out of there. Now.

"Help me!" he screamed and coughed. Surely a police officer would hear. For a small town as this, it wasn't heavily staffed, but they knew he was here. "Hey!"

The ground jerked upwards, slanted and threw him sideways away from the door. He slammed into a wall. Conduit panels and metal beams crashed around him, more cables snaking, and the shiny rock in the middle of the cell rose higher. He backed into the wall, staring at the thing. It was too colourful just to be rock. Amber… that's what it was: a solid chunk of amber shaped like a fucking dinosaur bone.

The lights surged and then went out. Only the moon now illuminated the cell, pushing its chill October haze in through the cracked glass of the barred window. More rumbles, more dust and debris filling the air…

He guessed this was it for him, death was close.

"Get me out of here!" He coughed from a ragged throat and spat. His eyes itched. Pressed into the corner, he blinked through the churning dust that diluted the moonlight.

Car alarms and crashes, and screams and shouts filled his head.

Again, he shouted, "Help me!"

The rumble subsided.

A strange silence seemed to follow, but was only the earth quietening: people still screamed and yelled. The alarms were still shrill, echoing. Somewhere further away, a coyote howled.

His heartbeat was like a cannon repeatedly firing in his chest and his breath came in rasps. And again, he coughed. Tears streamed down his cheeks. He wiped grit from his eyes and watched the dust settle. He was alive. Then he saw the door: the hinges had been wrenched from the wall and the metal bulk dropped, angling into the hallway.

It was as though it pointed to freedom.

Where were the police officers? Treading awkwardly, he shimmied past the length of amber and dragged a hand over it.

Smooth. And warm.

At the door now, he peered into the hallway and into the gloom. No one around. Lights flickered along the hallway, more of the ceiling angled and busted. It looked about ready to collapse. He rounded a bend and saw the first body. Part of the ceiling had crushed the man's head into a meaty pulp. A crimson pool had spread outwards, glistening to reflect a swinging fluorescent tube that sputtered life.

Chuck reached the main room.

Half the roof dipped inwards with buckled conduits, broken tiles and more tangled wires. Several fluorescent tubes swung lazily. He stepped past another body whose dead hands clutched a beam that pinned that person into the chaos of scattered paper and files. It was the lady officer who'd locked him in the cell.

Her dead eyes stared off past his head.

The crooked main entrance gaped freedom. As he neared it, from outside, the sound of misery poured over him. One of the glass doors had shattered. Glass crunched beneath every footfall as he stepped out into the night.

His breath plumed before him.

Little had changed in his time away, apart from several developing blocks beyond the outskirts. The police station was still one of a few large buildings. Before all this, his hometown always aspired to be something larger.

Now, those aspirations were a long way off.

Smoke billowed on the night, blending with the clouds, to hide a full moon. Fires raged through silhouettes of crumbled structures. And there was more… other things that did not belong here. Curves of glinting amber pierced the blacktop and pointed skyward. Some had torn up gardens and shrubs, uprooting trees. Several cars had overturned, hazard lights flashing. Residents were still fleeing from their homes, huddling in the streets amid shouts and screams and crying. A number of children wore costumes, and most had removed their masks to be comforted by a parent or sibling. Ghosts and ghouls and devils and skeletons of all shapes and sizes, now trod discarded candy into the pavement and sidewalks.

Chuck slowly shook his head, not knowing where to look, and whispered, "Happy Halloween."

* * *

Chuck made his unsteady way down the station steps as the ground rumbled again. Flaming buildings dotted the landscape, and great billows of smoke churned on the cold breeze. Out on the sidewalk, he didn't know which way to turn. Everywhere he looked, people were dressed for trick-or-treating, yet stood in front of burning and collapsing homes and shops. Everyone was aghast, watching as giant amber gemstones erupted around them.

Across the road, in a grinding and shrieking and heaving of jagged blacktop, another gemstone emerged. The streetlamp wobbled, bent and smashed to the ground in a scattering of glass and sparks. A group of little witches and a frantic mother screamed and backed off. They huddled at the roadside near a burning storefront, eyes wide, their whimpers loud on the night.

A cacophony of alarms and screams, of rumbles and explosions, filled the town.

Chuck had never before witnessed anything so catastrophic, outside of a TV screen or movie theatre. His heartbeat punched his ribcage.

Up and down the road, more of the town's residents crouched over fallen friends and family, crying at the roadside and on driveways further from the main street. Several parked cars were now on their sides, resting against great chunks of shining amber. Broken glass littered the street and reflected the moonlight.

Chuck followed the steps down from the station entrance, and out onto the uneven sidewalk. Yesterday there had been paving alongside the building, yet now each slab lay angled and separated. A cleft in the ground followed a jagged line toward another jutting hulk of amber that towered over the police station. His neck clicked looking up at it.

From around the corner, someone shouted, "Help!" The voice was small, female, and desperate.

He knew the station backed onto a parking lot that was shared with the general store and burger joint. Beyond that was farmland owned by his parents. He could be out of here in minutes and no one would know. But he couldn't leave yet, someone needed help. No doubt a lot of people needed help.

She called again.

Chuck ran towards the voice, taking him around the corner of the station and into the parking lot. Both the store and burger joint were infernos. The wall that once separated two parts of the lot had collapsed and as he approached, his skin prickled from the heat.

He squinted into the orange glare.

"Hello?" His voice echoed.

"Here!"

Finally, he found a woman – a mother? – pinned beneath a tree that had toppled with a wall. An amber shard had ripped up the ground. Chunks of brick littered the scene. And bodies, again all in costume: a witch, a devil, a pumpkin. He counted eight, all unmoving. Perhaps there was only one adult among the fallen.

This was like a punch to the gut.

A cloud of smoke scratched at his eyes and he coughed yet again.

The woman waved at him through the haze. Her face was painted like a black cat, now tear-streaked and blotchy. She wore a black outfit, not quite cat-like, and he wondered if her children were among the dead. Reaching her side, he yanked at the branches. Leaves flew and twigs snapped. Her black jacket had snagged, and a branch had trapped her leg. He grabbed it and heaved, his back screaming. She wriggled and something ripped as she freed herself.

Tears and dirt painted her cheeks. "Help me, please."

The stink of burning and melting drifted towards them.

Chuck opened his mouth to say something, but then the ground shook again and a bubble of amber rose up. The pavement cracked, heaved, and threw him sideways.

The woman screamed.

He scrambled up onto his knees and watched as a fiery energy sparked across the amber. Some of it had traced the cracked ground, racing towards her kicking feet.

Appearing like a lasso, the lightning jumped and shot straight for her.

She shrieked as that crazy energy coiled around her foot, burning into her boot and leggings. Beneath the crackling, leather and fabric bubbled and hissed, falling away in smoky wisps. The sparking energy intensified.

Chuck leapt up, his pulse throbbing in his neck. His chest was tight. He had to help her, but—

The sound of bones snapping. Skin and muscles shredding. Her flesh flew through the air and slapped across the amber, and it seemed to meld into it. Traces of what could have been electricity sent fiery sparks across the amber and her body, burning away the remainder of her clothes.

And the woman's skin ripped and churned in a red mess...

Just under the surface of amber, what looked like veins and arteries wriggled as though seeking the wet and glistening blood and mess of the woman that now dripped down it, following its contours. In a blur, both rock and flesh mingled with the arteries. It rushed across the surface.

His eyes darted left and right. He had to run. Now.

A teenager in a devil costume ran towards Chuck, screaming. His eyes shone white and wide from his red face, and a forked tail bounced along behind him. From the nearest lump of amber, a strand of fiery energy shot out. It coiled around his legs. His yell pierced the night, and his arms flailed. In a blur of sparks, it smashed him against the amber in a burst of orange and red. Blood, skin and skeleton splashed over it. Shreds of the red and black costume flapped on the wind.

All the way along the straight stretch of road beyond the parking lot, more hulks of amber erupted through the blacktop, reaching up for the sky. Each sparked with that electricity, jagged white and yellow patterns reaching out for the now-fleeing crowd.

No one was quick enough.

Their agony filled Chuck's head.

Feet tangled in fire, their screams brief as they melded with the amber.

He shrank within himself as more and more shards of amber burst up through the ground around him. More and more of that energy intensifying.

The way those shards curled down the road, it reminded him of vertebrae. It was like a fucking spine.

"What the hell?"

The row of huge vertebrae pulsed with an inner light, as yet another tremor rippled through the ground. The remaining structures toppled. Plumes of dust and debris erupted as the great shards of amber jutted upwards and tore through roofs. Most were covered in the stretched bodies of the inhabitants. As if pushed, each shard broke away from the ruined houses. They glowed, lighting the clumped mess of human remains. The traceries of veins and arteries, bright like autumn leaves backlit by sunshine.

More buildings crashed as the shards rumbled across the quaking ground, as though being dragged by invisible hands. Each one encased in spirals of energy. Screams echoed. A little witch spun through the air, that sparking energy looped about her flailing limbs. Fire spiralled and embraced her in an orange cloud. So many people, not all in costumes, were trapped in similar formations.

Towering higher than the five-storey building, those amber shards were forming a loose skeletal structure, joining the spine. Next, a pelvis. Legs. And behind it... were those wings?

All the while, that fire encased everyone, churning like phantoms, unsure of what form to take. They throbbed and twisted. Some squeezed together... and Chuck saw what was happening: collectively, everyone was transforming into organs. Lungs, heart, kidneys, liver, intestines, all shimmered in ghostly flame.

If he could run, he would've done so.

There was no sign of a skull.

In slurps and crunches, clicks and wet slaps, everything and everyone connected. Organs and bones joined. The sounds, as the amber slotted together, cracked loud in the night. More shards shot from the ground and pulled together, leaving gouges in the blacktop. Trees uprooted and crashed.

In the centre of the ribcage, as the final curve of amber closed up, the organs squelched and slid together, finding their place. The heart pulsed. Muscles fleshed out over the amber skeleton as its torso filled. The legs pulled tighter, inwards. Earth heaved as the claws grew. The arms flexed, long fingers twitched and curled into sparking fists.

Fire spat everywhere.

The stench of burning flesh filled Chuck's lungs, and it was all he could do not to spew.

Still only a mass of shaped muscle and bone, the *thing* pushed upright.

Something rumbled a little way beyond the town, out in the farmland.

He saw a great dome of amber, the largest of them all and the final piece of this monstrous puzzle, as big as a fucking house, erupt from the ground. A horned skull...

"You've got to be kidding," Chuck whispered. His back thumped against the station wall — evidently, he'd been stepping backwards all this time.

The skull burst upwards, shooting mud in every direction. A glistening redness clung to the amber surface and dripped, as white lightning carried it overhead. Dirt and mud and clumps of grass scattered the ground beneath it as it flew towards the skeletal structure.

Chuck squinted, watching it fly overhead, all the while arteries formed around it, rippling across the musculature. In a blinding flash, the thing connected with the spine. Veins wove like rivers across its body, intricate from head to tail. Then skin formed: a patchwork of leathery flesh, dark red with black streaks. Pulling taut, the skin stitched across the body amid licks of fire. Its feet stomped and sparks flew from claws. From its shoulders, sparking membranous wings creaked as they extended. Flames dripped from its flank. The horned head jerked left, and then right. The eyes shimmered a deep, but shiny, black, through so much fire and lightning and roiling smoke. A redness oozed from the sockets, dribbling down and its mouth full of glinting teeth of lightning and razors.

The thing, this demon, blinked. Those eyes, black as the death it promised, burned into Chuck's core. Fire sparked from the sockets. Its lips twitched and curved teeth parted. Smoking saliva dribbled over the gums, and hissed and sparked.

The demon rushed forward, its great feet smashing into the pavement...

In a blur of amber and black and red and lightning energy, it charged for him. Chuck's legs buckled, his knees smacking the ground and agony lanced up his thighs. The closer the demon, the smaller it seemed to be. Shrinking, smaller, smaller... messing with his perception. Nothing made sense... the pain subsided... the fire, the smoke, the shadows closed in... and the demon, now the size of an ordinary man, slammed into him.

He jerked backwards and his head cracked on the wall behind him.

The darkness, the churning of orange and black, of sparking energy, swept through him. *Into* him. Then silence.

* * *

Identifying Chuck's body was one of the hardest, if not most bizarre, experiences of my life. How he was encased in amber, I've no idea. The authorities have no clue either, and the whole town is still quarantined. Not that there's much left, nor any known survivors, apart from Ma and Pa. Needless to say, it came as a tearful relief to learn that my parents survived this bizarre quake and they both now remain indoors. From the little I've been told, the military are using the farmhouse and surrounding barns as a base, due to its perfect location on the town's perimeter.

I'd spent this past month with family over in California. Had I not been over there, I would've most likely been in town somewhere, hanging with my buddies. Probably the burger joint. Thinking of that makes my stomach churn. But I am not hungry. I wonder if I'd get to be fed soon, or indeed when they'd let me go home.

My head aches. So many thoughts crashing through my little brain.

When had Chuck returned home... and how the hell was he trapped in amber? No one else was. And apparently there is no other evidence of amber around the town. Plus, I'd overheard an officer saying no one knew where any of the other bodies are.

Apart from Chuck, his dead scream staring out from his amber coffin.

Too many thoughts...

Amber. Grandpa.

I remembered his story of amber. At least, some of the words of that story:

"Dillon," he'd told me, "special shades of amber allow us to speak with the dead."

"Really?" I asked, as I sat cross-legged on the rug beside his desk. I wondered why anyone would ever want to talk to dead people.

"Yes," he replied, and puffed on his pipe. "And some particular shades can be used to make things."

"Like what?"

"Demons, devils, any creature you want."

I remember how I laughed at him then; Grandpa could be so funny sometimes.

"Animals?" I asked. "Like rabbits and dogs and cats?"

Grandpa laughed with me.

Now, knowing my dead brother is in the next room, I think back to what I'd found on the outskirts of town.

A mile or so from the military blockade that unexpectedly awaited my homecoming, I'd needed a piss and so pulled over at the roadside – having guzzled so much water on the journey, I had been busting for ages and could not hold it any longer. After I zipped up and stepped back towards the car, I saw a gemstone glistening in the mud. About the size of my fist, it resembled one of those from Grandpa's shelf.

I didn't hesitate to lift it up: heavy, smooth, and surprisingly warm given the time of year. It was streaked with incredible black whorls like diesel had fused with the amber. I wrapped it in my towel that still smelled of chlorine and wedged it at the bottom of my travel bag.

As I gunned the engine to return to a hometown that existed beneath so much rubble, I recalled Grandpa's words all those years ago, those he'd uttered when he stopped laughing:

"The amber can do many wondrous things."

The End

Trick Turned Treat

By

Briana Robertson

Beauty is in the eye of the beholder.

Chicory glared at her reflection, seeing beauty, but acknowledging only flaws. Were she any other woman, she might be satisfied—even pleased. But the fact was, she wasn't any other woman. Not even close.

Turning to one side, then the other, she studied herself, noting every imperfection. Miniscule wrinkles marred the corners of her eyes and lips. Signs of thickening in her skin showed in her biceps and around her hips. Her breasts were drooping, and she counted three grey hairs peeking out of her ebony locks.

It's not time for this. It's too soon. The thought only aggravated her frustration. She should have had another year—*at least*—before she had to worry about this. But reality stared her back in the face. There was no help for it--something had to be done. Soon.

"Tomorrow. I'll do something about it tomorrow."

Chicory rushed through her nighttime beauty routine, making sure to avoid the mirror. She didn't need it; she'd been going through these motions long enough, she could do them blindfolded. After finishing, she slipped into a pair of silk pajamas; the shorts rode low on the hip, high on the thigh, and the thin-strapped top bared her midriff. She didn't understand women who slept in flannel nightgowns or ratty t-shirts; even if she wasn't currently taking a man to bed, she believed it necessary to look and feel desirable.

Pouring herself a nightcap of whiskey, she hopped into bed, sat cross-legged, and slid on a pair of black-rimmed reading glasses. The need for them might have bothered her, given her distaste regarding her other physical imperfections, but she actually liked her glasses. They added a bit of character, an odd sense of allure. They'd come in handy a number of times.

And not just for reading.

With a smirk, she grabbed her copy of "The Witch's Daughter," and settled in for the night.

***

The annoying, high-pitched whir of a saw ripped Chicory from an exceedingly pleasant dream; Damian's tongue had been working magic between her legs. Gaia, she missed that man. She missed most of them, in fact. But men were meant to serve a purpose—a purpose that did not include permanency.

The saw's scream jarred her from her memories, dousing them and the last vestiges of sleep. With a huff of irritation, she swung her legs from the bed, stood, and headed for the window. The red glow of her alarm clock caught her eye as she passed. 7:06. *Who the hell is running a fucking buzzsaw at 7am on a bloody Saturday? Gaia, the sun's not even fully up!*

Ripping the curtains aside, she squinted in the dim autumn light and threw the window open, prepared to give a sound tongue-lashing to whatever asshole had disturbed her.

The vulgar epithet died on her lips. Across the street, a young hunk hunched over a sawhorse, a white t-shirt stretched taut over muscular shoulders. Chicory propped a hip on the windowsill and studied him.

He was tall, six feet surely, though she couldn't be one hundred percent positive, given his stooped posture. Mid-thirties, most likely. Sandy hair fell in shaggy waves to just below his chin. A pair of worn Levi's rode low on lean hips, and...

That's quite the fine ass you've got there.

The saw bit through a two-by-four, sending a two-foot section clattering to the porch. The man's movements never faltered; smooth as silk, he adjusted the board and made another cut. Chicory watched for a long while, her interest growing with each passing moment. She had no idea who he was, but she vaguely remembered a moving truck parked across the street about a week ago. Whoever he was, he might be just what she needed--the perfect remedy for her current ... situation.

Yes, indeed. I do think you may do quite nicely.

Finally, the ceaseless buzzing stopped. Her new neighbor rose at the torso, bringing himself to full height, and stretched.

Yup. Definitely six feet. Probably closer to six-three.

And then, as though he sensed her presence, he looked up and over his shoulder. Turning, his gaze reached up, finding her in her window. She didn't shy away from his stare; rather, she held it, inviting it to stay. After a long, tense moment, she lowered one eyelid in a slow wink, then slunk back from the window and let the curtains fall into place.

***

August mopped sweat from his brow and took another, long swig from a plastic bottle of Dasani. Emptying it, he crumpled and tossed it into the blue recycle bin sitting beside the front door. Taking a look around, he huffed out a breath. The lumber was all cut and he ought to start carving and sanding; then again, he didn't imagine he'd be having visitors over for dinner anytime soon.

Unless ...

His gaze traveled up to the open window in the two-story Victorian across the street. There was a chance he might be making dinner for a female companion sooner than he'd anticipated, though an introduction was probably the initial priority.

She's a stunner, that's for sure. He hadn't seen much more than her face. Only a profile of her figure, really. But the way she'd boldly met his stare and given him that slow wink ... She was gorgeous, and more importantly, she knew it. Well, he'd never had trouble getting the ladies' attention, himself. Perhaps he should pay his lovely neighbor a visit.

First things first, dude. A shower, for example.

Grinning to himself, he headed inside and up the stairs. Stripping off his t-shirt, jeans and the snug, black boxers beneath, he twisted the showerhead and let it run hot. Steam mushroomed against the ceiling and fogged up the mirror. Stepping under the water, August hissed at the initial burn, then sighed as the heat beat into the tight muscles of his back and shoulders. Bracing his arms against the tiled wall, he let himself relax.

His neighbor's face bloomed in his mind and once again, she gave him that measured wink. August hardened.

Don't even think about it. You haven't even met the woman yet, for chrissakes.

August grabbed a bar of soap, worked up a lather, and washed the sweat away. The slippery slide of his hands did nothing to diminish his erection; rather, it lengthened. Determined to ignore it, August rinsed the soap away, then grabbed the shampoo. Suds dripped from his hair to his chest, then slid lower. Before he could stop it, an image arose in his mind of his neighbor on her knees in front of him, her lips wrapped around his cock, and his balls tightened.

"Sonofabitch!"

Unable to resist any longer, August gripped his hard shaft and tugged. With a groan, he leaned against the slick tile and let the fantasy in his mind take over. His neighbor continued to suck at him, her fingers curled into the taut muscles of his ass, her bright green eyes staring up at him. In his mind, he fisted his hands in her hair and pumped into her mouth. Faster. Harder. It wasn't long before August found release; cum jetted against his belly and his shout echoed off the walls.

Breathing hard, he hurriedly rinsed himself off and banished the image of the gorgeous woman who lived across the street from his mind. Stepping out of the shower, he toweled off and walked naked into his bedroom. Throwing on a clean pair of boxers, he flopped down on the bed. He'd planned on jogging across the street, knocking on her door, and introducing himself once he'd gotten cleaned up.

Yeah, that's *not happening.*

There was no way she wouldn't be able to figure out what he'd done; he was sure guilt and sheepish embarrassment would mar every feature of his face. He'd give it a couple days. Maybe more.

For now? He'd settle for a nap.

***

Chicory knew it was him the moment he knocked. Her lips curved as she took her time answering the door. Frankly, she was a bit amazed he'd waited three days. Another woman might have been worried he wasn't interested, but she knew better. He would have thought of her over the last few days and more than he'd intended; she'd made sure of it.

Flipping the deadbolt and pulling the door back, Chicory's lips curved into a well-practiced smile that oozed welcome and hinted at seduction.

"I was wondering how long you'd make me wait for an introduction."

Her handsome neighbor flushed; a soft red creeped up his neck and lightly brushed his cheeks, matching the setting sun behind his shoulders. "Yeah, I wanted to come over sooner, but things have been hard ... I mean, I've been busy jerking, I mean working! I've been working. I wanted to come sooner, but, oh shit, that's not what I mean. I mean ... Hell. Hi, I'm August."

The poor guy's face resembled a lobster, freshly steamed. Chicory couldn't help herself; she laughed. He blushed even hotter, so she took pity on him. Laying a hand on his arm, she smiled and answered.

"I'm Chicory. Would you like to come in?"

"Sure. Yeah. That'd be great."

She stepped back and gestured, inviting him in. Heading down the hallway, Chicory led him down to the small breakfast nook off her kitchen. A pumpkin sat half-carved on the table.

"Can I get you something to drink? Water? Iced tea? Something stronger?" She lifted a single eyebrow.

August grinned and sat. "Iced tea would be great, thanks."

"Lemon?"

"Sure. Sounds good."

Chicory nodded and headed into the kitchen. She glanced back at him as she gathered two glasses and filled them with ice. He was studying the room around him, careful to avoid watching her. She grinned and pulled a pitcher from the fridge.

He's off-balance. They always are when they can't get me out of their minds. I love it.

Filling the glasses, she returned the tea to the fridge and pulled out a lemon. Grabbing a paring knife, she deftly sliced the citrus in half, then carved off two thick slices. Wedging them onto the glasses, she crossed over to the open window. On the sill were several pots, overflowing with various herbs and spices. Tugging a few sprigs of mint free, she added them to the tea and headed back to August.

"Here you are."

"Thanks." He took a gulp and his eyes widened. "Wow, that's good. Not your regular glass of Lipton, I take it?"

"Nope. I create my own blends, actually."

"Really? That's interesting. What's in this one?"

"Oh, I can't tell you that." She propped a hip on the table and smiled.

"Why not?"

"It's top secret. Like the recipe for Coca-Cola."

"That good, huh?"

"You tell me."

August took another swallow. "It's that good."

"I know."

He laughed. "Guess I'll have to work on discovering some of these secrets of yours, then."

"I'm looking forward to it."

Her soft murmur had him blushing again and clearing his throat. "Your house is great, by the way."

"You've barely seen it."

"Well, I mean, what I have seen is nice, and…"

"I make you nervous, don't I?"

His gaze shot to hers and he let out a huff of breath. "A little bit, yeah."

"Good."

He took another sip of tea and looked away; he remained quiet and Chicory had a feeling he was searching for something to say, but wasn't quite sure how to respond.

They never are.

Finally, he broke the silence. "So … Getting ready for Halloween already?"

"I'm sorry?"

He gestured toward the table and her not-yet-completed jack-o-lantern.

"Oh, right. Well, it's a big deal in this neighborhood. Full of young families with kids. And as there's a long-running rumor that I'm the town witch, I like to go all out. Wouldn't want to disappoint them, now would I?"

"The town witch? Really?"

Chicory laughed at the look on his face as he tried to swallow down his latest gulp of tea. "Can you blame them? I mean, I live in a spooky-looking house—well, spooky enough, come October 31st—I grow my own herbs, own and run a holistic wellness shop, and I have an unnatural obsession with collecting crystals."

"So you're saying they're right?"

"I'm saying it's an easy assumption to make. Why? Do you believe in witches, August?"

"I ..."

She smirked, and he couldn't help but laugh at himself.

"No, I guess not."

"Well, that's a relief, let me tell you. So what were you working on the other morning? With the wood and the saw?"

"Oh, a dining room table."

"So you make furniture?"

"That and other things."

"Like what?"

"Mostly houses, actually. The furniture is more of a hobby. Building houses pays the bills."

"So you're a contractor."

"Yeah."

"Are you any good?"

"Damn good. I started my first business in Chicago when I was 22. Started a second branch in Springfield five years later. Stayed there another five years, and I just left it in the hands of my manager. Now I'm here to start a third one."

"Why St. Louis?"

August shrugged. "Seemed like the next logical place to go. The eventual goal is for MacGregor Construction to be a national business. But I'll settle for the midwest, for now."

"Wait a minute. MacGregor Construction? You're August MacGregor?"

Now August smirked. "Heard of me, have you?"

Chicory set her glass down and walked into the kitchen. A moment later she returned, a business card in hand. She handed it to him. "My home's been in the family for years, and it's due for some upkeep. I paid my uncle a visit to see if he knew anyone he'd recommend for the job. He gave me your card."

August looked down at the crisp white business card bearing his logo. "What's his name?"

"Leif Warner."

August considered. "A three-story Gothic just outside Chicago, right?"

Chicory nodded.

"I remember him. Good guy. Very specific about what he wanted."

"He is. And he seemed exceptionally pleased with your work. That's saying something, as my Uncle Leif isn't easy to impress."

"Well, that's nice to know."

"Yeah ... He had that work done about a year ago, didn't he?

"He did. He was actually the one who asked me if I'd considered expanding my business. I told him I'd already started a new branch in Springfield and did most of my work there. He suggested St. Louis as my next stop; even told me he knew some people looking to have work done he'd be willing to recommend me to. I wonder now if he meant you."

"It's possible."

Why, Uncle Leif, you sly thing. Did you send him here especially for me?

She'd give him a call to confirm it, but then again, she knew her uncle. He'd see the benefit of her being able to kill two birds with one stone.

"Well, I was going to offer you a tour anyway, but knowing now what you do, I guess we could consider it a business meeting. Would you like to take a look around?"

"I'd love to. Although, it doesn't necessarily have to be ... all business, does it?"

A tinge of heat mingled with the uncertainty in his gaze. *Trying to find your footing, are you? A bit of equal ground?* Good. She preferred her men *attempt* to exert some control over things. Even if their efforts were ultimately futile.

She gave him a slow smile. "I never said it did. Let's start with the kitchen, shall we?"

***

August couldn't keep his eyes from wandering to Chicory's swaying hips as they made their way through the house. *The place is beautiful, that's for sure.* It was old, so obviously there were some areas that needed a little TLC. But overall the home had been meticulously maintained.

As they made their way to the second floor, he couldn't help but wonder: *Will she show me her bedroom? And if so, what then?* He needed to knock it off. Even if she did show it to him, that wouldn't automatically mean it was some sort of invitation. Besides, he wasn't the type to sleep with a woman on the first date. *And I'm not sure this even qualifies as a first date, asshole. So get your head out of the gutter.*

Still, he was fairly certain a first date was on the agenda—hers as well as his. Her coyness was a tactic—one he was more than familiar with—but, he had to give it to her. It was working. If his inappropriate fantasies weren't enough to drive his interest, her body language and the innuendos beneath her words spoke loud and clear. She wanted him, but she'd insist on playing the game first.

Good thing he knew the rules.

"I'm torn about what to do with the upstairs bathroom." Swinging a door open, she stepped aside and let him take a look.

It was a small room, and dark. The toilet was backed into a tight alcove, hidden from the rest of the room. A wide, claw-footed tub rested along the left wall and opposite there was a small sink with a mirror above. The bathroom didn't have a shower or any windows. Still, she'd decorated it in a way that kept it cozy; homey and antiquated, rather than claustrophobic and out-of-date.

After getting a bit of a feel for the room, August turned back to her. "So what is it you're torn about?"

"Well, the house was built over one hundred years ago and I'd like to stay true to the building's original intent. On the other hand, I feel like the room could use an update. Nothing too terribly modern, but a few changes to make it a bit more accessible and usable. Know what I mean?"

"I do. I know exactly what you mean."

August meandered through the room again, looking at what was, visualizing what could be. "Here's what I might suggest. We could take the wall out that creates the alcove hiding the toilet. That would open the room up. I could build a platform here, adjust the plumbing, and add a showerhead here, a drain here." He gestured as he moved, trying to demonstrate for Chicory what he had in mind. "We'd move the tub up onto the platform; that way you'd keep the older feel but have the modern option of the shower. I would tile the platform; tile will hold up under the water better, but that way you wouldn't lose the rest of the hardwood floor. And if you were open to it, I'd add a skylight here. A skylight would detract less from the original design of the house while still giving you some natural light."

He turned back to her. "What do you think?"

She stood in the doorway, lips pursed. Her eyes darted back and forth as she gave a slight nod. "Yes, I can see what you're thinking. I think it's fairly genius, to be honest. A perfect melding of the old and new. You've got vision, August."

She sauntered over to him, placed her hands on his hips, and let her body slide in against his. "What else have you got?"

Before he could think twice, August fisted his hands in Chicory's loose locks, pulled her face to his, and kissed her. Her lips opened beneath his and his tongue delved into her mouth. She sucked at it eagerly, then nipped his bottom lip. August groaned, then backed her up until her back hit the wall. Breaking off the kiss, his mouth trailed down her neck to nibble at her collarbone.

He'd gotten her shirt unbuttoned while she attacked first his belt, and then his fly, when reason reverberated through his head.

What in God's name are you doing? You jackass! Stop!

His hands stilled. He leaned his forehead against the wall above her shoulder, his breath shuddering in and out.

This isn't the way. Not here, not now. I'm better than this, dammit. What the hell is wrong with me?

"Are you okay? August?"

He shook his head, then leaned back to look at her. "Yeah, I'm okay, it's just … Sorry, I should …"

He took a step back and buttoned her shirt back up. He glanced up at her, and his heart plummeted into his gut when he saw the hurt in her eyes.

"Don't you want to?" Her lip trembled as she whispered the question.

"Oh hell, Chicory, of course I want to." He gestured toward his cock, now straining for attention, as he carefully rearranged himself and did up his fly.

"Then why …?"

"Because you deserve better than a quick fuck in your bathroom from a guy you've only just met."

"What if quick fucks are my thing?"

He looked up at that and felt conflicting stirrings of arousal and disappointment. "Well, they're not mine. I like to know a woman's last name before I sleep with her. At the very least."

"It's Warren."

"Granted." He turned away and crossed his arms, trying to gain control over the situation.

"No, I get it, and I'm sorry. I shouldn't have put you in this position. It's just … Ever since I saw you on your porch a few mornings ago, I haven't been able to get you out of my head."

Well, we have that *in common at least.*

He came back to her. "I've thought about you, too. More than I should have. But still, I'd prefer we get to know a bit more about each other before jumping into bed. Don't get me wrong, I'm perfectly okay with that being the end goal. I just think we should wait more than twenty minutes before heading there."

"I can live with that. So what do you suggest?"

"How about dinner?"

***

Chicory smiled slyly as she watched August cross the street and enter his new house without looking back at her.

He's even better than I hoped; that being said, I think things are shaping up quite nicely. Men are so pliable. Like putty in my hands. It's so adorable when they think they're being noble; they have absolutely no idea they're no longer capable of thinking for themselves.

Shutting the door and flipping the deadbolt, Chicory headed into the kitchen. Pulling some kale, a variety of berries, and an apple from the fridge, she proceeded to toss everything into a blender. Stepping over to her kitchen window, she snipped a leaf here and a stalk there and added them to the blend. A couple of bay leaves, a bit of burdock. Even a calendula bloom, though the experts warned against ingesting the plant, due to its making most people sick. But again, she wasn't most people.

A couple of button pushes and about thirty seconds later, Chicory had a tasty smoothie that would bring out the natural highlights in her hair, smooth her skin, and aid in the image of youth. Pouring the contents into a glass, she took a sip and sighed. She noted the unfinished jack-o-lantern still on the table and shrugged. It could wait another hour. She carried her glass upstairs, entered the bathroom she'd only recently evacuated, and turned the knobs on the tub. Water gushed from the spigot and moments later, steam rose up to surround her.

Stripping down to nothing, she sank into the calescent water and sighed. After a few moments, she reached over to her jeans, pulled her cell phone from the pocket, and dialed.

"Something wrong with your crystal ball?"

Chicory laughed at her Uncle Leif's sarcasm. "Not a thing. But I'm in the tub at the moment."

"Not an image I needed, Chicory."

"Like it's not something you've seen before."

"Not the point, and you know it."

"Alright, I'll stop teasing. So, did you send him?"

"Did I send who?"

"Very funny. You know damn well who."

"And you know damn well that I did. So why'd you ask?"

She giggled, popped a foot out of the tub, and watched streaks of water trickle down her leg towards her knee. *My toenails need a fresh coat of paint.*

"He's absolutely delicious. Thank you."

"That was quick work. I figured it was getting to be that time, but I didn't know you were quite that desperate."

She knew her uncle was just giving her shit, but irritation flared in her chest anyway. "I wasn't. I'm not. I'm perfectly fine, as is he for the moment, and I could have found a new conquest on my own. When I needed one, of course."

"Don't I know it? Relax, Chicory. I was just giving you a hard time. Then again, you don't need me for that, do you? You've got August."

She grinned at that. "I could have had him today. But it's always better if I let them ripen a bit. He thinks it was his idea that we stopped, of course."

"Sure he does. Would you have it any other way?"

"Maybe someday."

Leif grunted. "Yeah, right. When Hell freezes over."

"Oh, you're probably right. Anyway, I just wanted to say thanks. I'm going to enjoy this one very much. I can already tell."

"Well, you're more than welcome. I gotta run, Chicory. Come see me sometime, will you?"

"Maybe over Yule. I've got a feeling I'll be busy come Samhain."

"I don't doubt it. Blessings on you, Chicory."

"And you as well, Uncle."

Setting the phone aside, Chicory sank shoulder-deep into the water, shut her eyes, and hummed. Her uncle had sent her quite the gift; she was looking forward to using it.

***

August woke with a raging hard-on. He rolled over and reached for Chicory, but of course she wasn't there. Over the past few weeks they'd been out a number of times: dinners, movies, a weekend trip up to the Chicago museums, drives over the river, up through Alton, and down the River Road to Grafton and back. Each day the sexual tension mounted, but for some reason every time they got close to reaching that point, August was overcome by an undeniable need to stop.

He didn't understand it; he'd never had trouble getting into bed with a woman before. He was always a gentleman, of course. He used protection, and if he wasn't planning on calling the next day, he was upfront about it. He wasn't one to pressure a woman into doing something she didn't want to. Then again, a lack of willing women wasn't one of his ninety-nine problems.

But with Chicory … God, he wanted that woman. And it was more than obvious she wanted him, too. *What is keeping me from sealing the deal?* He wished he knew.

Reaching down, he fisted himself and got to work; there'd be no getting on with the day until he took care of business. Envisioning Chicory's long locks curtaining their faces, their lips locked as she rode him, he rushed the hand job.

I'm all for sexual satisfaction, but damn, this shit's getting old.

He needed to get laid—if not by Chicory, then by *somebody*. Something to take the edge off, at the very least. Finally reaching climax, he moaned in resigned relief, rolled out of bed, and headed for the shower.

After a quick, cold one—no need to risk a replay of the morning's festivities—he walked into the kitchen, fired up the stove, and set some bacon to crackling. A couple of eggs followed, along with a handful of chopped potatoes. Sliding the finished food onto a plate, August poured himself a glass of orange juice and settled down at the kitchen table. Halfway through his meal, his cell rang.

Digging into his pocket, he pulled it out and hit "answer" without looking at the number. Chicory's voice immediately had him hardening, and he fought the urge to groan.

"What's happenin', hot stuff?"

He couldn't help but grin at the reference. They'd discovered early on they both shared a love of eighties' cult classics, and they'd spent a day having a Brat Pack marathon: *The Breakfast Club, Pretty In Pink, Sixteen Candles,* and *St. Elmo's Fire.*

"Morning, Chicory."

"Aww. Do I detect a sense of frustration this morning?"

How the hell does she do that? Somehow the woman always seemed to know what he was thinking. It was equally unnerving and intriguing. "It's nothing, I'm fine."

"What's the matter, babe?"

"Seriously, it's no big deal. Work stuff."

"Oh. Alright, then."

He knew she didn't believe him, but what was he supposed to say? *Yes, I'm frustrated as hell, because I'd really like to fuck your brains out, but for some reason known only to God, I've developed an unhealthy and extremely unwanted sense of chivalry.*

Yeah, that'd go over *great.*

He changed the subject, determined to let it go.

"So what's up?"

"I just wanted to find out if you had any special plans for tomorrow?"

"Tomorrow? Not that I know of. Why?"

She didn't respond. As the silence dragged on, August glanced out the window and got a good gander at her fully decorated house. Spiderwebs draped from the porch awnings and bushes. Gravestones popped out of the ground, along with skeletal hands and the occasional skull. With the flip of a switch, black lights would flash along the length of the porch, and a trio of stereotypical witches—old, ugly, covered in warts, and wearing pointy hats—crouched over a cauldron and would cackle ominously when anyone stepped too close. Chicory'd been working on it steadily for days. Hell, he'd even helped her with a bunch of it.

"Shit! Is tomorrow Halloween? Already?"

She laughed; her chuckles lost none of their charm through the ever-present cell phone static. "I'd have to grab a calendar and double-check, but yeah, I'm pretty sure."

"Dammit. I thought … How did I figure I still had another week?" Although he knew the answer to that. Besides getting the new business off the ground—and the flood of calls he hadn't truly expected so soon—he'd been so caught up in her, he'd completely lost track of time.

"Regretting the lost time?"

"Hell, no."

"Good. I'm glad. Anyway, I never open the shop on Halloween, so I was wondering if you might like to keep me company for the day? We could have a Michael Myers movie marathon, carve another pumpkin or two, I'll read your tarot cards. Then we'll hand out candy, obviously; my place is pretty popular on Halloween, if you can believe it. And afterwards? I'm sure we can think of something."

"No doubt. Wait a minute. Did you say tarot cards?"

"Yeah. It's an old family tradition. We still celebrate Samhein, too, but I enjoy Halloween, so I do both."

"Seriously?"

"Yeah."

"I thought you said you weren't actually a witch."

"I'm not. I'm a Gaian."

"Wow, okay. Pagan roots?"

"Celtic. Although, I guess technically it equates to about the same thing. Either way, you don't need to worry; there's no truth in it. It's just a bit of harmless fun."

If you say so. He didn't immediately answer, and she laughed. "Are you worried?"

"Maybe a little."

"Well, don't be. We don't have to if you don't want to. So what do you say?"

"Well, give me a second to check my planner ... Yeah, I'm good. What time do you want me?"

"Every second of every day."

His cock twitched. "Come again?"

"Oh, multiple times."

His cheeks warmed. *What am I, twelve?*

"Chicory."

"Alright, alright. Head this way whenever you get up and around. We'll make a day out of it."

"Sounds good. See you in the morning."

He hung up, then dipped his head and addressed his groin. "Knock it off. I don't have time for anymore of your shit today." *Good grief, I'm talking to my cock. I must be losing my mind.* That wasn't a revelation. Ever since he'd met Chicory, he felt like he was in the midst of a whirlwind; his life seemed to have lost all sense of direction. Work actually felt like work, for the first time in his life. He struggled daily to remain focused on his numerous projects ...

"Yeah, well, that's gonna change." This stint with celibacy had to end. She had her hooks in him, that was for sure. Even her last comment had underlying meaning, given his recent morning routine. *Whenever you get up and around.* If she only knew.

Standing, he took his breakfast plate over to the sink and came to a decision: Tomorrow would be the deciding factor. Either he and Chicory took this—whatever *this* was—to the next level, or he was walking away. Even if it meant he had to leave St. Louis to do it.

***

Chicory gritted her teeth as she rose at the sound of the knock at the door. *About fucking time.* She'd planned the whole day out and the asshole was just showing up now? At four o'clock in the fucking afternoon? What happened to "come on over whenever you get up and around?" She knew damn well he didn't sleep past eight in the morning, let alone hours into the afternoon. *So where the hell has he been?* She ripped the door open, the question on the tip of her tongue, along with more than a few choice obscenities.

She didn't get any of it said.

August barreled through the opening and kicked the door shut. Before she could respond, he'd grabbed her by the shoulders, spun her around, and slammed her against the door. His lips swooped down on hers with none of the gentleness or finesse he'd shown in the past. His tongue tore into her mouth, sweeping through with a level of violent aggression she hadn't known he possessed.

She went immediately wet.

She raised her arms to twine around his neck, her hands sifting through the hair at the back of his neck, but he yanked them away.

"No."

With one hand he locked her wrists together and pinned her arms above her head. With the other he reached under the hem of her skirt and yanked down her thong, then undid his own fly. His cock sprung free, its length jutting heavily against her belly. Continuing the assault on her mouth, his free hand palmed her ass, and in a smooth flash of movement, he lifted her, bracing her against the door as she wrapped her legs around his waist. With no hesitation, he thrust, burying himself to the hilt inside her. She couldn't contain the yell; it erupted from her throat, so loud she was sure the neighbors would hear.

She didn't give a damn.

Her back slapped against the door as he fucked her, hot and hard and without any consideration for her comfort. She didn't mind, but she did wonder.

How ...? She'd controlled him so well up until this point. Then again, perhaps she'd finally pushed him past his breaking point. It didn't matter. She was more than capable of improvising.

The friction between her legs as he slid in and out of her was to die for, if such a thing had been possible. She gave herself over to the moment, to the sex—to him—and simply enjoyed. A few glorious moments later, an orgasm blew through her, leaving her breathless. August followed immediately after, shouting as he twitched inside her. For a while, they panted in unison, August's head against the door and Chicory's drooped on his shoulder.

When August let her feet slide to the floor and finally moved to pull away from her, Chicory turned the tables.

"My turn."

Burying her fingers in the shirt still buttoned to his collarbone, she whipped him around so his back was against the door, then slid to her knees in front of him. Lifting his still semi-erect shaft away, she took his balls into her mouth and sucked. August groaned, and he hardened beneath her fingers. Letting her tongue fall against the bottom of his penis, she licked him from base to head, then lapped at the tip, still damp with a mingling of his orgasm and hers. She continued to tease for a long moment, then finally took him fully into her mouth. His hands fisted in her hair, but she reached up, grabbed his wrists, and pinned them against the door.

"No."

In full control of pace and pressure, Chicory brought him to the brink of fulfillment then backed off, again and again. She relished the guttural moans, mounting in volume and intensity, coming from the back of his throat and the struggle against her hands as he repressed the urge to rip free from her grasp.

"Dammit, Chicory!"

Still she sucked, the wet slap of her mouth against his manhood brash, yet arousing in her ears. Releasing one of his hands, she let her own slip between his legs to fondle his sack. With a shout and the slam of his free hand against the door, August came hard, his hips pumping as she continued to work him between her lips. She continued the suction until his shoulders hunched forward and he panted, fully replete. Catching his eye, she swallowed deliberately, then licked her lips, her expression that of a cat who just devoured an overly large canary.

He slid to the floor next to her, then stretched out.

"Sorry. I'll get up in a minute, I swear."

"Did I say anything?"

"No, but ... I'll get up. At least make it to the couch or something."

"Furniture's overrated."

With that, she slipped out of her pants, then straddled him.

"What are you ..."

She grinned at him, and his question, as she locked gazes with him and with a long, slow stretch, pulled her shirt over her head, revealing a delicate bra of inky lace.

"You didn't think we were done yet, did you?"

"God, Chicory, I don't think I can. Not yet. You gotta give me a min .."

His voice trailed off as she released the front clasp, revealed her breasts, then slowly brought a taut nipple to her lips. She trailed her tongue around the bud once, twice, then took it between her teeth and nipped.

"Fuck me." August groaned. His eyes rolled back into his head, and his hips lifted off the floor, pressing his returned erection against her wet core.

She smiled, a sly twinkle in her eye.

"That's the general idea."

***

Nearly two hours later, August lay spread-eagle and utterly exhausted on the carpet of Chicory's parlor. Chicory curled into his side, her head on his shoulder and a leg thrown across his. Scattered clothes lay haphazardly about the room; they'd finally managed to both get naked.

"I think I might be dead."

Chicory chuckled. "Not yet."

"You sure?"

She trailed a hand down to his now flaccid penis. At her touch, it immediately jumped to attention. He groaned, and she laughed.

"Positive."

"No more, Chicory. God, I beg you."

She smiled down at him, then pressed her lips to his. "I guess I can grant you a reprieve."

"Thank God."

"I feel like I ought to be offended by that."

"No, no. Not at all. I just ... a break ... Just a few minutes. K?"

"Okay."

She uncoiled her limbs from him and rose.

"Where you going?" He warbled the words as he fought to keep his eyes open.

"To get my vacuum."

"Vacuum?" He rolled his head to the side to look up at her.

"That's what I said."

"You don't think now might seem an odd time to be doing housework?"

"Well, I would, but you knocked over my plants."

"Come again?"

"If you really want. I thought you needed a break." She grinned down at him, mischief in her eyes, then took a step toward him.

"No! I do. I mean ... Sorry. I knocked over your plants?"

She nodded her head, indicating the antique end table standing nearby. Two pots were upended next to it, the carpet smeared with rich brown soil.

August thought back to the whirlwind that was the past few hours. Yes, he remembered now. At one point he'd had Chicory bent over that table, taking her from behind. He'd been a bit rough ... But then, so had she. Made sense the plants hadn't made it.

"Shit. I'm sorry. I'll ... I'll clean it up, just give me a minute ..."

"Don't worry about it, August, it's no big deal. I've got soil out back, so repotting them's no problem. I just want to get the soil up before it stains the carpet."

"Yeah, but I should do it. S'my fault."

"I think we're both equally to blame. Besides, I'd prefer you stay there and rest. The night's not nearly close to being over."

August groaned at her insinuation, then fell back against the floor and shut his eyes as she swayed naked out of the room. *How can she be ready for more?*

Six times. She'd made him come six times in the past three hours. If he didn't feel as wrung out as he did, August wouldn't have believed it. He was virile enough, but never before … *Six fucking times.* What was it about this woman that made him so horny? He just couldn't get enough. Even now, exhausted as he was, he hardened as he pictured her pushing the vacuum back and forth across the carpet, her breasts swaying with the motion, her nipples erect in the cool October air filtering in through the open window. When he heard the vacuum roar to life, he couldn't help himself. He cracked an eyelid to take a look.

Vacuum hose in hand, Chicory bore down on him, a look of cool determination—and the slightest hint of evil delight—in her gaze.

"What the …?"

Before he could move, Chicory shoved the cold, steel hose directly into his open mouth. The suction, violent in its force, ripped the oxygen from his lungs. Pain billowed, then exploded in his chest. *What the fuck?!?* August's eyes bulged and watered as he fought to draw a breath, but breathable air no longer existed. His lungs contracted, screaming in his chest, begging for sustenance, but the harder he tried to breath, the more the vacuum pulled at him. His chest and throat burned, the embers of a fire fighting for life. He clawed frantically at his neck, then his jaws, and finally his lips, trying to pry them away from the hose. His skin tore beneath his nails, but he barely noticed. The slight sting was nothing compared to the agony roaring beneath his ribcage.

God, it hurts! Make it stop!

As if she'd heard his thoughts, Chicory pulled the hose free. August immediately tried to inhale. He couldn't; his mouth simply gaped open and shut like a fish on land. His gaze shot thoughtlessly around the room, white dots dancing in his vision, searching for some kind of answer to his predicament. Seeing the hose move in Chicory's hands, he noticed blood and phlegm dripping from the opening.

His eyes widened in realization; she'd sucked out his lungs! His stomach churned. Bile rose up. His chest heaved. Only when his mouth flared and nothing came out did he understand his esophagus had taken the same route as his lungs.

Oh, God, somebody help me!

Seconds ticked by. His thoughts swirled in time to the pounding behind his eyes as he went without oxygen. Dizziness swept over him as his brain short-circuited. His eyes drifted shut …

They slammed open as Chicory thrust the hose against the bare skin of his chest. The vacuum's suction ripped him off the floor, causing his back to arch at an inhuman angle. August tried to scream as first the hairs, then the skin of his chest ripped from the underlying fascia and whipped up the hose, but of course, there was no sound beyond the snapping of his jaws. Blood splattered against his face, blinding him. He tore at the hose, managing for a moment to break its hold. The suction simply changed direction, catching hold of his left hand. His knuckles scraped against the unforgiving steel as his fingers flew through the opening, and black stars danced in front of his eyes when his wrist snapped and his whole hand disappeared, leaving nothing but a crude, gory stump behind.

Adjusting the hose, Chicory reapplied it to his chest. The sharp points of his ribs punctured through his pectorals, a macabre imitation of a wrought-iron fence, then splintered, leaving jagged tears along the muscles. Seconds later, his chest ruptured, splitting down the middle, and Chicory got to work destroying his innards.

She's killing me … I'm dying … I don't … want … to die …

His mouth hung open, unable to contain his grotesque and swollen tongue, blood and drool pooling, then trickling from the sides. Pressure throbbed behind his eyelids, threatening to pop his eyes free from their sockets. His vision greyed as August's back bent outward, further and further, his spine raising ever closer to the vacuum as his insides were sucked, little by little, through the small, but unstoppable hole of the hose.

A crack slapped across August's ears; just above his hips, his spine shattered beneath the pressure of the vacuum, leaving August to flop limply against the hose. For a mere second, a paltry sense of relief welled within the little that was left of him.

It's … over …

The momentary sense of peace dissolved as he continued to watch bloody ribbons of his flesh disappear. Though his legs now lay blissfully numb, the overall pain didn't stop … It intensified. Skin shredded and tore free. Bones shattered and deteriorated into dust. Organs burst and disintegrated.

Coherent thought ceased to exist for August. There was only unending agony. Blinded by vision now fatally black and with a silent scream that sounded only in his head, he endured in torturous silence as every last piece of him, right down to his last fingernail, was ripped away and sucked into nothing.

***

Still nude, Chicory carried the vacuum's pulp-filled canister into the kitchen. Pulling down her blender, she poured in the contents of what five minutes ago had been a fully-functioning August. *It's a shame, really. This one was* really *talented.* Then again, she'd had plenty to do with that anyway. She always did. She threw some vanilla yogurt, a handful of fresh strawberries, and a sprig of mint into the mix, then set the blender whirring. Shifting, she noted the slight soreness between her legs.

A damn shame.

She turned the blender off, then dumped the makeshift smoothie into a tall glass. Taking it upstairs, she stood before the full-length mirror in her bedroom. She downed the concoction, cringing as she crunched down on an intact tooth, but the grimace was replaced by a smile as she stared at the mirror and immediately began to change. The lines around her eyes and mouth evaporated. Her skin brightened, smoothed, and stretched taut over her muscles. Her breasts lifted, taking on the wondrous perkiness of her prime. The few grey strands in her hair, which hung in a wild tangle down her back, darkened and disappeared. As what remained of August flowed through her body, she watched herself transform, glorious youth reclaiming her.

With a satisfied purr, she donned a pair of jeans and a black t-shirt, then skipped back down the stairs. Stopping in the kitchen, she grabbed the massive bowl of candy she'd prepared earlier and headed for the front door, stopping to flip the switch that would set her Halloween graveyard alight. Barefoot, she stepped lightly onto the porch, the large cat eyes on her t-shirt glinting in the darkness. With a sigh of contentment, she settled on the steps, candy in her lap, and grinned in welcome as the first wave of ghouls and goblins came racing toward her door.

The End

.

Pumpkin Rex

By

Lisa Morton

Devin clutched the jack-o'-lantern mask in his lap as he looked out the car windows at the urban wastescape. "Is this part of town even safe?"

Maxx glanced at him from behind the driver's wheel. "Dude, it's Halloween. It's not supposed to be completely safe."

"I know, but...well, are you sure you're going the right way? These buildings all look...dead."

Devin couldn't think of any other word to describe the rundown warehouses and factories they'd passed for at least four blocks now. He was starting to wish he'd just stayed home; at fifteen, he might have been too old to trick or treat, but he could have found a party, or just watched horror movies. But he'd let Maxx talk him into his first rave ("c'mon, it's all ages, *and* it's Halloween, so you gotta love it"), and since Maxx was sixteen and could drive already, they wouldn't need a chaperone.

Maybe Devin would even meet a girl. That'd been part of Maxx's pitch.

Devin looked down at his mask and thought at least this Halloween wouldn't be a total waste. He'd saved up his allowance all summer for the mask, which was a full over-the-head hand-painted beauty complete with light-up eyes. Halloween was Devin's favorite day of the year, and this mask – called "Pumpkin Rex" – had a traditional, iconic look that pleased him. Devin was a Halloween fanatic – he'd read all the history websites and studied all the lore. To him, the carved pumpkin would always be the king of Halloween. He'd had the mask for a month now, sitting perched on a shelf in his bedroom, just waiting for this one night. He'd even bought a secondhand tuxedo jacket from a thrift store and a bright orange bowtie. Tonight *he* would be the King of Halloween.

Maxx, on the other hand…Zombie Elvis? Devin had to admit it was a good costume – Maxx even got Elvis's little hair curl down – but everybody dressed as a zombie these days.

As if on cue, Devin spotted a pair of the undead staggering down the street ahead of them. For a moment, given the dilapidated buildings, they looked startlingly like a scene from a post-apocalyptic zombie movie…then the illusion was shattered when one of them gave the other a playful shove.

"See? We gotta be almost there." Maxx gestured at the zombies as they passed, turned a corner, and sure enough – there was a line of cars waiting to enter a parking lot. A block down, lights flashed from one of the larger buildings, and now Devin could hear a throbbing bass beat, rumbling through the October night like the pulse of some ancient god.

Fifteen minutes later they'd parked, Devin had pulled his mask on, they'd bought their tickets, been searched, and entered the "First Annual All Ages Halloween Masquerave". Just inside they stopped, staring: before them was a world of colored strobe lights, hundreds of dancers gyrating to techno music, and a deejay dressed as the Grim Reaper.

"Okay, now tell me this isn't awesome," Maxx shouted, elbowing him.

"It's all right. Sure are a lot of zombies here, though." Devin couldn't resist the dig; besides, it was true. Half of the male attendees were zombies, wearing tattered clothing, pale makeup, and gallons of fake blood; the rest were vampires, cowboys, soldiers, and various celebrities. Devin was pleased to note only one other jack-o'-lantern, a cheap plastic face mask surmounting a t-shirt and jeans. Most of the women were dressed as sexy princesses, sexy fairies, sexy pirates, sexy cartoon characters…Devin felt like he was looking at one of his older sister's Victoria's Secret catalogs. The energy in the room was a palpable thing, impacting all of Devin's senses in a way that threatened to overwhelm him.

Maxx tapped his arm. "C'mon." He began moving through the crowd ringing the dance floor; Devin followed, threading his way among the tightly-packed wallflowers. He passed a twenty-something man buying and then swallowing a pill, and he felt a thrill of rebellion. *Wow, people are just taking drugs right out in the open here!*

They reached the lines for a bar, where they overpaid for cokes. Then Maxx led the way to an empty spot near a wall.

"This is great, right?" Maxx had to lean over and yell in Devin's ear to be heard.

Devin nodded, surveying the throng. Over half of the people around them wore glow bracelets or necklaces, standing out in the darkened space like thousands of jumping phosphorescent animals. The drums rumbled through Devin's chest, and his body vibrated in synch. There was something spiritual about the sensation, as if they were part of some vast ritual on the most magical night of the year.

The deejay came to a song with nothing but a rhythm line, which he spoke over. "Three hours now from midnight, when barriers fall and worlds collide, when transformation happens and we *become*. After a thousand years, are you ready?"

The dancers shouted approval, pumping fists into the air as a synth melody kicked in. Devin, though, was thinking about the deejay's words: *when transformation happens? A thousand years?*

"That was some weird shit," he shouted at Maxx.

Maxx shrugged. "These deejays love to spout this stuff that sounds like some freaky book or something."

Devin continued to watch the deejay, who looked up from his turntables for a second – and Devin had the uncanny sensation that the Grim Reaper was staring at him. As he watched, the deejay extended an arm, pointing, and Devin couldn't help but think the man was pointing at *him*. That wasn't possible; there was no way a deejay on a stage at least a hundred feet away had picked him out of a dark crowd, even with the light-up eyes in his mask. Finally the deejay lowered his arm, executed a bow, and returned to spinning records.

Devin shivered under his tuxedo jacket.

"Hey, are you listening? I said, check those babes out."

Devin shrugged off the chill before following Maxx's gaze to see a circle of three teenage girls standing away from the dance floor, giggling together. One was dressed as a 1960's go-go dancer, with short skirt and tall boots; another was over-spilling a skimpy genie outfit. The third, however, was the only female Devin had seen tonight who was covered head to toe: She wore a witch's costume complete with tall black hat, cape, and even had a puppet black cat cradled in one arm.

He knew instantly he had to talk to her. He just had no idea how to go about it.

"Okay," Maxx said, running a hand through his slicked hair and giving his jacket a little shake. "I dream of genie. Wish me luck."

Devin laughed, but watched carefully as Maxx approached the trio.

He stopped before them, struck an Elvis pose, and then did a passable hip-thrust. Two of the girls laughed. The witch rolled her eyes.

Devin liked her more by the second.

The girls conversed with Maxx, who finally looked back and waved Devin over. He came forward, suddenly realizing he'd never been this nervous on Halloween before. When he reached them, Maxx threw out a hand. "This is my friend, Devin." He was even affecting Elvis's accent.

The go-go dancer frowned at Devin. "What's with the mask? Is he like deformed under there or something?" The genie snickered in embarrassment and made a halfhearted attempt to shush her friend.

"I think that mask rocks," said the witch.

Maxx exchanged more meaningless words with the genie and the go-go girl, but Devin wasn't listening. He was looking at the witch, who was unexpectedly pretty under her green greasepaint and black wig. Finally Maxx gestured at the bar. "I'm going to buy these lovely ladies something wet. We'll be right back."

Devin barely acknowledged them, as Maxx and the other two girls left.

"Hi, I'm Kara," the witch said, and then, as the cat puppet bowed, added, "and this is Belial."

"Hello, Kara and Belial – Devin. And I'm not deformed under here."

"I didn't think you were. I love the way the eyes light up on the mask."

"Me, too. Do you...want to dance?"

Kara shrugged. "Belial and I don't really dance." The cat made a funny little attempt at dancing and then sagged in disappointment.

Devin laughed. "I don't, either. Pretty dumb that we both ended up at a rave, isn't it?"

She nodded, then said, "But maybe we could just go talk…?"

Devin felt 50,000 volts of happiness flare within him. "Uh…yeah. That'd be great. What about your friends?"

"What about yours?"

He looked behind him, but couldn't find Maxx and the girls in the dark and the bouncing crowd. He had his phone, though, and knew Maxx wouldn't leave without him.

"This way." Kara was tugging at his tuxedo; he let her lead the way through the crowd to a side room, where the noise levels were considerably lessened and conversations were happening. Conversations, and couples kissing. Kissing passionately. As he felt heat rise to his face, Devin was glad Kara couldn't see under the mask.

They found a quiet corner, where Devin took off the mask. Kara eyed his face, smiling. "No, you're not deformed."

He cursed himself for blushing again, and tried to stammer out a response when his breath caught in his throat:

The Grim Reaper stood behind Kara, watching them.

"Is that the deejay?"

Kara turned to follow his gaze. "Yeah. I recognize that skull mask. It's pretty good."

"If he's in here…who's running the music?"

Kara shrugged. "They usually have more than one deejay at these things."

Devin tried to look back at Kara, continuing the conversation as if he wasn't in a dark corner of a decrepit factory being stared at by a man dressed as Death. "Oh. So do you...you know, go to a lot of raves?"

"Not really. This is only my second one."

The attempt at casual conversation wasn't working. "Give me a minute here."

Kara watched as Devin walked to the costumed Reaper, who showed no response at his approach. "Hey," Devin said, realizing he had no idea how to handle this situation. "Do...um...I know you? I mean, I just wondered why you've been staring at us."

When the man spoke, Devin recognized the same smooth, modulated tones he'd heard over the song. "A thousand years have built to tonight."

Devin thought back over everything he knew about Halloween, but he couldn't think of anything important from the year 1017. "Why is that?"

The Reaper leaned in closer, his voice still low but bristling with excitement. "In 1017, in a small Irish village near Teamhair, where the Celts had once celebrated Samhain, the first real Halloween celebration took place. A group of peasants, overworked and exhausted from bringing in the harvest, decided to combine the new holiday of All Souls' Day with All Saints' Day and their ancient, beloved Samhain, and they drank and told fortunes and stirred up such furious energies that they invoked spirits. Certain forces were set in motion that night."

"How do you know that? I mean, I know a *lot* about Halloween, but I've never read that one."

The Reaper mask bobbed in amusement. "There's more to history than just books."

"So...what happens at midnight? You said something about 'transformation'?"

The Reaper nodded. "You'll find out. The energy is right, a thousand years have passed, and the time has almost come."

Another chill passed through Devin. "The time for what?"

The Reaper's grin widened, and Devin thought, *How did he do that? That's just a mask.* "The time for Halloween to take its dominion, for it to become more than one night a year of costumed play. Just a few minutes left now."

Devin shook his head. "No, it's just a little after nine –" He pulled out his phone, lit up the time

-

And saw it was five minutes until twelve.

"But that's...this can't be right, it's..."

He looked up, puzzled – but the deejay was gone.

Devin's head started to spin. He tried to turn, to find Kara, and he nearly lost his balance. She was there, though, supporting him, guiding him to an old wooden bench against one wall. "Hey, whoa there..."

Devin's whole head felt large and light, as if he were a balloon filled with too much helium. He wondered if he'd been drugged; maybe Maxx had slipped him something with the coke. Or Kara – what if she was a *real* witch and had cast a spell or something? No, that was ridiculous. He shook his head, trying to clear it.

"Should I get help?" She was leaning over him, concerned.

His vision cleared somewhat, and Kara's nearness centered him again. In fact, he was starting to feel good now. Not just good, but – ecstatic.

"I'm okay," he said. "Did you know it's almost midnight?"

She smiled. "The witching hour." The puppet black cat – Belial – wiggled in her arms. Devin didn't even care that he could see both her hands, that he knew she hadn't done that.

Devin realized he still held his mask in one hand; he didn't want midnight on Halloween to come while he was bare-faced, so he tugged it back on. Out in the main room, he heard the deejay intoning over low music, "We've created and channeled the necessary amount of energy tonight, and certain forces have been invoked. Thirty seconds to lift-off, everyone. Say goodbye to your old life and hello to a new world."

From somewhere, some carefully protected part of himself – call it his conscience, his *soul* – Devin heard silent shrieks, a voice telling him something was wrong, to go NOW, to run, get to the exit and then keep going, regardless of Maxx or his ride or the neighborhood (which would be safer than HERE)...but he looked at Kara, and he knew he'd stay, because she was where he wanted to be now.

So he listened to the seconds called out – "...SEVENTEEN...SIXTEEN...FIFTEEN..." With each passing number he felt new, newer. When Kara reached for his hand, he knew she felt it, too, that whatever the transformation would be in ten, nine, eight more seconds, they'd go through it together.

"...THREE...TWO...ONE..."

Devin's consciousness flared, a mental nova. When his vision returned it took him a few minutes to realize what it was: He felt bigger, more confident – and he was no longer looking out through eye holes.

But...

Beside him stood a witch – no, stood *the* witch, the most perfect Halloween icon he'd ever seen. Her skin was pale green, her eyes glowed with some inward crimson light, and the cat that leapt from her arms and circled her feet was black as pitch and lively as the Devil.

He heard screaming then – dozens, hundreds of screams – and other sounds, too: Moaning. Wailing. *Chomping*. He strode forward, briefly surprised by the length of his stride – he crossed yards with each step.

He saw pandemonium: Zombies – no longer boys in make-up, but real revenants, with glassy eyes and clawed fingers – were tearing apart the princesses and fairies. They ripped limbs off and raised them to dried, hungry mouths; they shoved through the crowd to reach for more flesh. Severed glow necklaces spilled phosphorescent liquid to the floor like the ichor of a slain angel. Soldiers and cops fired guns randomly into the crowd, more often than not hitting each other; vampires soared overhead and lunged for ballerinas, while werewolves tore into politicians and movie stars. Near the bar, zombie Elvis feasted on a severed foot still clad in a blue suede shoe.

He drank in the tableau, feeling neither horror nor panic, but instead...a *naturalness*. This was *right*. This was what he was meant for.

On the stage at the front of the room stood the Grim Reaper, motioning him up.

He glanced at the witch, who cackled in glee; together, they walked to the stage and ascended. The Reaper bowed to them, and then gestured to the mad scene below.

"Behold your Halloween kingdom, come to pass at last," he said, in his mellifluous voice, then added, "Pumpkin Rex."

The King was dimly aware that he'd once had another name, but that no longer mattered. He'd arrived at last, to rule over his realm with his witch-queen at his side. Starting from tonight, time would be obsolete and useless; it would always be midnight on Halloween, and the world would always belong to the October creatures.

The King smiled down benignly. The trick was his treat, and it was good.

The End

The First Shot

By

J. C. Michael

The sky was blue, the air crisp. Red and gold leaves gathered along the kerbstones, as sure a sign of autumn as the chill in the air. The marketplace was busy, cars filling the cobbles, people filling the footpaths. The whole range of ages: pensioners, kids, young women with their babies wrapped up against the October breeze. Amongst the hustle and bustle, Zach carefully propped his new mountain bike, a birthday present not yet old enough to be carelessly dropped to the ground, against the newsagent's window. The window display was dominated by fireworks and sparklers, with Halloween items—a plastic pumpkin, a witch's hat--sprinkled in-between. . There'd be more inside, including the glove he'd had his eye on, but things were different now, and had been since he'd found the note.

Hi Zach,

How's things? So, I'm going to cut to the chase. Would you like to take me to the disco after the bonfire on Saturday? I wish you'd asked me, I would have said yes! And now I feel silly doing the asking because I'm the girl! And what if you say yes just because I've asked, but you're not really that into me?

Okay, so, now that's out of the way, I had an idea. It might be stupid, I don't know, but I want to be sure you're serious. If, that is, you want me to be your date. So, Tuesday night, Halloween, I want you to bring me something, not so much a gift, more of a token, yeah, a token, that's a better word. It isn't about the cost, it should be something meaningful. Show me how well you know me and that you're sincere. Leave your offering by the war memorial in the church yard before midnight and don't hang around when you've left it, just put it down and leave. It I think you've proven yourself I'm yours for the dance (am I right in thinking Saturday's Mischief Night? I love all your old customs, and a bit of mischief too........), if not, I'll return your token and hope we can still be friends. You get one chance at this, so think carefully.

Take care.

Bree x

P.S. Don't tell ANYONE or you get disqualified o.k. DON'T TELL ANYONE.

He'd never had any idea she was interested in him, had always thought she was out of his league. It was odd that the note was typed, but she was American, and they did all sorts of queer things; the weird words and spellings that wound up their teachers so much, for a start. Besides, it was on a sheet of her pink notepaper. She was always jotting things down in her pad and never tired of telling people how you could only get that particular brand of stationary in the States.

"You've been eyeing that up all week, having second thoughts?"

The comment brought Zach back from wherever his mind had wandered. Mr. King was watching him with partial interest, and partial suspicion. There was a lot of shoplifting from the newsagents, but Mr. King should have known him better, since Zach had delivered papers for him for three years and never missed a day come rain or shine.

"Maybe."

"Bloody Freddy Krueger. Load of nonsense if you ask me. All them nasty videos," the old man shook his wispy white hair. "Rot your mind son, you mark my words."

Zach smiled, "You're the one selling it, and Rev. Hughes's daughter works in the video shop."

"Less cheek lad, and business is business. The money I make pays your wages doesn't it?"

"And then I spend it in here, and give it back to you."

That brought a smile from old Mr. King. He wasn't a bad sort, really; always gave the lads who worked for him a few quid extra at Christmas, as well as a can of beer for those over sixteen. Zach was looking forward to his first can: Stones, Tetley's, or maybe John Smiths, it didn't matter. He'd drink it with his dad on Christmas Day, like his older brother had when he'd had the 'round before him.

"And I'll gladly take it if you've spent long enough browsing."

Zach sighed, and took a crumpled five pound note from his pocket, his fingers brushing against Bree's note as he did so. His dad would have an old gardening glove and he could poke some nails through the end of the fingers, or he could tape some kitchen knives to them. It'd do. "I'll give the glove a miss, Mr. King, and take a box of..." He turned away from the Halloween display and looked at the chocolates behind the counter. "Roses. The box of Roses, please."

Mr. King reached up and took down the box. "Birthday present?"

"Just a gift for someone." The money exchanged hands, and the deal was done. To a fifteen-year- old boy a box of chocolates was the perfect present. Everybody liked chocolate. A niggling doubt told him perhaps he should have come up with something better, but it was soon put to the back of his mind as he left the shop and began to ponder how to carry the chocolates home while riding a bike.

***

Three cans on the floor. Three shots to take them down. One solitary can left perched on the log. Each can had a name, a name shared with one of the popular girls at school. The pretty ones. Rachel with her dark hair and smile, always full of fun and laughter, Jessica with the legs and arse that made up for her fried egg tits, and Wendy, whose chest was so developed you'd be forgiven for thinking she'd taken Jessica's share as well as her own when the boob genes were handed out. Those three were down. Down in the dirt where they belonged with a jagged hole torn right through each of them.

And then there was can four. No longer an empty Heinz baked beans can, but something more. The embodiment of all that she resented, all that she was envious of. The tin can represented the pinnacle of popularity within their small rural school, little Miss Perfect, the young lady blessed with long blonde hair, sparkling teeth, and a complexion as clear as a newborns backside. Miss Always-tanned and athletically toned. Miss Bloody U.S.A with the good grades and graceful manner. Miss Fucking- Annoying- Bitch Bree. All the fuss over Halloween this year was her fault. Damn Yank. All Hallows Eve had never been that important before; Bonfire Night was the traditional celebration, and Mischief Night the night for taking to the streets looking for trouble--not that she'd ever been allowed out. But then came Bree's excitable tales of "Trick or Treat" and bags full of sweets, or "candy", as she would say. Nothing more than an Army brat with no respect for custom and giving no thought for how things should be done. It was ridiculous...a childish excuse to play dress-up and go scrounging door to door. Even the teachers had bought into it, with the proviso nobody bothered any old people and didn't go into any stranger's homes. They said it was "an example of how two nations with a shared language could be so different". So different they were dumb enough to elect a half-arsed actor as President, according to her granddad. He'd never had time for Americans. "Bunch of cowboys who jump in at the last minute and think they won the bloody war single-handed," was his judgement. Mam said Grandma had liked the Americans who came over during the war a bit more than her overseas husband was comfortable with, (according to Uncle Frank anyway), and that was why Granddad couldn't stand 'em, however, Granddad's opinions were the ones that mattered to her, not those of the grandmother she'd never really known.

It was her Grandfather who had taught her how to shoot.

"It's your duty, lass, to be able to defend y'self, y' family and, if it comes to it, y' country."

She often heard his voice in her head, but it was stronger today; less like her imagination, and more like he was right there, whispering in her ear. Regardless of the comfort the voice brought her, it came with an undercurrent of unease. Though she had little time for the commercialised version of Halloween, it didn't mean she didn't respect its true nature: a time when the veil between this world and the next grows thin, and the normally impassable wall between life and death becomes a permeable membrane through which spirits can pass for one night only. Her mam had told her that, and she was the seventh child of a seventh child, which gave her knowledge of such things. Hearing the dead talk to you was a concern, even if it was somebody you loved with all your heart that was doing the talking.

"Now line up the last shot... steady girl," his voice was soft, and there was a smell of sweat and sweet snuff in the air as if he was right by her.

The voice was a calming worry, a soothing threat that all was well, but really wasn't.

"That might look like a tin can, but it's your enemy. You or him."

She could feel his strong arm around her waist as she looked down the barrel of the gun and lined up the sight. The gun felt light, just as it did when he used to take some of the weight for her so that she could hold it steady.

"It's a her," she muttered, as she slowed her breathing and took her finger from guard to trigger.

He'd been the gentlest man she'd ever known, kind and caring. But put a gun in his hand, or hers, and he changed. His experiences in the war had left a mark that never faded, as had the fates of his father ("gassed by them nasty Jerries,") and brother ("tortured by them vicious little yellow Jap bastards"). He used to say, "You have to be able to protect y'self darlin', from threats both abroad and close to home and there's no messing about when you've a gun in y'hand. It's there t' do a job, 'n' y' shouldn't have hold on it if y'aint gonna use it."

He'd taken her rabbiting with his .410, and promised to let her try the 12 bore when she was big enough. It hurt that his promise would never be kept; his passing away robbed her of the man and then the guns the police had taken away. They hadn't taken the air rifle, though. Nobody knew about that but her; a gift from the old man who'd told her to keep it loaded and keep it close. "Put it under y' bed and don't tell y' Mam or she'll 'ave our guts for garters."

"Under my bed? Really?" she said aloud, the year-old conversation now replaying itself in the present.

"Aye, lass. That's right. There's bad folk out there, bad lads in particular, and it's best to have protection and not need it than t'other way round."

She briefly wondered if her father had been a "bad lad"; he was certainly someone nobody ever wanted to talk about. But she wasn't thinking about bad lads at the moment. She was thinking of Bree Jackson, and as a green-eyed monster sat on one shoulder, and the ghost of her grandfather steadied her aim at the other, she took the shot, and a fourth can fell to the ground with a hole torn right through it.

***

At school, she felt like the invisible girl. Not attractive enough to draw attention, not ugly enough to draw cruelty. She was average at sport, academically adequate, and socially acceptable, when given the chance. Sometimes it was good to be left alone; at others, the isolation drove her mad, and only the internal voices kept her company. Tonight, she drifted through the streets, clearly visible in the white sheet with the roughly cut eyeholes, yet ignored by those she passed. Though they couldn't tell who she was, she could've been their best friend. She guessed she must have an aura about her, something that made people look the other way. It was a curse that one day she hoped would become an advantage--to be unseen in a crowd, remarkably unremarkable.

"Give me that Marathon!" shouted a Dracula, as he chased a toilet-papered mummy down the street.

She hurried, though she had plenty of time to get where she was going.

"Who the fuck are you supposed to be?" demanded somebody in a devil mask (that sounded like Phil Scarth) to Wendy Rees, who was wearing a tartan mini skirt and a top made out of a sack.

"Sawney Bean's Mr's."

Phil lifted his mask. "Who?"

"I don't know, it was my dad's idea. Come on, let's go to the playground."

A small piece of conversation overheard with disdain. Why did everyone have to have friends? Jessica was with them playing gooseberry, but managing to look stunning despite the zombie nurse outfit she wore, and no doubt Rachel wouldn't be far away. It was sickening. Why did *she* have to be the one walking the streets on her own while everyone else was in gangs of threes or fours?.

"Don't worry, love. The less people that get close to y' the less people are in position to hurt y'."

"Yes, Granddad," she answered.

"And you need to be on your own to finish off what you started, don't you?"

"Yes, Granddad,"

"Good." She felt his hand rest on her shoulder as she walked; a Halloween shade to keep her company, and a reminder that today, even if it was only for that one, single, day, she wasn't alone.

"Y' know wandering about i' this sheet, you'll scare the shit outta that darkie family that lives down ont' new estate."

She giggled. "You're not supposed to call people that any more, Granddad."

"My country. If the' don't like it the' can bugger off. Now 'a'n't we somewhere we need to be lass?"

She smiled. The rifle was awkward to carry under the sheet, but Granddad was right. Things to see and people to do. She picked up her pace a little bit more.

***

Had she intended to shoot him? She didn't know. What she *did* know was that she was shaking. Fear? Excitement? Adrenaline? All three? Was this the plan all along? No, it couldn't have been. She hadn't known how the boys would behave. Then why bring the gun? I. I. You told me to. Were you in danger? No, but Bree was. What do you care? I don't. Then why shoot? It wasn't right. What they were doing wasn't right. The dialogue was in her head.

"No, don't think like that. I'm here, it isn't in your head; I'm here, Granddad's here."

Tears joined the shaking; there was shouting somewhere in the distance.

"But you're dead. Am I insane?"

"There, there sweetheart. Y' no more barmy than anybody else in this world. You just go off to sleep and everything'll be fine. Things went just as planned."

The tower was cold, but sleep took her, and her dreams cemented in her mind the memory of what had happened.

***

It was a child's game. A plan with no defined outcome, at least she didn't think so. She certainly couldn't have foreseen how things would pan out, even as the daughter of a seventh child of a seventh child. But she had taken the rifle with her, and devised a costume that allowed her to conceal it as she had walked the streets. And she had taken a snipers position in the church without a second thought as to why. But why would she have done that if there hadn't been an intention, or at the very least, the awareness of the possibility that she may shoot someone before the night was out. Had she been guided? Or followed free will? It didn't matter anymore. What was done was done.

She'd stolen Bree's pink-papered notebook, and upon reading it learnt her secrets. She had then torn three pages from the book and prepared three notes... three very similar notes: one to Zach, one to Ben, and one to Tom. Was the aim to get the gifts? Perhaps. Was it an exercise of power, a way to control and manipulate them? Maybe. Or was it simply a way to cause trouble? A way to put a light to a fuse and stand back and watch the fireworks? That was probably what it was, too, but whatever the reason behind her charade, all three of them fell for it. All three delivered their gifts to the war memorial while she watched from the church tower. All three ignored the instruction to leave. All three ended up there at the same time.

"This is bollocks, man," declared Ben.

"Too fucking right it is," agreed Tom.

"What do you think she's playing at?" asked Zach.

"Dozy spastic," Tom snarled. "She's after the fucking gifts, isn't she? What did you bring?"

Zach looked at the ground and kicked at a pile of leaves as she watched from the church tower through her granddad's old field glasses. She could only just make out what they were saying.

"Well?" urged Ben.

"Box of Roses."

"Fuck me you're a charmer."

She felt sorry for Zach. He was there because she liked him, though he'd never paid her any attention, and *that* had made her mad, even if she did like him. She shouldn't have involved him, but she had. He was wearing a battered cowboy hat and a striped jumper, along with what looked like a rubber glove with four kitchen knives taped to the fingers. She sighed. It was a poor attempt at an outfit, but he still looked pretty fit. And he'd brought a box of her favourite chocolates. Those and Terry's chocolate orange.

"Time enough for that when you're older."

"Sorry," she muttered to the man who wasn't there, but whose tone of voice immediately drove any thoughts of romance from her mind.

The other two boys, however, were mean. Nevertheless, they tended to leave her alone-- her invisibility protecting her from them-- she saw how they treated others, and how they deserved to be treated themselves.

"Put down the binoculars, get the gun, and take aim at that little gobshite with the stupid thing on his head, but keep your finger off the trigger."

She followed her granddad's instruction without question. She trusted him implicitly. She aimed at Ben. He was wearing one of those rubber hats that make you look bald, but with lines drawn on it to form a grid and drawing pins stuck through wherever the lines intersected. A long leather jacket completed his outfit, a poor man's Pinhead that seemed oddly appropriate.

"What about you, y' prick?" Ben's cruel attention had now turned to Tom.

"I brought the bitch this." He grabbed at his crotch as he spoke. "The gift that keeps on giving."

"Yeah, giving fucking crabs."

"Fuck you, Ben."

A whisper in her right ear, "You should shoot that dirty shit in the balls."

"Now?"

"No, wait for it." Her granddad was lent so close, she could feel his whiskers against her cheek. She'd missed him so much.

"I'm glad you're here."

"I'm always here."

Down below Ben was continuing the conversation. "Fuck you more like, y' little wanker."

"So come on Romeo, what's in that little parcel?" goaded Tom, who was now taking his turn to taunt Ben.

"Silver bangle. Proper sterling and hallmarked too."

"Must be love, eh Zachy boy?" mocked Tom. He nudged Zach in the ribs as he spoke. His Jason Vorhees mask had risen up onto the top of his head and for a moment the empty eyes looked straight up at where she sat in the bell tower. It gave her a chill, but her granddad's arms were around her, just like when he used to bring her up here and they'd sit for a while after he'd wound the church clock.

"You can see all sorts from up here," he would say. "Life and death all set out below y'"

Ben was busy defending his choice of gift. "Love's got nowt to do with it. I'm just after a bit of action with that hot Yankee fanny of hers. Besides, it didn't cost me nuthin', I twoked it off me mums dresser; she's tonnes of this shit."

The bickering carried on for a while as her granddad held her close and told her to be patient and watch the drama unfold. Then decide if anyone needed to be dealt with.

"Why am I here, Granddad?"

"Because you've set up a house of cards, and now we'll see how they fall."

"Will I need to shoot anybody?"

"We'll see. But don't worry if that's how it turns out. It's easier to shoot a person than an animal. People do bad things-- nasty, wicked things. If you can shoot an innocent bunny, you can shoot an evil man. Or boy."

"But we ate the rabbits we shot."

"Not the ones sufferin' wi' mixi we didn't. We were putting them out of their misery and some people need putting out of their misery, too, or at least stopping from causing other folk harm. Anyway, here comes y' friend."

It was Bree. Her black and purple witch's outfit fit her perfectly, her long slender legs stretching below the thigh-high skirt in fishnet tights and her silver earrings and bangles glinting in the moonlight in a way that made her sparkle like a star in the night sky.

"Well, well, well," said Ben. "Come to pick a winner?"

"I've come for my notebook. Now which of you three's got it?"

The girl had an air of authority; a presence that, for a fleeting moment, generated the respect of her nemesis in the tower. A respect swiftly replaced with an envy that swung the barrel of an air-rifle to point at Bree's pretty, but angry face.

"Come on, sweetheart, you can't go shooting people out of jealousy. You're better than that. She's done nothing to you. She's just fuel you added to the fire."

Her granddad was right. Bree was only there because of the fourth note she'd written. A note she'd typed on another page torn from the stolen pad that offered the return of the rest, providing, of course, she attended the midnight meet. All the pieces were now in place. The stock of the rifle settled into her shoulder. She slowed her breathing and aimed at Ben. Then switched to Tom, and then back to Ben again. She imagined what it would be like to shoot one of them in the head with a real weapon, not the toy she was restricted to, and began to get excited; her heartbeat increasing when she should have been controlling it, keeping herself calm and her aim true.

What happened next, happened fast...

Ben showed Bree a sheet of her notepaper in his hand and demanded to know what she was playing at. She denied all knowledge of the notes the boys had received, as you would expect, since it was the truth, and lunged for the sheet of paper as he waved it toward her face. Ben was too quick for her, though, grabbing her and spinning her around and down to the ground. There was shouting.

Bree yelling at Ben, "Get off me!"

Ben snarling back, "You're gonna get what you deserve for dicking us about! "

Zach shouting, "Stop! You're hurting her!"

Tom shoving Zach. "What are you, bent? We can all have a crack if you shut the fuck up."

There was pushing and pulling. Was the aim to scare or hurt? To touch Bree up? To go further?

"See? They've shown what they really are—bad lads."

"You knew this would happen."

"How could I?"

"The dead know things."

"I'm not dead, I'm part of you. Now sort 'em out."

Shouting, screaming, four bodies mingled into one. The clock struck twelve, a shot rang out, then a piercing scream. She'd aimed for Ben, but Zach was holding his face and she knew she'd missed her target. How could she have? She never missed, the fucking clock! Tom was running. Ben was running. Bree was crying. Zach was on the floor. Her granddad was quiet. She crawled into a corner where it was cold. Her granddad comforted her, telling her that the first time is the hardest-- but it gets easier--and everyone misses sometimes... it's the just way the world works. As sleep began to take hold, his voice faded, and the approaching sirens seemed a world away.

***

She woke early. Though the police had been and left, she stayed hidden until mid-morning. Her granddad was gone. The blood on the grass wasn't. New voices whispered at the edges of her consciousness, introducing themselves as guests granted entry to her mind by the events of All Hallows Eve. She could ignore them...for now. They were insistent--and would have to be heeded eventually--but she was too drained to pay attention, and too cold and sore to care. As she slowly walked home past rows of dementedly grinning pumpkins and turnips, all of whom seemed to laugh at how she'd screwed up her shot, she determined she would never miss again.

The End

First Shot, is a short prequel to 'You Only Get One Shot,' a novella written by J.C. Michael and Kevin J. Kennedy

Hollowed Be Thy

By

Stuart Keane

"You can't escape, and there's no way out."

The woman said it matter-of-factly and with certain conviction.

She dragged the axe behind her, its vicious steel blade scraping the rough, uneven concrete. The weapon left a small trail of blood behind her, remnants of her recent victim, smearing the boring grey with a thin streak of bright vermilion. The woman was limping and laughing, the pain making her delirious and, coincidently, extremely dangerous.

She's already dangerous, thought Jacques. *The bitch has a fucking axe.*

"This basement has one way in and one way out. And you're heading in the wrong direction, sweetie." The woman laughed, the distorted sound echoing off the solid, dark walls.

Jacques didn't want to believe the woman's words, but the way she said it, and the tone of her voice, told him that he was in serious trouble. He knew he was heading into a dead end, but it was that, or take a blow from the axe.

The thought made him shrivel up inside.

Jacques retreated further into the basement.

He discovered a set of stairs and glanced into the haunting darkness below. Maybe he could find a dark corner to hide in, trick or flank her, and get behind her. If he remembered the way out, he could run past the crazy bitch. She'd have no hope at catching him with the busted knee. He half-smiled when he remembered kicking her. The sound of her kneecap popping had put a hopeful spring in his step.

A small victory, but a victory nonetheless.

He heard the woman's staggered footsteps behind him. Jacques gulped, took a final look at the stairs, and started to descend.

He had no choice.

The woman's words haunted him.

There's no escape.

That's what she wants you to think. Don't give in; you can get out of this.

Jacques hoped he was right, as he stepped off the last stair and walked into the darkness.

Something splashed under his feet.

Then his hands hit the flat, smooth wall ahead of him, signaling the end of the path. The cool, slick plaster blazed through his hot, sweaty palms, making him jolt in surprise and shock. He looked left and right; saw nothing but wall and smooth mortar-covered bricks, the same for the entire room. The swinging, dim bulb above exposed very little with its very small cone of yellow, blinking light. He was in a cubic room with one exit; the way he'd come in.

How many other basements do you know with more than one exit?

A cold pang shot up his spine. The squelching sound was getting louder, emanating from beneath him. He moved his feet and felt a soggy sensation fill his sneakers.

He looked down, squinting in the low light. His eyes focused.

The light swung back behind him, lighting the mess below.

Jacques screamed.

He jumped back, his sweat-soaked chamois shirt slapping against the mortar behind him. Jacques receded back, heading deeper into the dark room. A sour, coppery smell attacked his nostrils, sending a nauseous rippling to his stomach. His feet slipped and slid, and he fell, placing his hands behind him. A huge plop filled the air as his rump and hands hit the soaked surface beneath him. The vision of the mutilated corpse inches in front of him; his feet submerged in its eviscerated chest cavity, would haunt him for the rest of his days.

Or minutes. Maybe seconds.

"I see you found my abattoir. How fitting."

The woman stepped into the doorway. The light from behind cast her as a demented, hunched over silhouette. Her hair, nothing but black in the dimly-lit basement, hung scraggily over the dark form of her body. The unmistakable outline of the axe, tilted in her hand, leaning menacingly against her injured leg, and made Jacques moan in anguish.

He felt his bladder release; urine streamed down his leg, soaked his trousers, and flowed onto the sodden surface below him. As he backed away, he felt cold, dead, soggy flesh lick his slippery skin. The blood was everywhere. Nausea took a back seat to the fear riveting through his body. His heart boomed in his chest and his breath caught, coming in short, frantic gasps.

His eyes didn't leave the woman.

She took a step forward.

Jacques crawled back. "Why are you doing this?"

"It's my masterpiece. And it's nearly complete."

"What ... what masterpiece?" Jacques backed into another wall. Tears began to roll down his face, but he didn't realize he was crying. His attention was diverted to the horror before him, and some kind of adrenaline rush protected his sanity from his imminent fate. His body wasn't ready to go into shutdown. His eyes burned from focusing on his predator, the woman who was surely going to kill him.

"You'll see. You're part of it, Jacques. You've always been part of it..."

The woman stepped forward again, her left hand grasping the oak handle of the axe. Jacques noticed a low, wet swishing noise as she dragged her injured leg towards him. He would have prayed to the gods – had it mattered – and thanked them for keeping the room dark. The sound of the gallons of blood was bad enough, it wasn't something he needed to see.

The woman hoisted the axe into her hands and laughed.

"You don't have to do this … we can talk. You can let me go. No one needs to know…"

"Oh, but I do. It's of the utmost importance."

And with that, the woman swung the axe, lopping Jacques' head from his shoulders with one savage swipe. His heavy head, skull and skin and brain and sinew, spun into the air, sweaty hair whipping, and bounced onto the blood-soaked concrete with a sodden splash. It hit the wall with a solid *thunk* and came to a rest beside a dismembered arm. The woman looked down at the limb and noticed a rat chewing on the fingers. The rat ignored her as it feverishly devoured its meal.

She laughed and scooped up the blood-spattered head. Jacques's corpse toppled behind her, splashing in the blood that flowed around it. Its sliced neck hole sprayed in arcs, adding to the crimson floor. Moments later, it was a part of the room – another headless corpse that littered her soundproof, slaughterhouse basement.

"Mom, where's my shirt?"

"What shirt?"

"My best shirt, the blue one."

"It's on your bed, where I left it."

Jack looked behind him, in the reflection of his mirror. His bed was a mess; the duvet crumpled over and haphazard, the red sheets below wrinkled from last night's restless sleep. A pillow hung off the edge of the mattress. He walked over, turned the duvet and saw the shirt he was looking for. He picked it up by the hanger beneath its shoulders and placed it on the door handle.

With one firm stroke of his hand, he swished some dust from the garment. It hadn't creased. He smiled.

"Perfect."

"You find it?"

"Yeah, thank you."

Muffled footsteps came along the upstairs hall and Jack's mother appeared in the doorway. She leaned against the white woodwork and folded her arms. Her eyes brimmed with pride, and a grin turned her full lips. "Look at you, all handsome."

Jack jumped, splashing cologne on his white vest. "Jesus, Mom. You scared the shit out of me." He put the small bottle down and spread the scent around his body with roaming hands.

"Hey, less of the cursing in the house." She continued smiling. "Anyway, where are you going tonight?"

"I have a date. Remember?"

"Oh yes, with the woman from the bookstore. Where are you taking her?"

"I was thinking somewhere Italian ... Pirlo's maybe..."

"Nice. Very romantic."

A comfortable silence filled the air. Jack pushed his arms into the shirt, the cuffs flapping as he did so. He moved his arms up and down, loosening the ironed material. He removed it and put it back on the bed behind him.

"Tell me how you met again?" his mother asked.

"I already did."

"I know it was in a bookstore ... it's not a normal place for chatting to strangers. How did you meet? I mean like, the circumstances, you know?"

"Didn't I tell you...?"

"Yes, but it's so romantic. Like ...you couldn't write this sort of stuff. It's like a Harlequin novel, only better. And real."

"What the hell is a Harlequin?"

Jack's mother shook her head. "Never mind. Just tell me, please."

He sighed. "Nothing to tell, Mom." Jack buckled his belt. He checked his hair for the umpteenth time and grabbed the shirt. "I asked about a book at the counter, she was there when I did, asking for the same book." Slipped his arms into the sleeves. "We started chatting, we had a bit in common and she asked me out."

His mother stepped into the room, a frown on her face. "She asked you? You didn't tell me that."

Jack tucked his shirt in. "Is it important? Women do that, don't they?"

"Yeah, sometimes. Not often, but sometimes."

"So why the fuss?" Jack buttoned his shirt up and stepped back, holding his arms out. "What do you think? Too much?" He half twirled; checking the sides of his shirt, making sure it was tucked in properly.

"Handsome. My boy is all grown up. I'm so proud of you." She leaned in for a kiss on the cheek. Jack leaned away. "Gross, Mom." He smiled, sheepishly.

"She's a lucky girl." She patted him on the back, walked towards the door, paused, and turned back to her son. "Remember, you're taking your cousin, Scotty, trick-or-treating tomorrow. And don't be late, you have school in the morning. Have a good time tonight, okay?"

"I will. And it's college, not school."

"Love you, Jack."

"Ewww, sick." His mother narrowed her eyes in his direction. He noticed it in the mirror and their eyes met. Jack sighed. "Love you, too, Mom." She left, plodding off down the carpeted hallway. Jack clasped his watch around his wrist and took one final look in the mirror.

"Perfect."

Jack walked out of his room. Collected his cellphone and keys from the nightstand before flicking the lights off. He took the stairs two at a time and landed in the lounge. His mother was standing before him, looking out of the window, her fingers between two slats of the blinds. Jack frowned. "You okay, Mom?"

A small yelp. She turned and held a hand to her chest. "My God, now who's scaring people? I'm fine, a delivery truck for UPS just arrived." She looked at the clock on the wall. "It's nearly eight. A little late, isn't it?"

"They deliver at all times, Mom. Anyway, wish me luck."

"Good luck, you'll knock her dead."

Jack smiled and opened the front door. He walked down the path, checking his cellphone for messages. He nodded to the UPS delivery person who walked by. His mother appeared in the doorway as he climbed into the car.

Jack started the vehicle and drove off, heading into town.

The UPS person reached the door. "Mrs. J. Walker?"

"That's me."

The Italian restaurant, Pirlo's, was a small, independent bistro on the corner of Bachman Street. Situated between a butcher-slash-delicatessen and a grocer – both of which supplied the restaurant with the freshest ingredients and a sense of local hospitality – it was the perfect place for a first date.

Jack knew it well, and he'd been here with his parents in the past. Before his father had left them, he'd taken them for dinner once a month. They made the best spaghetti and meatballs in town. The marinara sauce was sublime, one of a kind.

Jack glanced at his date and offered a nervous smile. Emma returned the gesture and looked down at the table, her arms in front of her, hands in her lap, unsure.

Jack took a chance. "You look beautiful tonight."

"Charmer." She sipped her water and looked around, taking in the view. Jack felt a swell of pride. He knew Pirlo's was quaint, borderline exclusive, well decorated and romantic. The low music and the clatter of kitchenware lent the place an ambience of relaxation and peace. Jack had been here multiple times and never once had he felt rushed during his meal. The sign of a decent, family-run restaurant. Emma turned back to him.

"This is a beautiful place. Have you been here before?"

"Yes, with my folks. Several times. Never on a ... date."

"Well, I'm honored to be your first female dining companion."

"Apart from my Mom."

Jackass, he thought. Emma chuckled and sipped her water. Jack grimaced and looked away, feeling the blush spread across his cheeks. "I'm sorry."

"Not a problem." Emma observed, her wonderful eyes searching his and relaxing him. As if saying: *You're doing fine, I'm nervous, too. We're both nervous, this doesn't happen to us often.*

Jack hoped that was the case. He really did.

Emma was an attractive girl. Her brown hair, flecked with blonde highlights, curled at the edges so it caressed her petite visage. Every time she looked around, the locks swished silently against her face. Her stark brown eyes shone in the candlelight, and the homely luminosity bestowed the look of a supermodel. Her mouth was small, lips the right shape. Her nose was button-like, which gave her a striking aura of cuteness at the right angle.

Jack smiled on reflex. Emma glanced around once more. "Family business?"

"For forty years. Pirlo is the surname of the family. They make the best Italian food in Lake Whisper. Coming from experience."

"Ah, so you're a foodie."

"A what?"

"You like good food. You know what's hot and what's not." Emma said it like it was a fact.

"I know it's better than a burger and fries."

"An enema is better than a burger and fries."

Jack frowned. "What?"

Emma laughed. "That's a little exaggerated. Sorry, ignore me, it's been a long day."

Jack nodded. *Long day. Am I inconveniencing her?*

An awkward silence settled over them. Jack noticed a basket of bread on the next table and welcomed a distraction. *Maybe a waiter will bring one over soon.* He wiped his brow. "Is it hot in here?"

Emma reached across the table and placed her hand on his fist, which was opening and closing. Her touch was cool, welcomed. She wore flesh-colored nail varnish, which shone in the flickering candlelight. Her fingers were dainty, long, and slim. "Don't worry, Jack. You're doing absolutely fine."

"I am?" He grinned, half-believing her.

"I'm yours for the evening. I asked you out for a reason. If I didn't want to be here, I wouldn't be here. Enjoy yourself, I'm enjoying the company." With that, she leaned back and removed her arms from in front of her.

Jack's worries washed away and suddenly, the evening became a lot calmer. He breathed out, commending his luck in his head and grabbed his menu. He handed one to Emma and opened his own. They scanned the options, her eyes moving slowly, his already decided. Emma licked her lips. "What's good here?" She winked at Jack. "Coming from a resident expert..."

He chuckled. "The spaghetti and meatballs is excellent. The secret recipe sauce is the best I've ever tasted."

"Sold. I also need some garlic bread. Or is that redundant and boring of me?"

Jack chuckled. "Have whatever you want, who cares what people think?"

"True."

A waiter stepped over with a notepad. He didn't leave any bread. His pace was hurried, anxious, as if he didn't want to be there. Jack raised his head, smiling nervously at the newcomer. Emma watched Jack for a split second before joining him.

The waiter cleared his throat. "Would you like to see the wine list?" An English accent, which took Jack by surprise. The waiter's pointed nose and blond hair spoke of Scandinavian heritage. Maybe there was a shred of it in there somewhere. The waiter raised his pad. He didn't smile.

"Erm..." Jack fumbled, realizing he was underage. Emma slid her foot up his leg, distracting him. He gazed at her and she smiled. Her eyes turned to the waiter and Emma leaned on her hand, elbow placed on the table. "No, thank you. Can we get a bottle of the house red?"

"A wise choice, madam." The waiter walked off. Once he was gone, Jack hushed his voice and looked at his date. "We're underage."

"You might be. I'm twenty-three. How old are you?"

"Twenty. But..."

"Shhh, it's fine. Have you drunk wine before?"

"Homemade stuff ... once. And some beer."

Emma winked at him. "It's fine. Let's have some fun. Besides, it's nice to learn I'm not a total cradle-snatcher. Only twenty. You're very cute for a man just out of his teens. A great complexion, nice smile. Going into that bookshop was the best decision of my life."

"You're just saying that." Jack tried to follow up his statement, but couldn't think of what to say. Emma leaned in. "Yes, but it doesn't mean it's a lie. I'm an honest person, I speak the truth."

At that point, the waiter returned and showed them the wine. Without looking, Emma nodded. He placed the wine on the table and left. Jack glanced at his date; her smile was absolutely radiant. He leaned in. "I'm glad I went into the bookshop, too. Who'd have thunk more than one person likes 1984."

"It's only a classic. Shocking, really." Emma laughed.

And with that, the night flowed smoothly. They drank two bottles of house red – an oaky Merlot with a fruity aftertaste – and shared a spaghetti and meatballs with side orders of garlic bread and ravioli. The meal was plentiful and filling, and there was no room for dessert. The conversation was elegant, relaxed, and friendly. They split the tab and found themselves on the sidewalk two hours later.

"Tonight was great, thank you." Emma squeezed Jack's hand between her fingers.

Jack looked at her. "My pleasure."

Emma moved in close. "Look. I want to invite you back to mine … but I have an early day tomorrow. What say we hang out tomorrow night? You can come to mine, I'll make us some dinner and we can curl up while watching a movie."

"Sounds perfect."

Emma leaned in and kissed Jack on the lips. A jolt of electricity coursed through his veins. Her lips were soft, moist, with a hint of strawberry. The faint smell of wine tickled his nostrils. Her scent soon followed, engulfing him, making him close his eyes. Emma hooked her arms behind him and pulled into his body. The kiss became deep and forceful. Tongues delicately caressed one another.

After a few moments, they separated. "Wow." Jack wiped his lip with the side of his finger and gazed into Emma's eyes. Emma matched it, a look of lust betraying her dilated pupils. "Tomorrow … we can pick up where this kiss left off."

Jack nodded. "I'd like that."

He hailed a cab for Emma. A blue sedan pulled to the curb and he opened the door for her. Emma slipped a piece of paper into his hand. "My number. Text me."

"Sure."

She climbed into the car. Jack watched it pull from the curb, waved, and felt a sudden loss at seeing Emma leave.

This was possibly the best night of his life.

Then it dawned on him. The two bottles of wine, the amazing company, the succulent smell of Emma's perfume. His blood alcohol level. He stood helpless beside his vehicle.

"Shit, I can't drive home."

He took his cellphone from his pocket and dialed his house phone. He checked his watch. Just before ten, would Mom be in bed? The phone rang several times before clicking to the answering machine. *You've reached the home of…*

Jack hung up. "Shit."

Jack walked a few feet down the road and hailed another cab. Another sedan, yellow this time, veered and pulled to the curb. Climbing into the back, he directed the driver home.

Twenty minutes later, he was walking up his front path. He noticed the lights were off and the house was dark. Even the porch light was dimmed, which was weird. Mom always left it on to deter burglars. He shook his head and walked through the door. He didn't notice the door was unlocked as he stumbled through the entrance, closing it behind him. His head started to blur due to the wine.

He flicked the porch light on and stumbled up the stairs.

Within minutes, Jack was comatose on his bed.

The throb of a hangover stirred Jack from his deep slumber. A groan emitted from his lips, and quickly ceased when the sound became too much. He lapsed into silence – glorious, comforting silence. He pulled the warm duvet over his head and closed his eyes.

The shrill sound of the alarm clock almost gave him a heart attack.

He jumped out of bed, flung the duvet onto the floor, slid on it a little as it caught the carpet, and tapped the top of the clock. His eyes narrowed against the harsh sunlight that streamed through his blinds. Using a forearm, he shielded his eyes, ambled back to the bed and lay on its warm, comforting surface. He glanced at the clock.

It read 07:30.

"Shit." He realized college was imminent.

He pushed his face into the pillow and groaned.

After a moment, he realized he hadn't heard his mother. Normally, she would come in and wake him up, or prompt him, should he miss the alarm. After last night, he expected her to appear at the crack of dawn for an update. His mother was too curious.

Curiosity killed the cat.

But she hadn't come. He couldn't hear any of the usual sounds of the morning. No whistling or singing and no running shower. The smells were absent too. The fresh coffee, the sweet aroma of bacon and eggs. Her Celine Dion CD would sometimes be playing if she was in the mood. This particular morning lacked any Canadian crooning.

He heard nothing.

Absolute silence filled the household.

He listened harder; hoping his ears were simply affected by too many Italian grapes. He listened for a full minute.

Still nothing.

Which startled him a little.

Did she have a date he didn't know about? An early meeting? Jack rubbed his sore head, willing the hangover to vanish. His mother was right, she warned him to drink less because of college. He hadn't heeded her advice.

He thought of Emma, her beautiful face, the dream-like eyes. Her fragrance. The way she spoke, her lips turning at the corner; he wondered if she was aware of it. Such a wonderful evening.

He'd be seeing her tonight.

Immediately, he decided he was going to skip class. What's the worst that could happen from missing a seminar about different types of paper? The thought of class bells and slamming lockers and screaming kids was too much for him. His cranium pulsated on the pillow at the sheer thought. He leaned down, collected his duvet and pulled it back onto the bed. He smothered himself in it and closed his eyes.

Within seconds, he was asleep.

Jack swallowed half a glass of orange juice in a few seconds. His eyes wandered to the fridge and its assortment of magnets, leaflets and junk. His mother had left him a note, one he'd been told about last night. It completely skipped his mind.

It dawned on him now, though.

His evening with Emma might have to wait.

"Shit."

He grabbed his cellphone and swiped the screen, unlocking it. *Should I phone Emma or is that too needy?* Jack bit his lip, thinking.

He decided to text instead.

His fingers danced over the digital keyboard built into his iPhone. Within seconds, the text box read: *Hi, it's Jack. Thanks for a wonderful evening last night. Tonight: Trick R Treating with my cousin. Forgot about it. Raincheck? Xx*

His thumb hovered over the send button. After a second, he deleted the two kisses on the end and sent it.

No need to look pathetic.

Jack finished his orange juice. He took his toast from the toaster and plonked the slices on a plate. His phone skittered across the kitchen surface.

He had a text from Emma.

Hiya. No problem, come around after, if you want? Day off for me tomorrow. Late night could be fun ;) Last night was gr8. X

Jack felt a tremor of excitement sliver up his spine. She'd used a kiss on the end so he now knew the protocol. His tongue poked out as he constructed the reply: *Hello. No problem, can be around at 10? Shouldn't be out long. Tonight sounds like fun. I'll bring dinner. X*

He buttered his toast, sat down, and started to eat. He eyed the leaflets on the fridge. Nothing. No clues as to his mother's whereabouts.

Must have an early meeting. It's happened before.

Something felt a little off about it, though.

His phone jumped again. With a mouthful of breakfast, he read the reply from Emma: *No problem, food sounds good. Bring Pepsi and condoms. ;) See you soon xx*

Jack gasped out loud. His cheeks burned with embarrassment and he couldn't help but smile at Emma's audacity and forwardness. He'd noticed the lust in her eyes last night, but passed it off as the wine talking.

You were so wrong, he thought.

Jack clicked a quick reply: *Sure. Tonight can't come soon enough. Xx*

He paused and smiled. She'd put it out there. He changed the word come to cum. Feeling brave, Jack sent the message.

No going back now.

Jack finished his toast. After washing the plate, he slumped on the sofa and turned on the TV. He started to relax, not watching the shows so much as staring blankly at the screen. His mind was on the evening ahead. He might be having sex tonight.

He hoped so.

It was Halloween, after all.

Scotty was working on his third Snickers bar before Jack confiscated his earnings for the evening. He looked down into the plastic bucket. Scotty had enough sugar in there to start a diabetes war. Snickers, Twizzlers, Black Jacks, Baby Ruth's, M&Ms, Milky Ways, Twinkies and many more. With a mouthful, Scotty grabbed for the bucket. "That's my candy. Give it."

"You've had enough. Your mom will be pissed if you get chunks all over your costume. She paid good money for that."

"You said a swear."

"What? Pissed? That's not a swear."

"Is so. Dollar in the swear jar." Scotty spat peanut and nougat as he spoke. He finished the Snickers and put the rubbish in his pocket. "I'll tell Mom."

They stopped on the sidewalk. Jack sighed and pulled his wallet from his back pocket. Jack removed a five and put it in the bucket. "I'll do you a deal. Here's a five. That's a mountain of Snicker bars. You can keep it and I get to curse if I see fit, but you can't tell your mom, deal?"

Scotty thought about it, twisting his lips and creasing his forehead in thought. "Deal."

"Good boy." They walked for a moment, taking in the brisk, autumn evening. Jack looked down at his six-year-old cousin. He was dressed in a sheriff outfit, complete with gun belt, fake pistol, handcuffs and various other plastic gadgets. His brown shirt held a shiny, silver badge that read SHERIFF. His brown cowboy hat finished the getup, matching his brown trousers and shoes. He looked like the real deal. His gun belt clinked as he walked.

"What's chunks?"

"Huh?" Jack gazed down the street. A couple of little devils, one red and one pink, crossed the road. A group of child-like zombies accosted a man walking the opposite path, who fell over laughing, whilst a vampire and a Frankenstein held hands, chatting to one another. Several ghosts, portrayed by mutilated bed sheets, ran around making *oooooo* noises.

Halloween in Lake Whisper was a huge occasion; everyone got involved.

"What's chunks?"

"What are you talking about?"

"You said it just now. You don't want me getting chunks on my outfit?"

Jack laughed. "Oh, that. Yeah, if you eat too much chocolate, you'll throw up. Chunks is sick, puking. You've had three Snickers. Even *I* can't eat that many. You're a brave, but silly, little boy." Jack took the cowboy hat from Scotty's head and ruffled his hair.

Scotty scrunched up his tiny face. "Why didn't you get dressed up?"

Jack gave him back the hat. "I'm too old for this. It's for kids. Adults don't dress up, we do other things instead."

"Like what?" They turned the corner onto Scotty's street and soon reached his front gate.

"Making drinks and food, getting the sweets ready to give to all the sheriffs and ghouls and demons that knock on the door. Remember, if we don't keep the demons at bay, bad stuff happens. That's why you need to brush your teeth and say your prayers, okay?"

Scotty nodded, not saying anything. Jack felt a little bad for blackmailing the boy, but hey, in a world of torrential social media and imminent threat, some kids could be protected from the stark reality. He was just following his aunt's way of parenting.

"Can we go back out again? I didn't get enough candy."

Jack smiled. "I think you got plenty. Remember; don't eat it all at once."

Megan, Jack's aunt, stepped up behind them, her arms folded, a smile on her face. Jack winked at her. He turned to Scotty and bent down, looking him in the eye "And whatever you do, don't let your mother eat any, it's good candy for sheriffs who uphold the law." He handed him the orange bucket of goodies.

Scotty rolled his eyes. "Whatever." He laughed and skipped up the path, past his mother, and into the house. Jack straightened up and turned to Megan. "Any trouble?" she asked.

"None at all. Good as gold, as always."

"Thank you for taking him. It's nice to have some time alone with what's going on … you know, in the news?"

Jack shook his head. "What news?"

"Don't tell me you haven't heard?"

"Heard what?" Jack narrowed his eyes. Megan's face dropped like she was bearing some bad news. Jack noticed immediately. "Aunt Megan?"

A chilly wind picked up. Megan shivered. "It's cold. You'd better get home."

And with that, Megan started walking back to the house.

Jack frowned. *That was weird.*

Megan scooted up the path and disappeared inside.

Jack stood alone on the sidewalk.

The wind ceased a little. The laughter of children filled the dark, crisp evening. Jack looked along the street at the various Halloween ornaments, displays and memorabilia. One garden had a full graveyard on its lawn, complete with gravestones and a coffin protruding from the shattered earth. Several inflatable skeletons on various houses wobbled in the breeze.

Jack walked back the way he came.

He took out his cellphone and unlocked it. With a few dashes on the screen, he typed a text to Emma: *On my way, see you soon xx*

"This is an awesome house. You live here alone?"

"I do now. Was my folks'. They left it in the will."

"The will?" Jack gulped. "Shit, I'm sorry."

Emma nodded; her bottom lip trembled a little. "It's okay. I never really got on with my folks, anyway. We weren't that sort of family. Not the hug and pep talk and evening dinner types."

"Yeah, but still. Losing them at your age..."

"Can we not discuss it ... please?" Her voice wavered and Jack nodded, not saying a word. He sat on the soft, green sofa. Emma turned, wiping a tear from her eye. "Drink?"

"I'll have a Pepsi, please."

"Sure." Emma turned and walked into the kitchen. She vanished through a curved archway. Jack looked around the room. TV and DVD, fireplace — not lit — and a huge mirror hanging above. Ornaments on several shelves and plush, grey carpet. The blinds on the window were closed, the curtains hooked onto the wall. The room smoldered with a warm orange glow. It made Jack feel sleepy.

"We have DVD's upstairs if you want to watch something?" Emma walked over to the sofa and handed Jack a cold can of Pepsi. She was carrying a can for herself and some chips. She placed them on a small, wooden table beside the sofa.

"Sounds great."

"Have you got school tomorrow?"

"It's not school, it's college. But yes, I have. I can skip it, though. Brushstrokes are so boring!"

"What do you do?"

"I'm studying art, painting ... stuff like that."

"Won't you get into trouble for bunking off?"

"Bunking off?"

Emma smiled. "Otherwise known as skipping class." Jack watched her lips for a moment. He licked his own lip. The glow of the room cast a delicate orange hue over Emma's beautiful face. He smiled. "Ah, okay."

"So, will you?"

"Will I what?" Jack sipped his Pepsi.

"Get into trouble?"

"They won't even notice I'm missing."

"Good. I want you all to myself tonight."

"Then, I'm all yours."

Emma said nothing. Her smile turned into a grin and her eyes sparkled in the room's low luminosity. She stood up. "I'll dish up dinner."

"Sure thing, I'll help."

Emma walked through the arch again. Jack followed.

"Wow!"

The kitchen was huge. Every surface was made of steel or black marble granite and everything sparkled. The oven, a six-hob machine, sat boldly at the back of the room, parallel to a huge, central island counter topped with black marble. Various utensils hung above it, within an extended hand's reach. The double fridge was black and clean, so clean he could see a distorted reflection of himself in it. Every worktop was spotless and immaculate, bordered by smaller appliances like toasters, coffee machines and various foods like bread, cookies and spices. A knife rack sat angled in a corner.

Emma stepped over to two grease-darkened sacks that sat on the central island. A puff of steam rose from within. She took out two cheeseburgers, three portions of fries and a bag of onion rings. Emma laughed. "I thought you said you didn't like burgers?"

"I said no such thing. I simply prefer fine dining to burgers. There's a difference."

"Don't tell me there's an enema in here too?"

They laughed in unison.

Emma took two plates from a slot in the counter below her. She organized the food on the plates. "Want some bread?"

"Because a burger doesn't have enough?" Jack smiled.

"No, for the fries. Or a chip butty as the English call it?"

"Chips? They're fries."

"The English call them chips. Pie and chips, guvnor!"

"That's either informative or blatantly racist."

"Do you want some bread or not?" Emma leered, leaning on the counter, looking back over her shoulder. Jack ran his eyes over her form, the curve of her breasts, leaning over the food they were about to consume. The arch in her back, her shapely thighs – hardly contained in a pair of red jean shorts – and her toned, slender arms. She looked heavenly. Her hair cascaded down her back. His eyes met hers.

"I can eat it cold," he said.

Emma smiled. "At least something will be cold." She turned and walked towards him, her left leg gave way and she winced.

"You okay?" Jack asked.

"Yeah, I'm ... fine."

Jack stepped forward. "Why are you limping? It looks like it hurts."

"Nothing really. Popped a kneecap a few days back. No biggie."

"Did you get a doctor to check it? You look too young and hot to have arthritis but, hey, you never know."

Emma placed her hands on Jack's shoulders and kissed him. She wrapped her arms around his neck. Her skin was smooth and cool and smelt of strawberries. Her lips were moist and soft, her tongue urgent and probing. Her hands moved to his back and lowered to his belt buckle. With a few swift swipes, his belt was loose and his trousers clattered on the black tiles below. Emma was breathing hard. "Do you want me?"

"What do you think?"

Emma knelt down and took him in her mouth, his penis entered a warm, moist cavern. Her tongue flicked over his manhood, teasing the tip. Jack arched his back and groaned, placing his hand in her hair. Then it was over as she stood up and kissed him again. "Hmmmm, that's going to feel amazing when it's inside my cunt."

Jack moaned. "What's stopping you?"

"In due course. There's no point in rushing it. We have all night."

Emma took Jack's hand and slid it in her jean shorts. His fingers touched the soft, velvety flesh of her thighs before being forced higher. His fingers caressed a slick wetness and Emma moaned, closing her legs on his slippery fingertips. She took his fingers out and placed them in her mouth. She sucked them and slid them out slowly. "God, I taste amazing."

Jack's eyes were frantic now. "I bet you do."

Emma smiled, licking her lips. She cupped his balls in her palm and squeezed gently. Jack gasped and moaned, surprised and aroused at the same time. Her hand closed around his penis and she started to stroke up and down.

Her eyes met his, watching him. He saw a darkness materialize, fill her eyes, possess her. The smile on her amazing lips arched into a grin, then a grimace and finally a scowl. He heard her teeth clamp down, clattering against each other. The eyes were dark, but not with arousal.

They were dark with hatred and pain.

He didn't see her pull the knife out of her waistband.

She placed it under his erect penis and leant in close. "I wouldn't move if I were you."

Jack froze, lost in the sensation of her hand masturbating him to an erection. He looked at her face, which no longer glowed with joy or lust. Hard lines had formed under her eyes and mouth. Lines born from pain and neglect and suffering.

Her eyes were dark and void like in the fluorescent lights.

What the fuck?

Her warm palm released him and his penis sagged a little, lowering across the cool, unforgiving blade. The cold shock made him shudder. He gasped. All warmth and arousal seeped from his body within seconds. He felt his penis become flaccid and hoped the knife wasn't too sharp.

Emma placed her mouth by his ear. "Stand still. Very, very still."

Jack did as instructed. "Why..."

Emma chuckled. The laugh oozed with evil, brimmed with vehemence. "Why? Oh, that's the important question. Luckily for you, Jack, you're the last one, so I have no qualms about telling you. Shift to the right a little, will you?"

Jack, on tiptoes, at the behest of the twitching blade on his genitals, shuffled right. He felt a bead of sweat trickle down his forehead. He struggled to breathe, tried to keep calm.

Emma placed a hand on his shoulder, stopping him. "Right. Before we do this, one warning. I got my limp because the last fucker I dealt with – the last fucker who decided to fight and deny his fate – got clever. He busted my knee, but I cut his head off and left his body to the vermin in the basement. Now, tell me Jack, are you going to attack me if I take this knife away?"

Jack said nothing. Emma raised the knife, lifting his now limp penis an inch with the blade. He breathed in sharply. "No, no, no, no!"

Emma narrowed her eyes. "You sure?"

"For fuck's sake, *yes!*"

Emma removed the blade and held it to Jack's face. "You have fair warning. Now, pull your fucking pants up. Your cock is disgusting." As if to emphasize the point, Emma spat on the ground

232 | K e v i n J. K e n n e d y P r e s e n t s

beside her. Jack bent down and hooked his belt with his hands, pulling his trousers up. He buckled his belt, zipped his fly and brushed himself down. Emma stared at him, leaned in and opened a door beside him. "In you go."

Jack hesitated. His eyes were glued to Emma. He didn't move.

"What're you waiting for?"

"You first." Jack cursed himself silently for saying it. *She has a knife, you fucktard!*

"You think you're in charge here? *Get!*"

Jack flinched and stepped through the doorway. Emma shoved him in the back and walked in behind him. She closed the door. Blackness swallowed them completely. A plastic *snap!* and a light turned on overhead, dim, yellow.

Emma stepped past Jack and picked up a battered and blood-soaked dining chair. She placed it on the floor before him. "Sit."

Jack ambled to the chair and lowered his rump onto it. Emma nodded and stepped in front of him. She said nothing.

"What do you want?" Jack placed his hands on his thighs. *Keep calm; don't antagonize her. There might be a way out.*

Emma stroked her chin, waving the knife by her side. "Me? I have everything I've ever wanted … now. It took me some time, but I finally have it. My life mission is now complete."

"You're twenty three…"

"Wrong. I'm thirty-five. Fooled you once."

Jack's eyes widened. He didn't say anything. Emma chuckled. "Not bad, huh? I get by on my looks and my ways. I mean, look at you. You were a lovesick puppy with a literal bone when you turned up here tonight. Bet you couldn't wait to dive into my cunt. By the way, none of that make-up and beauty treatment shit works. Just water is fine, works wonders. Keeps my skin looking young. Mind you, that could be all the blood too…" Emma trailed off.

Jack didn't want to ask, but he had no choice. *Keep the conversation going.* "Blood?"

"Yes, I bathe in the blood of my victims. It's quite liberating. Feeling the warm, crimson fluids washing away the sweat and toil of the kill. I don't recommend it for hemophobics though."

Jack licked his lips. *The bitch is insane.* "So, you're a serial killer?"

Emma laughed, hard. Jack flinched a little. After a moment, Emma settled. "My, my, Jack. You know nothing. Nothing personal, people in general are born stupid nowadays."

Jack remained silent. He let his eyes roam the darkness, looking for a possible way out. Beyond the dim bulb that burned above his head, he saw just shadow and shapes. Nothing that resembled a door or window.

"You're looking for a way out? Don't bother. I've seen that look a hundred times. Well, five times to be exact. A hundred? I'm not a monster. I can control my urges … sometimes. But, people are predictable. Normally takes them a few minutes to start looking."

Jack moved his eyes back to Emma. She hobbled in close and leaned down in front of him. "There's nothing like a kill and there's nothing like soaking in the blood of someone who's spent their last moments on earth running from you, petrified or otherwise."

She leaned in closer.

Jack could see down her top, she wasn't wearing a bra. Before, this would have been arousing. Now, Jack felt sick to his stomach. Emma had her lips beside his ear. He could feel her warm breath on his neck. "Have you ever masturbated in a blood bath? I'm telling you, there's nothing like it. I'm a squirter, too, so that's always fun. Writhing in the hot blood of your victims and ejaculating into it. Heaven! I would recommend it, but hey, look where you are."

Emma stood up and hobbled away. "Besides, men wanking in the bath is fucking disgusting." She laughed.

"Why are you doing this?" *Cliché*, thought Jack. He couldn't think of anything else to say. He squirmed in his seat, sweaty and uncomfortable. With her back turned, he swiped at his forehead, wiping away the sweat.

Emma turned. "Is this the bit in the movies where the bad guy tells his whole plan so it buys the good guy some time?"

Jack said nothing. *Cliché indeed.*

"It is, isn't it? Very well, so be it. You know the difference between me and the people in the movies, Jack?"

"You have better tits?"

Emma howled. "You're a funny guy. I was thinking that when I drove away after our date. If I were a normal woman, I would fuck you five ways from Sunday, every day. What's the abbreviation? G.S.O.H? That word they put in the personal ads? Apparently, it gets women all wet and slutty. I can understand why, dropping our inhibitions and shit. We all love a funny fucker."

Jack remained silent. He continued staring at Emma. *Don't show your fear. Put her off and catch her out.*

"The difference is simple. I don't give a shit. I don't care about getting caught and I'm not going to leave you here in a burning building or a trap or whatever people use in the movies nowadays. Nope, I'm going to watch you squirm and kill you myself. Then, I'm going to fess up and display my masterpiece to everyone in the world." Emma walked over to Jack and cupped his chin in her sweaty palm. "So, I don't give a fuck about you. Whatever happens tonight, I *will* be killing you. You got that?" Emma released him.

"What if I try to escape?"

"You said you wouldn't?"

"What if I lied?"

"Then you're a fucking moron. Couldn't give a fucking shit either way. You ain't going anywhere. Besides, something tells me you'll want to stay for the show."

"What show?"

"I'm glad you asked. Shall we get started?"

Jack resisted answering and looked behind Emma.

"Once upon a time … there was a woman called Grace. That's me, by the way, Emma, pffft what a fucking pathetic name. Fooled you twice. Anyway, I had two parents. Loving, doting, caring. My parents were the fucking world to me. However, when I was fifteen, just blossoming into a woman, my parents died in a car accident. A semi-truck hit them head on and killed them. My life changed. On my eighteenth birthday, after a couple of hellish years in foster homes, the will and testament transferred over to me … and I received six million dollars."

Jack shuffled in his seat. Emma smiled. "By the way, my parents were filthy fucking rich. But, you read books and have a modicum of intelligence, that might seem obvious from my previous statement. So, I was rich and no longer needed care. I moved out and bought this house. It's been mine ever since."

"I thought you got it in the will?"

"Jack, what are you, retarded? Have you not yet figured out that I lied to you? You should dismiss most of the stuff I told you before I sucked your cock. It was pillow talk … so to speak. I was playing you. Now, where were we? Oh yes … so Grace is rich and lonely, and a bit pissed off. After all, her folks were taken from her and, as a result, she went into a foster home with a pervert and a whore. They treated Grace as such too … it wasn't pleasant."

"I'm sorry," Jack said, with conviction.

"Are you, really? Well, excuse me if I don't believe you. Deception is a common trait in my life. Keep it hushed. All of the 'it'll be alright' as he slipped his cigarette-tinged fingers under my nightgown and 'he doesn't mean any harm' as my foster mother touched me up and tried to pimp me to her drug pushers. You know what that can do to a kid?"

"Well, I meant it. I'm sorry."

"Fuck you."

Jack said nothing.

"Anyway, I had money to burn. Therefore, I hired a private investigator. Turns out, the police investigation into my parents' death was left unsolved. The guy got away with it. The police just couldn't be bothered to investigate. Therefore, he walked away. Turns out my parents' killer was fond of the bottle. So, I not only suffered at the hands of my foster parents, but the person who put me there – and probably didn't even know – was walking around, guzzling the hooch and shooting the breeze. Tell me, Jack, do you think that's fucking fair?"

Jack shook his head. He said nothing again. *Poor woman*, he thought.

"So, that was three people on my shit list. But, it gets worse. As well as the incompetence of the police, apparently the lawyers were bent, too. So not only did they fail my parents and take their money from my trust fund, but apparently, they thought we had it coming. Actual words from someone I spoke to about it. 'Rich people deserve what they get', I think was the correct expression. Obviously, the lawyer didn't know who I was. The state put a rookie on the case, too, all those years ago. A rookie who sold out to the money in my account and stitched my dead parents up because no one could defend them. No evidence, apparently. Traitorous cunts. Tell me, Jack, do you think that's fair?"

"I already said no. I'm on your side."

"Ha, nice try. You're actually kind of sweet … shame. Anyway, that's when I decided to do something about it. I started with the hit and run driver. I found him drunk in a bar, out of his face. He wasn't hard to track down. I turned up, showed him some cleavage and within minutes we were due to fuck in the cab of his truck. I slipped a pill in his beer, he fell asleep on my tits and I brought him back here. I chopped his head off and danced in the blood."

Jack felt bile rising in his throat. He held back, looking at the ground. Emma danced around him. "That make you feel queasy? Sheesh, I haven't even gotten started yet."

Jack nodded. Emma turned her back to him. He risked a glance again, looking for a way out. He wondered if he could escape through the door behind them. The way they'd come in.

Possibly.

It was a short run to the front door, out onto the drive and into his car.

Emma turned back around. "It didn't stop there. You're not wearing a wire, are you?"

A confused look crossed Jack's face. "Huh?"

"Just kidding. They say it in the movies all the time. I've always wanted to say that. Like jumping in a cab and asking them to follow that car. Epic. Anyway, next up was the police."

Jack balked in his chair, his eyes widened and he sagged. Emma noticed. "What?" Her prisoner said nothing, simply looking away in disgust. Emma smiled slyly. "They had it coming, did you not hear my story?"

"You killed a police officer?" Jack opened and closed his mouth, gasping for air.

"No, I killed two. I butchered them. They were so much fun. You know how much testosterone flies back and forth between two cops? My God, I thought I was going to grow a pair of balls just listening to them. I'll tell you, their descriptions of women? Puts porn to shame. Mind you, that just made my job easier."

Jack said nothing.

"Ever walk up to two cops, beer and chips flowing, and show a bit of leg? I thought they were going to bend me over right there in the bar. But, I managed to keep them hooked enough to get them back here. That's when the fun started. No, I didn't fuck them. I did make one of them fuck his partner in the ass with a strap on, though. Over and over, until his anus bled and his squeals faded to nothing. Massive internal trauma … mind you, the dildo was a cactus so…"

"You're fucking sick."

"No, I'm fine; I got myself checked out. Call me curious … yeah, that's a better description. Anyway, one of the cops ran away, into the basement, funnily enough. That's the fucker who popped my knee. I hunted him down and slaughtered him. Then I returned to the cop with a pain in his ass. He tried blocking an axe swing with his arm. I never saw a forearm slice so easily. His arm bounced off the wall like a newspaper smacking the porch. Hilarious. He fell into the bathtub, too. That's when I discovered blood baths."

"Emma…"

"Grace, Emma is such a disgusting name."

"Then why use … never mind, this is getting us…"

"Am I boring you? Is the weird, little rich kid annoying you with her stories? Well, fuck you, Jack. Fuck you and your righteous values. You don't know me."

Emma stepped forward and punched Jack in the face. The sound of the strike filled the room. Jack groaned as a glob of blood spewed from his lip and spattered his chest. Emma stepped back, waving her hand, shaking off the pain. "Fuck me, you have a strong jaw. It's going to be a shame to waste you."

Jack spat blood on the floor. "Why the fuck am I here?"

"Well, that's the important question. But first, let me tell you about my foster father. Now, my foster mother, she was a drug addict. She didn't know what she was doing half of the time; heroin does that to you. My foster father, however … he was teetotal. He knew every single sick, fucking thing he did to me." Emma shuddered at the thought. "So, he went next, but not before I lopped his penis off with a pair of garden shears."

Jack shook his head, his cheek swelling from Emma's punch.

"Which brings me to you."

Jack looked up. "What? What the fuck did I do to you?"

Emma grabbed his chin and planted a wet kiss. She drew back, licking the saliva from her lips. "You know, in a different time and place, I could have made you a happy man. I regret not having you inside me, fucking me, making me scream. But, you're part of the grand scheme. Nothing can ruin that."

Jack spat in her face. He withdrew a little. "Fuck you."

Emma's eyes glared with rage. "Want to play it like that, huh? Oh my, I'm going to enjoy this." She walked away and flicked a switch on the wall. A long, thin table appeared under the new light. Over it were several black sheets, each raised in the center by objects placed underneath.

Emma leaned on the edge of the surface and smiled. "You want to know the ironic thing? Ironic? Yeah, no, that's not the word. Coincidental? That might ring more true. You want to know what the funny thing is? Everyone involved in this, the pigs, the lawyer, the driver, they all shared a common trait."

"And what would that be?" Jack spat.

Emma smiled, remaining silent. She walked across to the first sheet and lifted it off. "They shared a common name."

Jack glanced at the unveiled object and screamed.

"Jack, I'd like you to meet Mr. Benjamin Jacks. The trucker who killed my parents."

On the table was a decapitated human head.

Jack recoiled. With the waft of the sheet came a putrid, rotten smell. It had no eyes and no tongue. The skin was white and cracked, yellowing in places. The hair was intact but ruffled, greasy. As Jack vomited down his front, he noticed a candle inside the head. Its yellow flame danced and glowed, bouncing around with the introduction of the natural air from the room. Yellow light shone from the eye sockets and the makeshift smile, a smile created by slicing deep, triangular furrows in the cheeks, creating a hideous, evil grin. Jack fell down and from this angle, he could see a hole in the top of the skull, viewed through the eye sockets; which he realized were now slightly larger and alien like.

A human Jack-o'-Lantern.

Jack groaned and backed away.

Emma laughed. "Do you like it? It's not my best work, I'll admit. I'd never used a scalpel or a bone saw until this point, so the edges are a bit rough. Don't think I did a bad job, though." She stepped across to the next black sheet. Her hand gripped the material. "Now, I would like you to meet the cops who couldn't and wouldn't. I present Jack Lane and Jacques Benzema."

Below this sheet were two heads, much the same as the previous; engorged eyes, flaking skin and enlarged grotesque smiles. However, these two heads angled inwards, facing one another. The tongues remained in the heads, leering from their dead mouths, touching one another in some grotesque undead kiss. Both were scalped, red raw skin showed above their eyebrows, removed to create a hollow within. Yellow flames flicked and licked within the empty skulls. Emma bent down behind them and grinned.

"Pretty proud of these. Fucking pigs got what they deserved."

Jack placed his arm across his face, half to cover his eyes and block any more vomit. A low, guttural groan resonated through his body. His stomach was performing back flips. He backed into a solid wall, restricted. His eyes wavered between Emma and the desecration on the tables before her.

She stepped sideways again.

Another sheet. Emma stopped smiling and gritted her teeth. "This one … this, I'm proud of. I relished this one. And I took my fucking time. Meet my foster Dad, Jack Phillips."

Emma removed the sheet.

Another head. One thing was clear, this head was more recent and the gouges in the face were precise, straight and streamlined. A lot of work had gone into the appearance. The face was painted with clown makeup. Yellow light burned bright in this one, casting a strange shadow from the mouth. Jack stood up and groaned again. "Oh dear, fucking God."

"Yes, that's his penis in his mouth. Look how it catches the light. Cunt stuck it in me enough times, turnabout is fair play, don't you think?"

Jack buckled, falling to his knees and cried. Vomit splattered the concrete beneath him. "You're … you're fucking … you … urgh."

"That's it, get it out. The best bit is coming up."

"Stop this, stop…"

"It's too late to stop. I've killed people – this is my masterpiece. It's nearly complete."

"You're fucking insane!"

"No, I'm normal, I got checks done. Mind you, it was a while ago. And I *did* kill my shrink. So, who knows?" Emma chuckled to herself. "Now, are you ready for the finale?"

"There's more? God, just stop this…"

"Not an option."

"Let me go…"

"You seriously think that would work?" Emma turned and pointed at the two kissing heads. "Jacques over there, he busted my knee. I chased him into the cellar and cornered him like the pig he was. He hurt me. You think if I do that to him, I would treat you any different?"

Emma let the question linger. Jack gulped, swiping his face with his arm. Emma stepped behind the final head. "Now, there's a story about this one. The lawyer, well, the lawyer was harder to find. It took a lot of digging and, finally, I found the bent sonofabitch that screwed us over. I was surprised too … not often that happens."

Jack spat on the floor. "I don't care anymore."

Emma grinned. "Well, you fucking should. You see, this person, well, this is interesting. You know this person. The others, the scum, they're strangers. Nobodies. The lawyer, however, is someone you know well."

Jack looked up, confusion on his face.

Emma lifted the sheet off. "I present to you … Mrs Jacqueline Walker."

The name sent a cold shock through Jack's heart. He felt every inch of his body stiffen and his skin broke out in an immediate sweat. His eyes widened and his scalp tightened. His bladder finally released, sending warm urine streaming down his clenched thigh. The name: he knew that name. His legs locked; a good thing, it meant he didn't fall back and slam his head on the concrete.

He knew the name well.

Emma threw the sheet down. "Your mother."

Jack howled.

His mother's head, the most recent acquisition to the puzzle, stood proud in front of him. Her brown hair was tied in a high ponytail. He noticed a small hole burrowed into the side of her head, just above the ear. Her dead, empty eye sockets and widened mouth sent repulsion through his skin and Jack shivered, then seized and fell back on his rump. The remainder of her bright red lips shone and he remembered her kissing him with them just yesterday. Her eyebrows were still as neat as he remembered. Yellow flames, the brightest of all, danced around inside her hollowed-out skull. She looked like a demon, her eye sockets and mouth blazing yellow and orange through the heat.

Jack cried.

Emma stepped over to him. "You mother was the worst of all. She took our money, changed her fucking name and moved to protect the one thing that mattered to her the most; her son. You. And for that, she will never be forgiven."

Jack looked up, his cheeks sodden with tears. He said nothing.

He noticed an axe in Emma's hand, hoisted by her side.

"I can't let there be any witnesses. I need one final Jack-o'-Lantern. Get it? Jack? I'm a laugh riot. See what I did there?"

"Fuck you."

Jack charged Emma, who sidestepped effortlessly. Jack flew by, crashing into the tables. The human Jack-o'-Lanterns toppled onto the floor, bouncing off the concrete with sick, hollow thuds. His mother bounced in his lap and rolled off to the side. Jack fumbled, pushing the heads away. He moaned whilst doing so, slipping on the sheets, losing his balance.

The axe plunged into his neck.

Blood erupted from his mouth. Liquid warmth started sluicing down his front.

As Jack died, he saw Emma laughing behind the axe blade that severed his throat. As the life ebbed from his body, he glanced sideways and saw his mother's head lolling on the floor. The candle had fallen over, setting her hair on fire. He reached out, trying to protect her.

It was useless.

"My masterpiece is nearly complete." Emma shouted in the background. Distorted, disjointed. Jack felt his ears resigning, the sound disappearing.

He coughed up blood, felt the blade shifting in his trachea.

He thought back to the bookshop, the excitement afterwards, the date.

I met a woman.

If only he hadn't asked for that book.

If only he'd ordered it online, waited a day or two.

He thought of his mother.

Curiosity killed the cat.

His eyes closed, the blood slowed, his arms lowered.

Never a truer word spoken.

The End

245 | Collected Halloween Horror Shorts

Dressed for Success

By

Peter Oliver Wonder

"This is bound to be the best, yet," Troy said to his smiling reflection in the mirror. "Christmas was a trial run and Easter really got the ball going—with bonus points for creativity—but they were both really just practice for this Halloween. This is the real deal, now." He continued to apply the various colors of paint to his face. Tonight would be the euphoric release he was looking for in every possible way.

Since he'd stumbled upon the makeup kit at that strange shop back in November, he'd yearned to use it, but didn't wish to arouse suspicion. While on a road trip, Troy had gone camping at the ocean. One day, he had gone walking along the streets of the small beach town and stumbled upon a gift shop like so many he had seen before. There were plenty of shirts, bottle openers, shot glasses, shark tooth jewelry, and lighters to satisfy anyone, but there was one item that stood out above all the rest. Oddly enough, it was on the floor near a trash can, and it was the only thing that wasn't branded with San Diego, or any other nearby popular location that may prove appealing to a far-traveling tourist.

When he'd reached down to inspect it, he was surprised to find it appeared to have been unopened. There was no cellophane wrapping, but when he'd opened the case, he saw that the makeup within appeared to be completely untouched. When he'd found it, he thought it was silly at first, but soon noticed it wasn't just average, girl-type makeup. It was high-quality, costume makeup. It was multi-tiered and had every color in the spectrum, with several different applicators included. When he brought it up to the register, the cashier was confused about the item, but had no issue with charging Troy twenty-five dollars for it. He wasn't entirely sure about the purchase, but thought he'd be able to get his money's worth, one way or another.

For Christmas, he'd made himself up as one of Santa's elves. It was pretty sloppy, and he was mistaken for a clown once or twice, but the makeup seemed to keep him in character the whole time he wore it. At the end of the day, he hadn't cared one iota about gifts or anything other than putting a smile on the face of everyone else. He was just so pleased to have spent the day as an elf. It was filled with joy and cookies and candy. For that one day, he felt as though he truly was an elf—the embodiment of the Christmas Spirit. Even his voice had gone an octave higher, without any effort at all. Though he'd enjoyed playing dress-up far more than he anticipated, it was months before he was able to don the makeup once more. It wasn't until he washed it off, that he noticed he had felt so different while the costume paint was covering his face

When Easter finally came around, Troy was ecstatic about getting to play dress-up again. He bought some silly ears and painted his face as a jolly Easter Bunny. He spent the entire day hopping around and doling out treats to young ones. When he applied the makeup, he didn't have to try to stay in character or act joyous. Candy even fell from his pockets on random hops—at least, he made the assumption that it was his pockets from which the chocolate balls fell. The makeup he put on seemed to cause him to take on the actual mindset of whatever it was he had dressed up as. When the costume makeup took over and literally transformed him, it was like the most fantastic drug he could ever imagine.

The happy costumes had been fun—he had enjoyed creating such enjoyment for the little kids that were around. But this was Halloween. Troy was excited to try something new and perhaps a little more sinister. This makeup wasn't something he was able to play with just any day. He might be locked up in the looney bin if he was parading around as a pirate or lizard-man or anything else, other than himself, on an ordinary day. This Halloween, he had something that he was so eager to try out. Sure, he could be a zombie or a werewolf, but he wanted to try something different. This was something that would be a mystery even to himself.

He applied shades of green and gray to his face and smoothed out his features with putty. He hid his eyebrows and covered his hair with a flexible cap. He enjoyed watching the transformation in the mirror but, as he looked more alien and less human, he found himself feeling confused and disgusted at the human features that remained. He felt that the colors he was choosing were inappropriate, and grew angry at his selection of green. He colored over his face with a darker shade and felt more natural. On the bottom tier of the makeup case, he found the contact lenses that turned his eyeballs completely black as though they had been filled with used motor oil. After he put them in and looked in the mirror, he finally recognized himself. Looking at the reflection in the mirror, he felt unsettled by the rise and fall of his chest, and so stopped breathing.

When it was finally complete, he had to force himself to remember there was a party being held by one of his friends in an apartment two floors down. He looked down and shut the makeup kit, then exited the bathroom. He made his way through the living room, seeing things as though he hadn't seen them in a long time; as though his life was but a distant memory, yet the thought of his destination was still firmly planted in his mind.

Troy exited through his front door, not closing it behind himself. With long, lumbering steps, he made his way down the hallway. He stopped in front of the elevator and looked at it. He knew it was a doorway similar to the one he had just gone through, but didn't know how to open it. He placed a hand on each door and tried to separate them, but was unable to do so. To his left, he saw a sign that read "stairs" above a door. After twisting the doorknob and opening the door, he found a pathway that led down and decided to see where it went.

The steep steps looked daunting. Rather than walking down them, Troy did what came instinctually to the creature he was dressed as—and what had now taken over his body—and hovered a few inches off the ground and gracefully glided over the steps in order to descend them. After two flights of stairs, he had little more than a feeling of what he was meant to be doing, but he knew to continue on his downward trajectory no more. Troy set his feet back on solid ground, opened the door, and exited the stairwell.

"Whoa, bro!" exclaimed a man dressed as a skeleton, who had turned to see who had just left the stairwell. "Come on, party is this way!" The language sounded strange in Troy's ears, but he did follow the skeleton-man as he made his way toward apartment 835. "That's an awesome costume, man. What are you supposed to be? Like, an alien, or something?"

Now almost under the influence of the makeup, Troy stopped right where he was in the hallway in order to better observe the skeleton-man who was speaking to him. He was filled with curiosity at listening to the beauty in the strange language that flowed from his mouth. The manner of dress for this particular human seemed rather peculiar.

The skeleton-man nodded. "Staying in character, huh? I have to say, that's really goddamn creepy, but I can appreciate what you're doing, bro. I'll see you in there, eh?" He waited very briefly for a response before ending the encounter, and heading through the doorway before him.

This doorway was something Troy was unaware of from his perspective and brought back to his mind the mission at hand. It reminded him that he was to attend a human gathering and he wondered what world of information he would gather from being in such close proximity to so many of these strange and wonderful beings. He hoped it would be the information he desperately needed.

"Troy, bro!" shouted the male owner of the domicile, from a long piece of leather-covered furniture. The man, dressed as a vampire, said, "Love the costume, man. That's some killer work you've done. You didn't really do that all yourself, did you?"

Unable to comprehend the language of the natives, he used his mind to reach into that of the vampire-dressed man doing the speaking. Just as he began to see what was being said, the thoughts were cut off and the human's mind was filled with intense agony. Watching the man in vampire dress contort in pain, he was intrigued by the scream that came from the surrounding members and the trails of blood that began to fall from each of the man's nostrils.

"Holy shit, what's wrong with Mark?" asked the male dressed as a caveman, sitting to the right of the vampire writhing around. Mark's eyes had now rolled to the back of his head, and two men were trying to shake him out of it.

"I think it's a seizure," a female, dressed as slutty penguin, suggested. "We need to call 911, like, right now!" A device was pulled from the small, red polka dotted bag that was sitting on her lap. Curious as to what her thoughts were, the entity, known only as Troy, entered her mind next. Inside, he found true fear and confusion, before everything erupted in excruciating pain.

"Oh my fucking God," exclaimed the male between the two victims of the unknown. Mark had ceased all movement, and the female was now beginning to bleed from her nose, as well.

"Holy shit! Is it you doing this, Troy?" asked the skeletal male he had encountered in the hallway. The accusation was followed by a shove of the shoulder. "You're the only one not freaking out right now. You're just standing there like a fucking freak, staring at people as their brains melt, or whatever. What the hell are you do-"

Troy didn't like the way this man was talking to him. It made him angry. To make him stop talking, he entered his mind—not to search for answers, but to defend himself against attacks that would, undoubtedly, be worse than the initial push. Was it always this way with humans? Would they all be quick to react to confusion with violence? For such an advanced race, there was nothing their anger could gain them, other than total loss.

It was just as Troy was about to release this last human, as he was beginning to feel pity for all of them, that all thoughts of letting these humans go anywhere dissipated entirely. His mission was meant to be one of peace and exploration, but these thoughts were strange and difficult concepts to him far before he had arrived on Earth. Never was he able to understand the point in looking to such a primitive race of quasi-intelligent life to find the answers that remained a mystery to all the truly advanced races in the known universe.

Even from afar, these stupid creatures still managed to get on his nerves. He had wanted to go to a place where new information may be learned. A place that may have real answers on how to stop the universe from collapsing back in on itself. Now, he was stuck with these breathers, and with an object permeating his chosen vessel. Never before, in all his time roaming creation, had he experienced such anger.

This frail form he was trapped in now would be incapable of the things he wanted to do. He wanted to lift this caveman off the ground and use him as a weapon to beat the rest in attendance into puddles of red goo. The mind, however, was found to be sufficient enough to manipulate the gravitational force around—something the humans seemed unaware they were able to do.

In a fraction of a second, everyone but 'Troy' left the ground, as if the artificial gravity had just gone out on a spaceship. Screams broke out from every corner of the apartment. Frantically, arms and legs flailed about as they tried to figure out how to regain control over their environment. The caveman withdrew his weapon and swung it again at 'Troy' as he began to float away. This time, the fork bent as it struck. The skin of the entity's host had turned as hard as steel. The caveman looked at the fork as he pulled it away, several thoughts ran through his mind. He looked back at the unnatural face in front of him. "What are you?" he asked, almost in a whisper.

The creature closed its eyes and focused. The bones in the host body began to break, so that the entire body structure could rearrange itself. The skin seemed to melt around the shape-shifting bones—the nostrils melted shut as the skull crumpled like an aluminum can. The makeup that coated the skin hardened and crumbled away from the skin as if it was an egg shell, revealing a dark, almost black skin with texture akin to a rhinoceros. For those brave enough to watch this metamorphosis take place, it was like watching an action figure melt to the ground in a microwave before being possessed by an evil spirit and rising once more. Internally, every cell was also reconfiguring itself. The brain was being rewired to properly house the foreign entity which was taking full control.

The energy being produced by this newly-forming creature could be felt by every nearby person. It stood on its four limbs, keeping its torso low to the floor. The tall and narrow head stood roughly three feet off the floor at its highest point. A woman on the phone with the police began shouting "Hello?" repeatedly, not realizing the device had stopped working. The lights in the apartment flickered on and off, before going completely black. Faint amounts of light from street lamps and stars trickled in through the windows.

In the darkness, the being seemed to nearly disappear. The almost-black skin blended in perfectly, but the oily eyes, which had drastically increased in size, reflected just enough light to be able to track the being—if you knew where to look.

With the inhabitants of the apartment incapacitated, due to a lack of gravity, the entity made its way to the window to look upon the world outside. Below, it saw the humans walking with their offspring through the streets. None of these people had the slightest inkling that this entire universe was in its final days. It was time to let them know about their inevitable demise so that they, too, would feel the unimaginable dread of knowing the unstoppable end was rapidly approaching.

Not knowing any of the local language, the alien being wanted to let the world know death was coming in the most obvious of ways. It walked toward the nearest human and grabbed an ankle that was floating at eye level. The human kicked the alien in the head repeatedly, but it seemed to have no effect whatsoever. As the grip of the long, slender fingers tightened, the human screamed louder and louder until the sound of the bones crunching was heard.

In a swift movement, the thin arm swung the screaming man through the window. Glass shattered outward and the jagged fragments remaining, scraped off pieces of the man's flesh. The gravity bubble seemed to end just outside the window where the man rapidly began to descend, screaming the entire way. With a simple thought, the sound inside of the apartment was muted entirely as the alien listened to those near the impact site. Initially, there was silence before a single scream pierced the night sky and made its way up to the eighth floor. After the first scream, more broke forth from the silence below. Once satisfied with this, the parasitic monster allowed the sound of screams and panic to continue, as it had previously, before it grabbed onto another human.

With its cold fingers firmly curled around the upper arm of a mid-twenties male, the alien jumped through the broken window. Once he was outside, the rest of the people in the apartment fell back to the floor, though all electronics remained non-functional.

The human trapped in the alien's grip, oddly enough dressed as a classic gray alien, was silent as he plummeted toward the ground. His thoughts were busy trying to make peace with the Lord before it was too late.

Upon landing, the confined man opened his eyes to find he had not splattered against the ground. Instead, the alien previously known as Troy, made a perfect landing, as though it had dropped only a few inches. As it did so, it let out a scream that shattered all windows of vehicles and buildings in the surrounding area. Then, it took the contents in its hands and threw the young man at the nearest group of humans.

More screams echoed down the street. Car horns sounded and tires squealed as they tried to flee from whatever horror show was ensuing. One of the women, near the area impacted by the costumed alien, called 911 and began shouting into the phone, "Help! Help! I think it's an alien invasion! We're all going to DIE!"

The End

The Halloween Phantoms

By

John R. Little

October 15

Ellen Weston was dreaming of a Caribbean cruise, full of laughter, exotic drinks, and Davey doting on her, as he always did. Mostly, though, she was just enjoying sitting on the deck of the ship with the sun beaming down on her. The feeling of having free time was heavenly.

It all evaporated when the bell's ringing turned out not to be from the cruise ship but rather the doorbell in her home.

"Damn."

She glanced at her watch. 9:35. Who the hell is here this late?

Maybe if she just ignored it, the person would go away. But, maybe it was important.

Shit.

Ellen got up from the couch and blinked her eyes to clear her vision. She couldn't see anyone at the door, but it was dark out. Dark, rainy, dreary.

I hate October.

The wind was blowing hard outside, accompanied by freakish whistling and howling.

Once again she wished for the comfort of her home in California. Autumn in Minnesota wasn't nice.

She walked to the door, yawning and stretching her arms. She cupped her hands to the narrow window beside the door, but she could only see her own ghostly reflection staring back. Her short blonde hair hung lifeless, just like she felt.

Her eight-year-old daughter, Julie, was sleeping upstairs and Ellen wanted nothing more than to be able to go join her. The damned alarm would be going off at 5:00, calling her to another day at work. Even though she was only 36, Ellen felt like she was 60. Davey's death still weighed on her like a pair of anchors crowded on her shoulders.

She still didn't see anybody out the window.

Fuck it.

She unlocked the door and pulled it open. The wind pushed harder, causing the door to almost swing open and crash to the side wall. Ellen caught it just before it hit.

Nobody there.

Figures. Stupid kids.

She was about to close the door when she saw the bag hanging on the doorknob. It was a black sack, made of some kind of light material, almost feathery to the touch. A few drops of rain beaded up and rolled down the fabric as it would off a bird. There was a jack-o'-lantern picture in the middle of the bag, bright orange, and almost lifelike. It creeped her out, but she couldn't help touching it. The image was silky and caused her fingers to tingle.

"Hello?" she called. "Is anybody here?"

She was shivering from the frigid wind, so she grabbed the weird bag and closed the door, being sure to lock it again.

"Mommy?"

Ellen stared at Julie as the little girl came down the stairs to the living room. It took forever to get her to go to bed each night, and now another hour of her own sleep would be lost.

"It's okay, sweetie. Just somebody leaving some Halloween stuff for us."

"Really? Who? Can I see it?"

Ellen knew it was pointless to resist, so they went to the kitchen.

"It's pretty!"

Ellen had to agree. She'd never felt material like this before, and the laughing eyes of the jack-o'-lantern seemed to warm the room up.

"Open it, Mommy!"

Ellen dumped the bag onto the table. There were a few candies, some chocolate bars, and a small toy that seemed to be a puzzle of some kind.

Julie grabbed a Mars bar and looked up at Ellen. She lifted her eyebrows and used those puppy-dog eyes that Ellen could rarely resist.

"Not tonight. I don't need you filled with sugar before bed. What's the toy?"

Julie picked it up, watching it glow with some type of internal lighting system. The toy was about four inches square and had a grid of numbers all mixed up on a screen. Julie seemed to instinctively know to use her finger to move the numbers around.

"I think I have to put them in order, Mommy."

"Okay."

"Who gave us this stuff?"

Good question.

Ellen looked back in the bag and saw a piece of paper still inside. She unfolded it and read:

#

Greetings! We are the Halloween Phantoms, and you have just been BOO'd!!!

You now have until Halloween to fill three bags with candy, small toys, stickers . . . whatever you like, and distribute them in secret to three neighborhood homes. You'll ring the doorbell and run away so they only have the bag and a copy of this note. If you don't do this, you'll suffer the wrath of the Phantom Curse!

Now that you've received your bag from the Halloween Phantoms, you must affix a note to your front door saying, "We've been BOO'd!!!" This way, nobody else can BOO you again.

Hurry with your bags! As time goes on, it'll be harder and harder to find homes that haven't already been BOO'd!

Be sure to leave a copy of this note with each bag you deliver.

Happy Halloween from the Halloween Phantoms!

#

Ellen just stared at the note and realized it meant more work for her. Figure out some stuff to buy, head to the dollar store or wherever to pick them up, find some bags (and where would she find something as nice as this one?), pack them all up, deliver the stuff to some random neighbors that she barely knew . . .

It was the kind of thing Davey was so good with but she sucked at. He was outgoing and friendly and knew all the neighbors. Some of them came to his funeral, but she didn't really even know more than a few of their names.

Now she was supposed to be a part of some neighborhood game or something.

Davey, I miss you.

It'd been six months since his death, but it seemed like six years. He'd had no life insurance, so to make ends meet, Ellen had to work a second job. The only other choice was to sell the house. Julie's home. The girl had gone through too much for that.

"Bedtime, sweetie."

"Awww . . ."

"Now."

As usual, "now" turned into forty minutes before Julie was actually in her bed. Sleep didn't come easily and when Ellen woke the next morning, she felt like shit.

#

April 9 (Six Months Earlier)

Ellen was watching a game show but barely paying attention. It was something where you had to guess the price of things, but she was never very good at it and her mind was wandering.

There was a storm outside that rattled her nerves every time thunder shook the small home she, Davey, and Julie shared. Every shake of the thin walls made her miss California anew.

She hated Minnesota. Sometimes she hated Davey for bringing them there. She hardly knew anybody, and for that matter, neither did he. He seemed to want to move just to recapture some childhood fantasy. Men and lost youths seemed to be a common problem with her friends, but none of them had been dragged a thousand miles to live out their husbands' fantasies.

The phone rang and shocked her from her thoughts. Probably Davey saying he'd be late. She thought he was out working in the field, but maybe he'd decided to get out of the storm.

Who wouldn't?

"Hello?"

"Mrs. Weston?"

She didn't recognize the voice, and a new blast of thunder gave her an earful of static.

" . . . to the hospital."

Hospital?

"What did you say? Who is this?"

She looked over her shoulder at the staircase, but of course Julie was at school, not in her room. Wasn't she?

"Please hurry. He may not last long."

He? Davey?

"What happened?"

Static filled her ear again, and then she had a dial tone.

"Davey?"

She hit speed dial #1 to call Davey's cell phone. It rang a few times before clicking over to his voice mail.

Two minutes later she was in her ten-year-old Toyota Camry racing to the hospital.

#

"He was hit by lightning."

"Are you serious?"

The doctor was a woman, about forty, and the expression on her face seemed to say, "Don't fuck with me." Even so, it was too hard to imagine somebody actually being hit by lightning.

"More than 400 people are killed by lightning every year in the U.S., Mrs. Weston. We usually get a few people admitted at this very hospital due to lightning strikes."

"He's going to be okay, right?"

She hesitated. "We're doing our best."

#

An hour later, at 3:28 p.m., the same doctor told her that her husband was dead. Ellen never had a chance to talk to him, to tell him she loved him, to say good-bye. All of a sudden, her complaints about the move to Minnesota seemed incredibly petty.

#

October 25

Ellen was tired. Dead tired. Her legs felt like jelly. Today was her 37th birthday and she could feel forty looming ahead of her. She'd woken up with a new determination to get back into shape and had just finished jogging around the neighborhood. It was a little after seven-thirty and she'd left Julie to read at home, figuring she'd only be gone a half hour.

Ellen had only lasted fifteen minutes before she had to stop and walk home. She felt sweaty and greasy from the run and just wanted to head back for a nice hot shower.

"Ellen!"

The clutch of women were a bit hard to see, since they were standing in the shadows. She squinted and saw three of them: the ABC Club. Annie, Bonnie, and Charlie were three girls who always hung out together. They rarely spoke to Ellen.

"Hi," she called. She wanted to fit in to the neighborhood, she truly did (she told herself), but somehow time and life seemed to intrude. None of the three had gone to Davey's funeral.

Ellen walked over and saw that they were all holding wine glasses, mostly empty.

"Did you get boo'd yet?" asked Bonnie.

"Boo'd?"

"Yes, you get a Halloween package and you pay it forward. Kind of a tradition around here." The way she said it, Ellen heard, If you don't do it, you'll always be an outsider.

She thought back to the bag that had arrived ten days earlier. She was supposed to hand out three bags of her own, but she'd forgotten about it as soon as she'd put the bag away.

"Did you all get one?"

Annie laughed. "You haven't looked around much, have you?" She pointed to her own house next door, and Ellen could see a white sign on the front door: WE'VE BEEN BOO'D!

She glanced at Bonnie's place (where they were standing) and a similar sign hung on her door, too. And Charlie's . . . and just about every other house she could see.

"I'll have to get onto it," she said without conviction.

Charlie leaned over to her, and Ellen could smell the red wine on her lips. Charlie put a hand on her neck and whispered to her, almost like a lover would. Her touch felt too familiar, and Ellen felt a longing for closeness and didn't pull back.

She tried to think of Charlie's hand being Davey's, but the words she whispered interfered with her daydream.

"You need to do it, sweetie." Charlie's breath warmed Ellen's ear. Ellen imagined kissing Davey, and how wonderful that always felt. "You need to. Don't skip it, because you'll always regret it. The first person to ignore the Halloween Phantoms always regrets it. They don't fuck around." Then in an even quieter voice she added, "But I do."

Charlie kissed Ellen's cheek and smiled. Ellen felt her face turn red and was grateful for the darkness provided by the twilight.

"I'll get onto it tomorrow," she said. She just wanted to escape from the ABC Club now, and she took a step backward.

She was going to say good night but surprised herself by asking, "Who started this thing, anyhow? Did one of you put the bag on my door?"

Bonnie took off her glasses and snorted. "Jesus, girl, don't you get it? This isn't a joke. Just do whatever the damned phantoms ask and you'll be fine."

"Oh. Well, okay then. I have to get back to Julie." She stared at the three women and saw no twinkle of an inside joke. Annie and Bonnie stared as if she had just grown an extra head. Charlie . . . . well, Charlie always looked at her with a bit of extra attention. "Good night," she said as she turned and walked back to her home.

The rest of the neighborhood was dark and quiet.

And every house she passed had a sign on the door saying they'd been boo'd.

#

April 14

Davey's funeral was held five days after he died. The coroner didn't do an autopsy, because the cause of death was obvious. Lightning didn't leave many doubts.

Davey had been six years older than Ellen, but even so, they never really talked about his final wishes. She hadn't known if he wanted to be buried or cremated, or any other things he may have wanted. The day before, she'd walked out to his "office," which was a corner of the barn.

When they moved to Minnesota, Davey somehow found a property in a small town that backed onto a large field. The bank had repossessed it from the previous owner, and Davey bought it for way less than they ever thought possible.

"Every guy needs a place to work on things," he'd once said. "This is my space."

The barn was empty except for that one corner he called his office. Davey had talked about one day raising cows but they'd only been living on the farm for a few months. The first year they were going to stick to growing a few hundred acres of corn. That sounded like a big enough challenge, and she pushed aside the occasional musing about whether he could actually pull it off on his own or not. Fortunately, Ellen had a job as a waitress and so could help with the finances while they got the farm up and running.

What would happen to the farm now? she wondered. She decided that was a problem for another day.

The office had a makeshift wooden table, built from old pieces of particle board and two-by-fours. The only nice part was a swivelling brown leather chair that was actually quite comfortable. She sat in it and imagined her husband sitting beside her, planning their little farm.

There were some papers on the table, but of course nothing that would give her any hint of his final wishes. It was mostly lists of things he planned to do, items to purchase, important dates for the harvest, that type of thing.

Ellen closed her eyes and thought of Davey, missing him terribly, wondering how he'd been so unlucky. If only they hadn't moved to Minnesota, if only he'd stayed inside when the storm struck, if only the lightning found a juicier target somewhere close by . . . if only.

She tried to pull herself from the fruitless thoughts and looked around the office more. There wasn't much more to see, other than a green plastic glass that he'd used for a drink of water on the day he died. There were two cardboard boxes below the table. She opened the top one and found only paper, pens, tape, and scissors.

The bottom box was more sinister. She had forgotten about the gun.

Davey bought it shortly after they moved to Roseville, worried about moving to an unknown rural town with no way to protect his family. He'd taken Ellen out to the far end of the field one day and taught her to shoot it. She remembered him smiling as she held her arms out to steady herself before shooting. "You'll never have to use it, baby."

She'd enjoyed the target practice, more than she could possibly have imagined.

Ellen picked up the gun now and held it out, as if to shoot an invisible intruder. Davey's lesson came back easily to her. She remembered the feel of his hand on hers as he helped to steady her aim.

Finally, she put the gun back, shedding more memories of their lives together.

#

October 26

Ellen believed not a whit about Halloween Phantoms, but part of her still did want to fit into the neighborhood and it bugged her a bit that she wasn't participating in the game. She found the note and re-read the instructions:

#

Now that you've received your bag from the Halloween Phantoms, you must affix a note to your front door saying "We've been BOO'd!!!" This way, nobody else can BOO you again.

Hurry with your bags! As time goes on, it'll be harder and harder to find homes that haven't already been BOO'd!

Be sure to leave a copy of this note with each bag you deliver.

#

Jesus, she hated crap like this. After dinner, she got into her car and drove through the neighborhood, looking at everyone's door.

There were no houses left that hadn't been boo'd.

"That's impossible," she said.

She drove back around the winding streets. Roseville only had about a thousand people, but surely not every single home had already been visited.

But after an hour, she gave up. She didn't see one solitary house she could boo, and frankly, she'd lost interest in trying.

"Fuck it," she said as she slammed her hand into her steering wheel. She drove home and threw the notice in the garbage.

#

October 29

The doorbell rang again at 9:35, exactly as it did when the stupid Halloween junk was left on Ellen's door. She closed her eyes and shook her head, knowing that once again, Julie would be leaping out of her bed to come down and see what was going on.

Ellen was in the kitchen, just finishing the dinner dishes. She walked to the front door and as she expected, Julie joined her shortly.

"Maybe it's more treats, Mommy!"

I'll be so glad when Halloween is over this year.

"Maybe."

Ellen looked out the window again as she had the earlier night but again couldn't see anybody. She pulled the door open, expecting to see a bag on the door handle but there was nothing there.

Instead, there were three figures standing at the foot of her front yard, close to the street.

"Mommy, who are they?"

Julie moved a little, so she was behind Ellen.

Ellen tried to make out the figures. Her house was smack in the middle section between street lights and she'd always hated that. She'd complained to Davey when they first moved in, but there was nothing either of them could do about it.

The three figures stood side by side, facing her. They were about thirty feet from her door, which Ellen was grateful for.

They wore costumes -- dark costumes with robes and hoods. The middle one wore chestnut brown while the two on either side of him were black. They just stared at her.

She couldn't make out their faces exactly, but she could see bumps and maybe fur below their hoods. The costumes were good, and she didn't like them at all.

"Can I help you?" she shouted.

Ellen was wearing a night gown and suddenly she felt very exposed. None of her neighbors were outside. She pushed Julie behind her and held onto the door, ready to close and lock it.

The three figures didn't answer her call.

"Hello?" she tried.

They didn't make a sound.

The middle one held a long stick in his hand that reached to the ground. As her eyes adjusted, Ellen could see that it was actually a piece of metal pipe, not wood. The other two didn't carry anything but they had belts and there were items inside the belts. She didn't know what they were. Rocks? Guns?

"Can I help you?" she tried again.

Then the middle figure started to walk toward her. He (She? It?) walked slowly and reached halfway to her, so that he was now standing in the middle of her lawn.

Ohmygod.

Ellen could feel her heart racing. Where were all the neighbors? Who could she get help from?

The figure just stood there and didn't say a word.

"Please. Who are you?"

She knew she sounded pathetic, but she couldn't help it. She'd never felt the need to protect herself before.

Julie pressed into her. "Mommy, I'm scared."

The ghoul (or whatever he was) lifted the metal pipe off the ground and then thumped it down. Again and again he pounded the pipe onto her lawn and she imagined him doing that to her dead body.

Okay, that's enough.

She leaned over and told Julie to run to the kitchen to get her cell phone.

When she looked back, the middle ghoul was walking back to join the other two, and they shuffled away toward the ABC Club and beyond. Ellen watched as they kept walking, and eventually she lost sight of them.

Julie brought her phone, but Ellen no longer felt the urgency to call the police.

"Mommy, who were they?"

"Just some teenagers out to scare us. Don't worry about it, baby."

"I don't like them."

"Me, neither."

"One of them looked like Daddy."

Ellen stared at Julie. "What did you say?"

"The one back there." She pointed to where one of the figures was standing. "The way he walked. It reminded me of Daddy."

"It wasn't Daddy. They were too small. They were teenagers. Likely some bored boys."

"Maybe girls."

"I doubt it, but I suppose it could have been."

Ellen closed the door, but neither of them got a good night's sleep.

#

October 31

Halloween continued to provide the blustery autumn weather that Ellen had grown to hate. The sky was overcast all day.

When she got home from work, it was already after 7:00, and Julie was champing at the bit to go out trick-or-treating. Too late, Ellen realized she couldn't be in two places at once, so she just left a bucket of chocolate bars on her front porch for the kids to grab when they came to her home, and she walked Julie around the neighborhood for an hour. Julie was dressed up as Minnie Mouse, and even Ellen thought she looked really cute. Soon Julie wouldn't want to do things like that, so Ellen took lots of photos.

When they got back home, the box of chocolate bars looked untouched.

"No kids?" she asked.

Julie just shrugged, and Ellen knew she realized there'd be more treats for her as a result.

Bedtime wasn't until 10:00. Julie took her time getting changed, and Ellen wanted to go through all the candy to be sure it was safe.

By the time Julie finally settled down and crawled into bed, Ellen was just grateful Halloween was finally over. It was the worst ever, only punctuated with bits of Julie's laughter as she walked around town collecting candy.

Ellen had a nice long bath and almost fell asleep in the water. She shook herself awake and was about to go to her own bed when the doorbell rang.

"Oh for Christ's sake!"

This time, she wasn't just irritated, she was full-force pissed off. She stomped down the stairs and pulled the door open.

This time there were only two of the ghouls standing at the end of her lawn. The one with the metal pipe was missing.

"Where's your leader, boys? Get too cold for him?"

They didn't move.

"Time to go home, boys. Halloween is over and now you can go back to church or whatever you do when you're not bullying people."

She thought of storming out and grabbing the little monsters, but then she heard Julie.

"MOM! HELP!"

The bone-chilling scream echoed through the house. Ellen turned and ran upstairs, not even bothering to close the front door.

She pushed Julie's bedroom door open, but the room was dark.

"Julie? Are you okay?"

Then she saw the shadow leaning over her daughter and she froze. Can't be. The missing Halloween phantom was on top of Julie. She could see the figure that was just a bit different shade from the darkness of the room.

It only took a few seconds for Ellen to get her wits back, and she hit the light switch.

There was no ghoul. Only Julie.

The first conflicting thoughts were gratitude that the monster wasn't there and fear about the same thing.

"Baby?"

She moved closer and saw the blood splattered on the white sheets. And the broken face. And the arms and legs twisted in ways they were never meant to twist.

Ellen collapsed.

#

November 4

The ABC Club attended Julie's funeral, as did most of the parents and children that lived close to Ellen. They all looked at her and told her how sorry they were, but sometimes Ellen saw another side to them: written on some of the guests' faces was an expression that said, "Thank God it was you and not me."

She ignored the neighbors and just mourned her little girl.

When she returned home, the place felt empty. It was like all the joy and happiness had been sucked out of her family home and all that remained was a rotted mausoleum of bad memories.

Ellen sat on Julie's bed for a while, wondering how her life could have been shattered so badly.

She closed the bedroom door and walked out to the barn, taking the opportunity to once again wander through old memories of her, Julie, and Davey.

"I miss you both so much," she said softly.

She was chilly even with a wool sweater. The sun was starting to go down, but she wasn't interested in heading back to the house. She wasn't interested in much of anything anymore.

The gun was still in the lower box.

Ellen hefted it in her hands, wondering what it would be like to pull the trigger. Of course, she knew that when she did it, she wouldn't actually know what it felt like. She wouldn't be around anymore.

The gun was polished steel, and it reminded her of the metal pipe the phantom carried.

She put the muzzle of the gun in her mouth and clamped her lips around it. There was a part of her that wanted her to stop, but she didn't pay much attention to it.

In her mind, she prayed to her Lord and said one last farewell to her little lost family.

The End

Halloweenland

By

Kevin J. Kennedy

The alarm hadn't even gone off when Zak jumped up out of bed. Not that Zak often set an alarm for Saturday mornings, however, this Saturday, it was only 7am when he decided to start his day. He had barely slept a wink anyway, and knew there was no way he was getting back to sleep. He had to get round to Wendy's house as soon as possible. He knew she was just as excited about tonight's events as he was and doubted that she would have slept much, either.

Wendy was Zak's best friend; they had always been friends from as far back as he could remember. Their mothers had been friends and had taken them to the same nursery, where Zak and Wendy had played together. Now, at the age of thirteen, they would often spend their time either getting into trouble or trying to get each other out of trouble. It wasn't that they were bad kids, they were just typical teenagers who had a knack for making bad decisions. They had both been on their best behaviour for the last two weeks to make sure that they didn't risk being put on house arrest by their parents. Zak and Wendy loved Halloween and this wasn't just any old Halloween... this was the Halloween that Halloweenland was coming to town!

The flyers for Halloweenland had started appearing around a month before. They were crudely designed, with a picture of a funhouse that looked like it had been drawn by a child and printed in jet black ink. The flyers looked like they had been ripped into shape rather than cut with a machine or scissors, and the paper resembled the cheap paper towels that companies buy when they don't care about their employees. Zack had found his first one in Cult Empire Comics, where he was picking up the new copies of Vietnam Zombie Apocalypse and City of Lost Souls. They had a pile of the flyers next to the cash register. Zak had picked it up because it looked pretty retro and cool, and thought he could add it to the assortment of random pictures, posters and art prints that were stuck to the pin-board above his chest of drawers. It hadn't given any details of what Halloweenland would be or where it was. The obvious guess was that a traveling carnival was coming to town for Halloween, but it turned out to be much bigger than that.

As the weeks passed, Zak and Wendy tried their best to find any details of Halloweenland online. There wasn't a single mention of it anywhere. They had busied themselves with deciding what costumes they would wear on the night of Halloween, regardless of where they ended up. Wendy settled on a 'Wednesday Addams' costume and Zak opted for an 'evil clown' costume. Wendy tried to talk him out of it due to her phobia of clowns, but he explained that Halloween was supposed to be scary and she would just need to deal with it. While she wasn't happy, she convinced herself she would be okay as long as she saw Zak with the mask off first.

The week before Halloween, everything was revealed. The old pier had been bought by an anonymous investor. The council put an advert in the local newspaper about how it would be refurbished and that it would create lots of jobs, not to mention additional tourism and revenue for the town. Apparently, the buyer was going to convert it back to its glory days and have it filled with various stalls and rides. As a special opening night, they were going to theme the mini- carnival as Halloweenland. The flyers became more extravagant, boasting cheesy slogans like 'If you come along, you'll never want to leave us,' and, 'The most terrifying Halloween evening of your life'. Zak could not wait. Part of the reason that Zak and Wendy's friendship had lasted into high school, while many others didn't make it, was in a large part due to their mutual love of cheesy, old horror movies. Zak's dad had a massive collection of horror movies from the eighties and nineties. Most were on DVD, but he even had an old VHS recorder set up in his study. Zak would often sneak in after his parents were in bed and watch some of his dad's old movies. The acting was terrible in some of them and the special effects were really bad, but Zak loved them, nonetheless. He had then started sneaking them out to Wendy, who would take them home for just the one night and watch them in her room, then they would swap notes the next day; that was when they were younger. Now, they just watched them together with each other and none of their parents seemed to pay much attention as long as they left their bedroom door open. That was the annoying new rule: no matter whose house they were in, they had to leave the door open. It really frustrated them both, that they were allowed no privacy just because they had gotten older, but they both knew you had to pick and choose your battles with your parents. None of that mattered right now, though. Halloweenland was coming to town.

As each day passed, in the last week leading up to Halloween, there were still very few details about the new carnival that would sit on the pier. Zak had expected to have spent the last week watching workmen refurbish the old pier, but nothing happened. It looked as bad as it ever had and was still a regular hang out for the junkies. The other thing that he found very strange, but no one seemed to be talking about, was the fact that there was no one building any rides. He started to wonder if it was going to be just a few small rides, and all the excitement would be for nothing.

On the thirtieth of October, Zack and Wendy walked out to where the old pier began; a place no one reputable in town ever ventured any more. The drunks and the junkies had made it their own and hung out at the end of the pier, knowing the police would never venture down there. Only the odd couple would wander halfway down on the way home from a night out for a quickie before they staggered home. You can actually divide the pier up by pairs of discarded panties down to where the broken needles start. Zak and Wendy looked along the pier as far as they could see, before their view was blocked by one of the old gift shops. It was made of wood and the weather hadn't been kind to it. The paint was cracked and the wood seemed to sag in places. Most of the panes of glass were broken or gone completely. Zak wasn't sure how they could get the place looking even semi-presentable by the next day, never mind safe for the public but he didn't care about that. It had been advertised everywhere, for a month. He knew that there was no way it wouldn't happen. It was only one more day. He would enjoy himself, even if it was a run-down dump.

***

Zak's brain was buzzing as he rang Wendy's doorbell. There had been an advert on the radio, just before he left the house about Halloweenland. Apparently someone had been there, first thing in the morning and was raving about how amazing it all looked. Zak found it a little hard to believe, considering the state the pier had been in just yesterday, but the reporter or radio DJ sounded convincing in what he was saying.

"Oh, hi, Zak. Come on in," Wendy's mum said, as she waved Zak inside. "Wendy will be down just now."

Zak walked straight through into the kitchen, as was his Saturday morning routine when he went round to Wendy's house. What wasn't normal was when Wendy appeared in the kitchen already dressed in her 'Wednesday Addams' costume.

"Uh, isn't it a little early for costumes?" Zak asked.

"It's Halloween, isn't it, dummy?" Wendy responded, rolling her eyes and glancing away. *'She really does look like Wednesday Addams'* Zak thought to himself.

"Well, yeh, but it's daytime…" Zak responded, wondering if he was arguing a point, or looking for a good enough reason to go put his own costume on.

"Look, we have a big day ahead of us and I just didn't want to have to come home later to get changed. This way I'm ready for whatever comes up and I don't need to be home 'til eleven tonight. My mum said since she knows I love Halloween, and because she knows the entire town will be there, I can have an extra hour. She said everyone in her work has been talking about tonight and that she doesn't know anyone who isn't going…" Wendy paused for a moment, slipping into one of her trance-like states, before she snapped back into reality and continued on an excited rant. "You know, we are going to have to queue for ages to get on anything. I think we need to be there early because people will probably queue, but if we get in first, we should be able to have a go on a good few rides before the pier fills up." As Wendy finished her excited chatter, Zak was still wondering if he should go put his own costume on.

"Uh, yeh, whatever you say. Do you think I should, maybe, go get my costume just now?" Zak asked, not really having listened to what Wendy said.

"Might as well. Will save us having to stop whatever we are doing later." As the words came out of Wendy's mouth, she felt a sense of dread, almost like sealing her own fate. Now she would have to spend the day with psycho-clown-guy. Maybe it wouldn't be so bad. At least she was getting to spend the full day with Zak.

"Okay, let's go back to mine, so I can get ready." Zak said, excitedly.

A few hours later…

When Zak and Wendy arrived at the pier, they couldn't believe the transformation. Not only was the entire pier filled with stalls and rides, but they had converted some of the old shops and everything looked like new. Neither of them could understand how the carnies had managed to do so much in so little time, but they didn't really care. They were amongst the first to arrive and had darted through the newly-built carnival gates after they had each bought a large reel of tickets. At first they hadn't even had to queue, but the carnival had quickly come to life as people of all ages descended on the pier with thousands of flashing lights. Calliope music played from each individual vendor, the tunes blending together in a happy melody. Bells and horns went off as the townsfolk won prizes at the stalls testing your skill or strength. Almost everyone knew that these games were rigged, and it was rarely skill that made you a winner, but people played them for fun and often to remember simpler times. All of the stalls and rides were painted with witches with black cats, jack-o-lanterns, vampires and the like. Some of them even had fake ghosts hanging with light-up eyes, and most of them had smoke machines hooked up, giving the flooring of the pier a layer of mist. Wendy just hoped they had gotten rid of all the needles, though she was pretty sure they would have, considering the job they had done on the place.

As night fell, and Zak and Wendy made their way between the revellers, they enjoyed the various smells that carried on the air. There were candy apples, candyfloss, roasted peanuts, freshly made doughnuts, crepes, chocolate-coated bananas, burgers, hotdogs and much, much more. Just about any kind of food that was bad for you, but tasted great was at the carnival. Zak and Wendy had grabbed a burger and chilli cheese fries when they arrived, but had decided to leave some of the messier snacks to the end of the night.

Wendy found that the scary clown costume that Zak had worn wasn't giving her the creeps. It helped knowing it was her best friend inside it and she knew him so well that no matter how he was dressed, she knew him by his movements and actions. On top of that, he had to keep lifting his mask up to eat. When they were walking down to the pier they had both agreed that they would leave the funhouse until after it got dark. They were now making their way to the end of the pier where the newly built funhouse had been erected. Moving through the crowd was slow, now that it had gotten so busy. Neither of them were in a rush and now that night had fallen they almost felt like they were in a different carnival. Darkness lends a feeling of magic to carnivals; the flashing, coloured lights, coupled with the enchanting music had them feeling like they were part of another world, even if only for a few hours. As the crowd got thicker towards the end of the pier, the two were huddled tighter together. Wendy took the opportunity to slip her arm through Zak's. It was something that she had never done before, but felt like this would be the perfect opportunity. Zak turned towards her, looked down at their interlinked arms and back up to her face. Wendy could see his cheeks had reddened, even in the dark, as his mask rested across his forehead. They had never been more than friends, but recently Zak had started to look at her differently, and after some careful thought, she had decided that it wouldn't be so bad if he was to ask to be her boyfriend. Zak could be pretty shy, so she decided a few days before the carnival that it would be the perfect time to try and subtly show him that she liked him more than just as a friend. She knew he had always had a crush on the Wednesday Addams character, hence the reason for her outfit.

As they walked between the stalls and rides, occasionally stopping to walk around the mini-arcades that had been set up, they both noticed that some of the carnies were pretty weird. They had both seen a fair amount of movies containing carnival freaks but hadn't expected to come across any in real life. Neither of them had seen any actual freaks yet, and the carnies operating the rides and stalls all seemed pretty normal, but every so often they would see someone who looked a little weird. They passed a Gypsy caravan with a strange little dwarf standing outside. He was calling out for people to come inside and have their fortune told by Madame de Rosemonde. Wendy thought about it for a little while and then decided it was better, not knowing. Something about the caravan and the strange little dwarf just didn't feel right. She couldn't work out what it was, but she had a feeling inside, that the fortune teller was real, unlike most, and Wendy wasn't sure if she wanted to know her future. Zak noticed her stop and hesitate.

"You want to go in?" he asked.

"No, I was just looking," she responded, before pulling him forward.

As they walked away, the fortune teller exited her caravan and stood next to the dwarf, named Doc. She had long red hair, her face was powdered white, and her lips were dark red. She was considered extremely attractive. Dressed in a typical Roman Gypsy clothing she leant against the side of the caravan and watched the two kids disappear into the crowd.

"Good kids, those two," she said to Doc, as she disappeared back into her caravan with a sombre look on her face.

Zak and Wendy were now struggling to push through the crowd. The bottom of the pier was much busier. A lot of people seemed to be heading towards the funhouse. When they finally arrived at the queue they sighed in unison. There had to be a hundred people and the strange-looking clown at the entrance seemed to be only letting groups of two or three in at a time.

The queue didn't seem to be getting shorter, when Wendy had a lightbulb moment that she hoped would make things go by a little quicker.

"I'm pretty cold. Do you think you could wrap your arms around me while we wait?" she asked, looking up at Zak, who was slightly taller than her, with her doe-like eyes. Zak, a little taken aback by the request, kept his composure and nodded. He had wanted to hold Wendy in his arms for a while now, but didn't know if she liked him back. As he stepped behind her and wrapped his arms around her, his mind went into overdrive. *Does this mean she likes me? She took my arm earlier. Or is she just cold, and didn't want us to get separated earlier?*

As Zak's mind raced, Wendy just enjoyed the feeling of being so close to Zak. She didn't know if they would have their first kiss that night, but she knew that it was definitely the beginning of something. Her heart pounding in her chest was enough to reassure her of that.

Before they knew it, they were at the front of the queue and they had barely spoken the whole time, both caught up in their thoughts of the future together without either being able to vocalise their feelings.

One of the most beautiful clowns that either of them had ever seen was stood at the entrance of the funhouse. Her makeup was white and black. It surrounded her eyes and mouth, her eyes darkened along the lids and a sharp line ran through both eyes from the brow to the cheek. Surrounding her pink, luscious lips was a thick, white rim that came to points at either side of her face, outlined in a thin, black line. The rest of her face had no paint on it. Her outfit seemed a little weird for a clown. She wore black and red pop socks, bare legs with little wine- coloured shorts with white lace around the leg holes. Her top was a black vest with a large blue silky bow around her neck. Her puffed-out, long, ginger hair was topped off with a gold top hat with a blue and wine oversized bow wrapped around it. She wore white lace cuffs on both wrists.

"Tickets?" the clown asked them. Neither of them had ever seen a clown look so sad. It wasn't the clown make-up that made her look sad. She just looked like she would rather be anywhere else than standing taking tickets for the funhouse. Zak stuck his hand out, holding two tickets. They had been paying each other onto rides since the start of the night, taking turns each. The clown just nodded her head to the side, towards the entrance.

The entrance to the funhouse was a massive goblin face, bright green and split down the middle. Zak and Wendy walked towards it and Zak pushed the doors open, ahead of them stood a long, dark corridor. With a last look at each other, they both stepped inside and the doors swung shut behind them. As soon as the doors closed, all noise from outside ceased. The chattering of the crowd, the calliope music and the various bells and buzzers that had been ringing out, was gone. The corridor had no lights, but there were tiny, little, white lights along the floor so they could see the walkway. They made their way along the corridor to the first turn. As they turned the corner, an almighty roar ripped through the corridor, as a man- sized corpse blocked their path. Neither of them screamed. The metal pole that was attached to its head, that swung it out from the wall, wasn't concealed nearly enough, not to mention that the corpse had a distinct plastic look to it. The rest of the funhouse wasn't much better. By the time they were walking down a corridor to the exit, both were feeling deeply let down by the claims the fliers had made.

As Zak pushed the doors open to the outside world they both noticed a few things straight away. The noise of the outside world didn't return. Where earlier there had been hundreds, if not thousands of people talking to each other at once with music playing from everywhere, there was now only a few separate calliope tunes playing from various points on the pier. It was now fully dark and most of the rides had been turned off, but more disturbing was the lack of anyone else on the pier. Nervously they both stepped out onto the walkway of the funhouse that led to the stairs to leave.

"So, you made it through?" the clown asked them.

"What? Where is everyone?" Zak asked, turning to her with a quizzical look on his face. "How long were we in there?"

For the first time, the kids saw the clown smile.

"You were in about fifteen minutes and technically everyone is still here. Well, most of them anyway."

"What do you mean everyone is still here?" Wendy asked, looking across the pier, trying to convince herself that she wasn't missing something.

"Well, the funhouse is a kind of portal. It feeds the carnival. Some who pass through come out of the exit, just like you two did, and others, the carnival decides to keep for itself. That's the magic of the carnival," the clown responded.

Wendy and Zak looked at each other for a second before looking back to the clown.

"You're fucking with us," Zak said. "It's some kind of trick, isn't it?" he said, with a pleading look in his eyes. He knew something was wrong, but was unable to believe what the clown was saying.

"Nope," the clown answered. "I've only been with the carnival for a little while, but it would seem that it's powered by souls. Nothing to do with me though, I just work here," she concluded.

"What, so you're telling me everyone else has been swallowed up by some crazy funhouse at a stupid carnival? Bullshit!!" Zak exclaimed, in a voice that was much less forceful than he planned it to be. Wendy was now holding his arm again, and pressed tight into his side.

The clown sighed. "Listen, I don't really give a fuck what you believe you little shit. It is what it is, just like most things in life. Not believing it doesn't mean you don't have to deal with it." The clown stopped talking and appraised the two teenagers. "Okay, this is how it works, as best as I've come to understand it. The carnival travels from place to place, never appearing for more than a day. The next day it's gone, as are all traces of it. Each time it leaves a town, it takes a few of the residents with it. It always has and it always will."

"So, where is everyone else, then? And what does the funhouse have to do with it all?" Zak asked, not sure whether he believed what she was saying, but unsure of what options he had other than to question her more.

"The funhouse is kind of the centre of the carnival, the power source if you like. The carnival doesn't just travel from town to town, it crosses planes of existence and sometimes even time-hops. Today we are here, but tomorrow we could be in the old west and the following day we could be back here again, on the very same day but in an alternate reality, that's only slightly different from this one. The carnival morphs into whatever fits the surroundings and time period. Sometimes it's a massive theme park and other times it's a tiny traveling side show. As I said, I haven't been here that long, but I've seen some pretty interesting things," the clown explained.

"This has to be some kind of joke. Did someone put you up to this? Someone from school?"

"Kid, look around you. Do you really think this is a joke? Everyone else is here. You two are here, too, but also not here," the clown said, looking around her. "You're here until the carnival decides if it's going to let you leave."

"But, I thought you said the funhouse decides? Aren't we free to go?"

"You are free to go, but the funhouse doesn't make all the decisions. It's just the centre of power. If either of you make it to the end of the pier, you will be safe. As soon as your feet hit concrete, you can go home and go about your life as always. Tomorrow a few people will be reported missing but that's nothing out of the ordinary. The carnival, and all traces of it, will be gone forever. I wish you good luck on your journey, my friends." And with that, the clown jumped straight up, with her arms extended, catching onto the balcony above. She was up and over the balcony with incredible speed and ease, leaving them standing alone.

"This can't be real, can it?" Wendy asked, looking at Zak with eyes that were filled with fear.

"I don't know. I mean, how would you fake this? Where the fuck is everyone? They couldn't have emptied the pier that quick. Let's just head for home. I don't think any good can come from hanging about here." They quickly descended the stairs, heading straight for the entrance to the pier. It looked much creepier with most of the lights off. The few individual tunes that were still playing, now seemed to carry eerily on the sea breeze, the delicious smells of the assorted foods from earlier now gone. Wendy slipped her hand down from their interlocking arms and clasped her fingers through Zak's.

"Let's move, quick," she said, picking up her pace.

They started to move quickly through the now creepy-looking stalls, steeped in shadows, making the carnival appear as if it had been abandoned for years, when suddenly three shapes stepped out in front of them. Wendy let out a gasp and they both stopped in their tracks. In front of them stood three clowns, Wendy's worst nightmare. More terrifying for her was the fact that each of these clowns had a carved pumpkin for a face-- not make-up to look like a pumpkin-- but what actually seemed to be a moving, living, possibly breathing, pumpkin face. Their mouths were carved exactly as they would be on a pumpkin that you carved for Halloween except Wendy and Zak could tell that their teeth were razor sharp. Zak grabbed Wendy's hand and started running, pulling her with him. They ducked between stalls and rides, moving as fast as they could while trying not to trip on all the electrical cables that were running along the ground. As they moved they could hear a strained, guttural laughing that sounded like it was coming from the roofs of the stalls above and behind them. As the kids came out between one of the burger bars and a novelty shop, they were both panting hard. Knowing they couldn't keep running, Wendy looked around for somewhere to hide.

"Look, over there," she said to Zak, pointing.

Zak smiled and they took off running together, straight for the shooting gallery. Both of them vaulting the counter and landing safely behind it. Zak quickly pulled two of the guns down from the rack. When they had played the game earlier they were both impressed with the force in which the ball-bearings fired out of the rifles. What they didn't know is if they would have any effect at all on the clowns.

"Stay down," Zak told Wendy. "I'll look and see if they've followed us."

As Zak began to peek over the counter he instantly felt something smash into his forehead, knocking him flying back on his ass. Wendy screamed again and crawled quickly towards him. Zak raised his hand to his forehead. "What the fuck was that?" Wendy touched her hand to his forehead. He winced. Bringing her fingers up to her nose and sniffing, she said, "It's pumpkin., They are throwing pumpkins at us."

"Are you fucking kidding me? We are running from these clowns and they are throwing pumpkins?" Zak said as the pumpkin-clowns seemed to laugh at him in their strange guttural way.

Wendy was shocked at the look of rage that crossed Zak's face; she had never seen him get angry before.

"Think this is all a big fucking joke, do they?" she heard him mumble as he crawled across the ground and retrieved his gun. This time he crawled over to the wall of the stall, and slid up behind the side of the window. "Wendy, throw one of those stupid teddies out the window and over to the side."

There were large plastic bags of teddies under the table she was lying next to. Ripping open the first bag, she grabbed one of the smaller teddies and crawled below the window to the stall. She looked over and Zak nodded. He had gotten a glimpse of the three clowns standing out in the open for a millisecond before the pumpkin had almost knocked his head off. *Just like a coconut shy,* he thought to himself. Wendy threw the teddy as hard as she could, without looking over the counter. As it left her hand, Zak spun around the side of the window, raising his gun as he turned, took aim and pulled the trigger. The clown in the middle's head exploded upon impact. Zak had no idea if it would even have any impact on the clowns, but it seemed that their heads weren't all that tough. The clowns on either side of the middle one turned from the flying teddy bear, towards their headless colleague. Zak took the chance to aim again and shot the second clown in the head. His aim was as true as the first shot. As the second clown's head exploded, the first clown's lifeless body fell to the ground. The third clown, having seen what happened ran straight towards the shooting gallery. Zak hadn't expected it and fired a shot that went wild. As he readjusted his aim and pulled the trigger again, the gun clicked, but nothing came out. Zak tried again just as the clown dove through the window of the stall and landed at Wendy's feet.

Wendy screamed, fell backwards and tried to crawl away, but the clown grabbed her by the ankle. Wendy, never one to just lay down, started kicking the clown in the face with her free foot, but Zak could see she was having to time it to miss the razor-sharp teeth of the animated pumpkin head.

Zak tried to get another shot off. He was at point blank range, but the gun just wouldn't fire. Having no time left, Zak spun the gun so that he held it by the barrel, and swung it with all his might at the clown's head. The stock had an equally pleasing effect on the pumpkin-clown's head as the ball-bearings did. While the head didn't quite explode apart as it had before, it'd burst in several places; chunks of the innards spilled out, spraying Wendy's legs before the clown fell on top of her. Zak wasted no time in checking that the outside of the stall was clear, before grabbing the clown by the back of its suit and dragging it from Wendy. He grabbed her hands and pulled her to a standing position.

"Euuchhhh!" Wendy said as she wiped the mushed pumpkin from her legs. It looked different from normal pumpkin innards, much more red, as if it had blood running through it.

"Are you okay?" Zak asked, sounding worried.

"Yeh, I'm fine. It didn't bite me. And thanks."

"Let's get the fuck out of here before any more of those things appear."

As if tempting fate, as the kids vaulted the window to the shooting gallery they started to notice more of the clowns appearing on the roofs of several stalls. Each wore a different style clown suit but they all had the same, large, pumpkin head. They had no eyes but a strange light inside the sockets that looked a little like a candle flickering. Each of them started to make strange gargled sounds. Zak and Wendy had no idea if they were communicating or if it was the collective sound of their hunger. Not waiting to find out, Zak grabbed her hand and started running. In his rush he had forgotten to lift the gun. It wasn't firing, but he could have used it as a club. Wendy however, *had* lifted the gun she had left lying next to the bag of teddies.

They sprinted down the centre of the pier, no longer concerned with trying to hide but instead going for the most direct route out of the Carnival. As they ran, Zak felt something lightly hit the back of his head before falling around his neck. His hands went up quickly to wrap around the yellow rubber ring that now hung around his neck. Slowing to a walking pace, with Wendy stopping to look at Zak to see what was going on, another hoop, green this time, came flying out of the darkness and landed perfectly around Wendy's neck.

"Are they actually playing ring-toss with us?" Wendy said, sounding a mixture of shocked and angry.

"Looks like it, let's keep going. We're almost there."

As they started to run again the rings began landing all around them and bouncing away. The clowns strange chatter was getting louder as they neared the entrance to the pier and then the kids noticed that the rings landing around them were on fire. All it would take was for one to find its mark and one of them were in for some serious burns.

"Keep going," Zak said, struggling to catch his breath. As they passed the last of the stalls and rides and entered the large open part of the pier just before the gate, they stopped in their tracks. In front of them stood three of the strangest-looking creatures they had ever seen. They looked like a mixture of an overly-muscular Rottweiler, with the head of a wolf, but the head and snout of the wolf-shaped face was also made out of pumpkin. Bright orange and lined like a pumpkin skin, just like the clowns' faces, except the dog-like creatures' jaws snapped much faster and had a lot more teeth. The bodies of the beasts were covered in jet-black fur, as if it belonged to a normal dog.

Not knowing quite what to do, and knowing they only had the one gun, Zak turned to look behind them. The clowns who had been lining the rooftops, had now formed a line across the middle of the walkway. There were twelve of them in total, and each was doing something somewhere between weird and terrifying. One of the pumpkin clowns juggled three mini-pumpkins that were all on fire, another was doing a pretty impressive nunchuck display, the nunchucks also on fire. One was walking towards them on his hands with both feet on fire. The fire seemed to cause the pumpkin-clowns no pain, but Zak and Wendy doubted it would be as painless should it touch them.

Zak turned back and forth quickly between the clowns and the dog creatures trying to work out which route was less likely to result in a painful death. As his mind ran a million miles a minute he heard the gun go off next to him. Wendy had taken a shot at one of the dogs while he was trying to work out what to do; she never had liked ditherers. None of the dogs dropped.

"You missed it," Zak said.

"I hit it, they just don't go down as easy as the clowns." As Wendy finished speaking, she took another shot, that Zak could see hit the dog, by the way its skull bounced back. It still didn't drop.

"Fuck!" Zak said, knowing they were in trouble. "Shoot the clowns. Maybe we can go back that way. Wendy spun round quickly and took aim and fired into the approaching wall of clowns. Two of them dropped at the one time, both on separate ends of the line. The first fell off his unicycle, crashing into the boards of the pier and the other just stood headless for a few seconds before falling forwards onto the chainsaw he carried. It took only seconds for the chainsaw to rip him apart.

"What the..." Zak started, as Wendy aimed again, and fired into the face of the one with the biggest pumpkin head, hoping he was some kind of leader and that his death would somehow render the others immobile. It did no such thing but again, two clowns went down. Zak looked back to see that the dog-like creatures were making their way towards them slowly, but he had no idea when they would break into a run. As he turned back towards the clowns, and Wendy setting herself up for another shot, he caught a glimpse of gold on one of the rooftops. On looking closer he could see it was the clown from earlier at the funhouse. He could barely make her out, but there was no hiding her gold hair and hat. He could see the barrel of a rifle peeking out from the darkness, though. As he turned back towards the clowns, two more of them fell to the ground.

Only six remained, but the dogs were now almost upon them. Zak ran to the closest stall and jumped inside. It turned out to be the hook-a-duck stall. It was filled with plastic ducks, floating in a spinning pool of water. There was pretty much nothing else in the stall, apart from the teddies for prizes and the long wooden stick with a hook on top of it. Zak grabbed the pole and jumped back through the stall window. When he got back outside, he could see the clown that appeared to be helping them had dropped down from the rooftop, and was moving towards the pumpkin-clowns. Wendy seemed to be messing with the gun meaning it had either stuck or she had run out of ball-bearings.

"Use it as a club," Zak shouted, as he moved towards the dog-like creatures. Two of them turned to Zak, while the other kept progressing towards Wendy.

"Behind you," Zak shouted. Wendy spun around and turned the gun over to use as a club. The pretty clown seemed to be doing fine on her own anyway. Zak was struggling to take his eyes away from Wendy when the first dog got close enough for him to take a swing. The pole he had was long and not the easiest to handle, but he only barely missed the creature's skull. As it made a strangled, growling sound at him, red mush-like chunks dropped from its maw. The other dog, seeing its chance, sprung at him. Swinging his stick quickly, he hit the creature in the ribs. As the dog landed, he realised the hook had stuck in the dog's ribs. Thinking quickly, he started to pull the dog backwards towards the stall he had come from. When they got in line with it, and using every bit of might he could muster, Zak swung his weight into pulling the stick as quickly as possible towards the hook-a-duck stall, dragging the dog with it and smashing it against the wall. The dog let out a not-quite-howl and fell to its side. The force of the dog smashing into the stall had released the hook from its side. It took Zak three goes, missing with the first two but the third time he crashed the pole down, the hook solidly sunk into the creature's pumpkin-like skull.

Wasting no time, Zak spun to see the other two dogs were closing in on Wendy. One at either side of her. The hook of his pole would not come free from the dead creatures skull and he had no time to find another weapon. Wendy was swinging furiously at the dog closest to her, which seemed to be keeping it at bay, but she was allowing the other dog to get closer to her. Without a second thought, Zak charged the dog closest to him and took the hardest penalty kick he had ever swung. The front of his foot crashed into the dog's ribcage and he felt the bones snap as it let out a bloodcurdling howl, the sound still gargled by whatever made up its vocal cords. It quickly turned to snap at him with its large, orange canines, but it was obvious that it was hurt. Taking his time to aim his next kick, Zak danced on the spot. The creature attacked again, Zak waited until it just missed him and swung another full-force kick, this time aiming for the creature's jaw. When his foot connected, its jaw snapped shut. As its teeth smashed together, part of its jaw broke off, landing between its two front paws. As Zak looked on, wondering what his next move was, Wendy came from nowhere, the gun held over her head and brought it down on the creature's skull. The first strike killed it instantly, but Zak watched as she continued to rain down blows. When she stopped, the corpse was almost unrecognisable. Zak looked over to where she had been and found the other animal lying dead, in a similar state. Remembering the pumpkin dogs hadn't been their only concern, he turned back to where that battle of the clowns had been going on. They were all dead, their bodies strewn all over the pier. He caught sight of the pretty clown, slipping between two of the stalls.

"Wait!" Zak shouted, before jogging to catch her. As he reached the alleyway between the two stalls he could see that she was gone, and he had no intentions of chasing her down the pier. Turning to go back and get Wendy, and get the hell out of there, he noticed a white, rectangular card lying on the boards of the pier. He reached down and picked it up and was shocked to see what was on it. The card had a sketch of both him and Wendy, and under the drawings were scribbled the words 'Look after these two. They're important.' On the back of the card was a printed signature of Madame de Rosemonde. Zak had no idea what it meant or why they were important, but he didn't really care. It was time to leave this place. He slipped the card into the only, tiny, excuse-for-a-pocket on his costume and ran back to get Wendy. She was still standing with the club raised, looking hyper-vigilant. She seemed to relax as he got closer.

"Let's get the fuck out of here," Wendy said, as she grabbed his hand and they ran to the edge of the pier. As soon as their feet hit the concrete at the edge of the pier everything went hazy for the briefest flash and then they were surrounded by hundreds, if not thousands of the towns-people. They all looked like they were in shock, some of them were injured, but it didn't look like many people could have been trapped on the pier. Zak and Wendy knew that by tomorrow reports would start to come in for missing people. Had everyone had the same experience or had it been different for each of them? Did the others receive help from some of the carnival folk or had it just been Wendy and Zak? Each of them had a million questions, but they weren't sure anyone would have any answers.

"Let's go to my house," Wendy said. "Hopefully, my parents have made it home okay and you can call your house."

"Didn't think I'd let you walk home by yourself, did you?" Zak asked, with the best smile he could muster under the circumstances. Zak wrapped his arm around Wendy's waist, pulling her in tight against him to keep her warm. His early shyness and worry about getting closer to Wendy seemed like absolute madness in light of the night they had just had. As they walked through the townsfolk, who seemed to be quietly making their way away from the pier, they stopped and turned back to have one last look at the carnival. It was gone. It had been gone the minute they stepped back on the concrete. The pier looked like it always had, rundown and in need of repair.

"Was it all an illusion?" Zak said, almost to himself.

Wendy put her arm out in front of him. The teeth marks were evident and the blood hadn't quite dried. "I don't think so."

"We need to get you to a hospital," Zak declared, sounding panicked.

"I'm fine. It barely caught me. I just hope I don't turn into a pumpkin," Wendy remarked, trying to sound jokey, but knowing that she was actually a little worried about it actually happening.

The next morning

When Zak got to Wendy's house, her mother had let him in, as always. He expected things to be somber, but she seemed her usual, chirpy self. When Wendy came into the kitchen, she quickly pulled him outside.

"What's going on?" Zak demanded.

"Aren't your parents the same?" she asked in return.

"What? Uh, my parents were still asleep when I left. Why is your mum acting like nothing's happened?"

When Zak had got to Wendy's the night before, her parents were already home. They were really freaked out and really happy to see the kids come in. They made Zak call his parents straight away. They had made it home safely, too, and told him to get a taxi straight home. Both sets of parents had known that neither of the kids had taken out their mobile phones, as they hadn't had decent pockets in their costumes to carry them, and hadn't wanted to lose them on the rides. Knowing the kids would have gone to one house or the other, the parents had gone straight home, knowing they may never find them in the crowd outside the pier. All four parents had spoken to their kids in length about what had happened to each of them, before they all headed to bed for the night, exhausted.

"They don't remember it. I noticed they seemed awful happy when I got up and knew it was strange, so instead of mentioning anything I just asked my mum if she had a good time at the carnival, and do you know what she said?" Wendy paused for a second. "She said *'Wonderful'*. Do you believe that shit? Wonderful!" Wendy exclaimed, exasperated. "I was kinda worried that you would show up and not remember."

"How could I forget?" Zak responded.

"Everyone else seems to have forgotten. I checked online. No mention of anything. I can't even find a mention of the carnival anywhere or a developer buying the pier. It's all gone."

"Fuck! What do we do?" Zak asked.

"What can we do? We're safe now and as far as I can tell we just act as if nothing happened."

"Let's go to my house." Zak said

At Zak's house

"It was definitely here. I'm sure I pinned it on the board." Zak said, rummaging around behind his chest of drawers to see if it had fallen. "I know I kept that fucking flier."

"It's gone, Zak, just like everything else. That carnival… it wasn't normal. It had some kind of magic running through it. How else would you explain a fucking living pumpkin of any type?"

"Shit! One minute," Zak grabbed the clown trousers from the night before. He reached into the little slit, that was lined with mesh, that masqueraded as a pocket, and he felt it straight away, the piece of card he had found after the battle.

'Look after these two. They're important.' was all it said.

They looked at each other. All traces of the carnival seemed to have disappeared apart from the card. What did it mean? Were they going to meet the strange, pretty, clown woman again? Was it Madame de Rosmonde that would cross their paths in the future? Or was it just a coincidence that the card was still there. Neither of them were in a rush to find out.

"So what do we do? Just act like nothing happened?" Zak asked.

"Well… We could always get cosy and watch one of your dad's old horror movies." Wendy said, with a little blush.

"You want to watch horror? After what we have just been through?" Zak asked, a little taken a back.

"Is there any other type of movie worth watching?" she said with a chuckle., " Besides, you can keep me close and protect me, but just to be safe, lets watch something old and cheesy."

As the kids made their way towards Zak's dad's study, they both knew that their lives had changed forever. As Wendy slipped her hand into Zak's and he clasped her fingers, they both thought that some changes were for the better.

Over the next few days

Several newspapers reported missing people, but none of the cases went anywhere. Nothing much changed in the town and people went about their business as always. The only one difference was that a clown had been spotted hanging around, with gold hair and wearing a gold hat. None of the townsfolk remembered the carnival, so it was chalked up to someone playing pranks or some weirdo trying to scare kids, but Wendy and Zak knew better.

"A clown with gold hair," he had said. "She's looking for us..."

The End

Halloweenland, is the first story in a series of interlinked carnival tales. Several authors are already involved in this project which will be a mixture of short stories and novellas. Keep your eyes peeled for 'Kevin J. Kennedys Carnival Tales.'

Afterword

By

Kevin J. Kennedy

Well, it looks like you have made it to the end of our little Halloween anthology. I hope you enjoyed it. Halloween has been my favourite time of year for as far back as I can remember. I think it is for a lot of horror lovers. It's a time of year when the stores are filled with the kind of things we would like to see on the shelves all year, an opportunity to decorate your house the way you would like to have it every day.

When I finished the Easter anthology, I wasn't sure if I was going to do another. There were quite a lot of problems putting the book together and I wasn't sure I wanted to go through it all again. I kept getting people asking me would I do a second Christmas anthology this year, but I decided to do something different, and Halloween seemed like the natural choice. After a bit of going back and forth, I decided to go ahead with it and was lucky enough to have several of my favourite authors interested in working with me again.

This is the third anthology in the series, all published within a year so I'm sure there will be more. I've had several suggestions on what the next book in the series should be, but, as of yet, haven't decided.

If you are enjoying the series so far, please consider leaving a review online. We all love to hear your thoughts and the feedback is always taken on board for future books.

Happy Halloween from all of us... We hope it's absolutely terrifying.

Author Bios

Christina Bergling

Colorado-bred writer, Christina Bergling knew she wanted to be an author in fourth grade.

In college, she pursued a professional writing degree and started publishing small scale. It all began with "How to Kill Yourself Slowly."

With the realities of paying bills, she started working as a technical writer and document manager, traveling to Iraq as a contractor and eventually becoming a trainer and software developer.

She avidly hosted multiple blogs on Iraq, bipolar, pregnancy, running. She continues to write on Fiery Pen: The Horror Writing of Christina Bergling and Z0mbie Turtle.

The horror genre has always been a part of Bergling's life. She has loved horror books ever since early readings of Goosebumps then Stephen King. She fell in love with horror movies young with Scream.

In 2015, she published two novellas. She is also featured in the horror collections Collected Christmas Horror Shorts, Collected Easter Horror Shorts, Collected Halloween Horror Shorts, Demonic Wildlife. Her latest novel, The Rest Will Come, will be released by Limitless Publishing in August 2017.

Bergling is a mother of two young children and lives with her family in Colorado Springs. She spends her non-writing time running, doing yoga and barre, belly dancing, taking pictures, traveling, and sucking all the marrow out of life.

www.christinabergling.com

www.facebook.com/chrstnabergling

@chrstnabergling

RICHARD CHIZMAR is a *New York Times, USA Today, Wall Street Journal, Washington Post, Amazon,* and *Publishers Weekly* bestselling author.

He is the co-author (with Stephen King) of the bestselling novella, *Gwendy's Button Box* and the founder/publisher of *Cemetery Dance* magazine and the Cemetery Dance Publications book imprint. He has edited more than 35 anthologies and his fiction has appeared in dozens of publications, including *Ellery Queen's Mystery Magazine* and multiple editions of *The Year's 25 Finest Crime and Mystery Stories*. He has won two World Fantasy awards, four International Horror Guild awards, and the HWA's Board of Trustee's award.

Chizmar (in collaboration with Johnathon Schaech) has also written screenplays and teleplays for United Artists, Sony Screen Gems, Lions Gate, Showtime, NBC, and many other companies. He has adapted the works of many bestselling authors including Stephen King, Peter Straub, and Bentley Little.

Chizmar is also the creator/writer of *Stephen King Revisited,* and his third short story collection, *A Long December,* was published in 2016 by Subterranean Press. With Brian Freeman, Chizmar is co-editor of the acclaimed *Dark Screams* horror anthology series published by Random House imprint, Hydra.

Chizmar's work has been translated into many languages throughout the world, and he has appeared at numerous conferences as a writing instructor, guest speaker, panelist, and guest of honor.

Please visit the author's website at: www.richardchizmar.com

Andrew Lennon is the bestselling author of Every Twisted Thought and several other horror/thriller books. He has featured in various bestselling anthologies, and is successfully becoming a recognised name in horror and thriller writing. Andrew is a happily married man living in the North West of England with his wife Hazel & their children.

Having always been a big horror fan, Andrew spent a lot of his time watching scary movies or playing scary games, but it wasn't until his mid-twenties that he developed a taste for reading. His wife, also being a big horror fan, had a very large Stephen King collection which Andrew began to consume. Once hooked into reading horror, he started to discover new authors like Thomas Ligotti & Ryan C Thomas. It was while reading work from these authors that he decided to try writing something himself and there came the idea for "A Life to Waste"

He enjoys spending his time with his family and watching or reading new horror.

For more information please go to www.andrewlennon.co.uk

Mark Lukens is an author and a screenwriter. He's had four screenplays optioned by producers in Hollywood, one of which is being developed into a film, and he's the author of many bestselling books including: Ancient Enemy, Sightings, The Exorcist's Apprentice, and Devil's Island. He's a member of the Horror Writers Association. He grew up in Daytona Beach, Florida. But after many travels and adventures, he settled down near Tampa, Florida with his wonderful wife and son, and a stray cat they adopted.

http://www.amazon.com/Mark-Lukens/e/B00G8GYUUG

http://www.marklukensbooks.wordpress.com/

https://www.facebook.com/Mark-Lukens-Books-670337796318510/

https://twitter.com/marklukensbooks

Suzanne Fox is a writer of both horror and erotic fiction which she manages to fit in around her day job as a nurse. She grew up in Staffordshire, England before moving, eleven years ago, to the beautiful county of Cornwall where she lives with her partner and three pussies: Cats, you dirty-minded folks! She loves the challenge of combining erotica and horror in her writing. Her work has been published in both print and online magazines with her short story "Hitting the Jackpot," coming third in a writing competition run by *Writer's Forum*. She has also had stories appear in several anthologies including *Collected Christmas Horror Shorts* and *Collected Easter Horror Shorts*. She is thrilled to a part of this latest addition in the series. Her writing credits also include short stories in, *Suite Encounters, Man behind the Mask, Tales from the Braided Pony, and Fuck the Rules.* Besides writing, she loves to dance, and drink wine with friends.

She had great fun writing her story, "The Devil's Fruit," and she hopes that you have as much fun reading it. Please join Suzanne on her Facebook page.

https://www.facebook.com/suzannefoxerotica/?ref=aymt_homepage_panel

Christopher Motz grew up on a diet of some of the horror genre's heavyweights: Stephen King, H.P. Lovecraft, Jack Ketchum, Richard Laymon, and Bentley Little, just to name a few. Writing at an early age, he often penned short stories to show to his parents, starting a life-long love of the written word.

Hailing from northeast Pennsylvania, Christopher lives with his wife, step-daughter, and miniature Morkie, Oy. His first novel, "The Darkening," was released in October 2016, followed soon after by a novella entitled "The Farm." His latest book, "Pine Lakes," was published in June 2017.

Christopher has several upcoming projects, including a novella to be released at the end of 2017, and a collaboration with Andrew Lennon entitled "The Pigeon" set for early next year.

www.christopher-motz.com

James Matthew Byers resides in Wellington, Alabama with his wife, kids, a dog named after an elf, and two tortoises. He has been published in poetry journals and through Jacksonville State University in Jacksonville, AL, where he received his Master's in 2010. His epic poem, Beowulf: The

297 | Collected Halloween Horror Shorts

Midgard Epic, is out now from Stitched Smile Publications, LLC. James designed and illustrated the cover and interior art for his debut novel at SSP, where he works as an in house illustrator. He also has a short story featured in their latest release, Unleashed: Monsters Vs. Zombies. James has won four Prose Challenges at www.theprose.com. He is published in Weirdbook Magazine and Grievous Angel ezine. He had a release coming out in early 2018 at Heroic Fantasy Quarterly. He won or placed in three of fifteen contests at the Alabama State Poetry Society. He continues to write prolifically, supporting anyone who wishes to place their hammering fingers to the keyboard anvil, becoming a polished wordsmith in the process.

Find James Matthew Byers at:

Twitter: www.Twitter.com/MattByers40

Facebook: https://m.facebook.com/Mattbyers40/

Wattpad: https://www.wattpad.com/user/JamesMatthewByers

Wordpress: http://jamesmatthewbyers.wordpress.com

Prose: https://theprose.com/JamesMByers

Steven Stacy has been writing since Junior School. His love for horror began when he watched 'A Nightmare On Elm Street ' at age 13 and decided Nancy was his heroine.

He graduated magna cum laude with honours, a joint degree in English and Creative English from the University of Bath Spa. He has written for numerous Horror magazines such as 'The Dark Side' and 'Gorezone', interviewing horror icons such as Robert Englund and Dee Wallace. For bellaonline.com where he is head editor of horror movies. For the sidekick cast, where he reviewed Catwoman comic books (he is a keen comic-book fan and collector of all things Catwoman; brought on by Michelle Pfeiffer's performance.) He loves Cats, The Little Mermaid, Tim Burton, Wes Craven & Drew Barrymore movies, and eighties music.

His favourite book is 'Cujo' by Stephen King, and he is currently working on his first major novel. Steven lives in Llandaff, Cardiff, with his cat, Isis.

Steven would like to say a huge thank-you to his Mum for all her help with this story, her honest critique and keen eyesight for grammar are amazing. Thanks mum! I love you xx

You can follow him on:

Facebook: https://www.facebook.com/stevenCJstacy/

Amazon Author Page: amazon.com/author/stevencaseymurray

Instagram: Username – blondarrow

Twitter: - @BlondArrow or @stevenCJstacy

www.screamhorrormag.com

www.bellaonline.com/articles/art37257.asp

www.thesidekickcast.com

Mark Cassell lives in a rural part of the UK where he often dreams of dystopian futures, peculiar creatures, and flitting shadows. Primarily a horror writer, his steampunk, dark fantasy, and SF stories have featured in numerous anthologies and ezines. His best-selling debut novel THE SHADOW FABRIC is closely followed by the popular short story collection SINISTER STITCHES and are both only a fraction of an expanding mythos of demons, devices, and deceit. The novella HELL CAT OF THE HOLT further explores the Shadow Fabric mythos with ghosts and black cat legends. For more about Mark and the mythos please visit www.theshadowfabric.co.uk

Briana Robertson excels at taking the natural darkness of reality and bringing it to life on the page. Heavily influenced by her personal experience with depression, anxiety, and the chronic pain of fibromyalgia, Robertson's dark fiction delves into the emotional and psychological experiences of characters in whom readers will recognize themselves. Her stories horrify while also tugging at heartstrings, muddying the lines of black and white, and staining the genre in multiple shades of grey.

In 2016, Robertson joined the ranks of Stitched Smile Publications. Her solo anthology, "Reaper," which explores the concept of death being both inevitable and non-discriminatory, debuted in 2017. She also has stories included in "Unleashing the Voices Within," by Stitched Smile Publications, "Man Behind the Mask," by David Owain Hughes, Jonathan Ondrashek, and Veronica Smith, and "Collected Easter Horror Shorts" and "Collected Halloween Horror Shorts" by Kevin Kennedy.

She is currently serving as Head of Dark Persuasions, the dark erotic branch of Stitched Smile Publications.

Robertson is the wife of one, mother of four, and unashamed lover of all things feline. She currently resides on the Illinois side of the Mississippi River, with a backyard view of the Saint Louis skyline, and is a member of the Saint Louis Writers Guild.

To find out more about Briana Robertson, please visit her website at www.brianarobertsonwri.wix.com/brianarobertson

Lisa Morton is a screenwriter, author of non-fiction books, award-winning prose writer, and Halloween expert whose work was described by the American Library Association's *Readers' Advisory Guide to Horror* as "consistently dark, unsettling, and frightening". She co-edited (with Ellen Datlow) the anthology *Haunted Nights*, which recently received a starred review in *Publishers Weekly;* other recent releases include *Ghosts: A Haunted History* and the collection *The Samhanach and Other Halloween Treats*. Lisa lives in the San Fernando Valley and online at www.lisamorton.com

J. C. Michael is an English writer of Horror and Dark Fiction. He is the author of the novel "Discoredia", which was released by Books of the Dead Press in 2013, and has since seen a number of short stories published in various anthologies. These have included "Reasons To Kill" in the

Amazon bestselling anthology "Suspended in Dusk" and "When Death Walks The Field Of Battle" in "Savage Beasts" from Grey Matter Press. He has also featured in the best selling Collected Christmas Horror Shorts, and Collected Easter Horror Shorts compiled and published by Kevin Kennedy, with whom Michael's has recently co-authored the novella, "You Only Get One Shot".

Taking his inspiration from Stephen King and James Herbert his writing frequently explores the dark side of human nature where moral boundaries are questioned, and the difference between good and evil is far from clear.

For more information on his writing please find him on Facebook, or take a look at his author profile on Amazon.

https://www.facebook.com/james.c.michael1

https://www.amazon.com/J-C-Michael/e/B00AX8BFIK

Stuart Keane is a horror and suspense author from the United Kingdom. He is currently a member of the Author's Guild, and co-director/editor for emerging UK publisher, Dark Chapter Press. Currently in his third year of writing, Stuart has started to earn a reputation for writing realistic, contemporary horror. With comparisons to Richard Laymon and Shaun Hutson amongst his critical acclaim – he cites both authors as his major inspiration in the genre – Stuart is dedicated to writing terrifying stories for real horror fans.

Feel free to get in touch at www.stuartkeane.com or www.facebook.com/stuart.keane.92 He can also be found on Twitter at @SKeane_Author.

Hidden in a remote location in California lives a man that responds to the name **Peter Oliver Wonder**. Though little is known about him, several written works that may or may not be fictional have been found featuring a character of the same name.

Devilishly handsome, quick witted, and as charming as an asshole can be, Peter has come a long way since his time in the United States Marine Corps. Making friends wherever he goes, there is never a shortage of adventure when he is around.

The works that have been penned under this name are full of horror, romance, adventure, and comedy just as every life should be. It is assumed that these works are an attempt at a drug fueled autobiography of sorts. Through these texts, we can learn much about this incredible man.

http://peterowonder.wix.com/peteroliverwonder

https://www.facebook.com/PeterOliverWonderAuthor/

@PeteOWonder

John R. Little has been publishing horror and dark fantasy stories for more than two decades. With his 17 books to date, he's been nominated for the Bram Stoker Award four times and has won once. His most recent novels are DarkNet and Soul Mates, and he is hard at work on his next novel. John loves to hear from his readers, either on Facebook or at his web site, www.johnrlittle.com

Kevin J Kennedy is the co-author of 'You Only Get One Shot,' and the man behind the best-selling Collected Christmas Horror Shorts & Collected Easter Horror Shorts anthologies. His short stories have featured in many other notable anthologies in the horror genre.

Kevin lives in a small town in Scotland with his wife, step daughter and two strange little cats

Keep up to date with new releases or contact Kevin through his website: www.kevinjkennedy.co.uk

Printed in Great Britain
by Amazon